CAROLINE SHAW   d
moved to Brisbane i   ild.
She currently lives w   rote
Cat Catcher, her firs   an.

Cat Catcher

CAROLINE SHAW

Library of Congress Catalog Card Number: 98-88890

A catalogue record for this book is available from the British Library on request

The right of Caroline Shaw to be identified as the author of this work has been asserted by her in accordance with the Copyright, Designs and Patents Act 1988

Copyright © 1999 by Caroline Shaw

First published by Bantam Books, Transworld Publishers (Aust) Pty Limited, 1999

First published 2000 by Serpent's Tail,
4 Blackstock Mews, London N4

Website: www.serpentstail.com

Typeset in Bernhard and 11/12.5 pt Times by
Midland Typesetters, Maryborough, Victoria, Australia
Printed in Great Britain by Mackays of Chatham, plc

To Andrew

Chapter 1

THE SIAMESE CLIENT

'You little shit!' Lenny inspected her latest scratch. This one was vicious, starting at the knuckle of her index finger and spanning an arc to the corner of her left wrist. A cat scratch, the blood in painful beads, the hairs on her arm standing up. If it had been a little higher it would have reopened the old scar. Lenny leaned back against the wall, squatting behind her desk, beyond which the Siamese Lilac Point spat hate.

She had taken it from its cage for a grooming session. There were two cats in the office at the moment, one clean and fresh and the other—this one—filthy. It stank from the garbage bins where she had found it rolling around in something sticky, collecting the trash it brushed against. Lenny knew its owners would want to see it neat and tidy, without the congealed wad of gum stuck in its neck fur, but it was a monster, hypersensitive and itching to escape. She had tried to groom it earlier in the week and scored a nasty bone-grazing bite to her little finger. She was only trying again now because if the Antolinis saw a dirty cat they might suspect that Lenny wasn't the angel of mercy they thought she was.

She looked at her hand. It was stinging and she saw her revenge glistening in the hard wad of gum.

She stretched out a leg. The cat went for her, missed. She jammed her swivel chair under one half of the desk, blocking the other side with her steel-capped boots. Cleo performed a quick montage of feline attitudes: hisses, hair puffing, back arching. The full ritual. Raked the leather boot where there was already a lattice-work of scratches. But Lenny had seen it all before.

'Live it up, furball.'

She had been stuck with Cleo Harrelson for a week now; couldn't get through to the owners (real estate agent dad and lo-trade, cocktail waitress mum). Something wrong there. He had smoked and looked uptight, but the Waitress seemed to really care as she filled out the application form, sucking on Lenny's pen, leaving a greasy ring of something cheap and red.

Lenny pulled a pack of cigarettes out of her jeans. They were Marlboros, the highest tar level. For a while she had been grading down; lights, ultra-lights: smoking like someone who treasured life, as though she wanted to prolong it, when it was more appropriate for her to smoke like someone who wanted a quick exit.

She glanced at the other cat. Renata 'Natty' Antolini was a seductress who purred long sultry purrs while grinding silky thighs round Lenny's calves. She was a one-year-old Russian Blue whose owners were falling over themselves with happiness and on their way to collect her right now. Natty seemed to sense it, sitting up straight, the silver bow around her neck setting off her dusky coat. She watched the stand-off like butter wouldn't melt on her salmon-pink tongue.

Lenny inspected her office, peripheral vision never leaving Cleo. Everything was tidy. She worked hard at that. She wiped the cheap furniture over with Dettol and/or Pine-O-Cleen each day to the point where it had started to bleach. The filing cabinets were from a fire sale, one with a scorch mark which Lenny turned against the wall. She knew the scorch was there and it niggled her. When she couldn't control the urge, which was frequently, she turned it around and went at it with ammonia.

It was a tiny office. The window let in a thin column of badly needed light. There was tinted glass in the door and a broken casement above. Lenny knew it was shitty. Shitty can be more than adequate. After all, her clients were four-legged and didn't care about architectural niceties. They needed only a bowl of water, a litter tray and some food. In this last area, Lenny's approach was pragmatic. She kept a cardboard box of 'no frills' tins hidden in one of the filing cabinets and a collection of the more expensive brands, 'Savoire Fare', 'Feline Gourmand' and 'My Ritzy', for casual display when the owners came to pick up and pay up.

Cleo farted. Lenny sighed, reached for a can of Scandinavian Forest. The day was winding down like a mechanical mouse.

She glanced at her bonsai. She had three—a Boxwood, an Azalea and a Juniper—arranged on a shelf along one wall. Above them hung a battery of fluorescent tubes and Alfoil reflectors. The trees needed at least ten hours of light each day. None of them was over twenty-five centimetres tall, all bent branches and twisted trunks. They were an important part of her psychological recovery after the attack, although as a rule she didn't enjoy 'nature'. You took a look at a magnificent vista and then what? Take another look? Bonsai was about control—the angle of each branch, the carriage of every twig.

Dr Sakuno would want an update on them soon. He had imported them from a shop in Kitayama, Kyoto. The first week she had nearly killed them, called his emergency number in the middle of the night in a blind panic. He had loved that, made a nasty little crack about Lenny's healthy expression of weakness. *Quite unnecessary to use the plants as an excuse*. Then he told her he didn't do after-hours consultations unless the patient was critical. He called her back in the morning with instructions. He made her wait because he knew waiting was guaranteed to piss her off and part of her therapy seemed to be—unless he simply enjoyed it—to piss her off. That and activity.

The Japanese, Dr Sakuno lectured her, were always busy with a hobby; always traveling, working, keeping the mind from fruitless contemplation of life. The way to *satori* could only be achieved through *physical* instruction. Too much thinking led to inevitable misery. And so she kept busy. She hunted missing cats.

H. Aaron Investigations was a one-room office in the back of Footscray shopping mall, its immediate neighbours a barber shop and an adult book store. If you wanted to plunge something into an orifice, porn shop king Mike Bullock had the something you needed. The inside of the shop was covered with posters of enormous boobs, the sort that looked like the plastic surgeon was myopic. Outside a sandwich board thrilled: 'No one is born a Great Lover! Enhance Your Love Pleasure—We can guide You to Nirvana!' Underneath in black marker Mike had written 'ID could be requested'. He had been busted and fined last year for selling hard-core porn to fourteen year olds.

Mike was a little Aussie battler: *I'm a doer, Lenny, not a thinker. That's what some people resent. I make things happen for me. This is a big beautiful country. You can do anything you want—if you've got the drive. I've got the drive, Lenny.*

He had asked Lenny out the second time he saw her. He was five feet tall with crinkly hair, poly-cotton shirts (with the emphasis on poly) and slip-on vinyl shoes (the kind with the fake gold horse bits). His accent was strongly northern English, but he was a dated flower of Australian manhood, a devotee of 'streuth', 'bonzer' and 'she'll be right'.

He had thought he had a real chance with Lenny. She was twenty-seven and borderline ugly. Her head was rounded like an egg and her teeth were crooked—especially the bottom row where she fought an ongoing battle against decay. Her hair was blonde and short, never more than an inch long. If she grew it, it went big and coarse. These days in matters of beauty she surrendered herself to Anastasia Cherbakov.

Anastasia was the barber. She had moved in a year ago and become Lenny's stylist of choice by proximity. She always dry cut, which was good because who had time for a three-magazine shampoo, rinse and set? Anastasia liked to talk about her family whom she was slowly bringing out from

Moscow. So far eight of them were living in a three-bedroom Collingwood apartment and only Anastasia worked. She was twenty-four, pretty in a swarthy way and she hated everything about Russia. It had been better under the communists, she moaned, at least everyone had food.

She was a minor master of the accordion. Clients waiting for a blue rinse to take would be treated to renditions of 'If I Had A Hammer' or 'The Road To Gundagai'. Old Italian men always requested the theme from 'The Godfather', but Lenny, who had asked for 'Smoke On The Water', was still waiting because Deep Purple was problematic on the accordion. Anastasia told Lenny on her first visit (a half-price Tuesday) that she wasn't looking after her hair properly and would be bald by fifty.

Cleo Harrelson was whining like a leaky tire. Lenny whined back. Her backside was going numb. She would look ridiculous if the Antolinis came to the door now. She smacked her fist against the desk. Cleo sniffed and ignored her. She was playing it deceptively cool, but if she got a chance this cat would trash the office. Not that any of the stuff was valuable. Even the metre-high Japanese cat with the raised welcoming paw was a cheapie from the Victoria Markets, although her story was that she got it from an ancient cat temple in Shikoku. The owners appreciated that.

The welcome cat stood near her Buddhist *butsudan*, a foot-square wooden hutch containing candles, incense sticks and a fresh mandarin. As a rule she kept the *butsudan* covered with a tea towel because she didn't want anyone prying. People were put off by rituals, especially weird, foreign ones. Once, when a cat owner had lifted the tea towel—*Hey, what's this?*—she had been forced to eat the mandarin on the spot to avoid an explanation.

Lenny reached into a drawer and took out a foil strip of aspirin. She put three pills on the back of her tongue and dry swallowed. Cleo Harrelson faked left then thrust out to the right. Lenny's expert hand caught the cat's neck and squeezed. Cleo gurgled and clawed at Lenny's eye. Lenny squeezed harder.

'Hurting?'

Someone knocked at the door. The Antolinis. Lenny shoved Cleo into her cage. Mr and Mrs Antolini, hugely successful fruit and veggie market owners and cat fanciers, swept in. Natty! *Mio cuore! Mia bambina! Mia angela!* They kissed their cat between its ears. It licked their tearful faces happily and they squealed again. Cleo Harrelson watched from the cat box with hard, defeated eyes and licked her paws to calm herself. It was pay-up time. Lenny said something about Russian Blues being her favourites. Mr Antolini, fat, fifty and festive, wrote a cheque that was even more than avarice anticipated.

'You the best detective in the world! *La migliore! Veramente!*'

They opened a bottle of label-less grappa for a toast. Mrs Antolini made the stuff in her garage and sold it to the rellies and friends for five bucks a bottle. She had brought a crateful for Lenny. Don't tell nobody, Lenny, *cara. E pericoloso, vero*? Dangerous! Lenny got the gist. She was dealing with the lettuce Mafia.

There was only one glass in her office so the Antolinis drank from Japanese teacups. The combination of aspirin and grappa was a good one. It gave Lenny a soft, cushiony feeling and she almost understood the Antolinis' happiness. Was this how people were supposed to feel?

After they left, she cleaned and Dettolled her hand. It was nothing once the blood was wiped away, nothing at all to get worked up about. If she felt a little sick it was only the grappa needling her empty stomach. She pushed up her left sleeve and looked at her scar. It was a pink line from elbow to wrist. Nothing to feel sick about at all now, two years on.

After the incident, after she had quit the Victorian Police Force, she wasn't faced with too many options. Junior clerk in a bank? Tram conductor? Serving espressos in Carlton coffee shops? These all required social skills Lenny hadn't bothered to learn.

She had locked herself in her apartment at first and done nothing. Ex-colleagues had visited once or twice before she discouraged them with blatant rudeness, and her mother had often popped in. Her mother liked to pop in. 'Thought I'd pop in!' Pop in and pop out, pop over and pop round. She had continued to pop despite Lenny's indifference. After a while they fell into a routine: Mrs Aaron popping in and popping a load of washing on, Lenny popping herself in front of the TV, no words exchanged.

She sat at her desk and flipped through the latest missing file: a three-week-old Chartreux kitten, which may or may not have been taken by the neighbour's Pit Bull, and a three-legged tabby—Honey Bubbles Ryan. A good client that one, easy to identify. Lenny generally picked him up at the fish shop ten minutes from home, hobbling along with a fish remnant in his mouth. The elderly owner was housebound and her help didn't think that looking for the cat was part of her duties, so the tabby was a regular. Lenny had a few of these habitual strayers, her bread and butter cats.

She figured the Chartreux was a lost cause. At three weeks old it was unlikely to have survived even a few days away from its mother. Its owners couldn't explain how it had got away from the rest of the litter. Lenny knew how, scrambling through that tiny hole in the garden fence for its first and last mistake in life.

She had seen the Pit Bull, but there was no chance of checking out the yard for evidence. Mr Maleny had slammed the door in her face. *You step inside this door, missy, and I won't be responsible*, he had growled. *Sarge doesn't like strangers, do you, Sarge?* Sarge snarled on cue.

No, she figured the kitten was already doggy-do and it was best to break the news to the careless family. Lenny made the call, got the usual response.

It had taken a while to build the business up. She had

placed her name in the Yellow Pages and waited by the phone to see who called. Originally, she had caught anything: dogs, cats, even a parrot. Once she had spent two days hunting a prize-winning rooster. She found its spinal cord on the lawn of a family with two Burmese.

But you need a very small niche to survive in this world and cat catching became Lenny's. She had a flair for it, perhaps because she saw right through cats—they were cunning and treacherous, cold and selfish. With this in mind she never let easy sentiment get in the way of her work. When she went down an alley and made contact with a cat it was going into her bag.

Slowly she had established a name; in feline circles she was someone who mattered. She got cards from cats at Christmas. Last year she had been invited to present a prize at the Royal Melbourne Cat Show. She politely declined. Too many of the competitors had felt her hands on their necks. It could have gotten nasty.

She looked at Cleo Harrelson. Rubbed her hand. No way was she keeping it for another week. She pulled the application form out of the filing cabinet. Real estate dad, Brad Holden, worked in Carlton and lived in Toorak. Lenny dialed the home number. A machine spoke: 'You've reached me and it's so good to hear your voice but I'm out of here right now. You be cool and leave a message, okay?' Backgrounded by Michael Bolton. He sounded like a real smoothie on the machine, not at all the uptight male who had come to the office with the Waitress. Maybe that explained it. Maybe he had broken up with the Waitress and neither of them wanted the cat. That made three of them.

She called his office, Carlton Prestige Homes, but the receptionist said Mr Holden was in conference with a client and would be unavailable for the rest of the day. Was it about a property? Mrs Lindsey-Forsyth was available ...

Lenny dropped the receiver and picked up the cat box. Cleo tried to get a paw through the front bars, claws extended.

Lenny went into the car park and put the box onto the back seat of her car, a lime-green Mitsubishi Colt and a zippy little hatch in its day, but fourteen years down the track a jerking rust bucket. Still, she prided herself on its level of hygiene. She cleaned it with the stuff they used to clean the inside of 747s, and there were no Garfields sucking the windows, no fuzzy dice, and no engaging stickers of any kind.

Carlton Prestige Homes was a small office in Lygon Street. It resembled an art gallery except for the 'No Student Rentals' in bold letters in the window. Lenny held Cleo Harrelson's cat box up.

'Look, Cleo—home!'

Inside there was a long, curved counter of yellow wood and a framed poster of a modern cityscape behind. The receptionist—a petite blonde with a winning smile—began her opening spiel then saw the cat box.

'No way, nooo way!'

'Cleopatra Harrelson to see Bradley Holden.' Lenny held the box over the counter. Cleo Harrelson spat something green.

'That's Tonya's cat, isn't it?' The receptionist put her hands on her hips. She was not a pretty woman but she had the lean-bodied look of the nineties, which meant nothing decent to eat and all her free time on the stair master. She was groomed immaculately, hair in a sharp, blonde bob. But it was all trashed by the nails-on-a-blackboard screech.

'It's Brad and Tonya's cat, yes,' Lenny said.

'Forget it. Tonya and Brad—Mr Holden—aren't together anymore. He doesn't want the cat. He told her.'

A door opened and Brad Holden came out. His eyes flashed, but he spoke in a jovial tone.

'Cheryl, what seems to be the problem out here? Mrs Hollander can't hear herself think, let alone sign the papers on her five-year lease.' Then he saw Cleo and pulled the door shut behind him.

Lenny put the cat box on the counter. 'You owe me four hundred and seventy-one dollars.'

'What?'

Lenny produced a bill. 'Six days of tracking at seventy-five dollars a day. I'm not billing you for the seven days I've been trying to contact you, but I am charging twenty-one dollars for the food and kitty litter.'

'Generous, aren't you?' he sneered.

'Look, Bradley, you can keep Cleo or not keep her. You can strangle her, beat her, skin her or shish-kebab her. That's not my concern. But I want cash, or a cheque or your credit card in my machine before I leave this office.'

'Or what—oouuuf!' He got a two-finger jab in the gut. He was soft. Not going to get Ms Lean Body in bed with that.

The office door opened and a pink-permed pensioner peeked out. She smelt of mothballs and Elizabeth Taylor's Passion. Lipstick bled in fine lines around her mouth and she fingered a strand of Mikimoto pearls cautiously. The five-year lease.

She spoke with the faux British accent old women sometimes affect. 'Anything wrong, Bradley?'

'Nothing at all, Mrs Hollander.' He turned elegantly, charm dripping like summer lard. 'Have you finished with those forms, dear?'

'Oh ... is that your pussycat?' Her face glowed. 'It's lovely. A Siamese, isn't it? My goodness me. My sister had one of those.'

'It's mine all right,' Holden picked up the cat box. 'Say hello, Cleo. How's my best little girl?' A nasty hiss. 'Daddy's really missed you, hasn't he?'

'Great, just a matter of my money then,' Lenny chimed in. 'Four hundred and seventy-one dollars. I think I will take cash after all.'

'No problem,' he gave her a smile. 'Cheryl, fix up this young lady, will you.'

'Certainly, Mr Holden.'

Holden put a proprietary hand on Mrs Hollander's back and eased her into the office.

The receptionist yanked open a drawer, pulled out four hundred and seventy dollars in crumpled, tenant-soiled notes and dropped them onto the counter. Lenny folded them into her wallet. She waited.

'My dollar coin?' she prompted finally.

'You cheap bitch!'

Lenny held out her hand. Take care of the pennies and the pounds will take care of themselves. Besides, she was cheap. And she was a bitch.

The receptionist slapped the gold disc down.

'Now get out of here before I call the police and take that animal with you.'

'I'm sorry, my job is done,' Lenny said. She went out into the sunshine.

She was ten steps away when the door opened and the cat box flew past her head and smashed onto the road.

Cleo Harrelson mewed, a soft nervous sound. Lenny was impervious to cat pleas and quite prepared to leave Cleo right there in the gutter. Still, she hesitated. There was something in the frightened blue eyes.

A group of shop owners, drawn by the excitement, was watching Lenny and the cat box with interest. A motorcycle cop pulled up outside a fish and chip shop on the other side of the street. He pulled off his gloves slowly, young and eager to intervene if necessary. Lenny sighed and picked up the box. She had her money. She could get rid of her client later.

Chapter 2

CRICKET, AND FLEECING A PENSIONER

It was the fifth day at the Melbourne Cricket Ground, New Zealand against Australia, and it looked like being a draw. Cricket was the only game in the world in which five days of determined sportsmanship could produce no result.

Lenny had discovered sport via TV two years ago. It required little concentration and coverage went for hours. What she had needed was a distraction. And TV sport was the biggest distraction of them all. She turned, within a month, into a 'Wide World of Sports' junkie. Plus that little beauty, 'The Footy Show'. Men talking and joking for a solid hour about football. Fascinating.

Subliminally she had become something of a sports expert. Men and women spoke eagerly of not knowing how they did it, it just happened. *I just knew it was gonna go in the net!* There was rarely a connection to thought. Sport was about instinct and ritual. Very Zen.

TV even had a sound. A hum, virtually indiscernible at first. The pictures and dialogue masked it. It was comforting. There were no surprises—well, occasionally the TV guide got it wrong and the late night movie didn't come on as advertised, but as a general rule TV could be relied upon to follow the rules, provide no more and no less than it advertised. A coloured friend.

Later she began to make forays to the stadiums. These days she had season tickets to the Melbourne Cricket Ground and the Melbourne Tennis Centre. Once a month, Dr Sakuno met her at the entrance gates of whichever sport was seasonal and they spent part of the day together.

Dr Sakuno didn't like Australian sport or the kinds of people who made up the crowds. *It's lower class, Helena san.* Lenny, however, was soothed by the growl of the crowds: *Kick 'im, Deano! Arghh, yur a fucking girl! Pull yur head in! Get yur heads up! Fucking Kiwi bastard!* She could watch the ball do its thing for two hours and go home feeling a pleasant buzz of blankness. Dr Sakuno could use the afternoon to get in a few of the one-liners he used as a substitute for meaningful therapy.

Dr Sakuno had a lot of patients and thought she was a time-waster. He advised her to be stoic and get on with her life. 'Get on with it' was a popular phrase in their sessions. He was showing her how to become Japanese, surely the highest form of life on this planet. What else did she want from him?

She glanced at him as he wiped his lips with a tissue from the tiny tissue packet he always carried in his pocket. He wore regulation navy pants and a white shirt—sleeves rolled down and buttoned at the cuffs, collar done up—and a dark blue Aquascutum tie with a silver tie clip. He carried a Hunting World shoulder bag. He was excessively thin with a wasp-like waist. She wondered how he could fit all his internal organs in there. Shorter than her, of course. Black eyes, black hair, gold Rolex. No other jewellery, no cologne and no hint of facial hair. She suspected he razored his whole face. It wasn't natural surely for anyone to be so smooth. He had told her that he found hairy bodies and faces disgusting. *Like animals, animals!*

'Last week on the news . . .' He didn't look at her. He knew about it, didn't want to mention it. He was afraid she was going to regress.

'I'm fine,' she lied.

'It's good that he's dead.'

'Yes.'

'I believe he took six bullets?'

'Seven. Four in the chest, three in the head.'

'And you are fine?'

'Fine.'

'Then it's time to stop finding lost cats.' He was taking photographs of the crowd with a Nikon F4 and a 70–300 mm Nikkor lens. He occasionally showed her his efforts: portraits of the underbelly of Melbourne life. He specialized in beer guts. *Your tribe is more exotic than ours. My relatives in Tokyo can't believe it when they receive my photographs.* He always laughed as though they were sharing a wonderful witticism. *When we Japanese come here, the first thing we realise is how fat you all are. We have an inferiority complex. We think the gaijin are superior. Then we meet you in your own environment and we discover that you are slobs. I learned that word in your country: slobs.*

'I like finding cats.' Lenny watched him zoom in on a huge middle-aged blonde in a rhinestone halter neck. Slobs? Maybe. But he couldn't take his eyes off them. The automatic lens whined and rotated.

Dr Sakuno didn't like her business, said it was pathetic. He didn't like cats at all. Lenny reminded him that Buddhists admired the cat's capacity for meditation. He countered that the cat was not listed in the original canons of Buddhism as a protected animal—*because while Buddha's funeral ceremony was taking place his cat fell asleep*. If a person needed a pet then let him have a dog. Preferably a Shiba, a furry golden Japanese breed: finest dog in the world, a national treasure. Not one of those Western creatures that barked all day and was allowed to roam the streets. That could never happen in Tokyo. He spoke fondly of the Japan death squads routinely rounding up strays. Seven hundred thousand a year.

'This week at the shrine I prayed that you would take the next step. Buddha is of course longing for you to do this. But you must be the one to do it.' When he spoke of religion his English became deadly formal. The Obiwan Kenobi of Zen.

'Did Buddha tell you what the next step is?' Dr Sakuno liked to drop Buddha into the conversation as though he had a personal hotline. But Buddha's advice tended to be vague. There was a lot of stuff about self reliance: the Zen sense of the alone. Buddha—as translated by Dr Sakuno—used the phrase 'get on with it' a lot.

'*Sa* . . .' This was supposed to be Japanese for 'Well . . .' but it always meant 'No'. It was a regular feature of their conversations, a popular answer to any question. Dr Sakuno continued, 'Verbal instruction is delusive.'

'Naturally.' A beautiful drive through cover interrupted their endless game. Deano had reached his half century and the crowd got to its feet. Dr Sakuno stood up to get a better shot of a large leopard skin lycra bottom wobbling three rows in front.

The umpires conferred and decided it was a good enough time to break for lunch. Family groups began to open eskies and take out foil-wrapped sandwiches and rolls. Dr Sakuno took out a *bento* in a blue and white checked tea towel. Lenny wanted the traditional MCG food—a cold in the middle, tepid on the crust meat pie.

She went down to the cafeteria, a sea of singlets and shorts. A large pink bloated face, ahead of her in the queue, looked back, eyes blinking under a Batman visor. It was MacAvoy.

Of course he couldn't do the right thing and glance away, pretend not to have seen her. He began to push his way back through the crowd.

As he got closer she saw a bigger gut than she remembered straining against his 'Gold Coast Movie World' singlet. The top of his head was going to be very painful the next day. His hair—the long left strands usually combed across to hide the bald patch—hung limply down the side of the visor. His dome was shiny red.

He was carrying a miniature TV with the antenna extended. Jostled by the crowd the picture was a fuzz of lines but the sound was clear.

'Len. Mate. Good to see you.' He looked around the crowd, perhaps realising at the last minute that she was not pleased to see him. 'Few of the lads here. Gazza, Paulie. You remember Paulie Rider?'

'Senior Constable Rider?'

'That's him. Sergeant now. Got a wife and two kids, eh? What? Sorry, mate,' as he bumped the man in front of him. 'Geez, what a picture!' He was blocking the queue and edged forward. He hesitated. He wanted to mention Michael Dorling's death, of course. But he didn't know how she would react.

'So ... he finally got what was coming to him.'

'Yes.' The newspapers had managed to get a photograph of the body, the head covered with a coat but a pool of blood clearly visible.

'Good ... good ... So what've you been up to?' She could see in his eyes that he—and everyone in the department— knew all about the cats. And didn't think much of it.

'I search for missing cats,' she said.

'Good on you. I like cats. Although the missus won't go for them. You know, the poodles ...'

She knew. He had bored her many times with anecdotes about his good wife's fondness for the world's ugliest dog: the giant poodle. Trimmed into grotesque style with droopy white curls, it was a vicious breed, its long snout filled with big savage fangs. The Tammy Wynette of dogs.

'So you're OK?' There was nothing provocative in the question. He cared about her. He always had. He had falsely perceived himself as the mentor in their relationship.

'Yes.' It was tempting to tell him to fuck off and be done with it but Dr Sakuno would say that was a loss of both control and dignity. Dr Sakuno had a thing about profanity and about public scenes. A thing about emotion period.

'What can I do you for, love?' The fat woman at the counter smiled broadly. Her hands were plastic-glove-free.

'C'mon, lovie. People waiting ...' Hands on hips now, smile thinning. The fingernails were dirty. There was something oily smeared across one hand too. Like creamy mustard or something ...

'Nothing.'

'Well don't stand in the bloody line then, blondie!'

Lenny was well away from the cafeteria when MacAvoy, sweating and juggling a cardboard tray of food, caught up with her.

'Len! Steady on!'

'What?'

'Why don't you come and sit with us?' He shrugged. 'Old times' sake.'

'I'm with someone.' She strode away.

Dr Sakuno was wiping his lips with a moist towelette. He looked significantly at his watch. He didn't want her to get the idea that this was a social occasion for him. The meter was running.

'So ...' She sat down, fingering the aspirin foil strip in her pocket. She decided not to tell him about MacAvoy. Generally she told him everything. He sucked it out of her with the tact of a vacuum cleaner, then offered no advice. *Because you must realise for yourself. No one can tell you.*

'How much for a mini TV?' she asked.

'Sony make a nice little one for the car. Under twenty thousand yen. I met Mr Morita, the founder of Sony, at a gathering in Nagoya once.'

The man next to Lenny was reading a magazine, looking at pictures of a bottle-blonde in peach-coloured underwear. Her legs were open to the camera and she wore a slack-mouthed pout.

'Waddya reckon, mate?' The man saw Dr Sakuno looking and turned the page towards him with a grin.

'Vulgar,' Dr Sakuno replied. 'A vulgar American woman.' He had a particular dislike for Americans. No restraint, he said, no control. *They try to force us to buy their low grade rice and cars. Their women are like their cars, big, loud and ugly, and their rice is inedible.*

'So,' he said to Lenny without missing a beat, 'the next step. When the opportunity to advance presents itself, you will recognize it. Whether or not you will choose to take up the challenge, I don't know. Did you watch the Sumo tapes this month? I have more for you.' He patted his shoulder bag.

'Of course. Musashimaru was great.'

Dr Sakuno shrugged: 'He will always be a gaijin.'

Gaijin: outsider, foreigner. Musashimaru, giant grim-faced hulk of sumo was Hawaiian born. He was popular and well-regarded but he could never receive the adoration meted out to a Japanese sumo star.

Lenny thought that she was gaijin even in her own society. Glad to be gaijin, she thought sourly.

Dr Sakuno had officially shot his bolt with his one nugget of Japanese wisdom. He had nothing more for her and lapsed into silence.

The remainder of the cricket was a lovely warm Sunday afternoon's anticlimax that produced the expected draw. Lenny bowed to Dr Sakuno at his car, an imported Toyota Crown Majesta that featured a satellite guidance system.

'I hope it's a one-day match next month,' Dr Sakuno said from inside the car, sucking on a Lark cigarette. 'This test match game—who can follow it?'

'Exactly,' Lenny said as he drove away.

She drove in the direction of her office, pulled over near the fish shop in Footscray because Honey Bubbles Ryan— the missing three-legged obesity—was wowling at the door. His tail swished back and forth and he scratched at the glass. Honey Bubbles didn't understand 'Sunday' or 'closed'.

Lenny opened her door and leaned out, a handful of cat biscuits in her palm.

'Honey Bubbles ... Yummy fish ... Mmmmmm ...'

Honey Bubbles Ryan waddled over to lick her fingers. She

grabbed his fat neck. He was blubbery underneath like a cellulite sausage with a furry overlay.

'Forget it, fatso,' she said. There was no point getting out the cat box from the boot. She had tried pushing him in before; she couldn't get the door to lock behind him. So she tied a chain to his collar and fastened it tight to the handle of the back seat. Honey Bubbles tugged on the chain, strangled himself, stopped, tugged again.

Mrs Ryan took ten minutes to get to the door on her walker. She was ninety-two, partially deaf and smelled of mothballs. But her eyes sparkled when she saw Honey Bubbles.

'Honey B! My dear old man. Home again at last. Oh, Miss Lenny, you come in and have some orange cake. I'm just having my dinner. I'll get my cheque book.'

Lenny followed her in. It was an awkward situation because when someone is doddering on a walker do you overtake them or dodder behind? There was an old war movie on TV. *Sink the Bismarck*, typical Sunday afternoon fare for those who didn't get into sport. Lenny had seen a lot of these movies because they were also repeated in the early hours of the morning. *Reach for the Sky*, *The Dam Busters* and *633 Squadron* were her favourites. British stiff upper lip in a uniform.

'I do like Kenneth More,' said Mrs Ryan. 'He reminds me of my ...'

'Husband, I know,' Lenny said. There was a photo on the TV of the late Mr Ryan in an air force uniform. Actually very little resemblance to Kenneth More, Lenny thought.

'His son's gone down in a plane.' Mrs Ryan looked worried. She took a long time to work herself into her chair and collapsed at the last minute with a soft whoosh.

'Don't worry. He gets picked up by a British ship,' Lenny said. 'I've seen it.'

'Oh, so have I, but it always gets to me. Seeing him crying

like that when he thinks no one can see him. And that lovely young girl watching the whole time.'

'Yes, it's a classic. I prefer *Reach For the Sky*.' Kenneth More as Douglas Bader, legendary double-leg amputee and World War II flying ace.

'Ooh, so do I. Help yourself to cake.' Mrs Ryan's shaking hands began to write out a cheque. 'How much then, dear?'

'Two hundred and twenty-five,' Lenny said. Three days of looking.

'Goodness me.' But she wrote the figure, ripped off the cheque and handed it over. 'Don't you worry about me, dear. George saw me right before he ...' Rapid blinking. Lenny forced down a mouthful of cake. 'He had the superannuation and life insurance. I'm set for life.'

She was eating her tea on her lap. It looked like it had been prepared the day before and been reheated today: a chop, mashed potato and tinned carrots. There was a slab of supermarket orange cake that was at the end of its life.

'More cake?'

'Thank you, no.' Lenny glanced around the room. Lots of antique pieces in here. The dealers would swoop when the old woman died.

Her glance lingered on the mantelpiece. There was a framed photo of Honey Bubbles in his days as a prize-winner. Hard to believe that this old pork wiener had once been the number one Mackerel Tabby American Short-hair in the country but there, next to the photo, was the faded rosette to prove it. The other photos were Mrs Ryan and her husband on their wedding day and children in modern Kodak snapshots who must be grandchildren and great grandchildren.

'My angels,' Mrs Ryan smiled. 'Is your grandmother still alive, dear?'

'Yes,' Lenny nodded. 'Yes. Definitely.'

'Good girl.'

Honey Bubbles rubbed against Mrs Ryan's leg and scored a piece of chop. He settled at her feet and chewed, wide girth spreading over the carpet. Mrs Ryan stroked his back.

'I don't know what I'd do without my old man,' she said. 'He's all I've got really.'

Lenny had heard that hoary chestnut many times but in this case it was patently true and she felt depressed. Why did anyone bother with relationships when they had to end like this: with one partner in the ground and one sitting old and alone with only an obese cat and Kenneth More to distract them.

'More cake?'

'No.'

The shopping mall was empty at this time on a Sunday. It was nearly six p.m. but with daylight saving it would be light for another three hours. The barber shop was shut, but the porn shop was open. Mike had explained that he did his best trade in 'the wee hours, when a bloke gets lonely'.

There was a new sign taped to the sandwich board: 'Just In: Philippine Love Slaves. One Aussie Bloke And Six Gorgeous Girls.' Mike stood in the entrance of his shop, smoking a Winfield Blue. He was wearing a sky blue nylon body shirt that clung to his love handles and showed his hairy nipples. His mint green hips thrust forward when he saw her.

'Gidday, gidday. Working after hours?' Despite all her best efforts, he liked her.

'Mmm hmm.'

'How about we—eh?' He looked back into the shop. 'Not there, mate. Not there. In the back. Jesus!' He gave Lenny a 'some people!' grin. 'Big sale. Prawn and Porn over in Essendon. They want the lot.'

'Don't let me keep you.' She got out her key and went to her door.

'Yeah ... well, OK.' There was yearning in his voice. She ignored it.

Cleo, imprisoned in the office cage, set up a venomous howl the instant the key turned in the door. She hissed and flung a claw out as Lenny passed by. Lenny picked up a plastic water container with a squirt lid that she used to water the bonsai. She let the cat have it.

'That's what you get when you can't keep your mouth shut,' she said. She had brought the cat back yesterday and put up an ad on the shopping mall noticeboard for a free Siamese.

She worked on the bonsai for a while. It was too hot yet to prune them but there was always new growth to be pinched and she was currently rewiring the Juniper. It had taken her quite a bit of practice to master the art of wiring. Too tight and the branches were bruised, too loose and it wouldn't do the job. She placed the Juniper on an upturned pot on her desk so she could look up at it. She rotated it slowly. The trunk still wasn't quite how she wanted it. She picked up her blunt nose wire cutters and snipped off the wire.

The rewiring done, she watered all three plants. This was still a challenge. Most bonsai died as a result of overwatering or drying out. Lenny tilted her watering can three or four times over the top of each plant, then checked the bottom to make sure the water was draining through.

Finally she looked for things to straighten. She had a little ritual every day of checking the room for precision. She got down and wiped a hand on the floorboards. She had ripped up the carpet when she moved in. Her hand came up clean. She would try again tomorrow. Surely it would be dirty by then.

The phone rang and her machine answered. She didn't pick up. It could be her mother. The greatest benefit of the machine was screening out her mother.

'Mr Aaron?' It was a young woman's voice. She sounded tentative. 'Oh. You're not in. I'm sorry. I suppose it's Sunday. I ... I just thought you might be in the office. I have a ... a cat emergency. I'd like to make an appointment. For as soon as possible. Is tomorrow out of the question? My name is Kimberly Talbott. Please do call me as soon as you can. It's absolutely crucial.' She left a Melbourne phone number and hung up.

Lenny wondered how many Kimberly Talbotts there were in Australia. Could it be the stinking rich one? Henry Talbott owned as much of the communications industry as the law permitted in Australia, and sizable chunks elsewhere. Nearly ninety, he was rumoured to be on his deathbed, back in his hometown to die. His twin children, Kimberly and her brother Kendell, were twenty years old, the product of a very late in life marriage.

Lenny knew the story. The twins' lives had been recorded faithfully in the *Women's Weekly*. The mother, Vivian Talbott, had wed Henry when he was sixty-nine and she just nineteen. Before the wedding she gave birth to the twins. Luckily for her the babies both had the Talbott family trademark: crooked little fingers on both hands. The family was never out of the news.

Lenny understood the fascination with TV and newspapers, how excited people became when they saw themselves, however briefly, in a wide shot on the tube. *Look, Mum! Look! There's Libby! Ooh I wish we had the video going!* TV was life affirming: I'm on therefore I am. Lenny had been 'on' two years ago, an experience she didn't want to repeat. She had been worried last week that her police file photo might appear on the news as part of the Michael Dorling coverage. It had not. But perhaps his death *had* been a sign, she thought. Perhaps Dr Sakuno was right and it was time to move on.

She looked at the cheap, gold statue of Buddha she had sitting on her desk as a paper weight. It looked serene: one hand stretched out. Giving or taking? Taking, Lenny thought. Everyone took so why should Buddha be different? She tweaked the gold nose and slipped the first Tylenol onto her tongue.

Michael Dorling had grabbed her in the police parking lot.

Right where his enemies plotted daily for his capture. She always knew he took risks. She wanted to be the one to catch him because she liked risk too. His capture would give her power and attention in the force. She was a good cop, but not popular with her colleagues—the Serpico Complex. She never took a free cup of coffee and wouldn't let her partners either. No one liked to work with her. But she did more overtime than anyone in the department and always had plenty of names on her arrest sheets, made the stats look good because she liked catching people.

Chapter 3

THE MILLIONAIRE'S DAUGHTER'S RAGDOLL

The next morning she didn't go into the office early to wipe it over as she usually did. She stayed home in her Astro Boy t-shirt and track pant pyjamas watching TV and eating cornflakes with powdered green tea.

She watched a children's show fondly. What a great job—wearing a fake fur suit five days a week. You didn't even have to speak! She wondered if the position of Humphrey B Bear ever became vacant.

Finally she called the number. She had to know.

'Hello?'

'This is Lenny Aaron.' Humphrey B was going on a picnic, getting very excited and, being mute, was for the twentieth time clapping his fur and vinyl paws, a hollow pat, pat.

'Oh? Oh! Thank you so much for returning my call. You don't know how happy I am to hear from you. I'm sorry I thought you were a man.' The voice had a whiny, breathy edge.

'What can I do for you?' Lenny said flatly.

'You are the cat investigator? I got your name from the RSPCA. They said you're the best in Melbourne. H. Aaron Investigations. Is that you?'

'It's me. What do you want?'

'Well, two things really. We've lost our cat, obviously. It's a Ragdoll. I got it a couple of months ago. It's been missing for a couple of days. I gather cats do wander occasionally but still ...'

'You said two things.'

'Oh. Yes, I did.' There was a long pause. 'I think someone

is going to kill my mother.' It was said with maximum drama. Lenny figured she was now expected to say 'I'll be right there' or 'You can count on me' and race over in her best gumshoe style. But what she actually said was:

'Will you be paying cash or by credit card?'

'Er ... cash, probably ...' Kimberly faltered. 'Did you hear what I said about my mother?'

'Yes, I can't help you with that.'

'I don't understand.'

'Ms Talbott, that's a criminal investigation. This is, as you know, a cat investigating firm.' Firm? Lenny was laying it on a bit thick for a one-room office. 'You got my name from the RSPCA, not Interpol, right? If your mother's life is in danger she needs to contact the police.'

'She won't do that. She's wilful. She treats it as a joke. I don't know what else to say. You must help me.'

'That's not true.'

'What about the cat then?'

'I don't think so.'

There was a long pause because Ms Talbott was not used to being refused.

'May I come to your office and discuss it with you? The telephone is so impersonal, don't you think? I know if we met you'd understand what I—' Lenny hung up.

She had stayed up late last night thinking and doing the housework. Now that the Antolinis' cat and the fat tabby were rescued, her immediate schedule was blank. There were always the outstanding cats but chances were they were dead in some never to be discovered gutter or 'not recoverable' as she told the owners.

It would have been easy to find the Talbott Ragdoll and give Kimberly an enormous bill. Tempting, she thought, as she watered her potted catnip.

She tried a little *Zazen* before she set off for the office. Dr Sakuno encouraged her to meditate every week. In the perfect state of *Zazen*, he told her, the mind became a blank, no thinking. Easy to achieve as a couch potato, not so easy otherwise. In her bedroom Lenny had a three hundred dollar tatami mat and she sat cross-legged, eyes closed.

Today's effort was worthless. Michael Dorling was intruding on her blankness. She gave up and wiped over the tatami with a damp cloth.

The Footscray shopping mall was crowded. Kimberly Talbott and a young man were standing outside Lenny's office. They were not together unless Kimberly's choice of partner belied her appearance. The man—mid twenties and dressed as Hollywood's idea of a clerk in brown pants, cream shirt and wide tie—was very upset. His face scrunched and he darted forward when he realized Lenny was going into the office.

'H. Aaron?' He was a bundle of nerves. Lenny nodded.

'Let's go inside, shall we?' she said, ignoring Kimberly who was watching her closely, doing the social arithmetic. It didn't matter, Lenny thought. Kimberly had come to her.

Mike Bullock was having a smoke in the doorway of the porn shop wearing a Tang-orange t-shirt and beige slacks. The hem on the left leg of his pants was coming down at the front and he had a creamish stain on the shirt.

'Lenny,' he gave her a nod, flicking his eyes at Kimberly. Lenny wondered if he recognized her or if he just fancied her long legs.

'Mike.' She opened the door and stepped into her office. The clerk filed after her and Kimberly Talbott followed him, at a distance.

Kimberly closed the office door behind her and said: 'Ms Aaron, I'm Kimberly Talbott.' It was a statement of wealth, of status, of certain expectations. Lenny didn't respond.

'I had to come.' She slid into the client's chair opposite Lenny's desk and slipped a Gucci folder onto the desk top. 'Of course,' she glanced at the clerk standing beside her who hadn't yet dared to speak. He was breathing heavily and had a sweat mustache. 'You must deal with this gentleman first.

He has something to say about ... a Scottish cat, wasn't it?' She was impatient to be first in line, clearly used to it, but she needed to present herself as amiable. The clerk started nervously when Lenny looked at him.

'Yes, I'm Frank. Frank Taylor. It's my cat, Queenie. A Scottish Fold. You know the breed I take it? Ears folded? Scottish Fold? I mean you do know 'em? Queenie's my pride and joy.' Kimberly Talbott's eyes widened but her face retained something approximating concern for her fellow man. She began a slow scrutiny of the office, eyes settling on the crate of home-made grappa pushed under a cat cage. Her mouth made what Lenny thought could be described as a moue.

'I know them,' Lenny reassured the clerk. Scottish Folds were smart and cute. Rather small, their ears folded forwards giving them the appearance of a stuffed toy or a cartoon cat and they had a deceptive character, pretending tranquillity while any animal smaller than themselves was hunted ruthlessly. She had tracked a couple. 'And your loved one is missing?'

'Yes, that's absolutely right. This morning I made her breakfast and opened the screen door. That's all it takes usually. The noise of the screen banging and she's in like a shot. Knows it's breakfast time. I let her out when I get up, you see. While I have my shower. So she can do her— business.' He looked at Kimberly who was clearly, unlike Lenny, a lady who would be offended at the indelicate mention of the faecal act. Kimberly was examining her fingernails on the desk.

'And this morning she didn't come back in?'

'Exactly! Exactly!' His hands were balled at his sides. 'I called and called and called! I walked around for over an hour yelling! I did the neighbourhood in my car! She's gone! If I don't find her ...' He burst into noisy sobs, skinny shoulders heaving. Kimberly took out a Chanel nail file and began to correct a microscopic flaw on her right pointer.

'Was she in heat?' Lenny asked. Mr Taylor blushed crimson.

'I keep her in when that happens,' he whispered. 'My goodness.' He glanced at Kimberly again.

Lenny gave him the spiel: there was no reason to panic. The cat was probably already at home. Cats liked to roam. They liked to hunt. Yes, even if you feed her well and love her. She's a cat. She's probably gone for a wander.

'No, she wouldn't do that. Not Queenie. I think someone's taken her.' He scrubbed his nose with a Kleenex Lenny forced on him. 'Will you, can you find her for me?'

'There are no guarantees in this life, Mr Taylor.' She pulled out a form, aware that Kimberly was listening, even though the dark, round head was bent over her nails. 'Why don't we get some details?'

It took him fifteen minutes to get the form completed. He was at first too upset to think clearly and then too earnest to hurry. It was important to him to get the details exact. Queenie Taylor was a cream Scottish Fold with—and this, Lenny knew, was a fault that would exclude it from competition—a large short tail rounded at the tip. Eventually Lenny and Mr Taylor shook hands over a deposit of two hundred dollars and she promised to telephone him as soon as she found Queenie or in three hours, whichever came first. He was weeping when he left the office, but he clenched both his hands together in a parting salute that seemed to signify both prayer and victory.

Lenny pulled out a Wet One and cleaned her hands. She placed the gilt-framed photo of Queenie Taylor on the desk. It showed Queenie in the garden, close up and pawing in vain at a tiny yellow butterfly.

She dried her hands on a clean white towel, tugged the new packet of aspirin from her pocket and dropped it into her top drawer. Then, reluctantly, she turned her attention to her second visitor.

Kimberly Talbott was unattractive. She had a spectacular

figure and expensive clothes, but the face was definitely a problem. How unlucky to have beautiful Vivian Talbott as a mother and inherit Henry Talbott's full jowls and bruised-plum eyes.

Even the crisp, white Chanel suit failed to help, except in one very obvious way. The skirt was micro mini and emphasized the longest, sexiest legs Lenny had ever seen. It was impossible not to stare at them. She forced herself to focus instead on Kimberly's hands which, pudgy and tanned, moved constantly as she talked, emphasizing the famed Talbott deformity: on both hands the little fingers bent inwards at a forty-five degree angle from the top knuckle.

When Kimberly's mouth moved, her hands moved—a helpless clutch at the throat, self-deprecating open palms.

'... so you've just got to help me!'

Lenny triggered the rapid-boil jug and prepared two cups and a teapot for green tea. The little Buddha's hand reached out to her. Taking. Definitely taking.

Kimberly placed a polaroid on the desk. It was of herself holding a Seal Point Ragdoll. 'Pretty, isn't she?' she said. 'I call her Marie Antoinette de Paris. She hasn't learned her name though. I really love her, Ms Aaron, although no matter what I do she doesn't have any affection for me. That's why she ran off, I'm sure. She spent half her time biting me.'

'I don't have any free time on my schedule right now.' Lenny was casual.

'You took the Scottish thingy case,' Kimberly protested. 'Look, if it's about money, I can pay anything you ask.' She glanced around the office. 'I'm sure I can.'

Anything she asked? Lenny thought about that new bonsai she had her eye on. And there was going to be a new selection of pots at the garden centre next month. Good pots were never cheap. As so often happens, greed smothered Lenny's doubts.

She said, 'Perhaps I can squeeze you in,' and pulled out a fresh form.

Kimberly knew little about her cat other than its name and breed. She wasn't even sure of its age. Lenny, going on the picture, thought it was about a year old.

'And it's been living in your apartment?' It was a Carlton address. Kimberly shook her head.

'No. Well, sometimes. She's really hairy. They shed, don't they? I'm supposed to brush her every day, apparently. Most of the time I leave her at the house in Brighton. We have a big garden there she can play in. Anyway, that's where she went missing. I'll give you the Brighton address.'

'Fine,' Lenny took the polaroid and paperclipped it to the form.

'Excellent,' Kimberly smiled. She took out two hundred dollars and placed it on top of the form. 'The retainer. And now my mother. I know it sounds silly but if I could explain—'

'No,' Lenny shook her head, 'it's not my area. I can recommend a reputable criminal investigator.'

'Aren't you reputable?' But the heavily mascaraed eyes slipped to the grappa again.

'When you've lost your cat, I'm your man.'

Kimberly took a little china cup of hot tea and placed it on the Hokkaido Snow Festival place mat on her side of the desk. She scanned the room hopefully, took in the cat 'wanted' posters, finally settled on the bonsai as the best bet for a safe topic.

'Are you interested in Japan? My father took Kendell and I to Tokyo when we were kids. They have highrise apartment blocks with those mattress things they sleep on hanging over every balcony. It's cement as far as you can see. Even the parks are grey. And it's so dense. They cram them in like ants. It's very ugly.'

Like you, Lenny thought. She wondered why Kimberly hadn't had more cosmetic surgery. Her nose had to have been done; her father's was raw and bulbous, Kimberly's tiny, Californian.

Kimberly gave up on the small talk. She opened the Gucci folder, took out a bunch of letters and slid them over to Lenny.

'If you could just take a peek. There are six of them, sent to the Brighton house. The one on the blue paper came on Friday.' She clasped her hands.

Lenny laid the letters out on the desk next to the polaroid of the Ragdoll. She sipped her tea. She hadn't seen a threatening letter for years, unless you counted bills. It might be interesting to see if times had changed and it wouldn't be a commitment to look.

They were typed on different machines and different paper. The envelopes were also different, postmarked Melbourne, various suburbs.

The tone of the letters was standard: 'I'll cut you open' was a recurring theme. So was 'Time's nearly up, bitch'. The blue letter added a final sentiment: 'this week!'. Lenny glanced at Kimberly.

'You see why I'm so worried now, don't you, Ms Aaron? My mother says this happens to people like us all the time and it's just a sort of sick joke or envy. I love my mother, Ms Aaron.' This was said vehemently. Too much so, Lenny thought. 'But she's not popular. She has her enemies.'

'Why isn't she popular?'

'Well ...' A pause. 'I'm sure you've seen her photographs. That sort of beauty makes people jealous. And also, my mother isn't very ... well, she has a lot of barriers. She doesn't encourage people to relate to her in a warm way.' Amateur analysis.

'So get her a couple of bodyguards,' Lenny said. She remembered that last year Vivian had switched on the Christmas Tree lights on Swanston Street. She had been given a short speech and a light switch to work with, but she used her props well and played that crowd like a pro. They surged forward like anchovies to pizza. Lenny, watching at home on TV, naturally, had leant forward herself. Vivian teased the crowd, fingers hovering above the shiny, chrome switch and when she finally flicked it on and looked up to the tree, her face framed in a tight, radiant close-up, the cameras didn't cut away to the lights for a whole second.

Kimberly was speaking again. 'Ms Aaron, you seem like a reasonable woman so I'd like to be frank with you, if I may?'

Lenny knew no one could really think she was a reasonable woman.

'You see, my mother doesn't want my father to get upset about this and I don't blame her. He's almost ninety years old.' Her cheeks turned pink. It must be embarrassing to have a geriatric father at her age. 'He's sick now and we're all worried that he might become weaker.'

'So?'

'So, don't you see, security men hovering around all the time would be a strain. My mother says she won't risk it. I talked to her about a private investigator but she says she won't do that either.'

'Why not?'

'She says it's nothing. Anyway, Annie Baron, my mother's assistant, agrees with her.' She was sulky now, mouth turned down. 'You have experience with this sort of thing, don't you? Your advertisement in the Yellow Pages doesn't say cats only.'

'It's an old ad.'

'I mean, I am here *mostly* about Marie Antoinette de Paris. Of course I don't really expect *you* to be able to help with my mother but I thought you could speak to her and pretend to be a proper investigator and then persuade her to hire someone else.' Kimberly stared at the floor. 'Perhaps she's right and I'm making a mountain out of a molehill.'

'When did she show you the letters?' Lenny made herself ignore the 'proper'.

'She didn't. We were at a party together last week and I needed aspirin. I get draining headaches. My mother always has aspirin so I looked in her bag and the letters were there. I suppose it was quite rude but I looked at them and now I'm glad I did. My mother's been going through this alone.'

'No one else knows about it?'

'No. Except Annie. She's no help with a thing like this.'

'Why not?'

Kimberly frowned. 'There's something ... wrong with her. I've never really asked about it. My mother's fond of her and she's good to Kendell—and me. I like her very much.' This was half-hearted. 'She's a bit slow, I suppose you'd say. Or is it something or other challenged these days?'

'I can't help your mother.' Lenny thought it was time to get this out of the way. She wasn't a cop. She was not even a private investigator. She was a cat catcher. 'But I may be able to find your cat.' Kimberly's hands spread wide in supplication. Quite a performance.

'Ms Aaron, I'm beseeching you—'

'That's nice. I've never been beseeched before, but it's still "no". Your mother is probably right. Letter writers don't often follow through. If you're really worried, you should get,' her lips pursed, 'a proper investigator. I don't think my talking to her is going to change her opinion, do you?' Lenny wiped her cup dry with a paper napkin and looked at Kimberly's. 'Drink up. I've got a busy day. I may get to your cat some time this afternoon or early tomorrow. Can I contact you anytime on this number?'

For the first time she saw a hint of real emotion on the other woman's face. The dark eyes narrowed with pure temper. Was she on the verge of a *grand mal* tantrum? Lenny hoped not. She had never had to physically remove anyone from her office before and didn't want to start with a Talbott. But, just in time, and perhaps saved by years of private schooling, Kimberly bit it back. She stacked the letters and slid them back into their folder.

She stood up and tucked the folder under her arm. Lenny dwelled briefly on the taut, shiny thighs. You could bounce dollar coins on them. She wondered if the arms were that good. And the stomach? Firm and lean or soft and silky?

Kimberly saw her looking. She opened her eyes wide then moved her hands deliberately away from her thighs. They gleamed across the desk top.

'If you could come out as soon as possible,' she said. 'I'm frantic about my cat. Poor baby. Do you think she's still alive? Perhaps the Scottish Fudge could wait?'

'Fold.'

Kimberly hesitated, pretended to read the 'wanted' wall.

'Perhaps when you come out to the house and if you see my mother you could have a talk, just in passing. Perhaps recommend someone. I know you said it won't help but it would mean the world to me.'

It was the thighs. There was something irresistible about a woman's thighs. Especially ones that were hard and cellulite free. Lenny liked to imagine the softer parts on the insides, cool and pale.

Her arm was aching. Two years of therapy and she was still feeling it. She wondered about hypnosis but Dr Sakuno shuddered. *Why ask for trouble? Helena san, hypnosis is futile. If you want to tell me, tell me. If not, not.* But perhaps subconsciously I want to tell you? Dr Sakuno always laughed at any mention of the subconscious. *So you have a sore arm! My shoulder hurts after golf! Do I bother you about it?*

Lenny began chewing off pieces of skin from the inside of her lips. By the end of the day she would have a blister.

She looked into the cage. Cleo Harrelson was pacing back and forth. Not much room to pace in that cage but she made a meal of it, tail swishing shittily when Lenny tossed in a fishy bite. Cleo was naturally suspicious. It wasn't feeding time and Lenny didn't give treats unless they were loaded with a strength-sapping potion. She licked it, mouthed it, spat it out, took it up again and finally crunched down.

The last supper.

Chapter 4

KITTEN-KILLING DAY

The pound was isolated on the outskirts of the city beside the highway that led to Werribee. The main building was a low, red-brick sprawl under a flat roof.

Jodie was in the reception nook. She was pretty in a K-Mart way and already, at twenty, plump around the jawline. Today there was a bag of potato chips and a packet of Iced Vo-Vos on the counter.

Lenny glanced at the cat box in her hand. Cleo was animated now. Perhaps the stink of death wasn't completely masked by the disinfectant.

'They'll be in in about half an hour, I think.' Jodie said, meaning Herb and Ross, the staff who drove the pick-up van. She was scraping the icing off the Vo-Vos with her fingernail and eating it. A pile of stripped biscuits lay on the counter. She pushed a copy of *Vogue* across the counter and pointed a sugar-frosted digit at Kate Moss. 'Would that hairstyle suit me?'

'No,' Lenny said, 'she's thin. A lot thinner than you.' She glanced down the corridor. 'Simon finished yet?'

'Not yet,' Jodie had a mini TV under the counter and was watching an entertainment update program. 'Did I tell you I'm going to be an actress? I'm doing a course.'

'That's nice,' Lenny headed down a corridor. Fat chance, she thought.

Simon looked up as Lenny entered. He had a kitten in one green-gloved hand and a syringe in the other. He waved the needle in a 'hello'.

'Lenny!' he beamed like a reliable torch, nudging back his wispy blond hair. He was about her own age and handsome in a soft way. His pointy chin was a little too small for the rest of his face.

Lenny put the cat box at her feet and glanced around the room. There were eight cages against one wall. Five were empty. The other three held a Pekinese, an Abyssinian, and a white moggie with a ripped ear.

There was a portable TV on top of a cabinet. The sound was turned down. It looked like an ABC educational program. Sunburned ten-year-olds trying to connect a series of wires and clips to make a light bulb come on. They pursed their lips and frowned. Lenny longed for a life that simple.

Today's death row victims were nervous, like cows at an abattoir who suddenly realise the cattle prod was a warm-up. It was, she thought, a little cruel to let them watch each other die, but Simon said you had to be practical. He didn't have the energy to go in and out of the door every thirty seconds. Anyway, he said, without malice, this way they could see it was quick.

'I'm looking for a Scottish Fold and a Ragdoll,' Lenny said and forced herself to not look away as he injected the kitten. It peeped and shuddered quickly into death.

'The Fold went missing this morning. It's female, five years old, has a red leather tag with "Queenie" on it. The Ragdoll is maybe a year old. Female, no tag.'

'Sorry, can't help you, mate. I don't think we have any Folds in the sheds and we haven't had a Ragdoll for over a year. But Herb's not back from the run yet.' He put the kitten into a heavy duty black plastic bag on a trolley. 'Pass me the Pekinese, will you?'

Lenny picked up the cage of the Pekinese which squeaked with fright. Simon opened the cage door and the little dog scuttled to him like a friend.

'Sorry, mate, two week limit.' The needle.

The Abyssinian went like a duchess to the guillotine; dignified, tossing a forgiving look to her executioner and a sad smile to the anxious crowd.

Simon looked over the table at Lenny's cat box.

'If that's a stray I could get rid of it for you now.'

'Hm.' Lenny picked the box up, placed it on the table and opened the door. Cleo stepped out onto the table. Simon was filling the syringe from a gleaming flask.

The phone rang in the next room. Simon placed the syringe on the trolley. 'I won't be a sec,' he said on the way out.

Lenny saw there was a small, red-lined cut just above Cleo's shoulder. It must have happened when the cat box was thrown onto the road. She looked round the room. There was a cabinet against the wall with a glass door displaying cotton balls, antiseptic and bandages. She removed a bottle of antiseptic and a cotton ball and swabbed at Cleo's shoulder before she realized what she was doing. The cat didn't flinch or scratch—it didn't utter a squeak. Then, to Lenny's absolute horror, Cleo licked her hand. She pushed it back in the cat box.

Simon bounced back into the room. 'OK,' he picked up the syringe. 'Shall we?'

'No.' Lenny picked up the cat box.

'No?'

'Maybe later.' Lenny blinked. 'I want to check out the cages.'

There were six sheds holding in total three hundred cages of various sizes. Up to about two-thirds capacity today, she thought, mostly valueless strays. There were no Scottish Folds or Ragdolls. Cleo Harrelson was silent during the walk.

Lenny was filling out a description slip for Queenie Taylor and Marie Antoinette Talbott when Herb and Ross arrived at reception. Herb was eating mini doughnuts from a big bag and offered them around. He insisted Lenny take the last chocolate doughnut. He patted his round gut fondly.

'Go on, Len, I'm stuffed anyway,' he groaned, a hamster peaking out of his green work shirt pocket. It sniffed nervously.

Ross Arbuckle came in a moment later, thirty-five and painfully thin. With moist eyes he held a hand to his stomach and winced.

'How's the ulcer?' Lenny asked.

'He's been on a cream diet for a whole month,' Herb said, shaking his head. 'Doesn't put on a stone. Now if I look at a doughnut ...' He grinned and took out a pineapple-iced hoop. 'Like this one ...' It fell into his mouth. 'Looking for anything special, Len?'

'A Scottish Fold,' she explained. 'Went missing this morning in the Clayton area. And a Ragdoll that's been missing for a couple of days now. Last seen in Brighton.'

'Brighton? Well, well. I've never liked Ragdolls. Ever picked one up? Urgh.' He shuddered. 'They feel all lumpy or something. We had a Fold in a couple of months ago, but it was claimed the same day. Now they're cute little buggers. Only dogs in the van today, though.'

'We've got four Labrador pups,' Ross said. 'They were dumped in a garbage bin behind Woolworths. If I could catch some of these ...' He turned away for a moment, hunted in his pocket for a large handkerchief. Herb shook his head sympathetically. Jodie sniggered and peered at Herb's pocket.

'Where'd you get the rat?' she asked.

'This is a hamster, Jodie, which I found in Cunningham Park. Must've got left behind by a kid.' Herb placed the rodent on the reception counter and it ran back and forth and stopped at the pile of de-iced Vo-Vos. It placed its tiny paws on the edge of a biscuit.

'Piss off!' said Jodie to the hamster, grabbing the biscuits away from it. 'Thanks Herb, I was gonna eat those after.' She watched the hamster do a couple more sprints across the counter. It was podgy and golden brown with a cute face. Finally, frustrated beyond human endurance, Jodie produced a cardboard box and used a notebook to flick the hamster inside. It squealed, landed with a soft thud and began to scrabble at a corner.

'Gross,' said Jodie. 'Simon shouldn't waste a needle on

this. I'll chuck it to the cats later.'

Ross marched around the counter and snatched up the cardboard box.

'Over my dead body,' he said.

'Whatever you reckon,' Jodie laughed as Ross carried the hamster away. She rolled her eyes at the others, drumming up support. 'What an old dag,' she seemed to say. She smirked with youth on her side if nothing else.

Lenny scrubbed her hands with hot water and disinfectant before leaving. She put the cat box on the back seat of her car. Cleo Harrelson was very quiet. Lenny poked a fish flavoured snack through the bars. Cleo let it drop in front of her face but didn't touch it, sniffed without moving.

'Snap out of it,' Lenny said, suddenly angry. She waited until the cat began to eat then started the engine.

She needed a pick me up. The pound had a way of sinking her chronic depression level to the bottom. She decided to go out to Brighton, to the Talbotts' house. Was it too much to ask the Talbotts for a hundred bucks a day? She thought not.

Central Brighton was a combination English seaside town and *nouveau-riche* hideaway; hair-rollers and high-rollers. The cars parked along the tree-lined streets were Mercedes, Volvos and BMWs.

She drove up to Cedars Court, a cul-de-sac with ivy-covered homes ranging behind native Australian bush gardens. At the end of the street was a tall hedge with a long pathway leading through it to the beach. Number twenty-two, even from a distance the biggest house in the street, was last on the left of the cul-de-sac behind a dark stone wall that was probably wired up to a security system. For weight, she figured. A bird or cat walking on it wouldn't trip the alarm, but a person would. The gates were iron and locked. Lenny buzzed.

'Lenny Aaron. I'm here about a missing cat.'

'Come right in, Ms Aaron.' A woman's voice, friendly.

Lenny parked in the circular drive. She looked at Cleo, who remained resolutely silent, and had an urge to poke a finger through the bars and stroke a small fur paw. She overcame it. That kind of bonding was fatal to someone in her line of work. She would end up like Ross Arbuckle with a house full of death-row pets.

'I'll be back.' She left both front windows down, the trees shading the car. She didn't want the cat to dehydrate to death now she had made a potential fool of herself over it.

The garden was lush, blue-couch grass, the pool, on the left of the house, a contrasting darker blue, some kind of lapis lazuli tile. The flowers were all native Australian: Christmas bells, orange everlasting and golden Guinea flowers. The trees were giants. Fifty years old at least, Lenny thought. There were no signs of digging and no plastic bottles of water. They obviously didn't have a dog here. It didn't look like the sort of place a cat would be welcome either.

Behind the pool there were changing rooms. Blue and white rubber rings were stacked against the wall and a white pool bed floated at one side of the pool. White wooden deck chairs dotted the grass. It reminded Lenny of *The Philadelphia Story*. Behind the changing room was a tennis court and behind that another building that looked like a small house.

The main house was a two-storey, square building in dark brick covered with creeping ivy. The double doors at the front of the house were open and a tall woman was waiting. Plump and about sixty, she was dressed in a severe linen frock. Faded blonde hair was rolled into a bun and she had a pink and tan smiling face. Her hands were heavy, capable, without nail polish or jewellery. She reminded Lenny of a nurse. She glanced at Lenny's car.

'My goodness we don't see many of those in this driveway,' she said. 'Good morning to you, I'm Margaret Gross, the Talbotts' housekeeper.'

'I'm Lenny Aaron.' She held back from responding to the crack about her car, sensing an origin in clumsiness rather than malice. Up close she noticed the woman's cheeks were more than rosy. There were a few broken capillaries and a little bloat around the eyes. Blood pressure or booze? she wondered.

'Kimberly told us you might come by today so we're all ready for you.' Ms Gross gestured for her to go into the house. 'Although none of us really know what to tell you. I mean, perhaps I shouldn't say this, but it is only a cat, isn't it? I suppose you make quite a lot out of it? Money, I mean.'

'I get by,' Lenny said. 'I don't need to see over the house unless you think the animal could have become trapped somewhere inside.'

'Is that possible? It is a large house.'

'If it's been three days now, it may be dead,' Lenny said. 'In which case you would smell it.'

'How unpleasant. I don't think I've noticed any nasty smells.' The housekeeper smiled. 'Do come in and meet Mrs Talbott and have a cold drink.'

In the living room at the front of the house, one large table held framed photos of the family in various stages. Early marriage shots showed Vivian already achieving her Jackie Onassis glamour.

'You must be Ms Aaron.' Vivian Talbott entered the room. People say it's what inside that counts, but Lenny would swap her inside for Vivian's outside anytime.

She seemed too young to be Kimberly's mother. She could pass for thirty and it didn't look surgical. Her black hair was long, straight and shiny. The tan was light and even and her violet eyes were penetrating. The lashes were thick and fluttered, at odds with the still, cool eyes behind them.

'I'm Vivian Talbott,' a long hand slid into Lenny's and gave it a hard squeeze. Up close she smelled of sandalwood and Lenny could see she was wearing a complete make-up. She wore an ivory blouse and loose grey pants, and dressed them up with a gold Bulgari watch and an enormous square cut diamond ring. She combined the colouring of Elizabeth Taylor with the physique of Faye Dunaway.

She folded herself into the couch opposite Lenny, took out a small paging device and a minute later Margaret Gross appeared at the doorway. Vivian asked for coffee.

'So, Ms Aaron—'

'Lenny.'

'Please call me Vivian.' Her voice was low and silky, 'strine trawling just under the surface.

'Kimberly tells me you're going to find her cat.' The violet eyes never moved from Lenny's face. 'She's at uni right now but I suppose I can tell you anything you need to know. It hasn't been here very long and frankly I'm not missing it. Look at this,' her hand drifted down to the carved teak leg of the sofa. There were several small scratch marks. 'Ruined. And she insisted on leaving it here. She decided her own apartment was too small. It's been very difficult. And now, as if it hasn't caused enough upheaval, the wretched thing goes missing. Do you suppose it's dead?' She seemed careless, even hopeful.

'I'm going to check the grounds and do a tour of your neighbours' gardens.'

'I don't mind saying I've got my fingers crossed,' Vivian's long hands were neatly folded in her lap. 'For death, I mean.' Her posture was relaxed but there was something about her that was unnerving, a distracted expression as though the cat was the last thing on her mind. Lenny hesitated. She thought of Dr Sakuno's advice: *Take the next step.*

'Kimberly mentioned some letters,' she said.

'Did she?' Vivian shrugged, but her eyes narrowed.

'Perhaps you need a criminal investigator,' Lenny suggested.

'I don't think so.'

Margaret arrived with a tray bearing a Royal Doulton coffee pot and cups.

'Thank you, dear. Lenny, will you have lunch with me? Maggie, tell Liz, will you?' Margaret exited. Vivian, somewhere in the space of the last thirty seconds, seemed to have come to a decision. She leaned forward, allowing Lenny the luxury of a close up.

'Lenny, this thing with the letters is really stupid. Just nonsense. I wouldn't even worry about it except that Kimberly won't stop nagging me. I'm not going to be topped. It's a ridiculous prank.' Vivian sighed, gazed out of the window at her garden for a while, thinking. It was a dramatic gesture, Lenny thought, but why not? If she'd had a profile like Vivian's, she'd want people to get a good look at it too. Vivian's jawline and neck were as tight and smooth as a young girl's. Lenny searched for scars. They would be up near the ears: tiny incision marks that were almost invisible unless you knew what you were looking for. Lenny knew. That was the sort of detail the coroner liked to point out. *Get in close. Closer! You see, there, behind the big scar— that's from the razor her husband used to slash her—but look, here, the old scar. Wonderful, isn't it? Cosmetic of course.*

Finally Vivian looked back and was smiling again.

'I'm a bit careless. People will tell you I'm a bitch. It's always been like that. I got letters like this once before, when I was in school. They turned out to be from a girl in my history class. I never even knew why. Some kind of teenage jealousy. I was unkind to her without realizing. Who knows? The point is, these things happen to people like me. It's nothing.'

'We should talk about the Ragdoll's habits,' Lenny said.

'Yes. Absolutely,' Vivian laughed. 'I'm bothering you with something you can't possibly deal with. I suppose you don't get many threatening letters in the world of cat detecting. Is that what you call it? Kimberly told me you have pictures on the wall of missing cats? Like a sheriff's office. It sounds bizarre. Let's certainly not talk about me.'

'Right.' Lenny drank her coffee. Her lipstick came off on the cup. Vivian's hadn't—why was that? 'But it wouldn't hurt to take precautions. Security guards ...' She wasn't sure why she was persisting. Perhaps it had been Kimberly's dig about a 'proper investigator' and now Vivian's 'something you can't possibly deal with'.

'My husband is in Melbourne at the moment. He's been ill this year.' She shrugged. 'He'd recognize a security team. He's not senile.'

'What's wrong with him?'

'He has cancer of the stomach and oesophagus. It's very sad. He'll die this year.' Vivian sighed, lit a Dunhill, hesitated. She leaned forward slightly. 'I don't want him to worry ...'

Lenny wondered what kind of relationship they had. He must like looking at her.

'Let me recommend someone,' she said. It was stupid to force the issue, to make suggestions at all. Safer to stay out of other people's business.

'No need.' Vivian shook her head. 'I don't believe they're going to try anything. Letter writers don't, do they?'

'So why did you keep the letters? Why not destroy them?'

'Ah,' Vivian laughed. She pushed the cigarette packet and Cartier lighter across the table. Lenny accepted and lit up. 'I don't know how you'll take this—I enjoyed them. Going out and meeting friends and all the time, lurking in my bag, these letters. It gave me a thrill.' She shrugged. 'I suppose that sounds pathetic. But sometimes it's very boring being Mrs Henry Talbott.'

'It shouldn't be difficult to identify the sender,' Lenny said.

'Really?'

'These kinds of letters are often sent by family or close friends.'

'In that case it would have to be friends,' Vivian said decisively. 'I have no family except Henry and the children. Henry has no reason to threaten me and the children love me.'

Love was no guarantee against violent attack, Lenny thought. Often, in fact, the reverse. Mothers beat toddlers to death because they wouldn't stop crying. Sisters attacked brothers with kitchen forks. Family crises were always the bloodiest.

'You talk like you have some experience,' Vivian finished a cigarette and began another. 'Is this some sort of trick? This whole cat thing? I mean Kimberly and that cat were not what I'd call close. The damned thing nipped at her every chance it got. She dumped it on me and now I'm supposed to believe she's *paying* someone to look for it when she could buy another one in a snap? Who are you really, Ms Aaron? Would you mind telling me that?'

'I'm here about the Ragdoll,' Lenny said quietly. 'Your daughter mentioned the letters and I said I don't handle that line of work now.'

'Well, I want to know why you think you can sit there offering advice. If you're just big noting yourself that's one thing but if it's something else I think you might tell me.'

'I used to be a police officer.' The words came out before Lenny considered their impact on herself as well as her host. Vivian stubbed out her cigarette, hard.

'I see,' she said. 'So it is a set-up. Kimberly got you here to nag me. Is the cat even missing, I now wonder?' She was annoyed.

'As far as I know, Marie Antoinette is missing,' Lenny shot back. She was getting angry. 'Look, I came here for the cat. I'm not interested in your letters.' That was a lie. 'I'm no longer a police officer. I investigate cats. Period. And your daughter's cat, frankly, is becoming more trouble than I care for. I'll give her the name of another investigator. Please don't see me out.'

'I wasn't thinking of it,' Vivian laughed suddenly. 'Please don't go.' Lenny waited. 'I'm sorry, I'm very rude. I'm really sorry. Please.'

Lenny stayed where she was. She didn't want to. What

was it about some people that made you feel suddenly unsure of yourself, as if in their presence you were in another country where your old rules and attitudes could be dismissed with a wave of a hand.

'Stay and have some lunch with me. We can talk about Marie Antoinette de Paris. Isn't that the stupidest name for a cat?' Another perfect smile. 'Please, Lenny?'

Chapter 5

THE LAP OF LUXURY

The kitchen was at the back of the house. It had windows on two walls looking out onto both the swimming pool and the immense trees shading the back garden. It was a grand scale kitchen with obligatory Aga stove and colonial table. There were two TVs, one by the sink and one mounted on the wall next to the table. Both were showing a Tom Selleck movie about Japanese baseball. Lenny had seen it. She didn't like anything with Tom Selleck even if it was set in *Nippon*. Dr Sakuno had seen it too and said it was racist, complete with jokes about Asian shortness, the inability of the Japanese to pronounce a rolling 'r', and squat toilets.

Lenny's mouth was full of gourmet lettuce and sun-dried tomatoes. Her head was swimming in Vivian's sandalwood scent. She wasn't used to spending time with beautiful women.

The cook wore a blue floral smock and a stainless white apron. Despite her age, she moved with an athletic spring in her step. She was slight with soft, curling, grey hair pulled back into a bun. A few wisps escaped around her face. She had once been pretty. The cook, Vivian explained, would soon be sixty-nine.

She served the meal politely but there was none of the housekeeper's fawning. Her manner was brisk, efficient and pompous. When Lenny moved her side plate to the right, the cook made a point of moving it back where it belonged. Vivian rolled her eyes for Lenny's benefit.

'Liz's been on Henry's household staff now for over thirty years,' she said quietly, drinking her second large glass of water with a handful of vitamin pills. 'We'd be lost without her. She's a great cook.' She paused to burp.

The insides of mouths and anything to do with the digestive
system had always been repulsive to Lenny. She couldn't stand to share cutlery or glasses. If she was eating an ice-cream and someone got a bite of it, she pretended she didn't want it anymore and gave it to them. As a result she had an undeserved reputation for generosity.

'Cold water,' Vivian said as though that explained everything. She leaned close to Lenny to whisper: 'She's a bit of a pain, actually. Her saintly routine gets on my nerves but I think we're stuck with her until she drops, although Carol, my son's fiancée, has other ideas.' She pressed a hand to her oesophagus. 'She says we have too many old people in this house. She calls it a geriatric home.' She sighed. 'She's very keen to make some changes. I can't really blame her. There is a bit of an oldie feeling around here, but Henry's fond of Liz and Max.'

'Who is Max?' Lenny asked.

'The gardener.' Vivian stretched out her hands on the table and looked at them. She glanced at Lenny's own hands. 'Yours are much nicer than mine, aren't they, and I spend a fortune on mine.' She chewed her lip for a moment then lowered her voice so it was barely audible. 'Listen, *would* you help out? Not with the cat. With me, I mean. The letters.'

'It's not my field anymore,' Lenny prevaricated.

'It might be *fun*,' Vivian cupped her chin in her hands and a smile moved over her face. It was flirtatious, made by someone who knew the effect her smiles had on others. 'I could pay *anything* you ask, you know.' Like mother like daughter, Lenny thought.

'Are you afraid you're going to be killed?' she asked.

'No,' Vivian smiled. 'But it's become an annoyance. If you find out who it is and we scare them into stopping, all well and good. Will you help me?' Vivian wiped her lips on a white linen napkin, oblivious to the olive oil smear she left behind. She was close enough to touch. Lenny swallowed her juice. Dr Sakuno's words pounded in her head. *Get on with it. Take the next step.* Perhaps Buddha was giving this time.

'Yes.'

Vivian activated her paging device and in a minute Maggie appeared in the doorway. 'Maggie, fetch Max here, will you? And prepare a room for Ms Aaron. She'll be staying with us for a week.'

'For the cat?' Maggie was surprised. She didn't know about the letters, Lenny thought.

'And to help me with my correspondence.' Maggie nodded and departed.

'I *won't* be staying,' Lenny said. She didn't like to wake up in the night and not know where she was.

'You could stay a few days,' Vivian said. 'I mean,' she lowered her voice, 'the last letter said "this week" right? So if nothing ... happens,' she gave another odd little blink of the eyes, 'then I'm all right. We can tell everyone you're my temporary assistant. Only Annie and Kimberly know about the letters. Please. A week.'

'All right, a week,' Lenny said. It was against her better judgment but she could triple her usual fee.

'I charge three hundred a day plus expenses,' she said. The figure came out of nowhere and was, she knew, her last try at rejection.

'Whatever,' Vivian smiled.

Max walked into the kitchen. He was in his sixties. The cook hurried to give him a plastic-wrapped plate of sandwiches and she slipped a Snickers into the pocket of his khaki dungarees. Her blue eyes were warm for the first time.

'You must be starved,' she said. 'I've made lemonade.'

'Great,' Max grinned. He squinted through thick glasses.

'Max, this is Lenny Aaron.' Vivian introduced them as he stayed back politely, eyes meeting Lenny's. 'Lenny, meet Maxwell Curtis, our gardener. He's a genius with plants. We owe this gorgeous garden entirely to him.'

'It's nice,' Lenny said although besides bonsai she couldn't care less about plants.

'It's better than that, it's marvellous,' the cook said. 'When we moved in here the garden was a jungle. Max is a miracle worker.'

'Liz,' Max smiled, 'that's too much. Mrs Talbott is the designer,' he said to Lenny. 'I carry out her ideas.'

'He's being modest,' Vivian said. 'Max, I'd like some flowers for Lenny's room.'

'No problem.' Max nodded. 'I'm finished with the weeding so I'll cut some new blooms for the whole house if you like.'

'Thank you.' Vivian smiled a 'you can go' smile. Max headed out onto the terrace at the back of the house, the cook behind him.

'Guess who has a crush on the gardener,' Vivian grinned. 'It's very sweet at their ages, isn't it? I don't think anything will come of it though. Liz has been after Max for years.'

'Do you have any reason to suspect either of them is writing the letters?'

'If you can think of a motive, you're better than me. Liz Dodd probably thinks I could come down a peg or two but she thinks that about everyone except Max. And *he's* a dear. He grows champion roses, you know. There's a white one: the Vivian Talbott,' she smiled wryly. 'It's exquisite.'

'And Annie Baron?'

'I suppose Kimberly told you horrible things about her?' Vivian said. 'I can tell you right now Annie is not the problem here. Kimmie is ... phobic about illness.' Another smile, this time the lips were thin, the eyes cool. Must be tough to be the goddess's ugly child, Lenny thought.

'Where is Annie now?'

'Shopping. I needed a few personal items. She's perfectly able to drive and use a credit card. She's not an idiot.'

'Kimberly said Annie doesn't want you to investigate the letters.'

'Did she?' Vivian was surprised. She hesitated for a moment. 'Annie knows I'm not in danger. She's very practical.'

'Do you always take Annie's advice?'

'Only when it's good,' Vivian laughed.

'Lenny,' she reached across the table, hesitated, pulled back. 'Annie has been with me for a long time. I trust her. Don't waste your time with her. She can be controlling sometimes.' She paused. 'But she's not a threat.' She sipped the water, looking away.

After lunch Vivian announced plans to go out for the afternoon. She laughed when Lenny asked if she shouldn't go with her.

'I think I'm quite safe shopping in Toorak. Look for the cat. Maggie will show you over the house.' She hesitated for a moment then put a hand on Lenny's bony shoulder. She was right to hesitate—Lenny didn't like to be touched. She had rarely been caressed as a child. Veronica Aaron had kept her hands to herself as though touching her child would burn her, and Ted had always been too sick to manage more than the odd hair ruffle.

But it was surprisingly pleasant to be touched by Vivian. In fact her shoulder tingled. The feeling went all the way up her neck.

'Lenny, I'm very glad you're staying. I'm sure Kimberly will be thrilled when you find her little cat.' Her eyes moved away. 'Lenny, I almost believe I could tell you anything. Do you get that feeling sometimes with people?'

The tingling continued, so warm and so pleasant that Lenny
had an urge to cover the hand with her own and press it more closely against the soft skin of her neck. It was so bizarre and shocking a sensation that it was almost paralyzing. She forced herself to speak.

'Is this part of the deal?' she asked flatly and dropped her shoulder to remove the hand.

Vivian's eyes widened, her face froze: prima ballerina rebuffed by stage hand. She recovered in a second and smiled.

It was fascinating in close up, the ability to switch her mood at will.

'Are you this tough with the cats?' she said softly.

They walked outside together. Lenny went to her car and took out the cat box. Cleo Harrelson mewed tetchily.

'You can't have that here,' Vivian said. 'It's been a nuisance having Kimberly's cat. We have the internal security system on at night. We had to keep it upstairs in Kimberly's room to keep it from setting off the sensors downstairs. It howled all night. Anyway, Annie dislikes cats. I promised there'd be no more.'

'Fine.'

Margaret Gross was happy to show Lenny around the house. Lenny smelled a whiff of whisky on the housekeeper's breath. Bingo! She must have forgotten the breath mints. They gave the cat some water in the kitchen. Lenny tied a lead to its collar and hooked it onto a table leg on the terrace. Cleo Harrelson lashed out with a paw and missed—definitely recovering from the morning's trauma.

'Will the cat be staying?' Margaret was doubtful.

'No,' Lenny said, although she had no idea what she was going to do with it for a week. 'Has Vivian ever had any pets here other than Marie Antoinette?'

'Goodness, no!' Margaret smiled. 'Never liked that kind of thing. The children had pony club, of course.' Of course. 'But we never have animals in the house.'

'Because?'

'Untidy,' Margaret said after a long pause. 'Vivvie likes things to be neat. Well, you see the scratch marks we've got now because of the cat? We had a dead finch in the middle of the living room carpet last week.'

'Vivian said Annie doesn't like animals.'

'Hmm.' The housekeeper's eyes squinted. 'It's not my place ...'

Lenny followed like a member of an art gallery tour as Margaret led her into the dining room. On the wall was an oil portrait of Henry and Vivian. Vivian, smiling, wore pearls, a 1920s dress and held a pale hand at her throat. The other hand rested on her husband's arm. Henry was seated in a big leather armchair and looked bullish and fighting fit, painted to look twenty years younger than he actually was.

Lenny didn't look forward to meeting him. She feared illness. She had seen Henry many times on TV but he had been out of the public eye now for over six months. She wondered who was running the business. Vivian? Kimberly? Was the Talbott empire linked to the letters?

On the right side of the house were Henry's study and the library. The study was locked. The library was shelves from floor to ceiling. Margaret commented that the children or guests kept bestsellers in their rooms but the library was reserved for 'quality'.

The books (Lenny pulled out a Thomas Hardy) looked brand new: no turned down corners, no pencil marks in the borders, no food stains or finger smudges. Novels were mostly the leather-bound variety and not made to be read.

'Do you take care of this house yourself?' Lenny asked. 'Who else is on staff?'

'I have a couple of young girls come in twice a week and we give the whole house a going over,' Margaret explained, 'but that aside, it's just me. Liz Dodd,' the name was ever so gently stressed, 'does all the kitchen work and table setting and clearing. We get in some young people to help out for dinner parties and if there's a big function, we cater. I'm cleaning and laundry. Annie Baron does Vivian's personal jobs and Eric takes care of Mr Talbott.' She paused to wrinkle her nose and look snooty. 'Max takes care of the garden. If there's a lot on, we hire a young man from Elwood to come in and give him a hand. A private company trims the trees once a year, of course.'

'Why are the regular staff so old?' Lenny asked and watched the housekeeper's affronted blink. Well, too bad. She had always been the bad cop in an interrogation.

'Mrs Talbott is loyal to her staff,' Margaret said through pinched lips. Her chin was up a couple of centimetres too.

'What do you think of Liz and Max?' Lenny asked.

'I don't know about *her*. She keeps herself to herself.' Margaret's mouth made a tight cat's bottom as she removed the *Works of Monet* from Lenny's hands and re-shelved it. She took a polishing cloth from her pocket and wiped the spine.

'Maxwell Curtis is a good gardener and he keeps out of my way,' Margaret continued. 'When you've worked together for this number of years you expect trouble. We've never had any because we understand each other.'

The rooms at the back of the house next to the kitchen were Margaret's own room, the cook's room and the bathroom and toilet they shared between them. Margaret's room was crowded with personal items. There were several embroidered scenes of European cities. A particularly large one of the Eiffel Tower hung over the television. Lenny searched for bottles of booze but there were none. She spotted a small cabinet with a lock next to the bed head. Ten to one they were in there.

The cook's room, although furnished identically, was spartan in comparison, with few personal effects on display. There was a bouquet of flowers in a glass vase at the window. A present from Max, Lenny thought. She wondered if she would find a framed photo of Max in the drawers next to the bed. Unrequited love could be a dangerous thing. Still, there was nothing here to suggest Liz Dodd hated Vivian.

Max, she was told, had a one-room flat behind the garage, next to his toolshed. Men were 'better alone' was Margaret's explanation. She added that Max took all his meals in the main house.

'God knows how many times I've had to eat roast beef and Yorkshire pudding because Max Curtis fancies it.'

'Who staffs the other Melbourne homes?' Lenny asked as

they went up the staircase in the centre of the house.

'Kimberly has a private company clean her place once a week.' Margaret walked along the corridor, gesturing at doors and stating the names of occupants.

Henry and his secretary, Eric, had rooms at the front of the house, overlooking the drive. Vivian had the largest suite and the best beach view. Annie was next to Vivian and Lenny was to be in the guest room next to Annie. Kendell and Kimberly had rooms on the left overlooking the pool.

'Mr Talbott's condominium and Vivian's Toorak house use a private cleaning company too,' Margaret continued. 'Of course I have to keep an eye on the Toorak house. Vivian may only be there once or twice a week but she likes it to have flowers and be aired. She's very particular about things smelling nice.'

They were in Lenny's room. On the right side of the house, it had a beach view but no balcony. There was a double bed with ivory linen and lots of little pillows. There was also an antique dressing table, a small writing desk and a very expensive set-up of TV, video, stereo and telephone.

Margaret gave Lenny a private extension number, a set of house keys, a list of family phone numbers and the codes for the house security system.

'Vivian said you would need these,' she said. 'It's all very elaborate for a cat hunt.'

'Hmm.'

'I'll unpack your things if you like when you bring them. Bring something posh for tomorrow night.'

'Hmm?'

'Vivian's having a dinner party for a few old friends. Semi-formal. Just something simple will do.'

Lenny scrutinized the housekeeper.

'Were you hired through an agency?' she asked. Margaret shook her head and laughed.

'Bless you, no. I've always taken care of Vivian. I used to work at Little Pines.'

Lenny wanted a cigarette, some green tea and a Tylenol.
'Little Pines?' she asked.

'The children's home.' Then Lenny remembered. In every story she had ever read about Vivian, she was 'The Gympie Orphan'. It sounded like an X File—The Gympie Orphan, The East Coast Bigfoot.

She pulled out a packet of Marlboro from her shoulder-bag and lit up. She felt annoyed with herself. They were doing a real number on her, especially Vivian with her charm school finesse and touchy–feely manner.

'What was your job at the home?' she asked. Margaret sensed the sudden hostility. She crossed her solid arms across her breasts.

'I don't see how my history has anything to do with you finding a poor little cat. Or *helping* Vivian,' Maggie continued. She looked suspicious. 'What kind of help would you be providing, I'd like to know.'

I bet you would, Lenny thought.

'How long was Vivian in the home? Why wasn't she adopted?' she pressed.

Margaret stiffened. It was supposed to communicate a haughty refusal to answer.

Alone in the bedroom Lenny flicked on the TV. Sheffield Shield: Queensland vs Victoria. Bewdy! And a great picture. Must be that big aerial on the roof. Her own flat's aerial was bent. Sometimes when the ghosting was particularly bad it was hard to judge the close line calls in tennis. During last year's men's finals at Wimbledon she had been forced to sit next to the TV holding the aerial at a forty-five degree angle during the final set.

She pulled out her pills and took two with a glass of water from the pitcher next to her bed. It would be nice to pull the curtains and spend the rest of the afternoon zonked in front of the screen.

But there would be no snoozing today. She had a job to do. She had cats to find.

Chapter 6

CREEPY'S CAT, LENNY'S MOTHER

At Clayton she stopped at a Seven Eleven and bought a small tin of 'Mon Petit' for the Siamese and a bottled water to share. Cleo tested the bars of her box with a paw.

'No way, fur face,' she said but a couple of pats later and the two of them were strolling together, Cleo Harrelson wearing a short chain attached to a chest harness.

Lenny started her usual procedure. First check around the owner's own home. Mr Taylor said he had searched but that meant nothing. An amateur never knew what to look for.

Mr Taylor lived in a one-storey house with a white picket fence and a handmade post-box. It had a ceramic cat placard glued on. The stencilled name said 'R. Taylor Esq. & Queenie'. Looked like Mr T and the cat had a groovy thing going.

She knocked on a neighbour's door. A petite Italian woman opened it. She was about thirty years old with black permed curls, rosy cheeks and a baby in her arms.

'Ma! Turn the TV down, will you?!' She yelled over her shoulder.

'Yes?' The woman looked at Lenny. Another child, about three years old, came to her legs and tugged at them, big brown eyes gazing at Lenny. It saw Cleo and squealed.

'Kitty!' It reached out a chubby hand.

'Alessandro!' Mama yanked the kid back. 'Don't touch it. It'll lick your face and you'll get a worm in your brain!' She raised her eyebrows at Lenny. 'Look, you're not a weird religion, are you? Because we're all Catholics.'

'I'm looking for Mr Taylor's cat. A Scottish Fold,' Lenny said. 'It went missing this morning.'

Someone called out from inside.

The woman turned. 'Nothing, Ma! Just Creepy's cat!' She looked back at Lenny. 'You're not a friend of his, are you?'

'No,' Lenny said. 'Have you seen the cat?'

The woman shrugged.

The next four houses produced the same response. Everyone knew about Creepy and his cat. Everyone knew it had folded ears. No one had seen it today. In the garden of the fifth house a ginger-haired skinny-limbed woman, ballooned stomach in a Peter Rabbit maternity t-shirt, was watering her grass. She had a toddler on the lawn. It was mashing a slug into the dirt. There was also a Rottweiler, untethered, a metre from the child.

Lenny was amazed Mr Taylor hadn't mentioned this.

'Excuse me,' she called over the fence. 'I'm looking for Mr Taylor's cat. A Scottish Fold called Queenie. Have you seen it?'

'No, I haven't seen it. No.' A glance at her dog. 'No.' Bingo! Lenny zeroed in on the dog's front paws, looking for traces of blood. Nothing. But Ginger had probably washed it off with the hose.

'We don't have anything to do with him,' the woman said. 'Stay, Rex! STAY!' Because the dog had caught Cleo Harrelson's scent and was growling. The toddler giggled and slapped Rex's nose hard:

'Wex ... ' The dog gave the kid a look.

'Jason, stop that,' the woman switched off her hose. 'Rex, heel. HEEL!'

'The cat disappeared this morning,' Lenny prompted.

'Look, we don't know anything, like I told you!' The woman put her hands on her hips. 'My husband doesn't let us have anything to do with Cree—that gentleman. If something happened to his cat it's his own fault. Shouldn't be out on the street, should it? They're destroying this country's natural flora.'

The woman bent down and picked up the toddler.

'Rex, inside,' she said. Then, when the dog didn't move: 'Now!'

Lenny found Queenie Taylor about a minute later. Around the corner from Ginger's house in a drain. Someone had lifted up the iron grate and dropped it in. It was half a metre down to the bottom of the drain. Lenny had to lie on the road and stretch in with her hand and it was wet and dirty, full of mulched leaves.

To her amazement she felt the cat move when she touched it. It gave the most pitiful bleat she had ever heard and when she pulled it out, she saw why. Rex had done a real number on it: three deep and open gouges on the side of its body and a bite wound to the back of the neck.

The cat cried against her chest. Cleo Harrelson mewed urgently.

'Bloody hell!'

She took off her jacket, wrapped up Queenie Taylor as best she could and walked quickly back to her car. She pulled out her address book: vets in the Clayton area. Bob Mulcahy.

She called Mr Taylor as she drove, told him Queenie was hurt and to meet her at the vet's. He hung up before she finished speaking.

It was a quiet day at Bob Mulcahy's offices, the only patient a sad-looking Labrador. Lenny strode past it and put her jacket bundle on the counter. The pretty receptionist picked it up and walked swiftly to the back room.

'Come through, Lenny,' she said over her shoulder. 'Bob! Code blue.' Their little joke.

Bob fingered the wounds with gentle hands. Mounted high on one wall was an old TV. It was tuned to 'The Bold And The Beautiful'.

'All right, little one. We'll fix you up. Don't you worry.' He reached for a needle. 'Anaesthesia might kill the poor little bugger, but she's not gonna let me clean her and sew her up without it. What was it?'

'Rottweiler,' Lenny said. She got no further because Mr Taylor rushed into the room, saw Queenie's torn open body and fainted. He woke up disoriented and tearful to find a cushion under his head and a dog blanket over his body. They didn't notice him at first. It was the wedding of the year on 'The B And B' and Bob, Suzanna and Lenny had their eyes glued to the screen. Mr Taylor had to mew faintly to get attention.

'Are you all right?' Suzanna, the receptionist, asked him. He jumped up and rushed to the table where Queenie Taylor had been cleaned, sutured and bandaged.

'Will she be ... ?'

'She's lost a lot of blood—Mr Taylor, was it?' Bob Mulcahy said. He stripped off his gloves and began to rinse his hands at a little sink.

'I'll donate anything she needs,' Mr Taylor said. Suzanna giggled.

'Yes, weeell, Mr Taylor. I'm sure Queenie appreciates the offer but we don't usually put people blood into cats,' Bob said kindly. 'I think we'll just see if she recovers naturally. She is a fighter.'

'She just needs a rest now,' Suzanna said. 'You come with me and we'll have a cup of tea.'

Bob wiped his hands and grinned at Lenny. She was using his sink and his hospital antiseptic soap to scrub her own hands. Cat germs. Drain germs!

In the reception area, the Labrador owner, Mr Taylor and Suzanna were having a cup of tea. Mr Taylor looked up at Lenny weakly.

'I can never thank you enough,' he said.

'Your retainer covers the pursuit,' Lenny said. 'But I damaged a jacket. I'll bill you for that.'

She headed for the city centre and found a park near the State Library. An hour later she emerged from the building with a pile of photocopies, old newspaper and magazine articles about the Talbotts.

She drove to Footscray, windows down, radio blaring, crunching an Aspro Clear without water. It fizzed up in her mouth and she swallowed it. She had put on the usual bold face for the vet but the sight of all that blood and the scalpel when he had removed that piece of skin that was too badly torn to suture ...

The traffic was bad. Serious horn honking. It had been a long hot summer. Variable was the key word for this city's weather. It might be cold in the morning and a heat wave by two p.m. Everyone complained about the weather, but in a proud, parochial way. 'Ah, Melbourne weather ...' The way people complain happily when the complaint is something that defines them and they know it.

At the Footscray mall Lenny bought a banana smoothie and a Scratch Lotto ticket at the newsagency. You scratched off a small metallic square. If you got the right answer, you won up to $25,000. Hers said 'money back or another ticket'. She got another ticket. Scratched. 'Money back or another ticket'. Another ticket. Scratched. Nothing.

She let herself into her office, unfastened the cat box and pushed Cleo into her cage. The cat wowled in protest.

'You're alive, aren't you? Think yourself lucky,' Lenny growled, tossing in a well-chewed cloth tomato with a bell in the centre. 'Here, live it up.' Cleo regarded the toy with disdain.

The bonsai were a problem. She couldn't leave them for a week. They needed to be checked regularly. And she couldn't trust her neighbours: she didn't want Mike Bullock coming in here and Anastasia would probably kill them out of sheer don't-give-a-damn-ness.

Lenny decided to take them with her. They might enjoy the ambience of 22 Cedars Court. She couldn't take the lights, of course, but her room at the Talbott house was brightly lit. She took the quick-boil jug and the green tea cups. She picked up little Buddha and tapped a finger against his head:

'I'm taking the next step. You better be right about it.' She shoved him in a drawer.

She had dusted the office thoroughly and carried the last of the bonsai to her car when Mike Bullock came out of the porn shop.

'Mike.'

'Gidday, Lenny. Gowin' away?'

'Mmm hmm.' She wanted to get to her car as soon as possible. It was a hot day and the bonsai would cook if she didn't transport them quickly.

'Vacation, eh? Got the old bikini out?' He ogled and she noticed his hair. It was newly permed in stiff crinkles like a potato chip.

'Did Anastasia do that?'

'Yep. It's a bewdy, isn't it? She's got great hands.' He winked and looked at the cat box in her hand. 'Taking 'im with yer? Cute little fella.' She thought for a moment of thrusting the cat into his arms and saying, 'Do me a favour, will you?'

'No,' she blurted. 'Anastasia is taking him.'

Anastasia, shaving an old man while she tried to watch the kids' afternoon TV on her portable, was not happy about the arrangement.

'What do you think this is? I'm looking like an idiot or something?!' She was using an old-fashioned razor on the man's neck—scrape, scrape—and his eyes were very wide. 'What can I do with a cat?!' Scrape, scrape.

'A week,' Lenny said. 'She's very well-behaved. I'll pay you for food—and a little extra for the inconvenience.'

'How much extra?'

'Twenty.'

'My equipment. This is a sterile environment!' So obviously a lie that it didn't merit argument. 'Bah! I'm stoopid! But for you, Lenny. For you.' For twenty bucks, Lenny thought.

Cleo Harrelson, her cat box on the counter next to the cash register, mewed curiously. Lenny looked in through the bars.

'I'll drop in and see how it is,' she lied.

'Do that.' Anastasia glanced back and nicked the man's throat. He gargled. 'Well, why are you moving?! You sit still, you don't get your throat cut.'

Lenny drove back to St Kilda to collect some clothes. She had decided to take her rice cooker and some *Koshihikari*, the finest grade of Japanese rice, with a pearly white mark inside. It was quiet at her block of flats. Everyone was employed this month.

Her flat was furnished minimally. An armchair and *kotatsu*, were in front of a huge TV in the living room. The *kotatsu*, a low, square coffee table/leg heater supported a stack of *Sumo Monthly* magazines. The mangy carpet was covered by a pale green *goza*, a thin tatami-style mat. The spotless kitchenette was hidden by a black wood and paper screen. Her bedroom had another *goza* and a futon on a pine base. The flat was scented with a combination of Domestos and incense.

Someone knocked at the door. Knock-knockity knock-knock ... knock-knock. Only her mother knocked that way. Perfect timing as always. Lenny yanked the suitcase off her bed and took it into the living room.

She peeked through the view hole in her door. It *was* her mother. She opened the door and pinned a strained smile across her dislike.

Veronica Aaron was forty-nine but looked older. She was short (Lenny got her height from her father) with a sloppy figure. She had got fat carrying Lenny. Her breasts drooped and her stomach retained loose rolls of saggy skin. Her face had a lost expression, a look of too many disappointments. Lenny was one of them.

Veronica had found and married the weakest man she could: Ted Aaron. Mr Bronchitis. Mr Pneumonia. For most of Lenny's childhood, Mr Asthma-as-a-life-threatening-illness. And now, inevitably, Mr Emphysema. Despite all this he was resolutely upbeat. Lenny loved him.

Neither of them bothered to say hello.

'Why did you take so long to answer? You know it must be me.' Veronica's voice had a sharpness that came from years of foiled communication attempts. Sometimes when they
spoke together, Lenny heard the same stridency in her own voice.

'I'm just leaving. I'm going away for a few days. I can't talk now. My trees are in the car.'

'You'd better give us your number in case anything happens.' Veronica had a perpetual fear of something 'happening'.

'It's not necessary,' Lenny said. 'Why did you come around? You didn't know I'd be here.' It was a long way from Box Hill to St Kilda and Mrs Aaron didn't drive. She was afraid of cars.

'You haven't phoned us for weeks. And then that terrible man was killed last week.' Dorling again. 'Why do you think I came round? I was worried about you. I thought you might be upset again. I left messages on your answering machine but you never bothered to reply.' There was, as always, a terrible loneliness under the complaints. Lenny defied the impulse to weaken. She had no affection for her mother. Wasn't it wrong to force a relationship? Nevertheless, she felt, as she did each time this happened, ashamed of her own coldness.

'I'm busy,' she said.

'Are you all right about him? That Michael Dorling? You're not being silly about it?'

'I'm fine.'

'Dad's on two canisters a day now.'

It was worse then. Lately she avoided going to visit him because it was horrifying to see him disappear.

She had expected him to die almost every day of her childhood and yet here she was—twenty-seven years old—and here he still was too. Hanging in there. There were times when she wished him dead so it could be over.

'I'll phone him,' she said. She would talk. He would wheeze.

'He misses you.'

'I know.' Lenny spoke carefully. She didn't want to talk about her father. It was one of the few things she could become visibly upset about. 'I told you I'll see him soon and I will. I promise. I have been busy and I am busy now—'

'Mum says you haven't visited her for months.' Veronica was nervous and she should have been. She was on dangerous ground. 'She's not going to live for ever, you know.'

'I know.' Lenny said it with true feeling.

Veronica's face reddened. Her eyes watered.

'She's been—'

'Let's not talk about her. Let's just ... not.' Lenny tried to sound reasonable and controlled but she heard the nervous, angry squeak of her voice and cursed herself. She had certain limits in any conversations with her mother, the prime one being that they did not discuss her grandmother.

She had talked about her family with Dr Sakuno. He said she should get a grip—a variation on 'get over it'. There was never any excuse for rejecting the family. *You've made a disaster of your own life, Helena san, and now you try to put the blame onto your relatives.*

'I only came around because I care about you, Lenny,' Veronica said to no response. 'Just remember, we're still your parents. You can always come to us if you need us.'

'Mother, please. I have things to do.' It was the 'mother' that ended it. She so rarely used it in conversation that Veronica Aaron was taken aback.

'Well, of course you have your job ... '

'Right.'

'Is it still cats then?' Clearly she hoped there had been a

change.

'You can make up a new job to tell the neighbours,' Lenny said and immediately regretted it. Now she had had the last word and it was a snide one.

She saw her mother to the door. It had been—she glanced at her watch—a three-minute visit.

'I'll call. I *will*,' she said. 'Tell Dad "hi".'

Her mother gave her a nod then went down the stairs.

Lenny put her hands over her eyes. Her face was hot. She tried Dr Sakuno's deep breathing technique and it helped. She remembered the sparkle of tears in her mother's eyes. Another chance lost.

She cursed her own behaviour. She had to learn not to react. Her mother had an enormous love of the melodramatic. Lenny's childhood had contained many shrieking scenes. They had both tried to hide their antipathy from Ted Aaron but he was not fooled: 'Lenny, your mum loves you. She's not good at showing it but you know why.' It had been a rare Ventolin-free day for her father. Lenny had spent the afternoon in the garden with him, the oxygen mask and mini tank close by in case pollen or pollution brought on a snap attack.

'Yeah, right, Dad.' She didn't look up from the book she was reading.

'Sparky, it's not right. You can't blame her for everything.'

'I don't. I refuse to discuss this any further.'

He was right though, she thought. Everyone was right. Her mother, Dr Sakuno. She was the one who had it all wrong. She was blaming her mother for being weak, for not protecting her. It was unjust.

Lenny drove back to 22 Cedars Court. Three teenage boys were playing cricket in the street. They looked at her old car curiously.

Lenny leaned out of her window.

'Have any of you seen a cat around here recently?' she asked. 'It belongs to the Talbotts. A Ragdoll.' The boys looked blank. 'Like a Siamese cat, but more fluffy.'

'Yeah, I've seen it inside the gate a couple of times.' One of the boys nodded. 'Why?'

'It's missing,' Lenny said. 'When did you last see it?'

'Dunno.' The boy grinned and his friends laughed.

'Fine.' Lenny drove past them.

She pulled into the driveway. Margaret Gross had given her an electronic device to open the gates and instructions to park in one of the two spare bays in the long wooden garage at the right hand side of the drive. It was full of European cars and the little Colt looked miserable beside them. Lenny patted its bonnet fondly. From the darkness of the garage, the house was dazzling. Sun bounced off its windows as she started to unload the bonsai.

She never tried to charm Michael Dorling. He liked that. He liked her brutal efficiency too. She was a fine addition to the accounts department, despite her lack of physical appeal. He liked her hands. Her one vanity. He noticed them immediately. He didn't fancy her, of course. His private life was filled with exotic women. But he enjoyed her personality. Good-looking men could never resist the one who didn't succumb. He had to make her like him. She thought he was handsome, but she wasn't charmed. Partly because it was her way, but mostly because it was her job—she was hunting him.

Chapter 7

THE HAPPY FAMILY

The quick-boil jug had lived up to its name. Lenny laid out her tea bowl and whisk. She had several types of tea with her but decided to go all the way and have *Macha*, the thick, bitter, green tea favoured by geisha and a feature at tea ceremonies. It had meant bringing the miniature Japanese tea bowl—because you could drink *Bancha* or *Mugicha* in a household mug if you wanted, but part of the charm of *Macha* was its presentation.

She drank three mouthfuls of tea. With her window open she could hear the sea and from around the other side of the house there was splashing and laughing. Someone was using the pool. Lenny went downstairs to check it out.

The cook was making bread in the kitchen. From the window Lenny could see a young man and woman in the pool. The man pulled himself out of the pool and flopped into a deckchair. It was Kendell Talbott, Kimberly's twin.

He was unattractive like his sister, but it wasn't so incomprehensible in a man. He had his mother's glossy black hair, but his was thinning. He would be bald at thirty. He had a great physique though, the six-pack stomach and lean muscles that were the current body of choice for men. Too hairy, Lenny thought. Even before Dr Sakuno's influence, she had hated body hair. Once, as a teenager, she cut off her blonde pubic hair with manicure scissors only to find it grew back coarse and itchy.

As Lenny watched, Kendell began to rub tanning oil over his muscles. While the rest of the country was living in terror of the hole in the ozone layer, he was actively courting cancer.

The girl, still in the pool, splashed him and called out:

'Kenny, come back in! Don't be boring!' She spoke with a Queensland country accent that reminded Lenny a little of Vivian.

Kendell tossed a rubber ring at her head and missed by a long way.

'Idiot,' the girl said, pushing back her wet hair.

Liz Dodd, the cook, watched Lenny watching them. She raised her eyebrows at the girl's shrieks.

The girl got out of the pool and sat on the low diving board, sunning herself and preening. Good ankles, Lenny thought enviously. Her own were like tree trunks. The girl was wearing a white bikini that made her suntan seem darker. Her hair was black, straight and shoulder length. She was no classic beauty but her features were small and regular and her smile revealed white teeth. Very, very even. She would have no trouble at all pulling floss between those.

Eventually, inevitably, Kendell gave up on the newspaper he was pretending to read and pulled the girl off the diving board into the pool. They kissed passionately. Lenny imagined germs from lunch and breakfast passing from one wet cavern to the next.

'Loverboy's latest.'

She turned and found a man standing next to her. He was light on his feet; she rarely had someone approach her without being aware of it. She glanced at his tan loafers then up to his limp blond hair. He was handsome without having any definable character in his face.

'Eric Hunter,' he said. 'Henry's private secretary.'

'I'm Lenny Aaron. I work for Vivian,' Lenny said. 'Is that Carol?'

'Yes,' Eric confirmed.

'Pretty,' Lenny said. She realized her arms were crossed defensively across her body and her hands had automatically made loose fists: her 'strike like a cougar' position. It looked as though she was relaxing but in a second she could lash out a fist and take down an assailant: pop a nose, burst a lip, double the size of an ear.

'Do you think so? She's from Gympie.' He said this as though it were a conclusion.

'What does the family think of her?' Lenny asked.

'Henry thinks it's a step-up from the working girls,' Eric laughed.

The cook made a tutting noise. When they glanced at her she was staring at a mangled bread twist.

'The staff don't approve,' Eric said. 'Carol makes it clear to all of them that if she has anything to do with it they'll be replaced. She calls them the wrinklies.'

'And Vivian?' Lenny asked. 'What does she think?'

'Two country bumpkins who hit the big time,' Eric said. 'Of course they're best friends.'

'What exactly do you do for Henry?'

'Whatever he wants.' He hadn't tried to be discreet. He had spoken loudly enough for the cook to hear everything. Evidently someone who thought he wielded some power.

As the old cook continued folding dough, Eric began to give instructions for Henry's dinner. Liz Dodd didn't appreciate Eric telling her what to do. Talk about mutual hostility, Lenny thought. Liz Dodd's voice rose as Margaret Gross entered the kitchen.

'I take my orders from Vivian, thank you very much. You're not running things around here quite yet, you know, whatever you may think.'

'Just do as you're told—'

'This is my kitchen.'

'Eric!' A deep voice boomed from another room. Henry Talbott must be home. Eric hurried out.

Liz Dodd wiped her floured hands, reached into a cupboard and took out a blender.

'Broccoli,' she said. Her strong hands made fists. Lenny watched as she took pieces of broccoli and began ramming them into the blender. It made a sickly, green mulch.

'You shouldn't be carrying on like that in front of new staff,' Margaret Gross told her. 'What kind of impression do you think Ms Aaron's getting?'

Lenny was wondering about the cook's retort to Eric Hunter. Did Eric think he had a stake in the future of the Talbott Media empire? And if so, had Henry given him that impression?

Kendell Talbott, dripping water, padded into the kitchen. He was wearing gold—a necklace, wrist chain, watch and a pinky ring with a polished, ebony stone. He had big hands with stumpy nails and the crooked little fingers like his sister. He was still in Speedos.

'Are you my mum's new assistant?' He grinned at her and took a Coke from the double-doored fridge. He slammed it shut and the whole thing rattled. 'Mum says she's got a lot on her plate.' He began to pour the drink down his throat. She watched his hairy Adam's apple move up and down like a piston. The drink was gone in a few seconds.

'I'm Lenny Aaron.' She held out a hand and a wet paw shook it in a grip that hurt. He was stronger than he realized but he was friendly. A boy in a man's body.

'Your fiancée is very attractive,' she said. They both looked out the window. Carol Connor was lying on her back on a sun lounge, large cat's eye sunglasses dropped across her face. The straps of her bikini were unfastened so that her shoulders could tan evenly. She was smiling at the sun.

'She's great, isn't she?' Kendell slurped at a new Coke. 'Best thing that ever happened to me.'

'Eric says she's from Gympie.' It was easy to slip into the routine: How long have you known? ... What is your relationship with? ... Although it would work better if she was on one side of a grey metal table and he on the other. And even better if the room was small and there were no windows.

'Yeah, she's a Gympie girl. But we met in Brizzie,'

Kendell said. 'I was on holiday with some friends. Friend of a friend, you know.'

Two country girls who hit the big time, Eric had said. Vivian and Carol were both standard issue Gympie girls. Kendell was probably in and out of 'love' all the time. Lenny figured a lot of girlfriends, a lot of sex. Somehow this girl had made it to the diamond ring.

They watched Carol dive into the pool. It was not done perfectly—a bit of the old belly flop—but she came up well. She knew she was being watched. Kendell grinned. He nodded at Lenny and grabbed two more Cokes from the fridge before going back outside. She watched him pull the girl out of the pool to kiss her again.

Voices sounded in the hallway and Lenny went to meet them. Vivian was tossing keys and sunglasses onto a table. She was elegantly dishevelled after driving with the top down. The woman with her was carrying stiff, shiny paper bags with the names of Collins Street boutiques.

Lenny looked at the woman who was fat but trying to disguise it in a tailored, navy dress. She looked up furtively at Lenny, ventured a smile. She was nervous.

'Lenny, this is Annie Baron, my assistant. Did you have a fun afternoon? All settled in?' Vivian nodded to Annie. 'Take those upstairs, will you?'

Annie said yes and smiled at Lenny. She had very blue eyes swallowed up in a large moon face and a wide torso that was at odds with her scraggy arms and legs. Her hair was pulled back in a severe pony tail.

Annie said, 'Nice to meet you, Lenny,' softly. Her hands grappled self-consciously with the shopping bag handles. 'Vivian says you're going to help.' She glanced at Vivian for confirmation.

'I'll unpack all that later,' Vivian headed for the living room, Lenny following. She kicked off her shoes, poured herself a vodka on ice and sat on the couch, finger-combing her hair and smiling.

'Get a drink,' she told Lenny and gestured for her to sit on the opposite couch. 'Met the gang?'

'I met Eric Hunter and your son. And I saw Carol swimming.' Lenny replied.

'Is Eric writing the letters?'

'What do you think?'

'Well, he hates my bloody guts.' Vivian shrugged and laughed. 'When Henry dies he's finished. I can't stand that type.' She paused and appraised Lenny thoughtfully. 'I'm not anti-gay. In fact ...' She smiled. 'It's his manner I don't like. He's funny about his family background. Henry checked him out ages ago. His father's a truck driver. I mean who gives a shit? I don't even know who my father is! But he's got this chip on his shoulder about it. He's a bastard with the other help.' She wriggled her toes, stretched her feet. 'He's a very ambitious boy though.'

'In what way?'

'He's made himself indispensable to my husband. Always there. Never takes a holiday, never has a sick day. On call twenty-four hours a day. Always ready with the business advice whenever Henry's flagging. He's managed to persuade my husband it's all motivated by affection.' She laughed. 'But you have to ask yourself why a smart, greedy, economics major would settle for playing bedside nurse to a dying billionaire?'

'You think he wants to run the company?'

'Of course! But he won't. Did you find the cat?' She smiled as though at a private joke, caught Lenny's look and laughed. 'I'm just thinking how silly it is that I have you here at all. I mean I don't care about the cat. I'm not going to pretend. And the letters are ... well, it's all very dramatic, isn't it? I feel like you're here under false pretences.'

'Did you have Carol checked out too?' Lenny asked.

Vivian sat up. She nodded, accepting the subject change easily.

'Yes, but it wasn't necessary,' she said. 'I already knew she was the right girl for Kendell.'

Annie came into the living room and took a seat on the chair next to Vivian's couch. She sat straight with her hands in her lap. It reminded Lenny of the housekeeper. They were two empty vessels waiting for Vivian to command them to life. Annie seemed free to enter the room just as she liked. Was that what Vivian meant by 'controlling'?

'Kendell has been a bit indiscreet,' Vivian fixed another drink. She shrugged. 'Women are his weakness.' She sounded like an amused bystander rather than his mother.

'Eric implied he preferred prostitutes,' Lenny said. Annie blushed and looked pained. Vivian clinked ice into her glass.

'It's true,' she said. 'We were all terrified he'd catch AIDS. It's not like when Henry was young and the worst you got was the clap. But we had him tested.'

'And he's fine,' Annie added.

'Since he met Carol he's been a reformed boy,' Vivian went on. 'He needs a strong influence.' She meant he needed a controller. Was Vivian letting the marriage go ahead because Carol Connor could keep Kendell on a leash?

'When you had Carol checked out, what did you find?' Lenny asked.

'She's from Gympie, a doctor's daughter. They sent her to a good private girls' school in Brisbane. She made some wealthy friends. That's how she met Kendell,' Vivian looked amused. 'She's not the letter writer, Lenny. For God's sake. She has no reason to dislike me. I've encouraged the wedding a hundred percent. I *like* her. We've a lot in common. Gympie girls made good. Isn't that what Eric-the-slug told you?'

Vivian went upstairs to shower and rest before dinner. She instructed Annie to wake her and told her which clothes to lay out for the evening. Annie, like Margaret Gross, seemed happy to be Vivian's little helper. Lenny decided *she* was not going to give the same satisfaction.

Annie offered to show her around the garden.

Lenny didn't have any interest in seeing the garden. Gardens were simply places where cats waited to catch other animals but she wondered if she might get some useful information out of Annie.

Carol and Kendell had quit the pool and it was quiet outside. They had left their white robes and pool toys strewn across the grass and Annie tidied them. She collected the empty Coke tins. Her round face began to sweat in the heat and she pulled a hankie out of her pocket to mop it.

'Hot,' she said. Especially for you, Lenny thought. Her eyes drifted up over the wide stomach and pendulous breasts. She realized she was staring, because Annie blushed.

Annie showed her the party house behind the tennis court. It was fitted out with a bar, stereo equipment and plump leather couches. There was a mirror ball on the ceiling and Lenny, looking down at her feet, realized she was standing on a mirrored floor with all its lewd revelations. She bet that was Kendell's idea.

'It's for the kids when they have friends over,' Annie explained. She smiled. 'Kenny used to have teenage parties in here. They don't use it much now. Kimmie thinks it's tasteless.'

'It is,' Lenny said. She took out her cigarettes and lit one. Annie moved an ashtray along the bar top.

Fat people were a threat. It was difficult to fight them. Rush them and you risked bouncing off as they used their girth like a fairground blow-up castle. Lenny recalled a bar fight where she had taken on a two-hundred-pounder with a smashed beer bottle in his hand. Ugly. It took six cops to get him into the paddy wagon. Lenny remembered how her hands sank deep into his fleshy arms. They had to cosh him into unconsciousness. Senior Constable Robbins lost two teeth to a fat fist.

'I wonder what happened to the cat?' she mused. Annie looked out to the pool.

'Yes, I wonder.'

'Do you suppose it's still alive?'

'I don't know,' Annie said in a small voice. 'I hope so.'

They strolled around to where Max's shed nestled against the far end of the garden. Beyond the trees masking the fence she could hear the sea hissing up to the sand. There were really two sheds. One was full of gardening supplies and the other had been turned into a miniature house with flowers in window boxes and a stone path winding to the door. A small greenhouse next to the sheds held a variety of rose bushes.

Max was outside the tool shed polishing a few of the bigger tools: a scythe, an axe and a scary-looking band saw. He looked up and smiled.

'Beautiful day,' he said. 'I picked some snow daisies for you, Ms Aaron. Not the flashiest flower around but I think you'll like it.'

'The garden is nice,' Lenny said.

'I do my best.'

'Have you seen signs of the cat anywhere?'

'Not a thing. I've sniffed around a bit. I reckon it's gone off for a wander. They do that, don't they?'

'Yes, they do.'

'He's a good man,' Annie said as they moved on. Everything she said sounded as though it had been learned parrot-fashion. 'He's been with Mr Talbott for a long time.'

'How long have you been Vivian's assistant?' Lenny asked.

'All my life,' Annie smiled as she found a ladybird on her hand. She drew the hand up to show Lenny. 'Is this lucky?'

Lenny flicked it off.

'Not anymore,' she said.

Annie covered one hand with the other as though stung. 'What do you mean "all you life"?'

Annie looked around for the bug.

'If you've killed it—' she said, worried.

'It's an insect,' Lenny said. Insects were creepy. She

looked around for somewhere to lose her cigarette, but the garden was immaculate. Annie held out one of the crushed Coke tins. The butt sizzled when Lenny let it fall.

'You know about the letters,' she said. Annie's hands lifted to her mouth.

'I don't know anything.' The blue eyes were frightened.

'Do you think Henry or one of the children wrote them?' Lenny prompted. Annie shook her head.

'No,' she whispered. 'Henry isn't like that. He's a good man.'

'What do you mean you've known Vivian all your life?' Lenny repeated the earlier question.

'Vivian and I were at Little Pines children's home together,' Annie explained. 'She looked after me and I looked after her. I was abandoned but I got to be with Vivian and I have the family.'

'Vivian's family,' Lenny said. 'Not yours.' Annie flinched.

'Yes,' she said, 'Vivian's.'

Lenny didn't follow Annie back into the house. Instead she spent half an hour checking out the garden for a corpse. It was not implausible that Marie Antoinette de Paris had been mauled by another cat and crawled off to die in her own garden. She foraged in the bushes but found no cat, alive or dead.

Chapter 8

DEATH THREATS AND ANNIE

Lenny examined the push button key pad that operated the security system for the house and grounds. There were motion sensors in every room on the ground floor and all external windows and doors were wired to the security system. If an intruder tried to enter, an alarm would sound and a signal would go immediately to the private monitoring station and from there to the police. At night when everyone was upstairs, the system was activated. Only the family and servants knew the code to arm and disarm it.

Of course if the intruder was ambitious, the whole family could still be dead before anyone arrived. Alarm systems were a deterrent, not a guarantee.

She went upstairs and took a cool shower. Her arm itched. Sometimes hot weather bothered it, made the new skin sensitive. The summer problem. In winter it was the metal pin inside that ached. She washed her hair and changed into a fresh black shirt then spent a long time cleaning her teeth. She always brushed twice—two applications of toothpaste—then used a spoon to scrape her tongue to get off the yellow build-up of food fur. Next came two mouthfuls of Listerine. It bit into her tongue like acid but she liked it. After the Listerine she flossed between each tooth, upper and lower. It was amazing how much dirt remained even after the brushing and Listerine, especially in the bottom, crooked ones.

When she was a teenager the family dentist (sensing Mrs Aaron's financial type) said no one even noticed the bottom row. Lenny spent the next fourteen years struggling with that day's decision.

She towelled her hair dry, rolled up her sleeve and

examined the scar on her arm. It was shiny and pink. Cortisone injections and vitamin E cream had helped. Now all she had to do was forget about it.

She lit an incense stick and a candle and held her hands together in front of the mandarin and apple on the dresser. She tried to think spiritual thoughts but nothing came to mind.

'I killed a bug.' A confession was meaningless to Buddha, a hangover from her Catholic upbringing. She chewed the inside of her lip. The skin felt ragged and rough from constant nibbling. 'I saved a Scottish Fold. That's about it.'

She combed her hair to the side and redrew her eyebrows then applied dark mascara. Although her eyes were brown, her eyebrows and lashes were naturally white-blonde. It was an unsuccessful combination of her parents' colouring.

She walked down the corridor and knocked at Vivian's door.

'Come in.'

Inside, Vivian and Carol Connor were playing with Vivian's purchases. There were boxes of designer clothes, shoes and bags strewn across the bed and floor: Versace, Carolina Herrera, Azzedine Alaia. Carol was wearing a new, white silk dressing gown over her clothes and striking a pose. She wasn't beautiful enough to model but she had the moves down. Vivian, a new hat on her head, smiled at Lenny and gave her an indulgent shrug.

Over the bed head was a small Russell Drysdale, the frame screwed to the wall on the left side so that it opened like a book. Behind it was a safe. Lenny saw a collection of documents and jewellery and fat bundles of cash. There was more jewellery on the bed.

'Playing with my toys,' Vivian said with a wry smile. 'Lenny, this is Carol. Carol, Lenny Aaron. She's helping Annie out with my correspondence for a week.'

Carol Connor gave Lenny a quick assessment and decided rightly that there was no competition. She didn't bother to smile. Up close the poolside prettiness was less apparent. She had opaque, lizard eyes, Lenny thought.

Carol gathered up a handful of clothes.

'Can I really keep this stuff?' The voice was ingenuous while the hands snatched and grabbed.

'Of course. You look much better than I do in it. I bought the jacket for you. Take whatever you like.' Vivian was a perfect benefactor. Carol grabbed more clothes and bags off the bed. She eyed the other things greedily.

She stepped past Lenny like she was invisible and left the room. Vivian laughed.

'I can't keep her out of my things,' she sighed.

'You could,' Lenny said, surprised at the edge in her voice. Vivian heard it.

'You look very sweet with your hair wet,' she said.

She gestured for Lenny to sit on the white ottoman near the window. French doors opened onto a balcony with a spectacular view of the sea. The sun was setting and the water sparkled dark crimson and flecked gold.

It had been a mistake to come with wet hair and no lipstick. Lenny felt vulnerable next to Vivian. She kept her face blank and sat in her best controlled manner, back straight, legs slightly apart at the knees, feet flat on the floor.

Vivian reached into her pocket and took out a folded envelope. A letter. She passed it to Lenny. She looked mildly irritated.

'This was at the Toorak house,' she said.

It was a plain white envelope, postmarked Toorak, with blue-lined paper inside. Typed on a word processor.

COUNTDOWN TO DEATH. THE FINAL HOUR IS HERE.
I WILL CUT YOU OPEN.

Lenny was disappointed. It seemed that contemporary death threats were still in the grip of a chronic mannerism. She folded the paper into the envelope and pushed it into her pocket.

'Who knows the Toorak address?' she asked.

'All the family and staff. There's a private cleaning company. A few of our friends would know it. I never give it out as a mailing address. There's usually just advertising junk in the mailbox.' Vivian leaned forward, violet eyes very close to Lenny, and squeezed her hand hard. The contact was scorching. Lenny pulled her hand free.

'Lenny, you've seen the security system here. I have the same system at my Toorak house. And believe me I don't wander down dark alleys in the middle of the night. I think it's a game. Someone wants to play with me.' She looked scared, though, despite her tough talk. Lenny wondered if she always got this close to people. She could see the tiny soft hairs on her face.

'Let's remember this is Australia,' Vivian concluded. 'If we were in New York, I might be worried. But—Melbourne!'

'It happens here,' Lenny said. Violence was common everywhere: wives with faces swollen up like blue pumpkins, pub brawls with smashed bottles replacing fists. Her own arm was a constant reminder. Violence was natural.

'Did you show Carol the letter?' she asked.

'No, why upset her? This is supposed to be the happiest time of her life,' Vivian said. 'I never had that myself, you know. The engagement time. All that nice, young stuff. I want her to have it.' She didn't sound sorry for herself, just matter-of-fact. 'I'm not going to let this nonsense interfere.'

'I want to know about the children's home,' Lenny said. 'Margaret Gross and Annie Baron were both there with you.' She waited for Vivian to look taken aback, some indication that here was something she shouldn't talk about.

'Do you think that's *strange*?' Vivian said with a smile. 'It feels natural to me. I never had any family so I grabbed onto two people I grew up with. I like them. They've got nothing to do with this. I swear to you, Maggie Gross would not write these letters.'

'And Annie?'

'Lenny, Annie is not the letter writer.'

'She's very attached to your children.'

'Of course, she's been with them since they were born. She's like a child herself sometimes. She loves little things.'

'Except animals.'

Vivian paused. Her lips closed tightly for a second.

'Animals bother her.'

'Why?'

'I don't know. I've never thought much about it.' The violet eyes fluttered. 'Lenny, it's not relevant.'

'You have to tell me everything,' Lenny said. 'I can't protect you otherwise.'

'Can you protect me?' Vivian asked softly. Her hand reached out but she stopped and, suddenly shy, pulled away. She laughed. 'I don't need protection. This is stupid!' She closed her eyes for a couple of seconds then spoke.

'When we were little girls, Annie killed a dog. It used to chase us on the way to school. It frightened me. Annie liked to be my protector. One day she waited for it and caught it in a bag. She's quite strong, you know. She put a rock in the bag and threw it in the river. We never told anyone. It belonged to a family in the town. There would have been big trouble.' She shrugged. 'I should have stopped her but I hated that dog. I was glad it died in the river.'

'Did she kill anything else?'

'I don't know. No.' Vivian pulled her cigarettes out of her pocket and lit one. 'We never talk about it.'

Lenny recalled Annie's gentle fascination with the ladybird. No signs of violence there.

'Insects,' she said.

'What?' Vivian stared.

'Does she hate insects?'

Vivian smiled, looked confused. 'I don't know. Probably she does. Everyone does.'

'Tell me about the children's home,' Lenny said again.

'My parents abandoned me when I was a baby,' Vivian

recited. She seemed neither ashamed nor pained by the memory. 'I grew up in a Gympie home—Little Pines. That's where I met Annie. We grew up together. She wasn't very bright but we took to each other. We didn't have much choice actually. Girls who had parents weren't interested in being friends with girls who didn't.'

'Was she always fat?'

'No, Annie wasn't always fat,' Vivian smiled. 'She got Cushing's Syndrome. She started to put on weight when she was about twenty. You've noticed her arms and legs are thin although her body is big? That's part of it. It's a hormone imbalance.'

'Is it terminal?'

Vivian laughed. 'No, she's fine. She had a course of radiation therapy that got it under control a long time ago. She didn't have a hundred percent recovery, I mean physically. You can see for yourself that she retained a fair amount of weight. But she's basically OK now.' A long pause. 'The endocrinologist advised us at the time to look out for mood swings or depression. But she's always had a tendency to be flighty. I think it's just her nature. I never noticed anything out of the ordinary anyway. And, as I said, it was a long time ago and she's fine now.'

'Did she ever start fires at the children's home?'

Vivian's eyes widened. 'No, she didn't. What do you mean?'

'Did she wet the bed?' Lenny pressed. Police psychology basic training on how to identify a psychopath: look for childhood psychosis. Animal torture, bed wetting and fire starting were symptoms.

'When she was little, I suppose. I don't remember ...' Vivian crossed a lean ankle over her knee. She had taken off her stockings and her feet smelled of roses. The toes were all small and she had no callouses. There was, however, a small red tattoo on the arch of the foot: yin and yang, red and blue. Tiny tattoos for women were a new trend, often on the breast or the lower stomach and always something exotic: a dragon or scorpion. The bottom of the foot was very sensitive. Bold choice for a needle.

'My little rebellion.' Vivian saw her glance and wiggled the foot. 'Let's get off this thing with Annie. Wet the bed, not wet the bed—Annie is devoted to me and I trust her. She wouldn't hurt me, quite the opposite.'

'Why weren't you adopted?' Lenny changed the subject.

'I was. A couple in Brisbane took me for six months but I wore them down. They gave me back. I cried too much or something. Maggie had to come and get me. So ...' she shrugged, reached for a Dunhill, lit up. The tiniest flicker of something showed in her eyes. Was it a painful memory? 'After that they didn't try to adopt me out again.'

'Why did you cry so much?'

'Some kind of hyperactive thing, I suppose. Maggie says it stopped when I was about two but by then I was settled at the home. Perhaps she didn't want to let me go again.' This time the smile was tight.

'There weren't many of us. Mostly boys and a few much older girls. Annie and I were about the same age. Her mother dumped her too.' She paused, far away. 'I *had* to bring her with me. What else was she going to do with her life?'

'Why did you bring Margaret Gross with you?'

'Isn't it obvious?' Vivian offered Lenny a cigarette and lit it for her. Their fingers touched.

'Maggie treats me like a princess. She always has. At the home I was her favourite. Probably it was the reason I didn't get re-adopted. She wanted me for herself.' Another pause. She kept a lot back, Lenny thought.

'It all worked out for the best. Old Mr Denny, the administrator at the home, criticized Maggie for showing me too much attention but she ignored him. She'd do anything for me. Why would I want to give that up?'

'Annie and Maggie don't mind talking about it.'

'Why should they? It's no big deal. Only my husband needs

to reinvent the past. According to the sanitized version in *his* newspapers, I didn't marry him for his money and he didn't marry me for the twins.' She sighed, blew a long line of smoke. 'It's all a long time ago, Lenny.'

'What about this party tomorrow? The letter writer could be one of the guests.'

'That's true!' Vivian laughed. She looked delighted. It was a complete mood swing. 'It's not a party. A dinner really. Just the family—if the children bother. Otherwise, Henry and me and three old friends. But,' she grinned, 'they've *all* got a hidden agenda. *And* plenty of reason to dislike me. It would be a real who-dunnit if I was topped tomorrow!'

'Who's coming?' Lenny pulled out a small notebook with tiny pen attached. The first half of the book was filled with feline trivia. Vivian smiled indulgently.

'Is this Miss Marple routine necessary?'

'Yes.'

'All right. Mike and Sonia Buchanan and Larry Burton.'

Lenny searched her mental tabloid. The Buchanans were the business stars of the eighties, big in the TV industry, had seemed for a while to rival even Henry Talbott, but there were too many lavish junkets for the press and hangers-on. They lost a lot of money in the 1987 crash. More recently their Hong Kong investments had proved disastrous. Black Thursday, rumour had it, had wiped them out and they were ready to declare bankruptcy.

Larry Burton. Lenny knew him well. 'Friday Night at Larry's Place' had been running from seven-thirty to ten p.m. every week for the past fourteen years. Before that it had been a weekend breakfast show called, strangely enough, 'Saturday at Larry's Place'. Then it had been strictly for the kids. Larry had been high energy, jumping around his brightly painted styrofoam set making the kids scream with laughter. Only Lenny had thought he was a dickhead.

Someone had decided Larry was wasted on the kiddies and transformed the show into prime-time, adult-audience TV.

'Friday Night' was born. But fourteen years at the top saw Larry balloon to twice his weight and lose that all-important energy. The show was on its last legs. Larry popped up in *TV Week* (one of Lenny's favourite magazines) discussing how he often thought of giving up the show, choosing a new host, getting on with his life. In denial, she thought. He was the sort of man who couldn't survive without his celebrity.

'What's your relationship with them?'

'Sonny Buchanan and I were best friends for a while a few years back. But that sort of thing never lasts. I get bored. I got bored. I didn't drop her but it cooled off. Now she and her husband are bankrupt. They probably think Henry will bail them out.'

'Larry Burton?'

'Henry's channel is pulling the plug on his show this year. It's been crap for ages now. Larry Burton's strictly a.m. from here on.'

'You don't like him?'

'Neither will you when you meet him.'

Lenny closed the notebook.

'You need to talk to the police,' she said.

Vivian exhaled with irritation. 'No publicity.' She relaxed, searched Lenny with those violet eyes. 'Lenny, there's Henry's condition to think about. The press can be so thoughtless, to put it mildly. I feel quite safe now. If you can find Kimberly's cat as part of this deal, wonderful. Although god knows what we'll do with it, because I'm not having it in here again. Why anyone likes cats is beyond me. You know I fed the thing once or twice and the next time I tried to pet it, it bit me. They're completely amoral, aren't they?'

'They have short memories,' Lenny said.

'You must be fond of them. It must be unpleasant finding one dead.'

'In my line of work the only way to be effective is to maintain a distance.'

'That sounds very cold.' Vivian seemed impressed. 'If you find the person who's writing the letters, fine,' she continued, 'but I'm not going to get all lathered up about it. That's what they want, right?'

'Maybe,' Lenny said.

'Lenny, it's all going to be all right.' Vivian leaned forward briefly, eyes bright. 'I'm glad you're here.'

Dinner was a buffet of salads and vegetables laid out in the kitchen. The family helped themselves. Kimberly didn't come home. Kendell and Carol ate by the pool, listening to CDs. She was talking about the wedding and was animated. It was going to be a grand function. Lenny listened blatantly at the door while she ate rice balls. Liz Dodd had said: 'Miss Kimberly says you like Japanese' as she proffered a small plateful and nodded at Lenny's surprised thanks.

'I just do what I'm asked,' she said. She was, thought Lenny, one of those people who prided themselves on being 'forthright' to the point of rudeness.

Liz took a big plate of food to Max when he appeared in the kitchen at exactly eight o'clock. They sat together and he told her about his day in the garden. Max was clearly her hero. If the gardener sensed her feelings for him, he gave no sign.

Eric took a plate of puréed green vegetables, baby food, to the study.

Vivian and Annie ate together on the patio outside the kitchen. It was shaded by tall trees and cool in the evening breeze. Vivian had her feet up on a chair. She saw Lenny watching them and smiled.

Lenny envied them their tranquillity. It was a long time since she had been relaxed or unafraid.

Chapter 9

TREKKERS AND STUFFED WOMBAT-HALVES

It was one a.m. The house was quiet. Lenny was reading her State Library research. Mostly society gossip columns. Several implied that Vivian was a social-climbing tramp. She also had the medical dictionary she had taken from the library downstairs. Cushing's Syndrome, she discovered, was rare. Less than twenty-five cases per million people per year. It was usually caused by a benign tumour on the pituitary gland and could be treated and often fully cured by surgical removal of the tumour or by a course of radiation therapy. Symptoms of the disease could include weight gain to the face, neck and torso, weakness of the arms and legs, excessive hair growth, ruddiness and *psychological damage*. Vivian had mentioned that. But she said Annie had always been flighty. Lenny wondered what that meant exactly.

She reached into her bag for a Tylenol. Her hand brushed a little card, a portrait of Mary and baby Jesus circa 1979. Lenny's first holy communion. The inscription read: *God is always with you, love Nana*. Two lies in one sentence because she couldn't imagine there had ever been a time when her grandmother had loved her and the feeling was mutual.

She stuck the card back into her wallet and plumped her brought-from-home Astro Boy pillow. She was restless. The answer was to pump eight or nine aspirin into her stomach, but her tolerance was now so high that even that might not do the trick. It was getting close to that time when she would have to have the nasty pill-free weekend, sweating in her bedroom then emerging pallid, smug and ready for a new start.

She dropped the papers on her bed and went out onto the landing. She wanted juice. A faint light spilled up the stairwell. As she reached the bottom of the stairs, she noted that the motion sensors for the rooms at the back of the house had been deactivated.

In the kitchen Liz Dodd, Max Curtis and Henry Talbott were sitting at the table watching an old episode of *Star Trek: the New Generation*, a Worf episode. Worf, Lenny thought, was not the best character. In fact for someone who was from a rich heritage of aggressive Klingon warriors, he was a bit of a drip.

The three of them were drinking glasses of iced milk. The wrinklies. Lenny thought of Carol Connor's assessment and smiled. Henry Talbott was a big man despite age and illness. His hair was wispy with bald patches. In the kitchen half-light the crags of his bulbous features were heavily shadowed.

Max saw her first. She stood in the doorway, blonde hair bright under the hall spotlight. He smiled at her and raised a hand.

Liz Dodd's face swung to Lenny's, irritated. Henry Talbott, seeing Lenny for the first time, sized her up. Apparently he didn't like what he saw. His dark eyes ran over her Astro boy pyjamas.

'What is it, Ms Aaron?' Liz Dodd asked.

'I need a drink,' Lenny said. 'I can get it myself.'

The cook jumped up, opened the fridge and grabbed a bottle of Evian. She walked over to Lenny and placed the bottle into her hand: 'There.'

Lenny nodded. 'Right. Thanks.'

She was at the bottom of the stairs again when Henry's leathery hand grabbed her shoulder. Nearly ninety but he still had a grip on him. She swung around and was hit in the face by the most rancid breath she had ever smelled (and that was even accounting for Granny Sanderman, who had breath like a pickled kipper).

This was cancer, she thought.

Up close his skin had the texture of porridge and there seemed to be some kind of decay occurring around the inner edges of his lips.

'You're my wife's assistant?' His voice rasped. Jabba the Hut, she thought suddenly. That was definitely the right tongue for a mouth like this.

'Lenny Aaron.' She stuck out a hand. He squeezed it hard, turned it over. She suddenly imagined him as a lover—rough, powerful and selfish, the way Jabba would have been with Leia.

'That fat cow Annie assists my wife so I wonder really why you're here, Ms Lenny Aaron.' He moved forward. It looked like he was going to try the Vulcan grip on her shoulder again. This time he would get a slap in the face.

'Henry, darling,' Vivian floated down the stairs, face glowing, nude body both hidden and emphasized in the palest of grey silk dressing gowns. It was shocking to see her next to this creature, impossible to imagine them married.

Lenny watched as Vivian linked her arm through her husband's and smiled at him.

'Henry, come up now. It's late.'

Henry grunted. He leered at his wife and pulled her close. They went upstairs together.

Lenny went back to the kitchen. Max was gone. There was a close-up of Picard on TV. Liz Dodd had tidied the table and was about to go to bed.

'When did you come here? When did you meet Mr Talbott?' Lenny asked her.

'I'm not interested in gossiping.' Liz Dodd said. 'You go talk to Miss Gross if you want that sort of thing.'

'I asked you a question.'

The little eyes widened in surprise.

'I was hired through an agency a long time ago, Miss Aaron.'

'*Ms* Aaron.'

'What's wrong with "Miss"? I've been Miss Dodd all my

life and I'm not ashamed of it. You young women wanting to turn yourselves into men. What you're thinking of is a mystery to me.'

'You're a trekkie?' Lenny ignored the spiel.

'It's trekker. There's no shame in it.' Lenny realized she was not joking.

'Are Max and Henry trekkers too?'

'I'm not obliged to tell you anything,' Liz Dodd rinsed the milky glasses. She reached for the off switch on the TV then paused as she took in the news flash.

Two teenage boys in East Melbourne had been arrested for setting fire to a cat. They had doused it in petrol and then lit a match. The cat ran for several minutes before it collapsed and died. A neighbour saw the whole thing and reported them. There was already a local outcry. The cat was a stray but each neighbour defended it as though it was their very own. One woman cried broken-heartedly. An old man shook his head at the cruelty of young people.

'What kind of person does something like that?' Liz Dodd asked, hands clenched on the table.

'You'd be surprised,' Lenny said. Last year she had caught a twelve-year-old boy in Brunswick trying the same trick. She managed to get her coat over the cat and got the flames out almost immediately. The cat survived with burned spots where it was unlikely to grow new fur. Lenny had found it a good home and hadn't thought about it since. She recalled now the cat's agonized mews as she drove at top speed to the vet's. Later she went back, tracked the boy and hit him hard.

The cook flicked the TV off. 'That's upset me, that has. I'll be thinking about that cat all night now. Poor little bugger.'

'I'm here to look for Kimberly's cat,' Lenny said. The cook prized herself on plain speaking. Perhaps she would respond well to it. 'And to help Mrs Talbott. I think someone in this household wants to hurt her.'

'Mrs Talbott is no concern of mine. I do my job in the kitchen and that's it.' She was defensive. 'Max and I just do our jobs. And we'll be keeping them no matter what *some* people say.'

'You mean Carol?'

'Do you know what she calls us?'

'No,' Lenny lied.

'She told Max to his face that he might want to start looking about for a new position! When he's worked here twenty-odd years and she's just put her foot through the door!'

'Where is Kimberly's cat?' Lenny asked.

'I'm sure I wouldn't know. It ruined the furniture. Mrs Talbott was very unhappy about it. I wouldn't be surprised if they dumped it. Sort of thing people do, isn't it? Abandoning responsibilities.'

'Do you have any evidence that someone in the family dumped Marie Antoinette?'

'I don't know anything about anything.'

'I think you know a lot.' Lenny said. 'I think you should tell me.' She tried to make her voice sound chummy but it was an art she had never mastered and it came out, she realized, like a threat.

Of course she had no intention of getting violent. Not that she had never hit an old person before. There had been a geriatric junkie waving an 'AIDS-filled syringe' (which later proved to be tomato sauce) as he held up a convenience store. Lenny and Danny, stopping off for morning tea snacks, happened in on the whole thing. Danny tried to talk the man around and then Lenny slapped a strong open palm into his face. The slap was enough to knock him to the ground where she was able to cuff him.

But that was a long time ago and she certainly didn't intend to brutalize the Talbotts' cook.

'Someone is threatening Mrs Talbott. Sending letters.'

'And you think it's me?' The cook sighed. 'Why would

I do that? I'd lose my job and then I wouldn't be able to see Max.'

'Perhaps it's Max then,' Lenny said.

'Don't you go accusing Max Curtis of anything! He's never hurt a soul in his life, he hasn't. There's plenty of people would like to hurt Mrs Talbott without you looking to blame Max. She likes to upset people. Anyone can see it. I don't approve of her and I'll tell you that much but it's not my business or my money and I'm not one to interfere.'

'But you wouldn't object if she was, let's say, cut open, would you?'

'That's a terrible thing to say. Are you ... ' the eyes narrowed. 'Are you with the police?' She hesitated. 'I'll tell you this much, something is going on around here. I've felt it for weeks.' The old woman nodded vehemently and hurried from the room.

Lenny saw Max at the kitchen window. He raised a hand and she went to the door. She pressed a code into the security pad on the wall.

'It's late, I know,' Max said, 'but I found a cat. It's down the lane a bit.'

It was cool outside and quiet. There was no one else on the street and the lamps were yellowish in the sea mist. The lane between the street and the beach was a long, narrow, pitch-black strip on each side of which was a natural wall of trees and bushes. Lenny glanced at Max who was carrying a torch.

'I go for a walk before bed,' he explained. 'On the beach. I take this in case there's trouble.'

'What kind of trouble?' Lenny asked.

'Just trouble,' he shrugged. She stopped at the entrance to the lane. 'What's the matter?' he asked.

Lenny wasn't going to admit to the ice cube of fear in her stomach.

'Nothing.'

They walked down the tunnel together in silence. Max

flashed his torch along the left bank at the bottom of the bushes.

'I spotted it just before. It's not attractive.' He stopped suddenly and Lenny slammed into him from behind. 'Sorry. Here it is.' He handed her the torch and she readied herself to whack him with it if he tried anything.

She bent down with the torch and pointed it into the bushes.

'What?' she asked. 'I can't see anything.'

'Lower.' Then she saw it: a cat's rear legs, tail and rump sticking out of the soil at the bottom of a bush. Someone had made a poor attempt at a cat burial and erosion had brought the half-decayed corpse to the surface.

'It's not Marie Antoinette,' she said.

'Really?' Max was on his knees beside her. 'How do you know?'

'The tail.' Lenny pointed. 'You can see the hair is still quite well-preserved and this cat is a short-hair. Marie Antoinette was a long-hair.'

'You're right,' Max nodded. 'She had a big bushy tail. Looks like I got you out here on a false alarm. I suppose I better re-bury it though. People around here don't like that kind of thing.'

'People around here?'

'Rich people.' He smiled. They were still squatting. Lenny got to her feet.

'Liz Dodd thinks there's going to be some kind of trouble here,' she said, but Max only laughed.

'Liz is a worrier,' he said. 'You mustn't take her seriously.'

'You don't?'

Max Curtis blushed like a schoolboy.

'Now I know what you're implying,' he said, waggling a finger in the torch light, 'but Liz and I are just good friends.'

'But you know her very well,' Lenny said.

'Twenty years or more,' he nodded. 'She's my best friend.'

They were walking together now, side by side, back

towards the house. 'Not finishing your beach walk?'

'The cat's bum put me off a bit.' He grinned. Lenny almost smiled.

'Does Mr Talbott always join you for late-night TV?' she asked. She was testing the waters about a possible connection between Liz Dodd and her employer. It seemed unlikely given the cook's clear interest in Max, but at this stage of the investigation it was best to cover all possibilities. Max paused.

'He's a good employer. I couldn't ask for better,' he said easily. But she hadn't imagined the sudden tautness in his body.

'That's what Liz Dodd says.'

They were back at the house gates which Max locked behind them. He paused again in the circular driveway.

'You just here for the cat then?' Not at all threatening, she thought. Nervous.

'And to help Mrs Talbott,' she said.

'There's no need to go upsetting anyone along the way then, is there?' He hesitated. 'I don't want to see anyone hurt.'

'You mean Liz Dodd? Is she having a relationship with Mr Talbott?'

'My god, no!' He laughed out loud, then realized where he was and covered his mouth. He glanced at the dark windows in the front of the house. 'Sorry. I'll be losing us both our jobs, though I'm not sure what yours is.' He sighed and rubbed his eyes, a poor mime of sleepiness. 'I'm not talking any sense. You just do whatever it is you're here for and I'll do my job and we'll both be happy as larks.' He held out his hand very formally for her to shake. 'I get feelings about people straight off, Ms Aaron, and I know that you are a good woman.'

Lenny let herself back into the kitchen and locked the door behind her. Before she went up she made sure the motion sensors for the ground floor were activated. At the top of the stairs she heard Vivian's whisper: 'Lenny, come on in and chat to me,' from the doorway of her husband's room.

'Don't worry,' Vivian added as Lenny reached the door, 'he's out like a light. Eric will be in here insisting on taking over once he's had his ritual four hours of sleep.' Lenny glanced at the bed. Henry Talbott was unconscious, tucked into bed, his head raised on two pillows and a stained white towel at his side. The room had the faint tang of a hospital ward.

'He's not really so hard to handle,' Vivian said with a smile. She squeezed Lenny's hand. 'Did you think I came up here to fuck him? He's long past all that now.'

'It's none of my business.' But Lenny didn't pull her hand away this time. Vivian noticed.

'You're sweet. Any luck with the cat?' she asked.

'No. Max thought he found it out in the laneway to the beach, but it was a false alarm. Another cat.'

'Dead?'

'Yes.'

'And the letters?' She moved to the oak cabinet that ran along one wall and poured herself a gin and tonic. 'Like one?' Lenny shook her head.

'Nothing yet. I think you should consider your servants as suspects though.'

Vivian began to protest when Henry shot up from his pillows into a sitting position and began to mutter, eyes wide and staring. Vivian sprang across to him and jumped onto the bed. She held him firmly with both hands and said: 'Shh, now. Shh,' with quiet authority. To Lenny she said, 'Don't be afraid.'

'I'm not afraid,' Lenny joined her at the bed and they worked to bring Henry around. Vivian patted his cheeks and continued to speak to him.

'Wake up, Henry. Wake up.' She looked at Lenny as the muttering continued. 'We should have a professional nurse now but he's terrified of that. It's the final stage, you see. He doesn't want to face his death. I don't blame him.'

They finally got him awake and forced some medication into him.

'You're fine,' she said. Although she was an efficient nurse, there was no trace of affection in her voice. Earlier, on the stairs, she had played the part of loving wife. It wasn't required now.

Henry ignored her and looked at Lenny, who had propped herself against the wall.

'Why are you here?' he spat.

'I asked her to keep me company,' Vivian told him. 'I told you: Ms Aaron is helping me out this week and you know Kimberly lost her cat. Ms Aaron is something of an expert in that line. She's going to find it for us.'

'Find it and skin it,' Henry ordered.

The command was not as odd as it seemed. Around the walls was a row of Australiana: an emu's shaggy neck and bald head, half a wombat, a whole koala, a kangaroo bust. Did he kill them personally, Lenny wondered. What sort of man stuffed half a wombat?

The door burst open. It was Eric Hunter, greasy-faced in crumpled red pyjamas, a sleep mask pushed up into his tousled hair. He rushed to Henry's side, plumped pillows with his fists.

'What the hell is going on in here?' he demanded. 'You know you're supposed to wake me if he has an episode!' His slender arms reached for a thermometer. Henry resisted him.

'I don't need it.'

'You don't know what you need.' Eric picked up the discarded syringe. 'You let me be the judge. How much did you give him?' He looked at Lenny. 'Why is she in here?'

'Oh, get out of here,' Vivian said to Eric, bored, or acting bored.

'Henry!' Eric protested. Henry and Vivian locked eyes. Vivian won. Her husband patted his secretary's hand gently: 'Go on, Eric. Get some more sleep.'

'You need me here with you,' Eric said.

'No.' Henry turned his head away. Eric hesitated, his expression halfway between betrayal and anger. He slammed the door on the way out.

'Try to sleep again,' Vivian said. 'You've never had a fit twice in one night. Anyway, Eric will be listening out for you. Sleep well.' She left the room.

Lenny uncurled from the wall where she had been leaning. She made for the door, but Talbott shot out an arm, wrenched her onto the bed next to him. She coiled her hand into a fist. Since the incident with Michael Dorling she had worked out more. Her upper arms were lean but well-muscled.

'You know Vivian was a whore when I married her? She kept me waiting the first time though. I practically raped her.' He smiled and saliva speckled his lip. He was aware of it but didn't try to wipe it away.

'I'm not interested in your history,' Lenny said coolly. 'Let go of my arm now. I'm going to assume all this is a reaction to your medication. But don't press your luck, hmm?'

'You like my wife? All the ladies like my wife,' he ran a thick finger across Lenny's hand.

She squeezed his wrist with her free hand, hard enough to make him grunt with pain. She pulled free easily and stood up. It would be easy to wait until he slept and then press a pillow onto the fetid face. She wondered how Vivian resisted the temptation.

'Listen,' she took a handful of his pyjamas in one hand and pulled hard so that she was almost strangling him. 'I don't like to be touched, Mr Talbott. I'd like you to remember that.'

'Bitches,' he said. His mouth oozed and he foraged in his covers for a handkerchief.

Eric Hunter had been waiting in his room with an ear to the wall, Lenny thought, because the instant she stepped into the corridor he was there beside her.

'Is he all right?' he asked and to Lenny's surprise there

was real concern in his voice. He saw her reaction and shrugged. 'I like him. What's wrong with that? No one else here gives a shit about him. They're all waiting for him to die so they can carve up his company. They just want his money. None of them loves him.'

'And you love him? You don't want his money?'

'I'd make a better CEO of the company than Kendell Talbott. I don't have a rich father to inherit my future from. My father drove semi-trailers from Brisbane to Sydney for forty years. Do you know what rich people ask you when they meet you for the first time, Ms Aaron? They say, "And what does your father do?" And from the moment you answer you're no longer a university graduate with the world ahead of you. You're the son of a truck driver. Period.'

'Quite a speech.' But Lenny knew what he meant.

'Henry Talbott trusts me. He likes me. This is my chance.' He entered the master bedroom and closed the door in Lenny's face.

Back in her own room, Lenny found Vivian sitting on the bed, amongst the little white pillows, Astro Boy behind her head. She looked a centre of calm, not at all perturbed by her husband's outburst. In her hands were the State Library photocopies.

She smiled, sleepy, flirtatious and summoning. Lenny recalled Kimberly at her office, flashing her sexy thighs. Mother and daughter had something in common after all.

'May I have some green tea?' Vivian waited while Lenny clinked the cups and teapot, opened the little tea tin covered with flowered washi paper. She sniffed the tea when offered it and said 'Mmm'. Lenny smiled her Lilliputian smile. Their fingers brushed. Lenny thought about giving those fingers a sharp flick, as she had the ladybug. Pleasurable or not, she didn't choose to be touched.

'I suppose you think we're a pretty strange family,' Vivian said, tapping a finger on a photocopy. She took a mouthful of tea and screwed up her face at the acrid taste. She had a thin line of green above her top lip, like a child at a milk carton.

'You have tea on your lip,' Lenny said. Vivian wiped the back of her hand across her mouth. Now she had tea and mouth germs on her hand.

'I don't think you'll find my enemies by foraging into the past.'

'Just being thorough,' Lenny said and held out a hand for the papers. 'Is that a problem?'

'I wouldn't tell you how to do your job. You're the ex-policewoman.' There was something mocking about the way she said it. 'Did you quit, by the way, or did they,' delicate pause, 'get rid of you?'

'I quit,' Lenny said.

'I see.' Vivian didn't ask the obvious question. 'I can see you as a cop actually.' She smiled. 'Did you rough Henry up after I left?'

'A little.'

'I try to be patient with him but he's a trial.'

'Yet you don't believe he's the letter writer?'

'Let's say I'd be stunned if you found evidence of it,' Vivian said. 'And do you really think my *servants* are threatening me?' She retraced their earlier conversation. 'Liz Dodd thinks I'm not suitable for my position,' she smiled, 'but Maggie adores me and Max is a dear, don't you think?'

She hesitated, sat forward on the bed and squashed Astro Boy between her knees and breasts.

'I sense something though ... That sounds like a rich housewife with nothing better to do than make fantasies for herself, doesn't it?' Her head drooped for a moment. 'But I really do feel something. Like I'm being watched. I can't explain it. After the letters started coming I was suspicious of everyone. At first I treated it as a joke but when they kept coming ... I started to imagine what it would be like to be trapped by someone who hated you and wanted to hurt you. You know? How you'd turn crazy. You'd do anything just to survive. I panicked.' She shivered. 'I was so rude to you when you came here about the cat but I do need you, Lenny.'

Lenny was still thinking about the bit that went *trapped by someone who hated you and wanted to hurt you.* She reached automatically for her shoulder-bag. She fingered her foil strip of aspirin as a comfort but didn't take one out. Later.

'Do you mind if we don't talk about it anymore now?' Vivian continued. 'It spooks me before I sleep, you know? I'm tired! If you were a man I'd ask you to carry me back to bed.' Lenny had never had a proposition from someone so beautiful. In fact she had never had a proposition from anyone she found attractive. Refusing had nothing to do with professionalism. Sex simply involved an amount of intimate touching that was unthinkable.

'I'm sure you can manage yourself,' she said.

Vivian locked eyes with her for a moment. 'Have I overstepped one of those boundaries again?' She looked tired but was trying to be a good sport. 'I must be more careful.' She slid off the bed.

'Do you think I'm a slut?' It was a question out of the blue but Lenny, used to Dr Sakuno's shock tactics, didn't react. 'I married an old man for his money. But Henry was never faithful to me.' She was bitter. 'He didn't love me, not for a moment. It was just a lucky pregnancy. I have nothing to feel guilty about, despite what the newspapers say.'

'He said he raped you.'

Vivian was silent for a moment. Was it still a painful memory? She rubbed a hand over her face.

'It's true. It's all true.' But then she shook herself and gave the carefree laugh, yawned.

'I thought he'd marry me if I withheld sex. I was very young and stupid. I led him on. He got drunk. It happened.' She smiled at Lenny's angry face, touched. 'Sweet thing you are. I had to sleep with him often in the first few years.

I don't imagine being raped by him was any different.'

She had her hand on the doorknob and turned to Lenny. They were almost touching in the half-lit room.

'I'm not sorry I asked you to stay,' she said, her voice caressing. 'Not at all. I feel really safe now that you're here. I mean that, Lenny.'

They said their goodnights and Lenny ripped open the foil on six tablets and pressed them onto her tongue. She slurped up the dregs of her green tea.

There had been two sets of books at Michael Dorling's computer software business. Lenny and the two other junior accountants had handed their work to the senior accountant, Mr Bob Baxter. He had worked in a private office that was locked when he was not there. Locks, however, had always been Lenny's specialty and, on her first opportunity alone in the office, she had taken under two minutes to crack this one. The safe had taken longer. The second set of books revealed a considerable margin between actual company profits and the amount declared to the government. A margin, Lenny calculated, in excess of two million dollars a year.

Chapter 10

TWO SMALL DEATHS

The next morning Lenny stood at the window and drank a big cup of *Mugicha* with three Aspro Clear to settle her head. Someone had to deal with yesterday's feline discovery. She would take a stroll before breakfast.

She walked around to Max's shed and found him already up, drinking coffee and reading the morning paper. He raised his mug and smiled.

'You're an early bird. Want a cuppa? I've got teabags or instant coffee.'

'No thanks.' Lenny suppressed a smile in return. 'Do you have a spade and a bag? I want to do the cat.'

'That's no job for a young woman. You let me handle that.'

'There's nothing masculine about holes, is there?' Lenny asked. Max studied her for a long moment and smiled again.

'Well, if you insist,' he said and went into his tool shed. He came back with a thick, black garbage bag, rubber gloves and a small spade. 'I've got bigger ones if this is too small,' he said.

'This is fine.' She took the things. He stood smiling at her, his hands in his pockets. Lenny half-smiled at him.

'You've been with this family a long time. You and Liz.'

He nodded. 'The happiest period of my life. I have serenity. I don't suppose a young person can understand that. Young people aren't looking for peace, in my experience.'

Lenny refrained from telling him how much she longed to find peace. 'Do you really believe everything's fine here, with the family?'

'Would you really take my word for it?'

No, Lenny thought. But before she could reply he spoke

again. 'I don't know what trouble you're expecting, Ms Aaron, but it won't come from me.'

'You're totally happy here?' she pressed him. It seemed important to dismiss him as a suspect.

'I'm happy here,' he said. 'I wouldn't cause trouble, not for anyone or anything.'

'Carol wants to get younger staff. Are you worried about that?' She imagined his polite face nodding as Carol had hinted to him that he should find a new job before he got the boot.

'Miss Connor is very young.' He sighed.

'Vivian's close to her. Do you think she's likely to acquiesce?'

'She very well may, she very well may do just that.' His eyes were momentarily unreadable. 'But I find it's best to take the future as it comes, Ms Aaron. One day at a time.'

It took five minutes to dig the cat remains out of the ground. She was poking the carcass into the garbage bag which spread across the pathway when a young couple in aerobics gear power-walked towards her heading for the beach. They glanced at the cat. The woman, mid-twenties with a horse-face on a tight body, bugged her eyes.

'What the hell is that?'

Her bull-necked boyfriend stepped in front of her.

'Can I help you?' he asked Lenny in a tone that meant the opposite.

'No,' Lenny stood aside for them to pass.

'Yuck!' Horse-face leapt over the garbage bag and walked on towards the beach. Her boyfriend stared Lenny down.

'Who are you?' He decided to bully.

'Mind your own business.' Lenny tied the bag on the cat remains and slung the bag over her shoulder.

'This is a semi-private beach.'

'Bullshit.'

He gave her another macho stare then made a contemptuous snort and followed his girlfriend.

Lenny pushed the spade, the rubber gloves and the bag under a bush at the beach entrance. She definitely needed her stroll now.

She saw the second corpse almost immediately. It was near the water's edge, on the damp sand. Two dead cats in one day. This had to be Marie Antoinette de Paris unless Brighton was turning into a Hammer Horror House for cats.

She crouched down. It was a Ragdoll all right. The body was already decaying. It had probably died at least two days ago, she thought. Its body was wet as though it had been washed up on the beach but that was odd because if it had been in the water for a while the bigger fish would have finished off most of it.

She left it there and went back to the house, taking the spade and garbage-bagged corpse with her. Max took it with a nod.

'It's all right if *I* bury it then?' he teased. 'I'll pop him in under the roses. It is a him, is it?'

'I didn't look,' Lenny said. 'Anyway, I need another bag and some more rubber gloves. I've found Marie Antoinette. She's on the beach, dead.'

'You're a dead cat magnet.' Max provided her with a fresh bag and pink rubber gloves. 'Poor Miss Kimberly. She'll be heartbroken.'

Lenny returned to the beach and scooped up the cat.

She found Kendell and Carol in the kitchen, complaining that Cook was late and what the hell was the story with breakfast today. Kendell had a cut finger which Carol was expertly band-aiding.

'Hold still, stupid,' she said when he tried to wave to Lenny.

Kendell smiled. He was, Lenny thought, the sort of good-natured type who would almost never take offence. No Einstein, but likeable. He was in swimmers again. She caught a whiff of his macho pong even across the room and thought it would be nice to see him in clothes.

'Can you cook?' Carol asked Lenny.

'Can you?' Lenny placed the garbage bag on the floor and poured herself juice.

'I was just *asking*,' Carol said. She stroked Kendell's meaty leg.

'I cut my hand,' he said.

'It's a scratch,' Carol told him. 'If you weren't so clumsy ...'

Kimberly walked into the room, high heels skidding on the tiles. She wore *fresco*-thick make-up and a pink Alberta Ferretti slip. The high breasts heaved up and out at the bodice.

'Hello, Ms Aaron. I'm so glad you're here with us,' she said. 'My mother is persuasive, isn't she?'

'Before anyone eats ...' Lenny said. She glanced down at the garbage bag. All eyes in the room moved to it.

'No ... Oh no,' Kimberly whispered.

'I'm afraid so,' Lenny nodded. 'It was on the beach.'

'It's not that cat, is it?' Carol said. 'Do we have to have it where we eat?'

'Poor little thing,' Kendell pitied. 'I'll put it outside, Kim.' He picked up the bag and took it into the garden.

Kimberly twisted her hands together.

'It's my fault. I should have taken care of it. Did it drown?'

'I don't think so. It looks like it's been dead a couple of days. I'm going to have a vet open it up so we can find out.'

'Spare us the details, thanks,' Carol protested.

Liz Dodd's door opened and she came out.

'Sleep in, Cookie?' Kendell asked. Carol rolled her eyes. The cook gave them a glance but said nothing and began to drag out pots and pans.

Kendell and Carol went back out to the pool to wait until everything was ready. Kimberly went off to her room to add another strata to her make-up.

Lenny remained in the kitchen watching the efficient old woman whip up a smorgasbord of bacon and tiny sausages and thin crisp toast with buttery soft eggs.

'Still think there's going to be deep dark trouble?' she provoked.

'You just stay away from Max.' The cook was earnest. 'Just leave him right out of it. Promise me.' Interesting how they tried to protect each other, Lenny thought.

'Leave him out of what?' she asked as Vivian came down for breakfast.

'Good morning, Liz. Toast, please.' Vivian slid into a chair at the breakfast table. She leaned in towards Lenny. 'I heard Kimberly crying in her room,' she added. 'The cat?'

'It's dead,' Lenny confirmed. Vivian sighed. She raised her shoulders languidly.

'Kimberly's a bit ... unsettled. She's not stupid. Very far from it. She's doing business law at Melbourne Uni. Kendell dropped out of his course! But she's always been too emotional. She's always at me about something. She had the worst tantrums when she was a child. Kendell was the same. He gave Kimberly a black eye once when they were six. She scratched his cheek open. He grew up able to control himself. She didn't.' She shrugged. 'I hoped a pet would help her— her psychologist advised it—but it didn't make any difference. I can't imagine why she's up there blubbing about an animal that bit her ankle to the bone.' Another pause. 'Dramatics.'

It showed a complete lack of concern for her daughter's misery, Lenny thought. But when Kimberly, hungry despite her anguish, joined the others at the table for breakfast, Vivian made an effort to be kind. She reached out a hand briefly to press Kimberly's. 'Lenny told me the bad news.' She looked at Lenny. 'What now? Do we just chuck it in the bin or is there a procedure?'

'Mum!' Kimberly glared at her while Carol smirked.

'There are pet cemeteries,' Lenny explained. 'You can have a full pet funeral, if you like. Or I can have the vet get rid of it after the autopsy.'

'Well, Kimberly, you'd better decide, although I'm not sure

I'm up to a funeral. I mean,' Vivian smiled, 'we barely knew each other.'

Kimberly sighed. 'The vet can do it, I suppose. Why are you doing an autopsy? Isn't that just for people? I didn't brush her much ... Can they die from too much fur?'

'Sometimes,' Lenny said. 'From furballs.' She doubted it in this case. There was something about the way the cat had been sprawled in the sand like a bedraggled question mark. 'But we should wait for the results.'

'If you think it's best, then we will,' Vivian said. She looked bored now.

'It's a lot of fuss over a cat, isn't it?' Carol couldn't stand not being the focus of attention any longer. She pushed her plate away so it clinked against her glass. 'I want a car this morning.'

'Take one of the Beemers,' Vivian said.

'I prefer the Merc.'

'Whatever you like,' Vivian grinned. A little secret between them, Lenny thought. The way their eyes met and held. There was some kind of intensity between them. Were they lovers?

Kendell and Carol left the room. Everyone in the kitchen heard the sound of his hand slapping her backside as he chased her up the stairs.

Vivian handed Lenny a small business card. 'Meet me here at two o'clock and we'll have a girls' day, on me.' She hesitated. 'You will stay with me for the full week? I need you, Lenny.'

'Liz,' Vivian turned to the cook. 'Thank you for breakfast. I won't be in for lunch.'

The cook nodded.

Vivian went off by herself. They heard a car start up.

Kimberly sighed.

'Please take care of my mother, Ms Aaron,' she said. 'Kendell and I would be lost without her.'

'Sure,' Lenny said. Kimberly glimpsed the skepticism and flushed.

'I'm serious,' she said.

'Whatever.' Lenny was beginning to regret eating the strawberries. The little seeds were sticking in the gaps in her bottom teeth. She had a compulsion to floss.

Annie Baron came into the kitchen. She smiled sympathetically at Kimberly and smoothed the young woman's hair.

'I'm sorry about your cat,' she said.

With her vivid blue eyes, she would probably have been pretty if she wasn't so heavy, Lenny thought. Kimberly mumbled an off-hand thanks and excused herself.

Annie watched her leave, still smiling, too dumb to see the snub or too kind-hearted.

'You would make a good mother,' Lenny said.

'Do you think so?' Annie seemed pleased at the comment. Pleased and amazed, Lenny thought, that someone should imagine her that way.

'Is Vivian a good mother?' Lenny continued.

'Vivvie is always very busy,' Annie said. 'But the children were looked after, I know that.'

'What was it like when they were born?' Lenny tried to visualize Vivian sweating and racked with pain, delivering twin babies, hating them for hurting her but knowing that everything depended on their being healthy, overjoyed to see them and then quickly relegating them to the care of others.

'It was a difficult time in our lives,' Annie said.

'You were at the birth?' Lenny asked. She recalled her research: Henry rejected Vivian until she could prove she was having his child. She went to the country to give birth and returned, triumphant, with the twins, crooked fingers and all.

'Of course I was,' Annie said. 'Vivian needed me. She ... she had a bad time. Nearly died.'

'Did Henry have the babies tested to prove they were his?' she asked. Annie nodded.

'They're his,' she said. 'They're his babies. They couldn't challenge that. There's medical proof. The fingers, blood tests. And, and D ... and ... D and A.'

'DNA?' Lenny suggested.

Annie lowered her voice and glanced in the cook's direction.

'She told me not to be afraid,' she whispered.

'Vivian?'

'Yes. This morning. She said everything was going to be fine because you're here. She said ... she said you suspect the staff.' Apparently Annie didn't place herself in that category.

'It's best not to take any chances,' Lenny said. Annie nodded urgently.

'That's what Vivian says. I'll watch *her* like a hawk,' she said, giving the cook another glance.

Carol and Kendell were dressed for shopping. Those were Vivian's clothes, Lenny thought, eyeing the ivory blouse and steel blue Armani pants. Carol and Vivian were the same size, even the same basic colouring, but however much Carol tried, she was never going to have her mother-in-law's classic beauty.

She strode past Lenny, Prada backpack slung over one shoulder. Kendell said 'See you,' and followed her out to Vivian's Mercedes to go shopping.

Lenny put the dead Ragdoll into the back of her car. She had rung Bob Mulcahy's clinic and he had agreed to take it that morning. The little Colt puttered out of the front gates and she felt liberated. She glanced back at the house as the electronic gates shut and made the car go faster.

At the clinic, Suzanna was busy. A young girl had found a parakeet mauled by her cat on her front lawn.

'Sibyl doesn't usually eat birds, honest.' This was spoken through a mist of tears and a mouthful of metal. 'It's still alive. I felt its heart beating. I think ... I think the wing is ... gone though.'

'All right. Thank you for bringing it in,' Suzanna lifted the little bundle over the reception counter. 'You go on home now. I'll get Dr Mulcahy to have a look in a minute and he'll telephone you after, all right?'

Lenny waited until the girl had gone out of the front door before holding out a hand with the garbage bag.

'Tell Bob I think it probably died two or three days ago. I found it on the beach at the water's edge but I'm not sure that it's a drowning,' she said.

'Thanks. I love autopsies ... not.' Suzanna stroked the bandaged bird absently. 'It's dead, of course. Funny how children can't tell, isn't it? Do you want to observe the autopsy?'

'No.'

'I'll give you a call then. At the office?'

'No,' Lenny wrote her mobile number on a slip of paper. 'You can reach me here.'

'Busy day?'

'I'm going to visit my grandmother.'

'That's nice.' Suzanna waved cheerily. 'Have a good day.'

There was little chance of that.

Tranquillity Gardens was a small hospice. It had thirty inmates, all post stroke or heart attack patients, aged between seventy and ninety-odd. A combination of obligation and affection kept the monthly payments coming in, but few relatives passed through the doors into that reminder of things to come.

Veronica Aaron visited twice a week and stayed for an hour each time. It must be torture for her, Lenny thought.

Trees hid the buildings from the rest of the neighbourhood. The locals liked it that way. Old people's homes, orphanages and schools for spastic people sent real estate prices crashing. The old people were locked inside because the place was understaffed and no one had time to chase escapees. Every patient had a security beeper attached to them. It reminded

Lenny of the anti-theft devices used in Target.

She signed in at reception. She had no gift of flowers or fruit. That was duly noted by a big man in a blue lab coat. His name tag said 'Jack'. He was reading a car magazine, circling Monaros with a red pen. His mini TV was on but he wasn't watching.

'You're here for Mrs Sanderman? You don't look like her.' It was a compliment. 'She's a real piece of work, isn't she?' He handed her a key attached to a card with the word 'visitor' scrawled on it. 'Do you know the way?' Lenny nodded.

At the end of the entrance corridor was a glass door. Through it she could see the main recreation room and its occupants. Their faces registered excitement, curiosity or—and this was the majority—absolutely nothing. She unlocked the door and went in.

It was a brightly lit room with six white vinyl couches, three of them surrounding a decrepit TV. A breakfast show was blaring. Three men in wheelchairs were parked in front of it. One was snoring and the second, a stroke victim, clutched a piece of paper tightly and gazed blankly at the screen. The third man was staring hard at the TV as he worked his way through a fat cigar. A plump, blonde nurse was doing the newspaper crossword as she polished off a cigarette and a cup of coffee. The smoking circle. Private smoking was forbidden. Personal supplies of cigarettes were kept in a locked cupboard and twice a day a member of staff conducted a nicotine session for interested parties.

The nurse was tired. 'Which one?' she asked, glancing around the room.

'Mrs Sanderman,' Lenny replied and the nurse's eyes widened.

'Well, you know the way, I suppose.'

Lenny knew the way.

A hand patted Lenny's arm fondly and she looked down at an old woman who had materialized by her side. 'Hello, are you my friend?' She was quite well-groomed in a pink dress with puffed sleeves. She had a pink plastic clip in her hair and smelled slightly of urine and stewed apples. Her physical presence was so slight that she shook like a cobweb.

'I'm here for Mrs Sanderman,' Lenny said gently.

'I missed you.' The woman gave Lenny's arm a welcoming hug, face scrunching. She had a lot of missing teeth. It spoiled her smile. And she had been eating chocolate recently.

'Mr Wilson, you bad boy!' It was a young voice. Lenny looked to her left. The toilet door was open and there was another young nurse, hands on hips, berating the eighty-year-old Mr Wilson. 'Get some of it in the toilet, will you! Oh, dear me.' She was down cleaning the mess when she saw Lenny.

She got Mr Wilson back in his pyjama pants, into his wheelchair and on his way down the corridor. Then she gently removed the old woman from Lenny's arm.

'Mrs Conroy, this isn't anyone for you. You've had your visitor.'

'My daughter's coming.'

'Mmm. That's nice.' A gentle push and the old woman was drifting away from them.

'I'm here for Mrs Sanderman, my grandmother,' Lenny explained.

'Oh, you're Lenny, then.' The nurse had brilliant blue eyes in a dark brown face. Aboriginal, Lenny thought, but those eyes were white. The name tag said Jenny Noyes.

'Is she all right?' Lenny asked, meaning her grandmother, but Jenny looked after Mrs Conroy and pursed her lips.

'Her daughter visits once a year, if she's lucky.' They walked out of the recreation room and down a long corridor. There were private rooms on each side, but not exactly private for none had doors. The staff had to be able to hear everything in case one of the inmates had an accident. All the rooms had TVs blaring. Lenny tried not to look either left or right.

'Your mother was here yesterday.'

'Hmm.'

'You don't visit us very often, do you?'

'Hmm.'

'We're all aware that your grandmother has some physical contact issues she needs to work through, but—'

'Hmm.'

'She is your grandmother.' Nurse Jenny said gently. 'She asks for you.'

They were outside room twenty-three. Lenny could already see Granny Sanderman on the bed. And of course the old woman knew she was here. She had a nose like a bloodhound. But she didn't bother to turn her head from the TV. She didn't have the sound up but she was laughing at the picture. It was an advertisement for Mars Bars.

'I'll leave you to it then,' Nurse Jenny whispered.

Chapter 11

THE CONSTIPATED GRANNY

'Grandmother,' she said from the doorway. The room smelled of prunes. Granny Sanderman was always constipated. Veronica Aaron brought fresh prunes and jars of prune extract but they had little effect.

'You,' Granny Sanderman turned her head. She was eighty-three and had long since stopped worrying about personal hygiene. If the nurses did not bathe her every night, she would, thought Lenny, be living in her own filth.

The hair, a grey-blonde colour, once waist-long and her 'pride and joy', had been cut off during her rehabilitation and never allowed a comeback. Her current 'do' was pudding bowl with dry strands hanging to the ears. The old woman had sharp features—she had once resembled her daughter—but in old age and following her stroke, her mouth had drooped so the bottom lip was permanently open. She had a dental plate but rarely put it in. Of her own teeth only three remained.

Granny Sanderman, Lenny thought, could hardly be popular among the staff. It was probably on her chart: 'Handle with care. May punch, scratch or attempt to bite'. Still, her physical power was not such a threat these days. Her evil mouth, on the other hand, worsened with age.

She never walked unless she had to. *It hurts my bad leg. Why should I? That's why your mother pays these bitches— to carry me.*

'My, my!' Granny looked at her as she came into the room. 'You're Veronica all over.' Granny hated Veronica Aaron more than anyone in the world. That hatred was her life's focus and, Lenny thought, her life force.

'The spitting image.' She had a laugh like a crow: 'Ark, ark, ark.'

'You're well then?' Lenny tried not to touch anything in the room.

'I'm old and I'm dying,' Granny said. 'I've got my problem again. I need someone to put their finger up my bum and scrape me out, that's what I need.'

'Hmm.' Lenny wondered if anyone really had to perform this irksome task.

'Who asked you to come? No one ever comes to see me.'

'Veronica comes twice a week.'

'*She* poisoned you against me! The bitch.'

Lenny pulled a tissue out of her pocket and used it to turn up the TV. She wondered if capable Nurse Jenny was listening outside, making notes.

It was true she was poisoned against Granny Sanderman but Veronica Aaron wasn't to blame.

As a little girl, Lenny had been wary of the Sunday visits to 'Granny's house' and always obeyed her mother's rule to 'not be alone with Granny'. Granny didn't liked Veronica. That was always clear. The tall woman smacked her daughter hard and often. *You're stupid, stupid! What's the matter with you?!* At the time, Lenny thought it was normal behaviour and wondered why Veronica never smacked her.

Granddad had been dead for a long time so there was only Granny, bringing out cakes and cookies and smoothing Lenny's white cotton 'church' dress and pulling her hair too hard. *Aren't you my angel?*

There was the inevitable reckoning at age ten when Granny found her granddaughter in the kitchen with a broken cup she was trying to hide. *Stupid, ugly girl! Just like your mother! Stupid little bitch!* And then hard smacks to the face and head. Six or seven blows received before her mother, terrified, burst in on them: Lenny sitting on the floor with the broken cup under her, holding her head and screaming.

She couldn't remember all of it anymore. She thought she probably blocked out the worst of the abuse her grandmother dished out, but she could clearly remember her mother standing to the side, shouting and sobbing but making no move to help her trapped child.

In the end Lenny, tall even at ten, struggled up and gave her grandmother a shove in the chest that sent the woman backwards onto her bottom. Lenny ran outside into the street, face red with handprints, and had the only hyperventilation attack of her life.

The Sunday visits continued. There was always the social pretence to be maintained but security was tightened. Granny Sanderman had crossed over a barrier that day in the kitchen. After that her hands flailed out angrily towards her granddaughter when she was angry or frustrated. Lenny learned to move quickly. She got a certain victorious pleasure from avoiding a blow.

She and Veronica never spoke a single word about that day in the kitchen and by some kind of psychic agreement they never mentioned it to another living soul.

Ted Aaron knew that his wife had had a 'difficult childhood'. Veronica confided a little in him but he was, Lenny thought, never aware of the extent of the problem. Granny was always different if he visited with them. Quieter, flirtatious. Although when he didn't visit she referred to him as 'that arsehole freak you married'.

Children of abusive parents, Lenny read, often become abusers. But not Veronica Aaron. She was not a spanker. Not, in fact, a toucher at all. She avoided physical contact. Like Granny Sanderman, Lenny thought, her mother was prone to fits of screaming and deceit but it never manifested itself in physical abuse. In fact Lenny could not remember a time when Veronica Aaron touched her in any way except to help her dress when she was very little.

It was a blessing for everyone when Granny Sanderman had her stroke. At first the old woman was in intensive care, critical for a week while Lenny and her mother waited. Veronica sat by the bedside at the hospital and arrived home each night with a pinched mouth:

'No change. Keep praying.'

Lenny, seventeen and wildly hormonal, went to church every day and knelt in the front row, a last ditch effort at Catholicism. *My grandmother's deranged. If you are god, I mean truly, you already know that, so ... if you're listening ... finish her.*

Unfortunately, Granny Sanderman made a miraculous comeback, and a month after the stroke was sitting up in bed, screaming her demands and complaints and covering Veronica with fresh marks. Ted Aaron shook his head weakly as she rubbed in her liniment.

'Sweetheart,' he said, 'you mustn't let her.' He suggested that Veronica was exhausting herself, spending too much time at the hospital.

'She's my mother,' Veronica said.

Lenny went to visit towards the end of her grandmother's hospital stay. She stood at the end of the bed, smirking.

'Been at your face again, spotty?' Granny always went for the jugular. 'What are you looking so smug about?'

She looked horrifying, Lenny thought. Amazing she could speak at all with her mouth all droopy like that. Her right arm and leg were permanently weakened. She would limp badly and her right hook was a thing of the past. Pity she had a mean left. The doctor said she would need constant care. He mentioned the personality change—of course he assumed it was a change. *You may find her inclined to occasional outbursts.*

'They're discharging you, Granny,' she said.

'About bloody time. C'mere.'

'Forget it.' She wasn't getting close enough for a beating. Despite Lenny's speed she'd had, during her adolescence, one or two nasty blows from those hands and Granny Sanderman always bought the rings with the keenest edges.

'Watcha smirking at?'

'You're not coming home with us, you know.'

'What do you mean?' The old woman was surprised. It was a glorious moment for Lenny, one of the few with her grandmother. 'That doctor says I'm to have care—constant care. Your mother says—'

'You're going into a home for old people.'

'Never.'

'You'll see.' Then she had to leave the room because Granny Sanderman, crippled or not, lunged across the bed and tried to kill her.

Lenny was certain that it was an absolute pleasure for her mother to put Granny away. Outside the family, people began to believe the old woman had died. Lenny always reinforced this idea: 'Yes, she's gone ... Yes, terrible ... Yes, I know ... Thank you.'

When she first went to the hospice she was thrilled. It was like seeing the old woman in jail. But after a while Granny found her place in her new world, recovered her nerve and became the person she was today: incubus.

Dr Sakuno insisted that she continue to visit Granny Sanderman. He believed in the family. Of course old people went senile and their opinions had to be ignored but that didn't mean abandoning them. They were part of what made you. You couldn't pretend you sprang clean from nowhere.

'Do you need anything?'

'Your mother says you're still with the cats,' Granny laughed. 'High ambition that. C'mere.'

'Forget it.'

Dr Sakuno said Granny had probably been mentally ill for years but that there was so much child abuse, *especially in western society*, that she had gone undetected.

'If you loved me ...' Granny Sanderman wheedled.

'I don't love you.'

'You love me or you wouldn't be here, darling. Come to see your granny because you love her, 'cos you're me all over. How's the arm?'

The question was no surprise. Granny had watched the

whole thing on TV. Lenny hadn't visited her for a year during that period. When she finally turned up again, the old woman dragged a nail down her own arm while making a horrible sucking noise.

'Fine.'

'He's dead. That Dorling. He's dead now, I saw it on the news. I bet you think you're safe now, but you're not!'

Lenny gave up. 'Take care of yourself,' she said, then walked back down the corridor. When she reached the recreation room, she leaned against the wall. She was concentrating on 'stabilizing her emotion' and the recreation room door key fell from her hand. Nurse Jenny came over and picked it up.

'Are you all right?' That remote, hospital concern.

'I'm fine, thanks.'

'Is Mrs Sanderman all right?'

'How long do people in her condition usually live?' She didn't disguise her feelings. Nurse Jenny gasped.

Lenny escaped.

Later she blamed the accident on her grandmother. She was still annoyed and wasn't concentrating. So of course she had an accident—a disastrous one. Backing into a parking spot behind the Footscray shopping mall she heard a yowl. She got out of the car, looked at the right rear wheel. And there it was: Renata, 'Natty'—the Antolinis' Russian Blue—pulped under the tire, its stomach churned up through its mouth. There was a lot of blood and a little girl eating ice-cream had witnessed the whole event.

This was her third corpse in one day. Perhaps Max Curtis was right, she thought grimly: she *was* a dead cat magnet. The witness—maybe ten years old—was pure spite. 'You're in big trouble now.' The girl had a round, freckled face and braids.

'No, I'm not.' Lenny used her 'grown-up' voice.

'Yes, you are.'

'No, I'm not.'

'Yes, you—'

'Will you go away!'

The girl's face got mean. 'I'll tell my mum.'

'Big deal.' That was stupid. What if it got back to the Antolinis? These people were cat maniacs. No telling what they were capable of. Lenny whipped five dollars out of her wallet.

'Here's a present,' she said.

The girl looked around the parking lot. It was empty. She snatched the money. 'Watcha gonna do with it?'

'You've got your money. It's none of your business.'

The girl shrugged and skipped into the shadow of the mall. Lenny took off her denim jacket and toed the cat onto it. Cat innards clung to her shoe. She couldn't even bill anyone for the jacket. She put it in the car boot, pulled out her radiator water can and washed the blood off the tire.

A woman and child with a trolley were heading out to their car. It was the blackmailer and her mother. The girl waggled a finger at Lenny behind her mother's back.

She drove down the road a bit, pulled over at a supermarket and bought some black garbage bags and string. She stuffed the jacketed cat inside three bags and tied the top. Obviously the next step was burial but that would have to wait.

She parked up the street from the shopping mall and went to her office. Mike Bullock was waiting, arms folded, an eye out for customers. Today he was a tribute to beige. His crinkle-perm was fuzzy.

'Problem, Len?'

'What?' She fumbled with her keys.

'The shoes, mate. The shoes.'

They were sticky with gelid blood. The key turned and she fell into the office, ignoring Mike's concerned blather.

She dragged out the Domestos and a Chux super-wipe and scrubbed at the shoes. She spent a long time at the sink cleaning her hands. They looked blood-free but you couldn't see germs. She never touched children or handrails. How many hands did the bank notes and coins pass through before they touched her own? At intersections she used her knuckle to press the 'walk' button on the traffic lights. A cougher or sneezer in her vicinity called for holding her breath and blinking rapidly for at least a minute.

She clicked on the answering machine. Two hang-ups.

'Me tabby's gone missing. I've 'erd about you.' Pause. 'Call yer back later, then.'

Lenny pulled out the card Vivian had given her. It was a Collins Street address. A plain white card with 'Madeleine's' in gold print.

The second caller said 'Hello, Sparky,' paused for a series of wheezes, and then she heard the sound of oxygen. 'Look, your mum's a bit upset about yesterday—'

He couldn't continue, couldn't breathe. Only a few months to go now, she thought. He was down to thirty-five percent lung capacity. The last time she had seen him he whispered to her that he was 'ready'. *I've made my peace, Sparky.*

She had sat with him through increasingly severe illnesses, altering the level of his oxygen when he needed it, reading to him and showing him schoolwork. But *outside* the house they had rarely shared a moment together that did not involve an emergency trip to the hospital.

She listened to him struggle to speak on the phone but it was beyond him and he hung up. She wondered if he ever wept bitter tears about their relationship, as she did.

She took the tiny tape out of her answering machine and put it into her top drawer in a box marked 'T. Aaron'.

She drove into the city, the bagged Russian Blue sloshing around in the back of the car. Thirty-three degrees. Mothers collapsed over strollers and hauled hot toddlers. Businessmen loosened their collars and flipped on Ray-Bans.

At two o'clock she was in the elevator of the Collins Street address. The top end, near the plaza, was the home of Louis Vuitton luggage shops and middle-aged women with artificially blonde bobs and gorgeous daughters. The men in

Collins Street were solicitors, financiers and orthodontists.

The Madeleine beauticians resembled fabulously made-up and coiffured nurses. They glided Lenny into a private room where two hours passed in ambient music, pure oxygen, green stinky mud, prodding fingers (not pleasant at all) and Lenny's hair-removal squawks.

Finally, newly perfumed, she was delivered into an open room. Vivian was having her finger- and toenails done and a beautician was arranging her box of paints on a counter. It was a woman-making production line. Lenny psyched herself up to be the reject.

'Lenny!' Vivian waved her to the vacant chair next to her. 'I heard you screaming.'

'Stubborn leg hair,' Lenny said.

'What's the news on the cat?'

'Nothing yet. The vet's opening it up today so we'll know by tonight. Unless it's poison, in which case we'll have to wait a day or two for results.'

'Very efficient, Lenny,' Vivian smiled.

A hairdresser appeared, her face a collection of perfect cosmetic planes. She looked down at Lenny's blonde tufts. The planes twitched away from each other. She seemed confused.

After they gave up on the hair they turned to her nails, cutting each cuticle and forcing it back into her finger with a spatula. 'Did you have a nice morning?' Vivian asked.

'No,' Lenny said, 'Ouch! OUCH!' It was her very first cuticle push.

'No pain no gain,' her manicurist said.

Cold-tea compresses and cucumber pulp were placed on their eyes. They were left alone to marinate. Vivian's hand reached across to touch Lenny's gently. The smallest caress.

'This is how I keep my looks,' she said dryly. 'It's very expensive being a great natural beauty. Are you enjoying it?'

'Not really.'

Vivian laughed. 'Has anyone laid a bear trap in my bed yet?'

'You should take it more seriously.'

'I can't believe it's someone close to me.'

'It could be. What about the children?'

'No.' Vivian's hand squeezed Lenny's hard before she broke contact. 'No, Lenny, I won't let you go down that route.

'All right,' she said finally, 'I'm not the world's greatest mother. And they're not model kids. But Kendell and Kimberly wouldn't hurt me. Kimberly was the one who persuaded you to come to the house, remember?'

To cover her tracks, Lenny speculated, but she let it go for the time being.

'And Kendell?'

'He's not dangerous,' Vivian said after another long pause. 'He's clumsy. And he's not the smartest man you'll ever meet. But he's not malicious. The children are not what I might have hoped for but I think any mother who's honest would say that. It doesn't mean there isn't a bond between us. I read somewhere that the bond between a woman and the children she gives birth to is unbreakable. Do you think that's true?' She seemed genuinely curious, as though she had given it a lot of thought.

Lenny, about to say 'no', thought better of it.

'I don't know,' she said. 'I don't have children. Annie said you had a bad labour.'

There was silence, again for a long time. Lenny tried to squeeze open an eyelid. Tea and salad oozed into her eyelashes. She closed the eye again.

'It *was* a terrible labour. Painful and long. Two babies. That was a surprise. One of them was behind the other, masking the heartbeat. Carol says that happens sometimes. It was twenty hours. I'm not very patient. I just wanted it to be over. Annie took care of me. We went to a small country hospital. There was such a lot of publicity then and I wanted it to be a private birth. I spent most of my pregnancy in the country. I wouldn't let Henry see me. I knew he'd hate that fat stomach!' She laughed harshly. 'In fact he didn't even try to visit. Just picked up where he left off with the other women. It was humiliating. Rejected by a seventy-year-old man.'

'Were you very fat?'

'A tank. I had terrible water retention. I swore I'd never have another child.'

Lenny heard a timer go off and the door open. Deft hands removed the treatment from her eyes and cotton pads wiped them clean. Lenny looked closely into the mirror, touched the skin tentatively. Did it feel softer? Did it look younger? Bloody right it did.

Vivian smiled at the pretty make-up artist.

'Hannah, just a light make-up for my friend,' she said. 'We don't want her looking like a drag queen.'

Driving back to Brighton, Lenny felt womanly, in the way she imagined women in magazine advertisements felt. There was not a part of her body that had not been cleansed, exfoliated and rejuvenated.

She looked in the mirror. They had gone for a 'no make-up' make-up: a base so sheer it was almost indiscernible, a skin tone lipstick, no blusher. Only the eyes were altered: beige on the lids with dark brown eyeliner and mascara. Lenny wiggled her lashes curiously. She wondered if she would ever be able to duplicate the effect.

The BMW pulled up suddenly and Vivian smiled through black cat's-eye sunglasses, red lips luscious and laughing. She waved and pulled away easily. Lenny gave chase but couldn't keep up. The Colt made protest noises and she was forced to ease back.

She wondered if Vivian had many lovers.

The Cedars Court kids were not playing cricket that afternoon. A gardening company had arrived to trim some trees that were brushing the overhead electrical wires. The tree-loppers were studying the angles, snipping and discussing. One of them was working from a chart. Lenny recalled how outside her apartment block, two men had taken fifteen minutes to chain-saw three metres off the ironbark.

She parked in the garage and experienced an unexpected coming-home sensation.

In her room she put the jug on for tea and clicked on the Sheffield Shield. She didn't need to but she took a couple of Tylenol anyway. It was time to kick off her shoes, hit the sheets and have a nice snooze before the dinner party.

It didn't happen.

Chapter 12

THE COOK DID IT

There were voices screeching downstairs, a cacophony of anger, shock and confusion. Lenny came down to the kitchen in best swat team form, half expecting to find a body on the floor. Fortunately everyone else was too caught up in the moment to notice her, so she could drop her dramatic pose in the door frame without embarrassment.

Liz Dodd was shaking her head. Maybe indignation. Maybe fear. Vivian towered over her holding a letter, pushing it into her face. Three guesses what that was. Max, holding a gardening fork, stood at the French doors. Lenny figured that a scene like this between staff and mistress was a very new experience for everyone in the room. Vivian, she figured, would pride herself on not losing control.

Kimberly, in a black leather Versace dress that looked straight out of an S & M catalogue, was protesting: 'Mum! Mum! Of course she didn't write it! Why would she?'

Lenny stepped into the arena. Vivian, still at a peak of rage, met Lenny's eyes. She waved the letter towards her.

'Look at this,' she said in a constricted voice. Her fingers gripped the letter so firmly, Lenny had to wrench it away.

It was pink paper, the letters cut from a glossy magazine and pasted in. It said 'Tonight! Bitch!' A flashy font had been used for some of the letters and it might even be possible to pinpoint the magazine.

Vivian was recovering. Lenny recognized her own often used breathing technique.

'Where's the envelope?' she asked.

'Here.' Vivian pulled it from her pants' pocket. 'It wasn't posted. It was in the mailbox outside. She must have put it in there this morning.' She pointed at Liz Dodd, 'I want you out!' The cook shook her head again.

'This is nonsense,' she said. 'Absolute nonsense. Mrs Talbott, you're upset so I'll give you some leeway, but this is ... nonsense.'

'I went into her room after I got the letter,' Vivian ignored the cook and directed her words to Lenny. 'I found this.' She held out a pad of pink paper.

'Max ...' Liz Dodd turned to him and he nodded and stepped into the room.

'There's been a mistake,' he said firmly. 'A misunderstanding. Perhaps if we can all talk about it?'

'She thinks I'm threatening her,' Liz said. 'I won't lose my job over this kind of nonsense. I work hard and I deserve better than that.'

Max touched her shoulder gently and she was silent.

Lenny examined the letter and the pink paper pad closely. Unusual stuff, expensive with a light texture and rough edges. They were identical.

Margaret Gross's eyes never left Vivian's face. She was ready to race in if needed. Annie Baron sat at the table, a half-eaten piece of cake in front of her.

'Is it your paper?' Lenny asked Liz Dodd. The cook glared at her.

'Of course it's my paper. What of it? I can buy paper, can't I?'

'Of course you can.' Max touched her shoulder again. He gave Lenny a disappointed look, as though she had let him down. 'Ms Aaron, I've known Miss Dodd for many years and I assure you her character is beyond reproach.'

Vivian stared at him. 'Max, thank you for your concern but I'm sure you have work to do. This doesn't affect you.'

'Don't you dismiss him like he's your servant,' Liz's eyes sparked. Max must have squeezed her shoulder hard this time because she winced and looked up at him.

'I am her servant,' he said gently. 'I do have the front to

water.' His tone was as polite as ever. He glanced at Lenny. 'You'll take care of her?' He meant Liz. Lenny was annoyed at the implied bond, as though they had some kind of connection, but she nodded.

Max bent down to the cook's ear and said something to her. She nodded. Then he left her and went back into his garden.

'I've done nothing,' the cook said to Vivian, trying to recover herself. 'I'm not young and I shouldn't be having these kinds of slurs made against me. It's not right.'

Vivian looked exhausted. She ran a hand over her eyes. Annie Baron and Margaret Gross both moved towards her, but she waved them off. 'Leave me be.'

'Get away, Annie!' Kimberly snapped. 'Mum, this situation is crazy! You have to call the real police.'

'Don't talk to me about crazy!' Vivian compressed her lips. Kimberly flushed and looked away. Vivian stepped back and took a long breath. 'We have guests coming.' Her voice was almost level again.

'Don't worry about a thing,' Margaret Gross leapt in. 'Everything's in perfect order.' The housekeeper looked smug. There was competition among the servants for Vivian's regard and the cook had been demoted to the lowest rung.

Vivian nodded. She put a hand up to her head, tired and pale.

'I'll be getting on with my job now,' the cook said, locking eyes with Vivian.

'I could fire you,' Vivian said.

'I've done nothing. Mr Talbott would never permit it.'

Vivian opened her mouth to refute this then thought better of it.

'It says tonight,' she murmured. She wrapped her arms around herself.

'Well, I don't know what it is you think I'm likely to do to you. I couldn't be bothered, to tell you the truth.' Liz opened a cupboard and began pulling out pots. 'Now I've a lot to do before dinner.'

Vivian's attention shifted back to her daughter.

'Kimberly, go upstairs to your room until the guests arrive,' she said.

'Mum!'

'Go.'

Kimberly stomped away, heels clicking down the hall.

Before anyone could speak further, Kendell and Carol appeared in the kitchen, their arms full of bags. Carol had also been beautified for the evening. Her dark hair was glossy and her lips, like Vivian's, were fire-engine red.

Kendell smiled at everyone and Annie beamed at him, always ready to make herself amenable.

'What's up?' Kendell asked. 'What's the matter with Liz? Not feeling the best?'

'I hope she's all right for dinner tonight,' said Carol. 'Someone better help me with these bags. There's more in the car. We went a bit crazy!' She laughed at herself.

Vivian smiled at the young couple, distracted from her anger.

'Have a good day? I want to see everything you bought. Let me take some of those.' She reached for a handful of bags. She was relieved to be diverted and eager to get out of the kitchen.

Annie took Kendell's bags and the four of them went upstairs. Kendell's voice dominated. He had seen a new Ferrari. Carol said he had to have it. It was him!

Lenny followed them up the stairs and called out:

'Vivian, I need to talk to you.'

Vivian turned reluctantly.

'Must you?' Carol said to Vivian. 'Tell her it can wait.'

'Can it wait?' Vivian asked.

'Tell her no,' Lenny said. Vivian smiled. Carol tossed her head and snatched her bags from Vivian's hands. She ran up the stairs, Kendell behind her.

Vivian sat down on the staircase. She rested her chin on her kneecaps and let out a little sigh as Lenny sat next to her. She let her hair fall forward to hide her face.

'Have I made a mess of it?' she asked, turning her head to smile. 'When I got this last letter I thought about what you'd said, about it being a staff member. I know it can't be Annie or Maggie. I figured it had to be her. I ransacked her cupboards. The paper's unusual, isn't it? It's not a coincidence, is it?'

'I don't know,' Lenny said.

'I should have told you first,' Vivian said softly. 'I lost my temper. Now there's an *admission* ...' She laughed and wrapped her arms around her knees. She looked vulnerable.

'Lenny, is it all going to be OK?' Vivian's voice was barely a whisper and Lenny saw with surprise the glint of tears in her eyes. 'Can't you just tell me it's OK?'

'It's not possible to guarantee anything,' Lenny said automatically. She had never been good at reassurance. Vivian stared and then laughed. A sharp laugh of real amusement. She sat up and the tears went from her eyes. The mood change.

'You are a funny thing, Lenny.' She stood up.

'Give Liz the night off,' Lenny said. It had been the reason she wanted to talk to Vivian. She wanted the old woman out of the way for the evening. Vivian shook her head.

'I need her for the dinner,' she sighed. 'I'm not going to give in to it. Fear, I mean. It's stupid. You're right, there are no guarantees in life. What's a piece of pink paper anyway?' She ran up the stairs lightly, turned at the top to smile down. She knew when to turn on the charm, each gesture timed for maximum impact.

Lenny went back down to the kitchen. The cook was stacking plates on the table.

'I didn't write any letters,' she said. 'No matter how many times she says it. I won't be losing my job for other people's mischief. She's got plenty of enemies without having to look in my direction.'

'Better get on,' Margaret said to the old woman. 'We have

to get the table set.' The cook nodded. She began to pull out the silverware and place it in a wicker basket to take to the dining room. Lenny and Margaret watched her.

'What was all that about?' Margaret asked.

'I don't know,' Lenny lied.

'What's in those letters then? What's going on?'

'Have you seen Vivian get that angry before?' Lenny evaded. She was wondering if Vivian ever got angry with her friends—specifically, with anyone who was coming to the party.

'She's got a temper, hasn't she?' Margaret laughed, easily distracted. 'You should've seen her when she was a girl. She could really let off steam. She was like a little queen at the home. Everyone loved her but she always made sure they knew who was boss. Still does.'

'What about Annie? Was she ever violent?'

'She's violent, yes,' Margaret said, eyes hard. 'We should have left her in Gympie. She would have been a lot better off.'

And you and Vivian would be best friends, thought Lenny. She had suggested that Annie was violent and Margaret had jumped at the idea. Still, Vivian said Annie was controlling. She determined to talk to Annie again and push harder. She was also thinking about Vivian's words to her daughter: *Don't talk to me about crazy*, and Kimberly's jumpy response.

'What was the home like?' she asked the housekeeper.

'Standard. Not enough money. No treats. Hand-me-down clothes.' Margaret nodded. 'I did my best to get Vivvie a few extra bits and pieces out of my own pocket. She didn't deserve to be done up in people's cast-offs like the rest of them.'

'Vivian says she was adopted.'

'The poor couple couldn't cope. I brought her back myself.' It was a happy memory, Lenny could see that. 'I suppose I was a mother to her, really.'

'Was there ever any trouble at the home?'

'Where there's kids, there's always trouble. The usual teenage stuff. Not the kind of stuff kids get into these days. Just cigarettes and some beer drinking. Nothing major. Biggest dramas around that place were illnesses. Kids are always getting appendicitis or such like. We had a boy who had a heart murmur—always giving us a scare. I was forever driving them into town to see the doctor.'

'Were Annie and Vivian ill?'

'Vivian had tummy upsets when she was a teenager.' A discreet pause. 'You know how it is for young girls during their special time. The doctor kept an eye on her, though, and she must have grown out of it. Nowadays she never complains.'

'And Annie?'

'The same kind of thing. Most girls complain about their periods at first before they get used to it. I remember Annie was always slow. I never liked that in kids. Dullness. It was unbelievable to me that she was ...' her mouth twisted, 'Vivian's friend. But she was always pretty healthy. They both were. I just thank god it was only Annie that got Cushing's Syndrome.'

'It's not contagious, surely?' Lenny asked.

'Luckily, no.'

'Didn't you want your own children?'

Margaret nodded. 'Can't have kids,' she said solidly. 'Found out early on. Came to terms with it. Didn't stop me loving 'em though. That's why I worked in the home. Got my nursing certificate and then straight into it.'

So she really had played mother to Vivian. No wonder she went to Brisbane herself to collect the rejected baby. Probably couldn't believe her luck and made damn sure no one else ever got a shot at adopting the little girl. And Vivian? Did she think of the housekeeper as a mother figure?

Margaret looked worried.

'Vivvie doesn't like talk about the past. The newspapers are unkind to her as though being an orphan is a crime! She's not like they say she is at all!' She hesitated. 'Why are you asking all these questions?'

'Vivian told you to help me with anything I needed—'

But there was no chance for further interrogation. The two young people who would assist Liz with the dinner had arrived and Lenny was forced to evacuate.

She went outside to the garden on the beach side of the house. The flowers near Max's cottage were a riot of colour: boronias, daisies, triggerplants. It was festive, like a flower show. Max, however, sitting at his bench sharpening tools again, was not happy. An axe lay at his feet while he rubbed at a trowel. He looked up as Lenny approached and squinted in the low sunlight. He reminded her of someone, she thought. Not her grandfather certainly. Both paternal and maternal grandfathers had died when she was very young. She had no memory of them.

'Ms Aaron,' Max nodded to her.

'Max,' she responded.

'Is she all right then?' He meant the cook of course.

'She's preparing dinner,' Lenny said. 'She's fine.'

'I shouldn't have spoken out like that.' Max sighed. 'I know my place.'

'For god's sake!' Lenny glared at him. 'This isn't *Upstairs, Downstairs*, you know.'

'You've never been in service, it's clear,' Max smiled. 'A fiery one like you wouldn't have the temperament.'

'What's between you and Liz Dodd?' Lenny asked. 'If you know something about what she's up to, you'd better tell me. She could get into real trouble.'

'Liz Dodd ...' Max shook his head. 'She's guilty of a soft heart, that's about all. You don't really think she'd hurt anyone? She's protective of people she ... cares about. She gets angry but it's just a front. She's a good woman, Ms Aaron. All this fussing.' He put down the trowel and began on the axe. 'I'll talk to her.'

'Is she writing the letters?'

'I haven't seen the letters.' Max blinked.

'Someone is threatening Mrs Talbott,' Lenny said. 'Does anyone on staff have a reason to do that?'

Max polished hard. The axe shone in the fading sunlight. Lenny could see her reflection in it.

'No,' he said and met her eyes. 'No, Ms Aaron.'

From Vivian's room came the sound of laughter. Lenny and Max both glanced up. Vivian had the glass doors to her balcony open and the chattering voices were easily audible. Carol must be modelling again. Vivian sounded relaxed.

Lenny's mobile phone rang. It was Bob Mulcahy at the clinic.

'Just finished up with the Ragdoll,' he said. 'I thought you might like to know the result. You were right about it being a couple of days since it was killed, and about it not being a drowning. Its spine was broken in a couple of places. Lots of little broken bones in the head and neck too. An odd one.'

'Car accident?' Lenny asked.

'Weeeell, you can never be certain, can you, but I'd say not. Looks like it was deliberate. My guess is—this is only a guess, mind—someone hit it against a wall or dropped it out of a high window.'

'Thanks.' Lenny had suspected as much.

'No worries. The bill is in the mail. You might be interested to know, we sent the little Fold home today. It's a bit early but the owner was hanging around so much ...'

Vivian came out onto the verandah wearing a ridiculously large white summer hat. She was modelling it and the others were laughing. She leaned over the balcony, lit a cigarette and looked out at the sea for a long time, smiling. Lenny didn't move but Vivian sensed the attention. She looked down and stared. Then Carol's loud voice demanded that she come back inside. Vivian smiled at Lenny, waved and went back in.

Max shook his head.

'It's not on,' he said. 'You're right, Ms Aaron. This isn't

Upstairs, Downstairs, and staff deserve respect. Liz has done no harm.'

'Perhaps the two of you should complain to Mr Talbott,' Lenny suggested, but Max was already walking back inside his tool shed.

Chapter 13

FEEDING THE SUSPECTS

The guests arrived at seven. The terrace had been transformed into a bar. A long white cloth-covered table held bottles and glasses. There was something glamorous about glass, Lenny thought. Certainly it was a change from the paper cups at the Police Union Christmas party, her last experience of a formal function. One of the two dinner staff, Sid, a guy of about twenty with slicked-back hair and a winning smile, was practising a flamboyant shaker style. He said with a wide, straight-toothed grin that he had a repertoire of over fifty cocktails. Lenny asked for a soda water to wash down the five Aspirin she had just taken.

She was wearing her most formal clothes: tailored green pants with a black blouse. She had been smoking in her room and smelt like a nightclub as her mother, who never went to nightclubs, would say. She had taken up smoking as soon as she left home. It was a little act of defiance and reassurance— her lungs could take it.

She didn't want to go to this party. Socializing was never a part of her life. She was incompetent at small talk and unable to smile politely at nothing without her teeth drying and her lips trembling with the effort. But she had to watch over things, earn her keep.

She was still frustrated by the latest pink letter, wondered if the writer was someone who would be at the dinner. Of course it was possible that the letter writer may not be a member of the family at all. It might be an acquaintance. It might be someone who had never met Vivian, had no connection at all. It might be a fan, someone who had seen her light the Christmas Tree or collected photos of her from the tabloids, someone who just wanted to feel their identity linked with hers through the messages.

Lenny also wondered to what extent her own reactions in the past couple of days had merely been to reacquaint herself with old routines, restake her identity as an investigator? She knew she was testing herself, running with the bigger cats again to see how it felt.

Kimberly was out on the terrace saying hello to the first guest, Larry 'Friday Night' Burton. He gave her a moist kiss on the cheek. Kimberly froze and whispered something, annoyed. Lenny couldn't hear but she watched the manicured hands flap. Larry's face was expressive. Almost as good as hearing the words, she thought. He registered lust, amusement, confusion and then anger. Old lover, Lenny thought, despite the age gap. He must be at least forty-five and looked older. He was too fat now to be a TV host. Didn't the camera add a kilogram or so? She wondered why he had become involved with Kimberly Talbott. Business or pleasure?

Kimberly was challenging a Helmut Lang mini dress in oyster silk. It had a push-up bodice and across the high part of the chest, a strip of dark lace, deliberately designed to give the effect of a woman whose bra has been pushed up over her breasts. And what breasts! This was the second time Lenny had seen them uncovered and they were no less appealing. Like a couple of little apples. Kimberly's long legs had never seemed longer. The dress had been altered, Lenny thought, or Helmut Lang had imagined a skirt so short that it revealed a flash of black panties if the wearer raised her arms. Kimberly topped it all off with six-inch Manolo Blahnik black heels with thin straps that laced up to the knee. From behind she was a goddess. Her hair was piled up in a series of elaborate curls and there was a bow encrusted with diamonds holding up the lot.

Mike and Sonny Buchanan were next onto the terrace, dressed in his-and-hers white. He looked worn, putting on a bold face. She looked like someone who was not nearly recovered from a nervous breakdown; her face was the colour of wood stain. They headed straight for the bar. Lenny noticed the way his hand gripped her arm to steady her. His eyes on her were impatient, her glance back icy.

Kendell and Carol came down together. Kendell got into a shaker contest with the barman. Carol had gone to town in a sleeveless Donna Ricci black dinner dress: short, high-necked at the front, transparent behind down to the lowest point of her back. It suited her and she knew it. She thrust out her pointy breasts and made a beeline for Larry Burton. Kendell, adding cream to his shaker, saw them talking but was unconcerned. He was fully occupied with the drink. He fumbled with the cocktail glass and it crashed onto the tiles. The female dinner staff, Nancy, a bottle blonde with buck teeth and a big bosom, glided in to fix the mess and Kendell laughed as though he had done something entertaining on purpose.

'Clumsy,' Carol said.

Vivian and Henry came down the staircase together. Eric must have had a busy afternoon. Henry Talbott looked immaculate in a lightweight wool suit. He was clearly dying, but the worst of the signs had been softened with grooming.

Eric walked behind him, watchful and protective. Vivian's arm rested on her husband's. Vivian, like Carol, wore a sleeveless, high-necked black dress. Not exactly the same designer or style but similar enough to make both women aware of it. Carol was tetchy since in comparison she was the lesser attraction. But Vivian, magnanimous in victory, reached for a champagne cocktail and laughed at something her husband said.

She excused herself and came to Lenny's elbow with two glasses of champagne. She held one out. 'Annie's super-special champagne cocktail. She did a bar course, if you can believe it.'

Lenny looked over to the bar. Annie was deep in conversation with Sid. She was animated.

Lenny shook her head at the drink.

'What? Not on the job?' Vivian teased 'Go on ...' And

with the make-up retouched and in her little black dress she was irresistible, like an Art Deco relief, holding out the glass as if it contained her own special essence which she was giving freely, with no strings, to Lenny. Lenny took the glass. Vivian beamed and drank hers in a single gulp.

'Everything's going fine, hmm?' She glanced around at the guests, the modern Melbourne hostess once more.

'Hmm.' Lenny was still thinking how perfect Vivian had looked in that moment of proffering Annie's cocktail. It must have shown on her face because Vivian said: 'Earth to Lenny ... Are you all right? *I* feel much better. I spent a little time with Carol. Now *she's* a confident young woman. She always reminds me of my own youth. Puts the spark in me.' She giggled, eyes following Kendell and Carol as they moved out into the garden.

'Let's just be careful,' Lenny said.

'Let's not!' Vivian shrugged. 'Let's say fuck them. Let them do their worst. What can they do to a girl from Gympie? Stop worrying. At least by confronting Liz I've brought it out into the open. She'll be too scared to do anything now, right?'

'The cat was deliberately killed,' Lenny said.

'That's a bit sick, isn't it? Why would someone kill that cat to get to me?'

'I don't know.'

'Cats! I have to keep moving. Duty calls.'

Sid and Nancy served dinner smoothly and silently. Margaret Gross hovered in the doorway with nothing to do except hover and hope something went wrong. The cook stayed in the kitchen. Lenny wondered what would happen if the cook suddenly burst into the room, screaming obscenities, and lunged at Vivian with a carving knife. If only life were that simple.

The meal was elegant: a cold salmon soup with mini crispbread, a salad, seafood, then melt-in-the-mouth steak. There was Key Lime Pie and fruit and cheese for anyone who wanted it. Lenny was surprised to find that during the seafood course there was a little *onigiri*, seaweed and rice wrapped around crab. She caught Vivian's eye and realized it had been prepared just for her. She felt touched. She had just sipped her wine, but her head was already light. She refused the dessert wine.

She was introduced as a personal assistant and instantly relegated to the bottom of the heap by the Buchanans. Larry Burton was drunk and willing to chat to anyone, but the has-been media moguls cut her dead.

As the evening wore on alcohol led them into new territory.

Guards were lowered and chatter became motivated. Larry Burton was the first to crack. Understandably, since he was drinking harder and sloppier than anyone else.

'The show's up there in the ratings, mate,' he said to Henry, leaning across Eric. Henry responded with a sad smile. They were both heading to the end of a long run. Henry mashed his vegetables with his fork until they were pulp, then used a spoon. Very classy. Everyone pretended not to notice.

Larry talked on and on about his being the longest running variety show in Australian TV history and his surprise at finding there was a fan club for him in the Philippines. No one responded. Lenny looked him over. His curly hair was cut in the same style it had been for the last twenty years and his clothes were as bright as the day-glo sets on his show. Tonight he wore his trademark red and green with thick gold baubles at his neck, wrists and fingers—a Christmas commercial. Everything about him was too broad and too vague. He looked, Lenny thought, as though he had been smudged.

She didn't feel sorry for him. She had watched *Friday Night at Larry's Place* quite a few times over the years and liked to imagine herself personally pulling the proverbial plug. Larry Burton was all used up.

'With another year we can really get the show back to where it was,' Larry reached the crux of the matter. 'I'm thinking about doing another Live from LA special.' Henry Talbott slicked up some gravy and didn't even glance at him. 'Remember that one, Henry?' Vivian patted her husband's hand lightly and switched her completely sober violet steel gaze on the drunken TV host.

'I'm sorry, Larry, I don't think anyone here watches your show anymore,' she said.

'What do you mean?' His bleary eyes showed he knew all right. 'You should look at the ratings, Vivian. The ratings. People are watching me.' Was his skin actually turning aubergine?

'But, Larry,' Vivian cut him off. She popped a tiny sautéed vegetable into her mouth. 'We're not.'

Larry was abandoned. His Todd AO face was panic-stricken. 'I'm afraid I will have to hear that from Henry himself,' he said.

Talk about setting yourself up, Lenny mused. It was thrilling. But Larry was beyond shame now, fighting for his career.

Henry looked up from his food again. He came up out of his stupor. Everyone waited.

'Larry, you and I have known each other a long time. I wish things could be different.' Henry's fork trembled in mid gesture. He looked tired. 'The show . . .' he glanced at Vivian, 'the show's a dog. It won't be renewed.' He went back to his vegetables.

Larry's ego took a while to realign with reality. He was having what Lenny always thought of as a moment of negative enlightenment. His down-the-tube future flashed before him. He turned to Vivian, frightened.

'Viv, talk to him!' He clutched at her as an ally. Vivian was amazed.

'You've had a great run, Larry,' she said. 'I'd have cancelled you three years ago. It's not personal, just business.'

'Fuck you it's not personal! Everyone here knows what's going on!' Larry shoved his chair back. His gut hovered over the table edge. There was going to be a scene. Lenny glanced around. Kimberly, horrified, stared hard at her food. Kendell was the only one unconcerned. He shook his head and said: 'I like Larry's show.' Carol gave him a look. Sometime before dinner they had had a spat, Lenny thought. Carol hadn't spoken to him all through the meal.

Margaret Gross oozed from the shadows, placed a big hand on Larry's shoulder and jammed him back into his chair. He went 'oof' as his backside hit the leather cushion with a loud slap. He stared at his dinner plate, looked occasionally at Kimberly. Had Larry been about to reveal his very personal connection with the Talbott family? Was that why they were cancelling his show, to pay him back for having the bad taste to screw their daughter? She doubted it. His show *was* a dog.

Vivian was wearing a matching diamond choker and bracelet from Bulgari. The chandelier light matched her own dazzle. Larry swallowed hard when he looked at her. She saw it but ignored him. Margaret deemed Vivian safe once more and went back to her place in the corner. Unexpectedly strong. Quite a useful person to have around.

They moved away from the table for coffee while Sid and Nancy whisked away the dinner plates. Carol put on some music and she and Kendell went out onto the terrace. It was dark now and the Mozzie-Zapper's blue-light bug frying became a feature of the rest of the evening.

Kimberly sat down beside Lenny on a couch. She was drinking martinis, had been drinking them all night. This close the Helmut Lang dress was almost irresistible. Lenny thought about touching the black strip across the breasts. Since she never thought about touching anyone, this was a very bizarre sensation and, she told herself, she had to stay off the booze for the rest of the night.

'Terrible party, isn't it?' Kimberly smiled. Her voice had modulated with the alcohol.

'Yep,' Lenny nodded.

'You look very smart,' Kimberly said. Trying to be nice, to be friendly, Lenny thought. Because Kimberly Talbott was clearly desperate for friendship.

'I got the results of your cat's autopsy,' Lenny said.

'Oh,' Kimberly sighed. 'I suppose I'm getting over it. What happened? Was it poison?'

'Someone smashed it against a wall.'

Kimberly slurped her drink. A teaspoon's worth splashed over the rim onto her frock and she dabbed at it with her hand.

'Why would anyone do that?'

'Animals get tortured all the time,' Lenny said. 'Some people get a kick out of it.'

'How horrible.' Kimberly looked around. She jumped up and her dress slid higher on her thighs. 'Poor thing. Do you suppose it suffered much?'

'I don't know,' Lenny said. 'I suppose if you had your spine smashed into a wall it would hurt a bit.'

'Yes ... yes, I suppose so. Did the vet take care of burying it and everything?'

'Yes. And everything. You'll get his bill attached to mine.'

'All right.' Kimberly was impatient to be away. She had not intended to talk about the cat, Lenny thought. She strode to the bar, long legs swinging.

Lenny went into the garden to get fresh air. It was dark now. The bar had been moved inside. She sat at a terrace table. Despite the Mozzie-Zapper, mosquitoes dive-bombed her ankles. She sat quietly for some minutes thinking about sleep. Then she heard Carol talking somewhere in the garden in the dark. The girl's voice was shrill. 'What are you playing at anyway? It's time you realized you do what *I* say.'

Poor Kendell getting another earful. Lenny was tired. It was a big mistake to have taken the aspirin. She could take some Sudafed to snap her out of it, but with the alcohol in her stomach that could be asking for trouble.

'Things are going to change around here—big time!' Carol's voice, a cold anger.

Lenny returned to the house. She looked for Vivian who came through the doorway to the hall. She saw Lenny's anxious face and laughed, moved towards her.

'You can't freak out every time I go to the toilet,' she whispered. She looked at her watch. 'Halfway through and I'm still alive. I think we can relax, hmm? Have you seen Carol and Kendell?'

'They're outside,' Lenny said. Vivian nodded. She moved over to Henry and listened to Larry begging him for a contract to appear as a regular on *Celebrity Wheel Of Fortune*. A truly desperate man.

Lenny slid into a chair. She realized that she was half asleep and must look it because the Buchanans began a private conversation right next to her.

Sonny was bitching about money: 'Ask him. That's why we bloody came. He'll help you, Michael. Do you think he doesn't know why we're here? He's not stupid. He always liked you. He'll help—'

'I'm not going to end up like Larry. I won't beg,' Mike Buchanan snapped.

'Don't be childish,' his wife's voice was impatient. 'They won't let you off with bankruptcy, look what happened to Alan Bond. You'll end up in jail.' She hesitated. '*You* could speak to Vivian ... '

'She was *your* girlfriend, sweetheart. Not mine.'

'I already asked her. She said no.'

Lenny opened her eyes and looked at them, tried to focus. They were opposite her on a couch, a matched pair of bottle-blondes, early fifties, very bronze, very vulgar.

There had always been rumours about them; he was gay, she was gay, they were in love, they hated each other and the latest: they were broke. That was true. Henry had destroyed them when he took over the channel they were mismanaging. Now they made a living out of regional TV contracts that didn't come under Henry's control.

'I'm going to the ladies.' Sonny tried to get up but her husband pulled her down.

'Not here, for god's sake!'

'Don't tell me what to do!' She yanked free, wobbled, and bumped Lenny's leg hard. They noticed her for the first time. She sat up straight and looked over Sonny's puffy face and nose. The skin around the nostrils was red, as though from a cold. But not a cold, she thought, cop's antenna twanging. Cocaine.

'Sorry,' Sonny sat down with a thump. For a bony woman she had a large bottom, the unfortunate pear-shaped body type. She smoothed her white silk pants. 'Sorry. Look, we were just ... talking.'

'Shut up,' Mike told her. 'You're pathetic.'

There was a scream. A shrill, horrified scream from upstairs. It went on for a long time and was followed by more of the same, drowning out the Mozzie-Zapper's electric tics.

Lenny stared around the room. Vivian was gone. She ran for the stairs.

Chapter 14

A BIGGER DEATH

Her legs were disconnected from her brain. It was the wine. She wasn't functioning normally. She stumbled on a couple of steps, hit her shoulder on the banister and cursed. And all the time the gut-wrenching screams continued.

She went straight to Vivian's room. It was going to be there. Even half sloshed she knew that. Everything had led to this moment. Someone had been threatening to deliver a body and Lenny knew that when she reached the room, it would be a body she found.

The bedroom door was open. Kimberly stood just inside. It was from her stretched lips that the screams came. She was hysterical. Lenny shoved past her then stopped. Her head swam. She was going to faint. She felt cold sweat break out all over her body.

The doors to the balcony were open and outside, face down on the terrace, was Vivian, lying in what must have been most of the blood from her body. Her black dress was glistening with gore. The long limbs were coated in too much scarlet gloss, as though she was participating in an avant-garde installation. Damien Hirst's 'Dead Lady'.

The axe was embedded in Vivian's back, haft sticking up at forty-five degrees. The blade was wedged into her spine.

Lenny staggered over. Her legs were like cotton but she was rapidly sobering. Her tongue felt thick and furry. There was something familiar about that sensation. Her feet reached blood and she bent down carefully. It was easy to lose your balance and end up sitting in blood, something not appreciated by the boys and girls at the lab. Tampering with evidence. She shouldn't even be touching the body, she knew, but she had to see.

Kimberly made noises of extreme hyperventilation: 'It's Mum! Oh god! Oh god! Is she dead?'

'Of course she's bloody dead!' Lenny snapped. People didn't survive an axe in the back.

'Don't shout at me!' Kimberly shouted.

The body was warm. The dark hair was soaked with blood and this close she could see why. The first axe blow had killed her, almost severing the neck from the shoulders. Lenny
could see the smashed bone. Only a few shards of skin joined the neck to the shoulders. The second blow had been unnecessary. She pushed back the hair. The face was bloodied but discernible.

'It's not your mother,' Lenny said, turning to Kimberly. 'It's Carol.'

And then Vivian appeared in the doorway with the others, the group fighting each other for front row seats. Lenny scanned them. Everyone accounted for except Sid and Nancy, Liz Dodd and Henry Talbott. Vivian, white-faced, stared at the body and at Lenny crouching beside it.

Kimberly had cupped her hands over her mouth, trying to breathe her own carbon dioxide. Eric Hunter appeared a few seconds later. He looked across the room at the body and, unlike the others, his face registered neither surprise nor horror. He simply stared.

Kendell sobbed against Annie's plump bosom. Lenny couldn't see his face. Annie's big eyes, terrified, looked to Vivian for reassurance.

Vivian was trembling. She knew what was obvious to everyone. It was her room. A young girl lay there, styled in imitation of her. It was meant to be her on the balcony floor with an axe in her back. She looked at Lenny helplessly, covered her face with a hand and stumbled.

Lenny was at her side in a moment and got her out of the room, down the hallway and into Lenny's own bedroom.

Margaret Gross followed. She was shocked but, as a nurse, handling it better than the others. Vivian allowed herself to collapse in the motherly arms.

'Where's Annie? Is she all right?' she asked. 'Where *is* she, Maggie?'

'I don't know. Stop worrying about her. You worry about yourself, my angel,' Margaret stroked the dark hair gently. In full mother mode, Lenny thought grimly. Why would Vivian wonder about Annie now?

'It was Max,' Vivian whispered. She shuddered. 'It was him all along. I never thought of him. I never ... Why? God—'

Max?

Margaret tucked Vivian into Lenny's bed. Stroked her hair some more, soothed her by making little wood pigeon noises.

There was blood on Vivian's arm. It had come from Lenny's own hands. They all stared at it. With a 'tut' Margaret reached for a handkerchief from her own pocket and, to Lenny's horror, spat on it before rubbing at the arm.

'You—' Vivian said bitterly, looking at Lenny. She was weak, still in shock. She turned her head into the pillows to hide her face. Lenny felt the sensation of panic well up in her. Failure. Fear.

'It's not hygienic,' she said.

Margaret looked up at her. 'Eh?'

'You shouldn't ... ' She meant the spit, the wet goob from Margaret's mouth now being worked lovingly into Vivian's bloodied arm. But she couldn't make herself clear and Margaret turned from her. Vivian kept her face pressed into the pillows.

Lenny instructed Margaret not to leave Vivian for a moment and told her to lock the door behind her. Margaret nodded.

'Is it still dangerous? Was he after Vivvie?'

'*Of course he was!*' It came from Vivian. Lenny closed the bedroom door.

There was no one in the corridor and the door to Vivian's suite had been discreetly closed. Lenny opened it. The body lay exactly as she had left it. Now that she knew it was Carol, she felt no fear of the body itself.

Was it Max? Was he outside now, somewhere in the dark, terrified at what he had accomplished?

It was quiet in the house. What the hell were they all doing? Had anyone bothered to call the police? Lenny half fell down the stairs.

No security alarms, she realized. During the party the guests were in and out of the terrace all night so the door and window sensors and the ground floor motion sensors had all been deactivated. Only the sensors on the garden walls and the gate were activated.

Her hand shook on the phone but she got through to the emergency operator and was transferred to the police.

'I want to report a murder.' Her voice was, she hoped, steady.

'Where are you now?' Constable robot-voice on the phone. Probably thought it was a prank. They got quite a few.

Lenny gave the address and the family name. She felt the little pause and spark of interest. *Talbott*.

'Are you still at the scene of the crime?' This time the voice was enthusiastic. The other on-duty constables would be listening in now. The phone room was a big bore.

'Yes.'

'Is the perpetrator still at the scene?'

'I don't know.'

'Your name please.'

'Lenny Aaron.'

'That's a blast from the past. Not *the* Lenny Aaron?' Oh god. Was her picture on the academy wall?

'Can we get someone out here, Constable? I mean sometime tonight?'

'No need to take that tone, madam.'

She hung up. She knew with sickening dread what would

happen now. In fifteen minutes the house and grounds would be full of police wanting to know what she was doing there. The cat catcher.

Her hand was still bloody. She wiped it on her pants and pushed the sleeve of her blouse back to look at the old scar. There was no blood on it but it throbbed.

She shouldn't have touched the body.

She went through to the lounge room. There was a collective soft gasp as they saw her. Her feet and lower legs were still speckled with blood. She looked back. Faint bloody footprints followed her down the staircase.

They were congregated near the antique fireplace. Henry Talbott was at the centre of the group, in a chair. He looked Lenny straight in the eye but a shock like this wasn't good for an old man. His eyes moved restlessly, often seeking out Eric's for reassurance. Eric bent down to speak quietly into his ear. Lenny recalled his blank face at the bedroom door, eyes on the body, emotionless.

Kimberly stood near her father. Her face was swollen from crying and her hands squeezed each other. Annie hovered next to her.

Kendell sat in another chair. He was stunned, kept wiping a hand across teary eyes and shaking his head to clear it. Larry Burton stood behind him, drinking. Sid and Nancy hovered at the edge of the room by the windows, their eyes enormous. There was still no sign of Liz Dodd.

The Buchanans, Mike and Sonny, were desperate to leave. She had her bag and Mike was rattling his car keys but both hesitated, waiting for permission. No one knew what to do at a murder scene, Lenny remembered. People waited for a leader.

'Is Vivian all right?' Annie asked. Her eyes were huge. More than frightened, Lenny thought. She looked *guilty*. She had always looked guilty. What the hell was going on here?

Lenny nodded. 'Nobody leave the house. The police are on the way.' She pulled out her wallet and showed her ID card. 'I'm an investigator.' But not a real one. She expected someone to say it any moment, expose the persona she had been busy fabricating.

'A detective.' Kimberly enlightened the others. 'Mum's been getting death threats. She hired Ms Aaron to protect her.'

'You've done a fucking fantastic job, haven't you?' Larry Burton laughed snidely and raised his greasy glass in salute.

'We're leaving,' Mike Buchanan pronounced.

'No, you're not,' Lenny said. Buchanan stopped in his tracks.

'You gutless wimp,' his wife said. She rummaged in her bag, searching for her stash.

'Just stay together until the police arrive,' Lenny told them. 'Nobody goes anywhere until then.'

Henry Talbott looked angry at the command but said nothing. Annie glanced at him.

'Can I get anything for you?' she asked. Henry looked at Annie as though she were both crazy and revolting. She blushed and stepped back. Kendell reached for her hand and held it. Annie leaned down to him.

'It'll be all right,' she said. 'It was an accident.'

Kimberly snorted. 'Someone *accidentally* cut off Carol's head?' She reached into her stiff bodice and pulled out, to Lenny's amazement, a cigarette and a tiny silver lighter shaped like a gun. It was something out of a James Bond movie and so sexy Lenny was almost distracted from the real action. But not quite.

'What do you mean an accident?' she asked Annie.

'Nothing,' Annie blushed.

'They were trying to kill my mother,' Kimberly said. Her hair had come awry during her breathing attack and the elaborate curls hung down in clumps. 'Who would want to kill Carol? She was nobody.'

Lenny buzzed in the police when they arrived at the gate and met them at the front door. Outside the fence, Cedars

Court was already crowded with floodlights and red flashing patrol cars. Press vans and journalists were being moved back by young constables.

This was the kind of call-out police men and women dreamed of: the celebrity murder. Flash bulbs went off. It was difficult to make sure your best profile was to the camera while at the same time doing your job, Lenny recalled. She stepped back out of sight. She had no desire to see her face in the paper although she knew that it was inevitable.

She told the police where the body was and handed over all the letters. She told them it appeared to be Max's axe. No, she didn't know the motive.

Ron MacAvoy came with the first wave of police who began to unravel the scene—photos, evidence bags, fingerprints. MacAvoy was no longer the MCG cricket slob. Now he was in his official capacity as police slob. His brown suit was crushed and he wore a cream-coloured shirt with red pinstripes.

MacAvoy flicked on the giant TV. All the channels were showing the Talbott house. He spotted himself arriving in a pre-taped segment. He grinned.

'Geez, am I that big?' He patted his gut.

'Yes,' Lenny said.

MacAvoy wet his lips and whistled, looking at a Monet. 'Picasso! Classy.'

Lenny's head was throbbing. She craved drugs: Tylenol, Aspirin, something stronger.

'Any of that blood yours, mate?' MacAvoy looked at her rolled-up blood-flecked pants. She had wiped her shoes with a tissue.

'You know it isn't.'

'I saw your Jap boyfriend at the cricket.'

'He's not my boyfriend.'

'Oh well, I just thought ...'

'MacAvoy, we don't have to talk.' She turned from him.

'I watched *Shogun*. You ever seen it?' MacAvoy made a

quantum leap. 'James Clavell? You know? Doris has all the books. Richard Chamberlain's in it. You seen it?'

'Yes. It's crap.'

After that they waited in uncomfortable silence for a long time. He was guarding her, she realized. Was it possible they considered her a suspect?

Ron MacAvoy was one of the police who had visited her in hospital after her 'incident'. He had held her hand when she was too weak to prevent the liberty. His eyes had been full of tears and concern. And he had tried to persuade her to fight on. *It happens, Len, mate. Bad guys win sometimes. We can nail the bastard. Testify, mate. We can put him away.* She told him to fuck off and leave her alone. Danny Hoyle was the last to stop visiting. *I'm not going to come anymore, Len. It's not helping you. In fact, I think it's hurting you.* She wondered if he thought about her sometimes.

A young police constable appeared at the door. MacAvoy roly-polyed over. They spent several minutes conferring.

He came back to Lenny. 'We're all going downtown, mate. Just routine, I reckon. We've got the killer,' he said.

'Max?' she said. What kind of evidence did they have? Had Max just wandered back to his cottage and waited? It seemed wrong to her. Life wasn't that simple.

'Max,' MacAvoy agreed. 'They reckon he was after Mrs Talbott. She's asleep. Housekeeper gave her a sedative. Doctor's staying with her for a bit though. And Talbott's got a security team coming in. Guess you're out of a job, mate.'

'How solid is the evidence?'

'It's him, mate. No question.'

'Motive?'

'Ahh,' MacAvoy tapped the side of his nose mysteriously. 'We're taking the old girl in too,' he said, 'Liz Dodd. She's in on it, I reckon. Went for Senior Sergeant Riley.'

'She's in love with him,' Lenny said. 'She's trying to protect him.'

'Bit old for romance, aren't they?' MacAvoy who, Lenny thought, probably hadn't had sex with his wife for years, looked doubtful. 'I reckon there's more to it.'

'Maybe,' Lenny shrugged. She didn't see Max Curtis and Liz Dodd as axe-wielding maniacs.

Finally they were moving. Lenny joined the others in the hallway. Henry looked exhausted, out of it. The caterers were trying to look appalled but were thrilled, talking to each other in soft voices. Nancy giggled and Sid hissed at her to shhh. They were keen to get out amongst the press. Everyone knew a photo op when they saw one. Mike Buchanan was using his mobile phone, complaining to his lawyer. Kimberly and Kendell walked together in a joint daze. For once they seemed truly twins, shoulder to shoulder, occasionally glancing at each other. Kendell reached for her hand once to squeeze. She permitted it. Kimberly's dress drew a lot of press attention. The murder would be page one but Kimberly's tits would be page three.

Annie was behind them. She looked very tired. It was late, Lenny thought, and they had all drunk too much. They were going to look a sorry sight on tomorrow morning's breakfast news bulletins.

In the garden there were police cars everywhere. The grounds was lit up like a night match at the MCG. Helicopters were hovering. Reporters shouted questions. *Who's dead? This way Kimberly, sweetheart! Aw c'mon* ... Scuffles broke out.

There was a yell over at the garage followed by a rush of activity. Blood had been found in the back of one of the cars. Manly poses were struck in the garden. Thumbs touched guns, voices deepened, swaggers enlarged. A new speck of blood found and everyone was Dirty Harry. Lenny knew what it was and groaned. MacAvoy, eyes darting, was already jogging towards her. He was breathing like a man with tuberculosis. He shouldn't run at all with his beer gut and smoke-filled lungs. But the eyes of the other men were upon him.

'Len, huh, huh, mate, huh, huh,' he huffed. 'The, huh, Colt's, huh, your, huh, car, huh, isn't it?'

'It's a dead cat,' Lenny said flatly.

This was confirmed by a loud 'Urgh!' over at the garage. Someone had finally gotten the bag open and smelt it, seen the fetid remains of Renata Antolini. She had forgotten to bury the Russian Blue and now it was back to haunt her.

Lenny slid into the rear seat of a patrol car. Oh joy—she was sharing with Larry Burton. He leered drunkenly and placed a hand on her leg. Lenny bent his index finger back almost to breaking point and he shrieked. Constable Snelling in the front passenger seat looked back warningly.

'Mr Burton, I'm asking you to restrain yourself, sir.' He exhibited the extra politeness police always used when they disliked someone. The more loathsome the person, the more extreme the good manners. Like a test of will.

'Restrain myself! Like bloody hell! You little prick!' There was a tussle as he lunged forward and the constable was forced to grapple with him. Larry Burton copped a nasty jab to the cheekbone. He gasped and fell back, holding his face and blinking like a startled lamb. Unused to being hit.

'I'm sorry, sir, but it was necessary. Are you going to give me any more trouble?'

'Erg ... '

Lenny turned her head away. She looked straight ahead. She felt the brightness of flashes going off as the car pulled out of the main gates. Then the blue and red lights came on and the siren started. Hey, hey boys, we're away!

Lenny took out her badge and put it on the desk in front of the senior accountant. He thought for a moment that it was a joke. Then he turned grey.

'You'll get immunity,' she promised.

He started to cry. He was a little plump. Always had a half-sucked Freddo Frog or Caramello Koala on the desk.

He started an asthma attack. She had to help him with his Ventolin. It reminded her, of course, of her father but did not give her pause. He made a grab for the books and ran into another room. Locked the door. Simultaneously squealing and gasping. Eeeee! Noooo! Huff, huff, huff. Eeeee! Grind, grind ... She smashed the glass door with a chair but he had the paper shredder jammed with the leather binders before she reached him. He sat on the floor sobbing.

'You've killed me.' Huff, huff.

He refused to talk to her further. She collected the remains of the books. They were badly ripped, but she thought there might be enough there. Not exactly the crime of the century but if they couldn't get Michael Dorling for importing and distributing heroin, they could at least arrest him on charges of tax evasion and fraud.

Chapter 15

A CERTAIN NOTORIETY

Lenny sat on the pier at St Kilda beach, dangling her legs over the side. Cleo Harrelson was sprawled at her side, licking her paws then using them to wipe her face. Next to them two men had caught a handful of tiny fish.

'We should go further round, mate. They aren't biting here.'

'Give it time, mate.'

'Yer watchin' *The Elephant Man* tonight, Gaz?'

'Naa,' Gary shuddered, jamming a worm onto his hook. 'Angie doesn't like deformed stuff. It's bad luck, because she's pregnant.'

'Oh, yeah.'

'How did he get that way anyhow?'

'Yer what? Wait—I got a bite ... No ... nothing.'

'The Elephant man, how did he get, you know ... ?'

'All bumpy? I've seen it before. His mum gets run over by a herd of elephants while she's pregnant.'

'You're joking!' Gary was fascinated. 'Don't tell Angie that, Baz, she'll freak.'

'No joke.' The fisherman noticed Lenny. 'You seen it, love?'

'That's the stupidest thing I ever heard,' Lenny said.

Barry stared at Lenny. He looked out at the flat water as though making an important decision and took a big breath: 'We're off, mate. Pack yer stuff. We're off round the bay,' he said. 'Some people don't know how to have a good time.' He bent to pick up his basket. Cleo Harrelson shot out a paw and raked his arm, her accompanying hiss magnificent, fur rising like helium.

'Jesus Christ!'

But it was true, Lenny thought as the men walked away. She did not know how to have a good time. She knew how to tranquillize herself but that was not the same. She stroked Cleo Harrelson absently. The cat wriggled and shook her off.

Small groups of people wandered up and down the pier: mothers with infants and toddlers, older children wagging school and a handful of couples either on a flex or on the dole. Everyone (everyone *else*) was happy. They were laughing and smiling, wheeling bicycles, eating ice-creams, reading newspapers. Last week's headline had set the whole country buzzing: 'Talbott's Love Child—Axe Murderer?'

That had been the big secret MacAvoy had been unwilling to divulge and, she had to admit, it was a beauty. Max Curtis, it turned out, was not just a humble old gardener. He was, in fact, Henry Talbott's son. His birth certificate and a tell-all letter from his long-deceased mother had been found in his shed when the police took it apart.

It was six days since Carol Connor had been axed and Max's face was plastered over the TV every night. He looked indignant and frightened. At least Lenny thought so. She supposed that to the general public he looked like a nutcase killer. He was being held in the City Remand Centre, bail had been refused.

The evidence was strong against him: his prints on the axe, Carol's blood found in spatters near his door and on his shirt, pants and boots stuffed into a drawer in the tool shed. And the motive, of course.

Max's mother was one of many women from Henry Talbott's youth. Their relationship was brief and, or so the press implied, Miss Curtis was paid off and dispensed with. Oddly, Max didn't have crooked little fingers.

Friday Night at Larry's Place had been replaced by a repeat movie with no announcement about its return to programming. Its host was said to be 'unavailable for comment at this time'. Shots of a handcuffed and drunken Larry had been in every newspaper. Lenny figured he would quietly slip into the has-been category. This meant popping up on the Logies next year to accept an honorary award for services to the industry and an obligatory standing ovation. He was finished.

The Buchanans had flown back to Brisbane after their police interviews. Photos of them heading to their private plane showed them surprisingly sombre.

Lenny had been back in her own apartment since the day after the murder. The police released her mid morning after a series of bullshit questions. That part she had expected. They found her investigation of the missing Ragdoll particularly amusing.

'You catch animals, then?'

'Cats.'

'Yes.'

'You mean ordinary cats?'

It was MacAvoy as good cop, Bill Williams as bad. She remembered Williams from the police academy. He had bullied the smaller women. Lenny knocked him flat on his backside in hand to hand combat.

'*Cats?*' Meaningless repetition is a Kafkaesque requirement of interrogation. She remembered his tone of voice. It always had a sneer in it.

'Yes.'

'I remember you, Aaron. *Ms* Aaron.' He bared his teeth. They were oversized with enormous incisors. She remembered that about him too. In the hand to hand, before she downed him, she thought he would bite her. He growled.

'I bet you do,' she sat forward.

'I always said you wouldn't last in the force. Too much ego. But—cats!'

MacAvoy didn't look up from the floor.

'Am I a suspect, detective?' She was too tired to spar. Her eyes ached and she felt sick in the stomach.

'You tell me.' Bill drummed his dirty-nailed fingers on the metal table top.

'You're not a suspect, Len,' MacAvoy cut in.

'So don't waste my time.'

Her police training made it all very easy. She knew the routine.

No one said a word about blame but she knew they thought it. Even MacAvoy, who was trying to be 'in her corner', was embarrassed. Here she was again as a loser in a high profile case. This time a member of her client's family was dead.

'Second big crime for you then, Aaron.' Bill Williams rubbed his arm lightly. Incisors rested on his lower lip.

'You have food in your teeth,' she said. It was true. Something meaty, she thought. Stringy and brownish anyway. It was the first thing she noticed when he sat down at the table to question her. It was the first thing she ever noticed about anyone.

'Eh?' His tongue roamed horribly across the fangs. 'Where? Have I got it?' He looked at MacAvoy, made a big grin. 'Have I got it?'

'No, the other side,' MacAvoy pointed at his own teeth for example. 'No, not there. That's it.'

Good manners required a simple thanks, but Williams wasn't interested in good manners.

'You really think you're smart, don't you, girlie?'

'Bill, she was just trying to be nice.'

'Bullshit!' Williams thumped the table. The letters bounced. MacAvoy grabbed them.

It went on for another couple of hours before they released her.

That was six days ago. A cheque had arrived in the mail. Two thousand one hundred dollars: payment for a week. The cheque from the Talbott Ltd accountants on Vivian Talbott's behalf, was accompanied by a note: payment for 'investigative

services' that were no longer required.

Thursday's paper contained a photo of both Marie Antoinette de Paris and one of Lenny herself. She was referred to as 'the family's private detective, Ms Helena Aaron, 27', pictured in a long shot, getting into a police car. She looked drunk. A great advertisement for business. Friday's paper brought further revelations of her career on the police force and—this time there was no escaping it—the Michael Dorling connection. Friday's paper also detailed her current employment situation under the caption 'Cat Woman'.

She had always thought that to face publicity again would be intolerable. But time had worked a little magic. She read about herself in the paper. She relived Michael Dorling's attack on her. She didn't break down.

She called Dr Sakuno to be on the safe side. Perhaps she should get an extra session. But he was leaving on two weeks vacation with his family.

'*Sensei*, do you think I should come in?' she had asked.

'We don't have an appointment.'

'No, but—'

'Helena san,' he sounded impatient to be off. She heard his secretary yattering in the background. 'See me in a month at the usual time.'

'Really?'

'Be your own lamp. I'm hanging up.'

So he was off for two weeks R and R and she was left to her own devices. Be your own lamp!

To gain privacy from the press, she unplugged her phone. And when her mother inevitably knocked on her door, she just didn't answer. She wasn't in the mood for sympathy.

'Lenny, are you in there?' This after knocking solidly for two minutes and angry because she knew damn well Lenny was in there. 'Lenny, this is childish. Lenny, please. I'm worried about you. Lenny! Can you hear me?'

She could hear. She was sitting in the lounge room. She had the TV on and was watching *Breakfast at Tiffany's* with the sound down low and wondering if Orangey, the cat star of the movie, had scored residuals.

Her car had been impounded for a couple of days while forensic checked the bag of cat remains. Fortunately that gruesome detail eluded the press. The police finally returned both her car and the dead cat. They had the nerve to look peeved as though she had been wasting their time. That night she dug a hole in the miniature flower bed at her apartment block and buried the cat.

As for her own opinion of the crime, she didn't have any evidence to contradict the police hypothesis: a son living within the family for years and yet not a part of it, treated as a servant while his brother and sister received everything money could buy. His own mother abandoned while Vivian Talbott, young and beautiful, got herself a husband. Max finally cracked.

Lenny had considered the idea that Carol was the intended victim. But who would want to kill Carol? She had offended the older staff, called them the wrinklies. She had told Max to look for a new job. Max. Whichever way Lenny looked at it, it still came back to Max.

She had spent the week in a state of restlessness. She didn't have the bonsai to distract her. They were still at the Brighton home. Nothing could be removed. She tried to explain to a constable outside the house that they needed careful handling.

'Dwarf trees?' He looked uncertain. 'Geez, I don't know. It's not my thing. Glen comes on at six. He grows chrysanthemums. I could ask him.'

She expected them to be dead when she saw them again.

The victim received the least press attention of all. Carol Connor wanted desperately to be special but even in death she was just 'the woman mistaken for Vivian Talbott'.

Carol's parents, a Gympie GP and his wife, had been told the body would not be available for some time. There was one small shot of them looking inconsequential, devastated and confused.

Lenny butted out a cigarette in her empty Coke can. It was getting quiet on the pier. Dinner time. Family time.

Lenny

rarely took up the invitation to eat with her parents. Her father was too weak to feed himself. The last time she visited him, he gazed at her from his usual place on the non-allergenic couch, eyes twinkling although he was unable to say a word. Each attempt brought a new attack.

It was impossible, she thought, to save the situation. Her father was dying. He had always been dying. She couldn't visit him now, not when she was so obviously the loser again.

She had decided to investigate Vivian's case. *Finish* the investigation. Dr Sakuno would approve. He always supported action over words. Answers could only be found in oneself, not from the words of others. There was only self-reliance. *Be your own lamp, Lenny.*

She parked the Colt in the shopping mall car park. There were two middle-aged journalists at the door to her office. The photographer got a shot of Cleo Harrelson, strutting her stuff on her chain. Mike Bullock, resplendent in baby blue crimplene, stepped out from behind his sandwich board.

'C'mon, give the lady a chance.'

The journalists ignored him. The one with the camera had been getting a wide shot when Lenny arrived. It would look classy—a porn shop, her office and a rundown barbers. The journalists fired questions: Was the old man screwing his future daughter-in-law? Was Larry Burton screwing Vivian?

'That's no kind of talk for a lady,' Mike Bullock said. He scuffled with the journalists who laughed and pushed him into his sandwich board.

'This your boyfriend, Lenny?' one of them asked. They snapped a couple of pictures of Bullock. Lenny shut the door in their faces.

She checked the mail. There was a letter from the *Sun* newspaper wanting her to contact them as soon as possible. She ripped it up.

She left the office and drove to Carlton, Cleo in the cat box. Lenny played a hunch. She parked outside Kimberly's apartment block close to Melbourne University. There was a lone security man at the main gates. Lenny watched him take down her licence plate number. She turned off the ignition and waited.

Kimberly showed up at three in a blue BMW. She raised a hand to the guard as she pulled up behind him. He got out to talk to her.

Kimberly looked across at the Colt through purple-lensed shades. She was attractive from a distance, the tall body in canary-yellow Chanel with black accessories, legs obscenely long in a thigh-high skirt and Frankenstein heels. How the hell did she fit in with the t-shirt and baggy shorts set on campus?

Kimberly walked across the road and knocked sharply on Lenny's passenger window. Lenny wound it down slowly.

'What do you want, Ms Aaron? I know you're not working for my family anymore. You were fired.' Her face was almost in the car.

'I want to know who killed Carol Connor,' Lenny said.

'I believe it was that man trying to pass himself off as my *brother!*' It had been a very nasty shock. 'Look, Ms Aaron, I don't mean to be rude, but you were hired to protect my mother. She may be alive but it's no thanks to you, is it? And my brother's fiancée had her head chopped off.'

'I can see you're heartbroken about that,' Lenny spat back. 'Don't try to tell me that you liked Carol. It's bullshit.'

Kimberly squeezed Lenny's car window frame, her hands big and stumpy, the crooked little fingers adding to the ugliness.

'Look—'

'I am going to find out who killed Carol.'

'It was Max!'

'Perhaps Max, perhaps not.'

Kimberly hesitated and looked around at the guard. She knew something, Lenny was suddenly sure of it.

'Get in,' she said. Kimberly hesitated again then signalled

the guard that she was fine and opened the passenger door of the Colt. She got in and looked around at the plastic fittings and cream velour car seat covers. It was, Lenny thought, probably the first time in her life she'd been inside anything more humble than a Volvo. She held her Louis Vuitton Speedy Bag primly on her lap, eyes widened in horror as she took in Lenny's cheap cassette player and Sharp radio.

'God, this thing is tiny.'

They were very close to each other in the car. Kimberly would look better without all the pancake, Lenny thought. And yet, like her brother and her father she exuded a strong sexuality. She had slept with Larry Burton. Who else did she sleep with?

'I was rude,' Kimberly said finally. 'I'm sorry.' It seemed genuine. Their eyes connected. 'But I can't help you, Lenny. I don't know anything. Honestly.'

'You wouldn't have got in the car if you didn't know something,' Lenny said.

The busy hands mangled the Louis Vuitton bag.

'This has been a very difficult week for me,' Kimberly said, looking straight ahead. She moved her bag a little to the side, exposed a thigh. 'There are all these things I didn't know about that I have to deal with. My family is—'

'Really fucked up?' Lenny said helpfully, pulling out a cigarette and lighting up. Kimberly looked sad.

'They're still my family,' she said.

'Oh please,' Lenny said. 'You're not going to tell me that deep down you really care for that old bastard?'

'Do you mean my father?'

'Give it up.'

'What?'

'Kimberly,' Lenny flicked ash out of the window, onto the pavement. 'Why don't you cut the act. I don't buy it. Your father and mother don't give you the time of day.'

'Don't say that!' Kimberly protested. 'You think you know *everything*, don't you? You don't have any idea.'

'So tell me.'

'I have a class. I have to get my books—' Kimberly grabbed the door handle. Lenny put out a hand to stop her. Her loose white sleeve rose up and the pink line of her scar was visible to both of them for a few seconds. Kimberly stopped. She was fascinated, like a kid seeing a crippled person for the first time and following them up the street to look. Lenny wrenched her arm back.

'I read about you in the paper.' Kimberly was embarrassed. 'That terrible man hurt you, didn't he? And he never even went to jail. I'm sorry for staring.'

'Sure.'

'I can cut class,' Kimberly said finally. 'Come up to the apartment.'

Chapter 16

KIMBERLY TRIES TO HELP AND LARRY DOESN'T

Kimberly's apartment was on the top floor. Couches and chairs were cream-coloured leather, tables held glossy picture books of art and design side by side with legal and economics textbooks. Glass bowls were filled with yellow alpine daisies and there were silver framed photographs including one of Kimberly in black and white. The photographer had used all her skills to make Kimberly look delicate. The softening filter she had used was so strong that Kimberly seemed to be in the centre of a fuzzy cloud.

The apartment floor had black tiles, shiny as a mirror. The lounge room carpet was subtle pink and cream.

'It's a late 19th century Agra,' Kimberly commented and looked happy for a moment. 'The furniture is all Rose Tarlow,
my favourite, and the floor is polished granite tiles. From the Andes.'

'Whatever.' Lenny flopped onto a couch, lit up again. Kimberly's face fell.

'Don't let that thing out,' she said as Lenny put the cat box down. 'I don't want any more scratches on my things. It's terrible to say this but it's kind of a relief that Marie Antoinette is gone. She broke my Tina Chow vase. And the litter tray stank the place out. Sometimes she got runny shit in the hair around her bottom and I had to wash it out in the sink. God! What a disgusting experience! It got under my nails.' She paused. 'I suppose you know all about that. I suppose you're back at your usual work since my mother fired you.'

Lenny didn't respond. Kimberly flushed.

'Do you think I could have a cigarette?' she asked.

Lenny tossed her the Marlboro packet. Kimberly pulled out her toy gun lighter and lit up. She looked around nervously, settled on the giant panoramic TV and switched it on. Oprah Winfrey's face appeared.

'Do you think the person who killed my cat also killed Carol?'

'I don't know,' Lenny said. 'Do you?'

'How would I know? I'm sorry I got you involved in all this. Although you know a thing or two about cats, I'll give you that.'

Kimberly sat on the ottoman puffing on her cigarette, long legs splayed out. Her skirt was pulled up. She fingered the cover of a Modigliani book on the coffee table in front of her.

'I like beautiful things,' she said, beginning to drum on the book with her fingers. 'Are you sleeping with my mother, Ms Aaron?'

'No,' Lenny said. 'Did she say I was?'

'Of course not,' Kimberly sighed. She shook her head.

Lenny said nothing.

'I can see how you might be my mother's type,' Kimberly said.

'Really?'

'I know that she has affairs with women.' She began to wriggle out of her Chanel jacket. Underneath she was wearing a very exciting Chanel bustier.

'Like who?'

'Sonia Buchanan.' Kimberly was contemptuous. Her upper arms, as Lenny had noticed at the dinner party, were slender and firm and she had lovely shoulders, lightly tanned but without freckles, not sloping, not too square.

'Did Vivian tell you that?'

'I heard them fighting on Tuesday.'

'At the party?'

'Yes.'
'What time?'
'I don't know. After dinner sometime.'
'Where?'
'Ms Aaron—'
'Don't bullshit me!' Kimberly jumped out of her skin.

'Don't shout at me all the time,' she said. 'They were in my mother's room. I listened at the door. Sonny was yelling. She and that creep want my father to give them money because they've managed to get themselves bankrupt. My mother won't let him. She never gets soft about money.'

'Get to the lesbian bit.'

Kimberly flinched. 'Sonny said my mother owed her.'

'What did Vivian say?'

'She said ... she said just because she'd ... fucked her a couple of times didn't mean she had to pay for it.' Kimberly was red faced. 'She said it wasn't worth it anyway. Then she started laughing.'

'Did Sonny threaten her?'

'I don't know. I got out of there. I was embarrassed. I know they used to be best friends a few years back. At least I thought it was just friendship then.' She blinked back tears. 'God! I used to be so jealous because my mother spent all her time going out around town with Sonny Buchanan when she didn't even notice I was alive ... ' She laughed bitterly. 'Can you believe that? When I was a child I would have done anything to get that sort of attention, even for a moment.'

'So you think Sonny killed Carol, thinking it was your mother?' It was tough to ask a strong line of questions when the interviewee was leaning forward, showing off her nifty little breasts. This was a body that could, in the right circumstances, distract you from the face. Kimberly must rely on that.

'No. I think Max did it,' Kimberly said.

'Your brother.'

'He is not my brother!' Kimberly was in complete denial. 'He's a lying old man and he's going to jail.' She scrubbed her eyes with a tissue. 'God! All those years living right under our noses. He could have killed all of us.'

'Vivian's sure it was him?'

'It's obvious. It's his axe and he tracked blood to his own door for god's sake! It was all over his clothes! The police asked me about Liz Dodd. They think she's in love with him.'

Lenny sighed. 'Did you see Sonny and your mother downstairs after their fight?'

'I don't remember. I think so. I was drunk.'

Lenny's head was beginning to ache.

'Is Larry Burton your lover?'

'He's nearly fifty!'

'I saw the way he looked at you.'

'I hate him.'

'Right.'

'I do!' Kimberly exploded, swung her arm and a pretty cream lamp, one of a matching pair, smashed onto the granite tiles. 'Fuck! It's a Mattaliano.' It sobered her and she nursed her hand as though it was broken, the sudden spurt of temper fading quickly. 'He took advantage of me.'

Sure, Lenny thought.

'I was eighteen and he was on TV. Stupid, right? But it was like only two or three times. He has mirrors over his bed. Isn't that sad?'

'Isn't he married?' Lenny asked.

'So?'

Lenny knew Larry Burton was married to Helen Harmon, the 'Bundoora Budgie' of childhood songstress fame. Unfortunately she had grown up a Plump Parrot.

'I'll need his address,' Lenny said. 'Did both your parents know you slept with him?'

Kimberly nodded, humiliated.

'He *told* my father. He thought it would give his stupid show a chance. He said I threw myself at him!!' Lenny glanced at the other Mattaliano lampshade. It could go any minute. 'What a creep! He's not my type, you know.'

'Did your father speak to you about it?'

'My father never speaks to me, Ms Aaron. I'm invisible.' She blinked back more tears. 'That stupid company! I know he's going to leave everything to Kendell. I know that—it's not ... I'm top of my year at uni, you know? But it's meaningless to him. Eric has more of a chance of becoming the next CEO. My father wouldn't trust a woman to operate a calculator.'

'Do you really believe your father would make Eric the next CEO?'

'Eric believes it. He's been angling for it from the start. Sucking up, pretending to be devoted.' She shrugged. 'I think they do like each other, some Spartican, Master–Slave thing, I imagine. But my mother would never allow Eric to control our company. He may be able to get Kendell under his spell, but with my mother around ... She'll get rid of him in a second.'

'Did Vivian talk to you about Larry Burton?'

'She didn't care. My mother calls Larry Melbourne's number one arsehole. She's been after my father for years to cancel his show. She said Larry made passes at everyone and she couldn't believe I'd fallen for it. She even told Annie about it.'

'Isn't Annie one of the family?' Lenny knew that Kimberly would rise to the bait.

'Of course not! She's my mother's assistant.'

'Larry Burton's address,' Lenny reminded.

Kimberly reached into her purse for a sachet of business cards, took one out and put it on the coffee table. Lenny stood up and reached for the card.

Kimberly jumped up and the two of them were close enough to touch. Their eyes connected again. To Lenny's amazement she felt the frisson of sex. It was Kimberly's body. Certainly she felt no interest at all in the face or in the whining personality.

'Lenny, I . . .' Kimberly whispered. Lenny tried not to look at the gently heaving breasts. She felt a little dizzy.

'What?' Her mouth was bone dry.

'You could stay a while . . .'

'I need to talk to Vivian,' Lenny stepped back and folded her arms.

'My mother's not seeing anyone. We're all going to Europe. We have a house. I'm sick of this country right now anyway. Do you know how far we are from everything? Some of my friends in the States still think this is Austria. You have to get out to the real world every couple of months or go crazy, don't you?'

Lenny had never been outside Australia. 'I can't stay,' she said.

'Well, another time.' Kimberly turned away, tried to sound casual. Lenny looked down and got a clear view of lemon lace panties reflected in the shiny, black tiles.

Back in the Colt Lenny tried not to think about the attempted seduction. It was unsettling to imagine that right now she could be curled up in bed with Kimberly. Or on the couch. Or the floor. Or wherever it was people ended up doing these things. Touching each other.

She drove to Canterbury. Larry Burton and Helen Harmon lived in a mock Tudor home behind a large grey stone fence. Matching BMW convertibles snuggled in the gravel driveway.

Cleo at her side, she pressed the buzzer.

'Yes?' A woman's voice.

'Lenny Aaron to see Larry Burton.'

There was a long pause.

'My husband doesn't know you Miss—did you say Aaron?' It was the Bundoora Budgie and she sounded clipped. 'Perhaps you could call the channel. Ask for Lesley Taylor.

She's my husband's secretary.'

'I met your husband at Henry Talbott's party last Tuesday,' Lenny said. There was a second pause and then the gate opened.

Helen Harmon met her at the door. She wore a t-shirt and track pants with an apron around her waist. Her blonde hair with its too short, straight-cut fringe was shoulder length and shiny. Her pudgy face looked much older than thirty. Too many years of TV make-up and stress. She was wrinkled around the eyes and must have to wear a hefty corset under the stage costumes, Lenny thought. She held a whisk in one hand. Lenny could hear two TVs on different channels.

'My husband says you're a detective.'

'That's right,' Lenny lied.

'For *cats*. I read about you in the paper. You were in the police car with my husband.'

'Not by choice, believe me,' Lenny said.

Helen Harmon shrugged. 'He's down there, second on the left. He's drunk. If that animal scratches anything, you pay for it.' She went back to the kitchen, closed the door and turned up her TV. She was watching *The Simpsons*. A good episode: Krusty the Clown was arrested after a set-up by his jealous assistant, the evil Side Show Bob. Bart would come to the rescue. Lenny had it on tape.

Larry was in a large oak panelled room. On the back wall there was an enormous blow-up of himself in which he was holding a Logie, grateful and humble.

He sat in a sunken lounge suite, a velvet quadrant with a bar trolley in the middle and a giant blaring TV at one side. He wore jeans and a red Chinese dressing gown that was unfastened. His hairy stomach hung low over his jeans. He was, as his wife had said, drunk.

'Oh yeah, I know you.' He waved a bottle of gin at her. 'The ugly bird who didn't say much in the car. Betcha got fired.'

'That's right.' Lenny untied her Dr Martens and climbed into the lounge suite. Cleo jumped next to her. Larry Burton stared at the cat as though in a trance. 'But so did you.'

Larry held the shit-eating grin, consummate professional that he was, and poked at the cat with his bottle. Cleo pawed it half-heartedly. Then, sensing Larry wasn't worth any effort, she settled into the couch. She stuck one leg up at a ninety degree angle and licked her bum. Larry leered at the cat with what he probably thought was warmth.

'I love animals,' he said. 'But Helen won't have 'em in the house.' He was looking for sympathy. 'She says cats are destroying the natural wildlife? D'ya reckon that's true? I mean, there's a lot of fucking birds out there.'

Lenny said nothing, though she did agree. She didn't want to share opinions with Larry Burton. The TV was behind and to the left of her head. Larry could watch them both at the same time. Her face was competing with a re-run of *Roseanne*. Roseanne's edginess was infectious.

'You were fired? Right?'

'I'm on vacation,' Larry swigged his gin. 'What is this? You invade my privacy like you own the joint and lay it on the bottom line to me ...' the clichés rapid-fired, '... thinking I'm a bloody mug. But I know about you. You're that cop who got her arm chopped off—you're cat cop.'

Larry laughed at the screen behind her. Lenny looked. It was a commercial for pork products, animated pigs singing gleefully about wanting to be miniature sausages. Funny how animals always seemed thrilled to be processed into food.

'Did you argue with Vivian?'

'Did Kimmie tell you that? She's another bitch. An ugly bitch.' He smiled. Lenny imagined the mirrored bed. Why would someone with Larry's body want to watch himself have sex?

'Does your wife know you had a relationship with Kimberly?'

'I've fucked about fifty women since we got married.' He took another gulp of liquor. 'Why would she worry about Kimmie Talbott?'

'Did you fight with Vivian on Tuesday?'

'No way.' He pulled the drinks trolley closer to his legs. 'The gardener killed her, believe me.'

'Did you see anyone else arguing with Vivian?'

'Yeah—that little poofter. Derek.'

'Eric?'

'Derek, Eric ... The *poof*.'

'What about him?'

'He was in the hallway having a hissy fit with Vivian. Quite a tantrum. I was pretty pissed so I missed the best stuff. She was laughing in his face, but. Threatened to sack him.'

Lenny was surprised he could remember anything, the way he had lolled against her in the back of that police car. When they got out downtown, a camera strobe went off in their faces. Wednesday's page three photograph had shown them close together, the caption reading 'Larry Burton and friend'. She shuddered to think there were people in Melbourne who now thought she was sleeping with him.

'Did you ever have sex with Vivian?' The question surely stretched the bounds of taste given the man-mountain reclining in front of her. To her relief, he shook his head.

'Vivvie doesn't fuck anyone unless there's something in it for her,' he burped. 'I never had anything she wanted.'

Larry took a mouthful of gin and watched a promo for his soon-to-be-former employer with its exciting theme, space age visuals and 'celebrities'—newsreaders, current affairs hosts, soapie stars; a litany of the mildly accomplished. A week ago, Larry had featured in it too. Now he searched for his face in vain.

He flopped back. If he hadn't been one of her least favourite TV people, she might have felt something for him.

He let his glass slide onto the carpet. 'Should be her dead. Not the kid. Vivian fucks with everyone.'

'Did you know Kimberly's cat was killed?'

'Yeah?' He shrugged. 'I never even saw it. We never did it at her place. Probably killed itself anyway. I know I couldn't live with her. Or she killed it herself because she got sick of it.' Lenny waited. The silent treatment worked. Larry Burton couldn't contain himself. 'Don't let that little girl bullshit fool you. Kimberly is dangerous.'

'You don't say?'

'I do say! She stabbed me with a pencil when I broke up with her.'

'You broke up with *her*?'

'Yeah. Why? What did she say?' He sneered. 'I couldn't put up with her anymore. Too clinging. Anyway, apart from the body she's nothing special.'

'She stabbed you?'

'Would have had my eye out if I hadn't been quick.'

Lenny left Larry watching a medical soapie. His eyes never left that glowing wall of glass. She wondered if Helen Harmon was going to divorce him, citing career differences when she was really saying *Piss off, loser*.

She drove home and parked outside her apartment building, venetian blinds wriggling around her. She was the star attraction of this place now. No one wanted to have anything to do with her but everyone wanted a look.

She ate *yaki soba* at her *kotatsu* and watched a highlights package of the day's sport. Dessert was a mini cocktail of Bayer Aspirin and Codral Cold & Flu tablets. Cleo Harrelson wolfed down Turkey Whiskettes.

After dinner she cleaned the flat with Domestos. Underneath rubber gloves she wore soft, white cotton ones. It absorbed the sweat from her hands. When you cleaned as often as Lenny did you couldn't afford to get sweaty. You could pick up a rash if you weren't careful. Although the Domestos fumes made her a little faint, it was an excellent way to cap off the day.

She was avoiding thinking about Kimberly Talbott, breasts peeking from the expensive bustier, prolonged legs open. Her voice whispering, *Lenny* ...

The portable TV next to her futon hummed cozily. She was nodding off to a late repeat of *Deep Space Nine* when the phone rang. Veronica Aaron got lonely at night when her husband was sleeping and she was by herself in front of her TV. Her mind turned to her daughter and she would call for a chat. Lenny didn't like chatting and didn't like knowing that she and her mother were both sitting wide awake in the middle of the night.

She hesitated then picked up the receiver.

'Yes?' Cleo Harrelson stuck a head around the bedroom door. 'Out!' Lenny yelled. The cat sniffed and withdrew to its cushion.

'Ms Aaron? This is Henry Talbott.'

'How did you get this number?' It must be pretty important or he wouldn't be calling while *Deep Space* was on.

'You're still investigating the murder. Why?'

'I asked how you got this number.'

'Oh, a phone number is not difficult to get, Ms Aaron,' he said. 'Do you think Max killed that girl?'

'No,' Lenny said and realized that it was the first time she had really faced it. She didn't believe Max was guilty.

'What do you want, Ms Aaron?'

'I want access to your family,' she said. 'I want to interview everyone who was at the party. I'm going to prove that your son is innocent.'

There was a two minute pause in their conversation. A Ferengi pilot was creating an ugly scene at the Deep Space bar. Eventually, Henry spoke again.

'The police are sure it's Max.'

'Are you?'

'He's nothing to me.' There was a long pause. His laboured breathing reminded her of her father. She tried to figure his angle. How did he feel about Max Curtis? Did he look back on all the times the two of them had talked and realize what Max must have been thinking?

'I'll see you tomorrow, Ms Aaron.'

He didn't wait for a response. Lenny put down the receiver.

She rolled herself up in her quilt and fell asleep, the TV still talking to itself.

Chapter 17

LENNY FOR HIRE—$40,000

She slept badly, Henry Talbott and Michael Dorling moving around in her dreams, both of them touching her, stroking her softly on her arms and her face. She couldn't stand to have hands on her face. She always thought about the fingers dipping towards her mouth. She woke finally to daylight and a spotless flat. She couldn't even distract herself with cleaning.

She drove to her office with Cleo Harrelson. The porn shop was closed but Anastasia was already open. The journalists were not there. Lenny, cat box in hand, strode into the barber shop.

Anastasia looked up as the Siberian oxen bell clanked over the door then turned her attention back to her client. 'Look, look at this mess!' She tugged at the woman's roots. 'I told you—you perm the crap out of your hair and this is what you got.'

'You should learn some tact, young woman.' Her client was about forty-five in a pleated skirt, silk blouse and a single string of pearls, her hair the consistency of a Brillo pad.

Anastasia eyed the cat box. 'Don't bring that thing in here, Lenny. Look at this and tell me, am I a miracle worker?' She tugged too hard and held up a frizzy clump of grey hair. 'I comb it and it comes out! I think you should be at the doctor right now, lady, not here.'

'I wish to leave if I may,' her victim wavered, but the barber's hand rested heavily on her shoulder.

Lenny put the cat box on the counter near the till. 'I have an idea,' she began. 'You see, I don't get anyone in the office who hasn't already got a cat or hasn't just seen theirs stiff as a board, and I don't know if I'm going to be able to get this one off my hands—' She knew she was babbling.

'No.'

'Ten dollars for the day. Leave it here, near the magazines, and let your customers see what they think.'

'Lenny, I'm a very busy woman.' She looked at Lenny's reflection in the mirror. 'I thought of something new.' She gestured with her scissors at a pamphlet on the trolley where she kept her instruments. The hand on the cover had two-inch talons decorated with petals and rhinestones, the sort of thing the locals did to tourists in Bali, after they gave you the Bo Derek hair.

'I could do this in here. Good money. It costs about two bucks for product and I can charge twenty. I'll practise on you. You've got good hands.'

'Fifteen.'

Anastasia turned away from the mirror and faced Lenny directly. 'You have to cope with this yourself, Lenny. I am not a cat's ...' She stared at the ceiling, searching for the noun, '... pimp. You know what I think? I think you love this one. Yes, and I think you can't decide how to do because your love has made you blind.'

Lenny bolted. She walked swiftly down the corridor to the open double doors to the car park, opened the cat box and shook the cat out.

'Go! We're through.' She looked at the box—it would turn into a guilt object. She tossed it into a giant, orange Coles dumpster.

Cleo Harrelson stared back curiously. For the first time in days the cat was standing free in the open street. No box, no chain, no hand on its neck. It stretched and arched its back. It wandered up to Lenny and rubbed against her legs.

'Fuck off!' she said and hurried back into her office. She shut the door, making sure she wasn't being followed.

Fifteen minutes later Mike Bullock knocked at the door and came in without waiting for an answer. Lenny, in the grip of a cleaning mania, raised her rubber gloves: I'm busy. He was undeterred.

'Haven't seen you much lately, mate.' He said it like a question. He had a way of looking at her as though he really cared, as though they were old friends. He was waiting to be confided in, asked for help. There was real concern in his eyes.

'Yeah, well I'm busy.'

'I read the story about you.' Mike fidgeted. 'Big time stuff.' She didn't let him into her office often and he was grateful and curious. He stared at her Japanese posters. 'What happened to yer Siamese?'

'I got rid of it.' She gave him her best repellent stare and walked towards him, forcing him to back up towards the door. At a certain point he would have to turn round and use it or risk bumping into something.

'Well, if there's anything you might need me for ... ' He wandered back to his shop.

Lenny groaned. Mike Bullock thought he was in love with her. Did he really think they were a suitable match?

She listened to her answering machine messages. Number one was a missing Norwegian Forest Cat. Easy to find that one, she thought, just look for the huge, shaggy tail. Call number two was a missing Birman. Interesting. She had never tracked a Birman before. They were descended from cats once venerated in Buddhist temples. It was said that the first specimens lived in Burma and had been protected by the Grand Lama.

She wondered if she had time to look for a cat. She wrote down the telephone numbers and slipped them into her wallet.

In the car park her eyes searched for Cleo Harrelson. Gone. Obviously it was no more attached to her than she was to it. That was great! She slammed into her car.

She got caught in traffic on Flinders Street. A car had been bumped by a tram right at the intersection with St Kilda Road. A tow truck was fighting its way through. Drivers soon became impatient. Fuck the guy who was crushed! Just get the goddamn traffic moving! Lenny was onto her second Marlboro in five minutes when the police officer signalled her to U-turn into the opposite lane.

The traffic was jammed on St Kilda Road. It was difficult to change lanes without incurring streams of abuse. But, finally, she parked outside Henry Talbott's apartment building.

It resembled a private hotel. Eight stories tall. She looked up from the street. There was a wide balcony up there with what seemed to be trees. He would have a great view. Lenny's own flat was at the back of her block. Her kitchenette window gave her a view of another block of flats and a laundromat.

A security guard stood at the entrance. As Lenny approached he spoke into a mobile phone then nodded at her.

'Ms Aaron.' He was a deep-voiced, six foot six guy with shoulders like a tank and a neck like a bullfrog. 'Gotta see some ID.' He examined her driver's licence then looked her over.

'Are you carrying?' He meant did she have a gun. She shook her head. She had not as yet been required to shoot a cat.

'Gotta check you before you go up.' He meant he wanted to frisk her. She stepped back.

'No chance.'

The guard gave her a hard stare. She stared back. He reached for his cellular and dialled: 'I've got a Ms Aaron down here. She's refusing the body check.' Pause. 'Mmm hmm. Ahh haa. Yup.' He nodded: 'He says no exceptions.'

'Fine,' she turned and began walking away.

'Hang on a tick!' The guard panicked. 'She's leaving! Hey! Wait a sec!' She turned. 'He says go up.'

He punched in a number on a security pad at the door and they went inside. He punched in another code on the wall pad and the elevator doors opened. Lenny stepped in alone. It was a smooth, noiseless ride to the top. When the door opened she saw a second guard. This one had settled himself on a long cream couch. He had a Coke, a mini TV and a bunch of auto magazines.

He was half reading and half watching the Sheffield Shield. Lenny paused for a moment to pick up the score. Tasmania was not going to win.

She waited while the guard punched in another number at the condo's door. The lock snapped open.

She stepped into a large open space with full-length, tinted windows along one wall. Outside, the balcony was a good fifteen feet wide and filled with greenery and wooden patio furniture. It looked like a garden. A man and a woman were sitting outside. It was Kendell Talbott but Lenny didn't recognize the girl. A blonde. They were both in swimsuits, sunbathing on deck lounges. The glass was soundproof but she saw a ghetto blaster sitting on the table next to a tray of drinks.

Off the main room was a network of corridors. Somewhere down one of them must be Henry Talbott, Lenny thought. She looked around the ceiling. No obvious cameras but she felt very much on display in the centre of the room. She took a seat on a green leather couch.

She sensed that Vivian had had no hand in decorating this place. The Cedars Court house was hers. This was Henry's bachelor pad. The giveaway was a large stuffed emu next to the bookcase.

She knew he was there immediately but didn't react. She had trained herself not to jump out of her skin. It gave people too easy an advantage. But the hair on her neck prickled and her nose twitched. She could smell him.

She turned her head slowly to face him. Henry Talbott nodded at her from a corridor entrance. He was dressed for home in a white shirt and grey pants with old men's brown slippers. Without the power-dressing suits he looked smaller and more his age, like someone's great grandfather. He had been under a sunlamp recently to boost his tan, but there was no disguising terminal illness. His eye sockets were hollow and his eyes were dull. Lenny decided he would be dead within a month.

'What the hell do you think you're playing at?' she asked coldly. 'They wanted to search me. *You* asked *me* here.'

'Ahh ... Eric is worried ...' Henry waved a hand. 'He's just trying to protect me. The only one who bothers.'

He took a chair opposite Lenny's seat on the couch. It took him a minute to ease into it and he touched a hand to his stomach. He wasted no words.

'Can you prove Max Curtis is innocent?' He didn't have much vocal projection and she had to strain to hear him.

'Not yet. But I believe he is.'

'Why?'

'The situation at your house on Tuesday was too easy. No confession. No witnesses. I think it's a set-up.'

'So you think one of the staff or guests tried to kill Vivian?'

'Yes,' Lenny said. 'Or one of the family.'

The bulbous eyes didn't move. He took a long time between words and his speech was slow but not hesitant. She had read that people with cancer began to decay inside long before they actually died, but the reality was more shocking than she imagined.

'Vivian likes to play.' Henry dabbed a cloth to his mouth. Lenny forced herself not to look away.

'A lot of people don't like her,' she said.

'I don't like her.' He smiled. He was quite still but she didn't forget how quickly he had grabbed her. She was ready to defend herself this time. She kept her body tense and her hands coiled—be ready to strike like a cougar.

'Do you have any idea who tried to kill your wife?'

'Vivian pisses everyone off,' Henry replied.

He glanced out to the balcony. The ghetto blaster must still have been on because the blonde girl was dancing. She was slender but had large breasts barely concealed by a red bikini. They were bouncing. Must be painful, Lenny thought. Without music it looked surreal.

'New girlfriend?' she asked. Henry didn't answer but he looked hard as the girl's breasts bobbled.

'What did you think of Carol Connor?' she tried again. He took a long time to answer.

'She reminded me of Vivian twenty years ago. I told Ken not to marry her. He doesn't take my advice. He's his mother's boy.' This was the first sign of emotion from him. He reminded her of Kimberly for a moment.

'You didn't like Carol?'

'Vivian liked her. Vivian told the boy to marry her.'

'Kendell wasn't in love with her?'

'No.' He glanced out at the balcony again. The blonde had stopped dancing and was sitting on her deck lounge applying more tanning lotion. 'Being engaged didn't stop him seeing his other women. Not for a second.' He smiled at the idea. 'He'd do anything to please Vivian though. He's not smart. Not like Eric. Eric graduated top of his class without any money behind him. Everything he's achieved has been by hard work. I have to drag my son into the office. He has no head for business. Eric could run my business with one hand behind his back. He's helped me this last few months. Helped me run things. He's ... a good man. If he was given a chance he could really do things.'

'What about Kimberly? She's studying business.'

'Women!' he spat into his cloth. He clutched at a chair arm and squeezed it.

'Why did Vivian like Carol?'

'Same type,' he said.

'Type?'

'Whores.'

She didn't rise to his bait. She imagined him in the back of a horse-drawn carriage, his hand on the ivory knob of a Malacca cane.

'You said Vivian was a virgin when you met,' she reminded.

'She was after my money.'

'Well, what did you expect?' Lenny laughed in a sarcastic way. It was calculated and it worked. She finally sparked his attention.

'You think I was lucky to get Vivian?' he asked. He looked evil. She had provoked him. Like the night in his bedroom. He didn't like anyone to dish it back to him.

'Yes,' Lenny said.

Kendell and the blonde came in from the balcony. They were laughing, both greasy from the tanning lotion. The music from outside was loud for a couple of seconds until they closed the sliding door. They both looked at Lenny and Henry. The blonde kept smiling but Kendell stopped in his tracks, looked at the blonde then at Lenny. Sprung badly. The girl went down one of the corridors. She called his name and he padded after her.

'Eric argued with Vivian at the party,' Lenny said to Henry. She was trying her bad cop voice. She liked to imagine that it was 'the voice' as used by Paul Atreides in *Dune*, and that those who heard it were compelled to respond.

'Vivian's a dyke. Dykes and faggots don't mix.' This was sometimes true but hearing it from his lips made Lenny want to deny it. At least now she was sure Henry knew his assistant was gay.

'Vivian is a lesbian?'

'She fucks women.'

'Such as?'

He rattled off a few names: all well known women in Australian society, including Sonny Buchanan. Either he was keeping tabs on his wife's affairs or she took delight in telling him everything.

'And this began after you were married?'

'She came to Melbourne with my son and daughter and I married her,' he said. 'She set up house like a queen. She was nothing when I met her. She was no more than that fat cow she brought with her.'

'You don't like Annie?'

'Don't like ugly women,' he gave her a penetrating stare. 'Annie Baron is an ox. I turn around, she's there. Are you interested in my wife, Ms Aaron?'

'No,' she stared him down.

'She won't waste herself on you,' Henry said with a sick smile. 'My wife only beds down when she wants something.' Larry Burton had said the same thing. Lenny forced herself to show no reaction to his comments.

'Liz Dodd dislikes Vivian,' she said.

'Doddie's a tough woman,' Henry said finally. 'But too old to swing an axe.'

'Was she angry when you married Vivian?'

'Why would she be?' His eyes narrowed in comprehension and he laughed. 'I don't fuck my help, Ms Aaron.'

'Are you planning to include Max in your will?' She was always pulled back to the idea of money being behind the murder. 'Are you planning to include Eric? Who's going to take over the business when you're dead?'

'I'm not dead yet.'

'Right.' They stared at each other, neither giving in.

'I don't talk business with outsiders and you shouldn't talk so tough, Ms Aaron. Last time it got you in trouble.' Her arm. He probably liked thinking about that: her tied to a chair, a victim, being cut open.

'I need to talk to Vivian, Annie and Margaret Gross,' she said coldly. 'Also the Buchanans, Liz Dodd, Max and the two extra staff that night, Sidney Ailsworth and Nancy Denver.'

Henry was lost for a moment. He was losing contact with life. One night soon he would drift away.

'Mike Buchanan will do what I tell him.' He dragged himself back.

'And the others?'

'I'll arrange it.' But Lenny suddenly wondered if he had any power left.

'If Max is cleared, I'll cover your expenses plus twenty thousand,' Henry said. So he wanted to employ her. She should have guessed. His solution to everything was money.

She considered telling him she wasn't doing it for the money. And that was true. But it was foolish to reject cash.

'Forty thousand plus expenses,' she said. The figure meant nothing to him. She could have asked for two hundred thousand, she thought.

'He's a master gardener,' Henry said. 'Wins competitions ...' He was drifting again.

He fell asleep right in front of her. Was there panic in the international business community? It must be apparent at a sniff that Talbott Ltd was about to undergo a changing of the guard. She wondered if he was really good for the forty thousand. She should have got it in writing ...

Chapter 18

THE GIRL WITH THE RISING INFLECTION

Kendell and the blonde were in the kitchen, a wide room at the north of the building with a view of the city centre. Lenny, used to cooking in the tiny kitchens of rented flats, drooled over the gleaming stainless steel cabinets and wooden bench tops.

Kendell was making sandwiches. The counter was spread with plastic-wrapped bread and assorted fillings. He had already spilled mayonnaise on both the counter and the floor. The girl sat on a bar stool watching him, breasts upwards. Her face was animated when he looked at her and blank as a doll when he didn't.

Kendell saw Lenny and his face fell. The girl looked over her shoulder and smiled. Nothing in *her* head except plain old instinct, Lenny thought.

'It's your turn, Ken,' she said. She glanced at the big ham and avocado sandwich he had just made.

'D'ya wanna sandwich while we talk?' Kendell asked as she took a seat at the counter next to the blonde. Of course it was unprofessional to accept.

'Sure,' she said. 'But I'll make it and I'll need a clean knife.' She didn't want his hands touching anything that went in her mouth.

The blonde, mindful of the size eight figure under the silicon boobs, nibbled a cracker.

'I'm Karen?' she said in a voice with rising inflection. 'I'm Ken's friend?'

Lenny accepted the pickle jar Kendell offered. 'Thanks. I'll need a clean fork. We have to talk about last Tuesday. About Carol.'

'Carol's dead. Talking isn't going to change anything.'

'Do you mind using a fork?' Lenny said as his fingers dipped into the jar.

'Wha ... oh, right.'

'You had an argument with Carol at the party. On the terrace?' she prompted when he obviously didn't remember. He shook his head.

'You were cheating on Carol and she was angry about it,' she pressed. Given what Henry had just told her about Kendell's other women, this seemed the most likely reason. Kendell looked away and Karen giggled. She was leaning on the counter,
breasts sitting on the surface having a well earned rest. Was she the woman who had caused the argument in the garden?

'Carol was really bossy sometimes, you know,' Kendell said. Lenny groaned. He was going to do his father's trick of answering every question indirectly.

'Were you angry with her?' she asked.

'Sometimes ...' he chewed his lip. 'I wasn't a very good boyfriend. Mum said it didn't matter as long as we got married. Carol always bossed me.' His face registered annoyance at the memory. 'She acted as though I'm stupid or something. That's not right from your girlfriend.'

'Did you love Carol?' The million dollar question. Kendell hesitated, looked at his sandwich.

'Yes, of course,' he lied.

Lenny remembered the two of them at the Brighton house, at the pool laughing and kissing. But behind the scenes neither loving the other. The whole thing held together by Vivian, determined that it would go ahead. Why? Because Kendell was out of control? Because she needed to restrain him somehow? If Carol had been her master plan, then it hadn't been working.

'Did you want to marry her?' she asked.

'She was pretty,' Kendell answered. He was lost in his memories for a moment. 'We had a lot of good times

together.
I just wasn't a very good boyfriend. I let her down. She was always angry about that. She made me angry. But she was so pretty ...' He smiled. Karen's face froze, instantly alert that he was happily describing another woman. She sat back with a jerk, breasts bounced back up, refreshed.

'But you didn't want to marry her?' Lenny pressed on.

'I asked her to marry me,' Kendell said. He started buttering more bread. 'I would have gone through with it. She was all right, Carol. She made me laugh at myself. And Mum said ...'

'What?'

'Mum said it was time I got married.'

'Why?'

'She liked Carol. Annie liked her too,' Kendell gave a goofy smile. 'She said Carol was really pretty and we were a lovely couple.'

'Do you like Annie?'

'She looks after me,' Kendell said. 'She's always been my friend.'

'I'm your friend, Ken?' Karen interjected and stroked his arm. The pink tips grazed his black hair. Lenny noticed that one of the nails was broken and filed much shorter than the others. Little discrepancies like that drove her wild.

'Did you go upstairs with Carol at the party?' Lenny asked. 'Did you go into your mother's bedroom?'

'No ...' he was tentative.

'Why was she in your mother's bedroom?'

'She was always playing with Mum's things. She said Mum's room was nicer than mine. She and Mum were real friends. I thought that was great.' Kendell sighed. 'I don't like it here. Dad doesn't even have a cook. Just Eric. Eric makes it pretty clear he hates me.'

'Did you see anyone argue with your mother at the party?'

Kendell hesitated and then nodded. 'I listened,' he confessed. 'I was in the hall but they didn't see me. I stayed quiet. It was dark.' He stopped eating. 'Larry said something to my mum.'

'What something?'

'He wanted Mum to save his show. He acted like it was all her fault Dad wanted to cancel it. He said he knew Dad would let him fade out gracefully with another couple of years' run. He said Dad would go for it if Mum kept her mouth shut. He said Mum had it in for him because of,' he hesitated, 'Kimberly.'

'What did your mother say to him?'

'She said it was nothing to do with her or Kimberly.'

'I mean, was she angry?'

'No, she was laughing. She said some stuff to him.' He hesitated again. 'She said she was glad his show was cancelled. I liked that show.'

'Was Larry angry with your mother?'

'Yes.'

'Did he threaten her?'

'He said he wasn't going to let his show be ... fucked over. No matter what happened.' Then, in an incredible moment of unbefuddled lucidity, a light dawned in Kendell's golf ball eyes. 'Do you think *Larry* killed Carol?'

'I don't know,' Lenny said. So Larry Burton had lied when he told her he hadn't argued with Vivian the night of the party. She wondered if he really believed Vivian was standing between him and continuing TV existence.

'Who do you think killed Carol?' she asked.

'I don't know either.' It had been too much to hope that the spell would last. 'I don't reckon it was Max though. I like Max. He's a good gardener.'

'How long had Carol known about your cheating?'

'Aw—' His big fist slapped onto the counter, upsetting the salt shaker. 'I dunno. I *don't.*'

'What about Vivian? And don't say "I dunno".' She gave him a look not unlike the one she gave pesky cats.

'Mum said it was OK—'

'How long?!' He jumped. So did the blonde.

'From the start.'

Eric Hunter came into the kitchen, puffing. He looked tired.

'Ken. Help me lift your father,' he said. Working for Henry must be a barrel of laughs, Lenny thought. Kendell hurried to help.

'I'll see you in the front room in fifteen minutes,' Eric told Lenny.

Lenny and Karen were left alone in the kitchen. Karen let out a heartfelt 'phew' and sagged all over. She reached out for the remaining piece of buttered bread and wolfed it—one of those women who won't eat in front of men. She grinned at Lenny as though they shared a sisterhood.

'This place is great, isn't it?' she enthused.

'No,' Lenny said. 'How long have you known Kendell?'

'A week? He came into Circle K last week for petrol? He looked really down? I said "cheer up, mate"? He liked that? He met me after work? And took me out? In a Merc?'

'A *week* ago?' Lenny couldn't hold back her surprise. 'When exactly?'

'Wednesday afternoon I s'pose?'

He picked up a console operator the day after his fiancée was hacked to bits.

'So what really happened to your arm?' Karen ate a whole pickle in one mouthful. Lenny noticed that her teeth were pointy. All of them. Almost as though she'd filed them that way for effect. It made her look ... carnivorous.

'None of your business.'

Karen did not take offence. 'Think *I* could wind up in the papers?' She sounded as though it would be the thrill of her life. She looked down the corridor. 'He's got a good body, don'tcha reckon?'

'No,' Lenny said again.

Karen was halfway through her second pickle when Kendell returned. She gulped it down fast, but Kendell didn't notice. He was worried, looked at Lenny.

'Dad's really sick, isn't he?'

Lenny nodded.

'Kimmie says Dad's gonna give me his company. She's the one who should run things. Not me. She's the one with the business head. I've never wanted to do that sort of thing.'

'God, you're lucky?' Karen interjected. It was a jiggle opportunity and she took it. Kendell looked at her voluptuous figure and smiled.

'Eric's waiting for you,' he reminded Lenny. Karen slid off her stool and bounced over to her man. They went off together.

Lenny put two pieces of spearmint gum into her mouth and chewed solidly for a minute then wadded the gum into a napkin and left it on her plate. She cupped her hand over her mouth and breathed out, directing the breath up to her own nostrils. Not pickly.

When she returned to the main room, Henry was gone. They must have gotten him into his bed somehow. Eric now occupied his chair. He had placed a briefcase, a mobile phone and a small mini disc recorder on the ebony coffee table in front of him. He sat upright, feet crossed at the ankles, hands linked in his lap. He looked intense. Lenny bet he ground his teeth. She had that problem herself: the sudden realization that your jaw is aching, incredible pressure and then you discover that your back teeth are clenched like a vice. It was similar to waking up in the morning with your hands so clenched that your nails had dug grooves into your palms. Hers sometimes bled.

'I'm taping this,' he said as Lenny took her seat on the couch again. She waited while he set up the tiny Japanese machine. He nodded finally, sat forward.

'It's three o'clock, Tuesday the 15th. Present are myself and Ms Lenny Aaron, a private investigator. Ms Aaron, say something for level check, please.'

'Something.'

Eric leaped forward and rewound the machine. 'Very original,' he said. He pressed record again. 'Well, Ms Aaron, I believe you wish to speak about last Tuesday night.'

'Yes.'

'My job requires me to devote myself to Mr Talbott. I had little time to notice anything else.'

'That's garbage,' Lenny said. She pulled out a cigarette. The packet ripped and a few cigarettes fell on the table. At the same time the mini disc recorder made a tiny squeak and stopped working. Eric grabbed the machine and began pressing buttons. Nothing happened. Lenny gathered up her Marlboros and lit one.

'Batteries?' she suggested the obvious answer. He dropped the micro machine into the briefcase.

'This presents a problem.'

'Oh, don't be an arsehole,' Lenny had had a long day. 'I'm not a cop.'

'You used to be a cop,' he said. 'You're the one who messed up the Michael Dorling case. People don't forget, you know.'

They sure don't, Lenny thought. She wished someone would think of a new way to provoke her.

'You argued with Vivian at the party,' she said. 'Did you threaten her?'

'Like I'd tell you!' he said. Good point. Usually she didn't ask stupid questions but she was tired. She always hated Perry Mason shows, Perry asking each suspect 'Did you kill Mrs So and So?' As though the killer would say: 'Oh, go on then, yeah, I did it'.

'Vivian's going to dismiss you when Henry dies,' she said. 'You think he's going to include you in his will. But if he doesn't, your only chance is to manipulate Kendell. Vivian would never permit that. Of course if Vivian were dead you'd have a clean run.'

Eric stared at her for a long time without speaking. Not the reaction she had hoped to provoke. She had wanted to make him angry, reckless. Instead he simply said: 'I didn't kill Carol Connor. And I don't spend my days thinking about Henry's will. He and I are friends—as much as that's possible when one person's paying the other.'

'You've been employed by him for how long?'

'Seven years.'

'What's your job these days? Nursing?'

'Pretty much. I trained as a nurse for a couple of years then switched to economics.'

'How did you meet Henry?'

'I was working for one of his regionals in New South Wales. He was doing some publicity out there. He needed a new PA.' He raised his hands, let them fall.

'Lucky break,' Lenny commented.

'You make your own luck.' Her needling was beginning to take effect.

'How do you keep his condition out of the press?'

'Amphetamines for public appearances. Heavy duty pain killers. And,' he smiled grimly, 'breath sprays.'

'They're not working. What will you do when he's dead?'

'Not a relevant question, Ms Aaron.'

'When Kendell inherits everything with Vivian controlling him, you'll be left on the outer—right? Plenty of reason for you to feel angry.'

'But not enough to kill anyone,' he countered. 'Why don't you ask Mrs Buchanan if *she* felt "angry"?'

'What?' Lenny played dumb.

'Vivian and Sonny Buchanan had a relationship a few years ago. Then Mike Buchanan lost everything. So Vivian dropped Sonny.'

'Because?'

'She wasn't interesting anymore. Vivian's only attracted to people with money or people she can get something from.'

Larry Burton had said the same thing. From him Lenny had taken it as sour grapes but Eric Hunter had no sexual interest in Vivian.

'You're so sure this is about the company,' he continued. 'You think someone wanted to kill Vivian to get at the money? I suggest you follow the trail up to Brisbane. Ask the Buchanans about their finances. Everyone knows they're bankrupt. But Henry's got a soft spot for Mike Buchanan. They did a lot of good business together. He wouldn't ruin them. He told me that. Only Vivian ...' he shrugged. 'She wants *everything*. Any little crumb going spare, she has to take that too.'

'Why doesn't Vivian like you, besides the obvious?' Lenny asked. It was time to turn up the heat on him.

'What the hell does that mean?!'

'Oh come on.' Lenny finished a cigarette and lit another. Her fingers fumbled a little. 'You're gay. You thought it was a secret?'

To Lenny, gay men were a fact of life. Like straight men, there were the good, the bad and the ugly. But sometimes it was useful in an interrogation to use sexuality as a weapon, because some gay men were uptight about it. Far more so than gay women. The women became tougher the more you pushed. The men dissolved quickly into defensiveness. Eric didn't answer. He was the sort of person who thought he controlled his identity. He looked annoyed that the information about his sexuality was out there, freely available.

'Vivian doesn't like anyone except herself to have control of the family's life,' he said coldly. He also lit a cigarette, a long thin More. It was a delicate movement and brought Lenny's eyes to his slender hands and nails. They were delicate but he was, she thought, big enough to swing an axe. 'Henry relies on me now. Almost completely. Vivian hardly bothers with him. And he needs help. Most days he can't function without injections and massive doses of pills. He won't have a private nurse so I'm on duty twenty-four hours a day. And I'm not doing it for the money. Not *just* for the money, Lenny. He needs someone. He needs *company*.' He turned his head to the window, avoided her eyes for a moment.

'It's possible to care about someone even when you're using them,' he said finally. 'It *is* possible. I've done my best for Henry. I do my best. Vivian doesn't like it. Fuck her.'

Eric followed her out to the elevator. The guard was eating a sausage roll and nodded to them. He was surrounded by empty food wrappings.

Eric had something on his mind. He was too close to Lenny for her liking. She stepped back from him deliberately. They were the same height but he was weedy. She wasn't afraid of him. He stepped forward again, close enough to touch her, even grab her.

'Step back,' she warned.

'My private life is my own business,' he said. 'My sexuality has no bearing on this investigation.' She agreed with him. It had just been an investigative tool. He was quite right, but she couldn't think clearly when he was standing so close. Too close. It couldn't be permitted.

'Step back.'

'Or what?' His hand enclosed her arm, rubbing the scar underneath the material. Lenny felt her skin quiver.

'Get off me,' she said.

The grip on her arm tightened. The pressure on her arm began to transfer and accumulate in some other place, mushrooming into an old terror.

Lenny's right elbow connected with his nose. There was a loud popping sound and blood spurted. Eric screamed.

'You broke my fucking nose!' He had blood on his hands and speckled on the white shirt. She couldn't see his nose because his hands were covering it but she guessed from the pop that it was bad.

The security guard rose, sausage roll with sauce still in his hand. His mouth opened with surprise and he hovered ineffectually. Lenny was a midget next to him. He could crush her with one giant hand. They faced off warily. She was planning a kick to his groin, old faithful, when it came to her that the guard was in a real bind. He was the kind of guy who didn't hit women, a real drawback in his line of work.

'What are you waiting for?' Eric yelled at him. His hands dropped and she saw his askew nose. She had broken six noses before in her police career and this was definitely the most comprehensive.

The guard decided, against his better judgment, that he was obliged to make a move against her. He stepped forward. She felt a little surge of fear and readied herself for impact but she was saved by Henry Talbott. He was up from his nap. Quite a sight with his hair on end and his face bleary.

'Leave her,' he told the guard, who shrank back immediately. Henry propped himself against a wall. 'Eric, get inside and call a doctor,' he said gruffly. He wasn't going to back him up. Thank god, Lenny thought. She could be charged with assault. Eric hesitated, furious, then went back into the apartment.

'Was that necessary?' Henry asked.

'Larry Burton,' Lenny said. It hadn't been necessary. Of course not. She just couldn't stand to be touched, to feel imprisoned. Her response had been uncontrollable. Her hands were trembling and she balled them tightly.

'Eh?'

'Why did you cancel Larry Burton's show?'

'The show's not bad, but times change. I'll find something small for him to do.'

'Did Vivian persuade you to cancel the show?'

'Vivian has no power over me, Ms Aaron. None.' Henry's breath was heaving. He was still half asleep. That was good because in his right mind he was a lot more scary than Eric Hunter, and Lenny wasn't up to another grabbing.

She signalled to the guard to punch in the code to the lift. She wanted out of this place.

'I need to see Liz Dodd and Max—and Vivian,' she said.

Her voice wasn't shaking. It sounded very even and controlled. If only she felt that way.

The lift came and she stepped in, turning back to face them. The guard was munching on his sausage roll again. He was relieved that the crisis was over and he didn't have to muscle a girl. Henry's eyes didn't blink. The lift door closed in his face.

Lenny drove immediately to a chemist and filled a prescription. Dr Sakuno let her have this stuff for *emergencies* and this was one. She asked the chemist for water and took two pills on the spot, then sat outside her car for ten minutes doing the deep breathing technique. The tranquillizer washed through her veins.

She berated herself for the incident. It was ridiculous to break a man's nose because he held her arm. Dr Sakuno would say she was allowing her emotions to rule her, a dire criticism, and he would be contemptuous that she had fallen back on prescription drugs after a long stretch without them.

She drove home quickly and ran to the toilet, stuck her fingers down her throat and brought up the half-digested pills. She wiped her hot face with a flannel and lay on her futon watching Kurosawa's *Ran*. The swords disturbed her a little but the residual sedatives in her system were a big comfort and she was snoozing comfortably when the phone rang. She felt no concern as she reached for it.

'Hullo?'

'You bitch!'

'Look, I'm sorry about your nose. Really. Genuinely sorry.' Drugs made her benevolent. She yawned.

'Not as sorry as you're going to be.'

She slipped further under her doona. She was going to have a heavenly sleep, a no-dreams, semi drug-assisted sleep. She was impatient for it to begin.

'What do you want?'

'You can see Liz Dodd tomorrow—and Max too,' Eric said. Even with a flattened nose he was still Henry's faithful drone. He gave her a phone number to call: Max's lawyers, Smith, Smith & Breslin, were also taking care of Liz. Henry must be footing the bill for all that. She wrote the phone number carefully on a notepad next to the phone then slid her hand back under the covers.

'Anything else?'

'If I get a chance, I'll cut up more than your fucking arm, so just watch out.'

As she dozed, she wondered if Eric was the killer. If he was, she could expect an axe in the head sometime tomorrow. Ahh well ... better get some sleep. She heard herself snoring.

Chapter 19

AN EASY $75

She woke at six a.m., puffy faced, thick tongued and headachy. Feeling a little guilty about Eric's nose and the drugs she had taken the night before, she took a cold shower. She spent six minutes scraping the dirt from her tongue.

She drove to her office not allowing herself to be angered by the incompetent driving of everyone else in Melbourne. She was considering her last moments with Henry Talbott the previous night. He had not admitted that Vivian had anything to do with the cancellation of Larry Burton's show. But he had seemed regretful, promised some small industry job for Larry. Perhaps Larry sensed that ambivalence and thought that with Vivian out of the way he could persuade Henry to change his mind.

Outside her office door, Anastasia and Mike Bullock were huddled together. He had an arm around her slender shoulders. He saw Lenny and drew his arm back. He didn't want Lenny to think he was two-timing her.

'Lenny!' Anastasia ran towards her and would have made physical contact, except Lenny pretended she was fishing for her keys. 'Something terrible has happened.'

'What?'

'The Siamese, mate,' Mike Bullock stepped forward. 'You should prepare yourself for a shock.'

Lenny sighed. 'I'm always prepared.'

'The little fellow's had an accident.'

Cleo Harrelson had been injured somehow and they thought she cared? She did not. Not at all.

'Where's the body?' she asked.

'It's not dead!' Anastasia made the sign of the cross. 'We took it to Mr Wellington.'

'I found the poor scrap over the road a bit.' Mike's lip trembled. 'Musta got winged by a car. Broken leg, I reckon. And its little face ...' he blinked hard. 'Hrrruumph ... Wellington asked about cash or credit, by the way.'

Anastasia snapped out of sympathetic grief as an old man hovered at the barber shop door. 'Be right with you, Mr Jacobs,' she called.

Lenny turned to go herself but Mike Bullock coughed behind her. She took a breath and turned to face him.

'Anastasia is ... just a friend. Just so you know.'

She gave him her sourest smile. 'And just so you know, I am not now nor ever will be remotely interested in you.' She left him gaping. Now, if she could dispense with that cat once and for all ...

Wellington's office was within walking distance. He sewed fast and preferred payment in advance.

His clinic, small and not clean, was packed with pet owners. A black and white TV in the waiting room showed a repeat of *The Henderson Kids*. The old woman assistant (cunningly disguised as Wellington's geriatric mother) was assessing the damages to a budgerigar that lay on the bottom of its cage: 'No, that one's gone, dear. No, it's stiff. You take it home and bury it. No charge for looking, seeing as you're so pretty. Remember to feel for a pulse and put a little mirror to the beak. Check for breathing.'

She moved on to a runny nosed Doberman: 'Got a bit of a chill, hmm? You know the injection costs a little extra this year, dear? All right then. Lenny! How lovely!' Her smile exposed the wire around her dentures. 'Oberon is just taking care of your little kitty now. You go in.'

'It's not my cat. It's a mistake,' Lenny muttered.

'Oh my goodness. Oberon won't like that. He's already given it the anaesthetic, dear. And you know how much we charge for that—'

'Nevertheless ...'

'You talk to Oberon.' Mrs Wellington turned to a very fat and unhappy looking Corgi. 'Who's been a bad boy? Little tummy-wummy all full of chocolate again? Are we going to need another pumpy-wumpy?'

Lenny walked through the hanging beads and past the kitchenette to the 'surgery' at the back of the building. It had once been a living room. The floor was mustard and the walls brown floral paper. In the centre was a raised operating table and a sixty-year-old man in a blood-splattered white gown. He was short, pot-gutted and had a way of smiling and looking angry at the same time. Some kind of squint, she supposed.

He was splinting Cleo Harrelson's leg, so he would be billing her for X-rays too. The cat's head was swathed in bandages.

'Lenny, I've saved it!' he twitched at her. The whole face spasmed. 'Hell of a job. Front leg might still have to come off. Looks like a bike hit her. If it'd been a car she'd be finished.' He laughed heartily. 'Lost the eye though.' He gestured down and to the left and Lenny noticed a glistening eyeball sitting on a bloody paper towel.

'That's not my client,' she said. 'There's been a mistake.'

'Mistake?' The squint morphed into a savage leer. 'I don't think so. Your friend, Mr Bollocks—'

'Bullock. He's not my friend.'

'Another mistake?'

'Look, I'm not paying. It'll be here for *days* recovering.'

'Yes. It is going to cost you.' Squint. Squint. 'Give this to Ma on your way out.' He handed Cleo over, lying still in a wicker basket. 'Come back one week.'

Lenny looked down into the basket. Cleo Harrelson's fur was wet where the vet had washed away the blood. A closed eye moved under the lid. Was Cleo having cat dreams? Lenny stroked a finger against the cat's tummy gently. She had seen this kind of thing many times. Escapee cats often ended up under the wheels of a car or bike. She thought that she had become immune to it. Of course when it was one of your own ...

'Bloody hell,' she murmured.

'Send in the Corgi, will you.' Wellington reached for an enema tube.

Mrs Wellington took the little basket.

'Are you all right, dear?' She looked at Lenny.

'Of course I'm all right. I don't think I'm liable to pay for this. It's not my client.' But when Cleo twitched in her sleep she reached out a hand to stroke the tummy again. Mrs Wellington looked omniscient.

'There, there, dear. Grief takes us all in different ways. I'm just going to pop it on your monthly account. That'll be the least worrying for you.'

Cleo mewed. Lenny realized her hand was still stroking and yanked it away. 'Nuisance,' she said softly.

Back in her office, she had a desperate need for activity. She rang the owners of the missing Birman. The Woodruffs lived in North Fitzroy and she drove to their house.

They lived in one of a neat row of renovated terraces with polished iron fences and bars on the lower windows. Across the street were a colourful bar promising *tapas*, a delicatessen with wooden chairs and canopied tables on the pavement, and a real estate office that looked more like an antique showroom.

Mrs Woodruff, young, short and very pregnant, led her into the living room at the back of the house. The interior was pale grey and there was a preference for Shaker style wooden furniture and educational toys. A two-year-old was watching Humphrey B. Bear.

Mrs Woodruff gave Lenny a cup of percolated coffee in a pink mug with teddies on it and a large eight by ten glossy of Mr Silky. He was a Seal Point Birman with the typical golden cream coat and white gloves. The face, ears, tail and paws were dark brown.

'It's been two weeks now.' Mrs Woodruff was calm but

her eyes dampened a little. She glanced at her toddler protectively. 'Gabby's been really upset. Mr Silky's her best friend.' Gabby banged her toy drum and screeched with insane laughter as Humphrey tried on women's clothes.

'How did you get my name?' Lenny asked.

'My vet recommended you,' Mrs Woodruff explained. 'You have the best reputation.'

'I see,' Lenny said. 'You realise it's not cheap. Seventy-five dollars a day, plus expenses.'

'What exactly are expenses?'

'Well ...' Lenny hesitated. 'Petrol, for one thing. I may have to feed the anim ... Mr Silky. Then there's damage to my clothing and car.'

'It sounds acceptable,' Mrs Woodruff said. 'I think we can afford to hire you for a week, is that all right?'

Lenny nodded. The toddler was at the TV screen trying with its fat hands to remove the rolling credits from Humphrey's face.

They shook hands at the door. Lenny said she'd be in touch. A week wasn't long. If she didn't find the cat, it made no difference financially. She would provide them with an account of the search and an itemized bill. She rarely had a client refuse to pay. She had a good record: she returned sixty percent of pets to their owners. Some as carcasses, it was true, but wasn't it better to know the awful truth than to always wonder?

Mrs Woodruff held Lenny's hand longer than was necessary. She looked concerned and Lenny realized it was a concern directed at herself.

'Hmm?' She pulled her hand free.

'I'm sorry,' Mrs Woodruff blushed into her brown curls. 'Ms Aaron. I thought I recognized your name. You're the young woman in the newspapers, aren't you?'

'Yes,' Lenny said.

'I remember the case. Two years ago, wasn't it? I was a social worker at St Vincent's at the time.'

'Hmm,' Lenny squirmed.

'Well, thanks for coming over.' The perceptive Mrs Woodruff realized she was saying all the wrong things and stopped. 'You'll be in touch?'

'Right.' Lenny couldn't get into the Colt fast enough. She sensed Mrs Woodruff watching from her pale grey doorway, and hastily started the car.

She slammed on the brakes. About two hundred metres from the house, sitting on the pavement and looking exactly like its photo—including red collar and name tag—was Mr Silky, the Woodruffs' cat. They were going to think she was the best detective ever, Lenny thought.

She pulled over to the kerb and opened the passenger door gingerly. You had to be careful with cats. Dogs were morons. They would lollop into anyone's car. Cats were naturally suspicious.

She pulled some cat snacks from the glove box.

'Here kitty ... here.'

Mr Silky stared her down. He looked at the snacks but wasn't going anywhere near the car. She had a cat box in the boot, but she'd have to grab him first.

'Mr Silky ...' she wheedled. They locked eyes. She reached for a little handful of catnip and that did the trick. Some cats tranced out on the stuff. Mr Silky eased over slowly. He had been eating on the wild side judging from his breath and he was filthy. He reached out to paw the catnip onto the ground, lowered his head to sniff it. Lenny grabbed him. He tried to claw her and hissed. Still holding him, she got out of the car and recovered the cat box from the boot. She pushed Mr Silky inside.

'Stupid,' she said and tossed the box onto the back seat. She should go back to the Woodruffs' terrace right now, take the seventy-five dollars and revel in her good fortune. Money for nothing.

But she didn't want to face Mrs Woodruff's gentle assessment again so soon. Mr Silky mewed tragically. He gagged and the cat snack barfed up onto the back seat. Great.

'You stink, mate,' she said. Like all pets who escaped from a good home, Mr Silky had gone mad. He was living on the edge and loving it. She really should clean him.

She had to park a long way from Collins Street. The cat box got heavier and heavier.

She went into Collins Towers. The guard at the main desk did a laughing double take at the cat and waggled a finger at Lenny.

'Sorry, miss. The little fella will have to wait down here.'

'No problem.' Lenny handed over the box. The guard began to poke a finger through the ventilation holes, then wrinkled his nose at the gastric smell. Lenny was already on her way to the elevators. Ascending, she saw Mr Silky being fussed over by a crowd of office staff.

On the fifteenth floor every office was part of Smith, Smith & Breslin. Reception consisted of an ebony desk with an attractive, middle-aged woman behind it. She took in Lenny's black jeans and tan corduroy waistcoat over a white t-shirt. Maximised her eyes.

'Lenny Aaron to see Elizabeth Dodd,' Lenny said. The receptionist led Lenny to an interior reception area lined with Georgian couches, and directed her to wait. Lenny examined the walls where there were several large paintings of Englishmen in silk pantaloons and cravats standing in front of marble arches that didn't lead anywhere. White greyhounds snoozed at their feet.

The receptionist returned two minutes later and showed her into a large office. A man was standing behind a desk that resembled a dining table for ten.

Liz Dodd sat in a leather armchair. She was not wearing her big white apron today. She sat with a straight back, knees and feet pressed together, head erect.

'Ms Aaron.' The man stepped forward and shook her hand in a firm, no-sexism-here kind of way. 'I'm David Breslin.'

He was greying, jowly and overweight, disguising it with an exquisitely tailored suit.

'Mr Talbott informed our offices that you'll be handling the private investigation of Ms Connor's death on his behalf. Our client, Ms Dodd, has indicated her willingness to support your investigation.'

'Being that we all want the same thing. We all want Max free, *don't* we?' Liz Dodd looked hard at Lenny.

'Have a seat,' David Breslin gestured to the leather chair angled next to the cook's and Lenny sat down. The lawyer took a seat at the desk.

'Well,' Liz Dodd gave Lenny a grim smile. 'So you *are* a detective, sort of. You managed to find that dead cat at least. Why haven't you told the police that Max is innocent?'

'He has no alibi,' Lenny said. She reached for her cigarettes. 'According to his statement he was in his room alone all night. No witnesses. The murder weapon was his axe. Blood was found outside his room and on his clothes and he has a motive. What makes you so sure he's innocent?'

'Ms Aaron, I caution you,' David Breslin interjected. 'Please do not smoke in this office.' Lenny ignored him.

'Max told me the truth about his mum and dad years ago,' the cook said. 'His mum left him a letter to read when she died. She said Mr Talbott was his father. He broke and reset his own fingers, you know, so that they'd look straight. He didn't want to be anything like the man who'd deserted his mother. He was very angry then, he told me. Only later on he wanted to see his dad. Not for money. Never that. He's not the sort of man who's interested in things. It's people he cares about. Fate. Max believes in fate.'

'I see,' Lenny said, smoking. 'But you're going to need some proof of that. A lot of people would find it hard to believe that Max wasn't jealous of his brother and sister. Or that he didn't hate the woman who replaced his mother. Perhaps he never had any bad feelings towards anyone. Perhaps he just told a friend his sad story and the friend was angry on his behalf. Maybe he is innocent but maybe you're not.'

'Ms Aaron!' David Breslin cautioned anew.

'Don't try to blame all this on me,' Liz Dodd said. 'I'm an old lady and I haven't done anything wrong.'

'All right. You tell me who to go after. Ashtray?'

David Breslin took out an alabaster ashtray and pushed it across the desk.

'I don't know who did it.' The cook squeezed the handle of her black vinyl handbag. 'It has nothing to do with me and Max. We just do our job. Mr Talbott knows that and he appreciates us. He'll take care of us when all this fuss is over. We'll be back at the house just like before.' Her eyes watered. 'I got Max and Mr Talbott spending time together. Max wanted to stay out in the garden and just see his father on the off-chance once in a while, but I said that's not good enough. A family should be together. I said *tell* him. But he never would. He didn't want to spoil things for the others. He didn't think they'd understand.'

'Someone used your notepaper to write the letters to Vivian.' Lenny said.

'Not me.'

'Didn't you hate her?'

'Why should I?'

'Because you're in love with Max.'

The cook sat up even straighter and fidgeted.

'That's not a fit topic of conversation in front of a gentleman.' She glanced at her lawyer. 'You are no lady to speak like that.'

'I'm no lady, all right,' Lenny agreed. 'When this goes to court you're going to have to answer questions tougher than mine. You're in love with Max and you are protecting him.'

'I do my job and I don't make trouble.' The cook evaded. 'I've never been trouble for Mrs Talbott. Never. When she and the babies came into our house I kept my mouth shut. Two babies in the house at once and no professional nanny, just Annie. And Mrs Talbott was no kind of decent mother. Only interested in parties and the like. But I never said a word.'

'Annie always looked after the babies?'

'And Maggie Gross. She's a *drinker*.'

'Did Vivian recover from the pregnancy quickly?'

'She went down to a size eight wedding dress in a month.' A sour smile.

'What happened when Annie got Cushing's Syndrome? Who took care of the babies then?'

'She still did. She insisted. She was all right. Just a bit weaker that's all. She put on weight faster than anything I've ever seen though. When she first came to the house with Vivian she was already heavy so it must have been starting in her then.'

'Did she develop any peculiar moods? Depression?'

'She was obsessed with those babies, I can tell you that. But it turned out to be for the best being as they weren't getting any attention from their mother.'

'Tell me about the party last Tuesday,' Lenny said. As far as she remembered, the cook did not come into the dining area after the guests had arrived. She set the table for dinner and then supervised Sid and Nancy in the kitchen.

'I was in the kitchen all night.'

'Did you see anyone go out onto the back terrace, around to Max's cottage?'

'And come back carrying an axe? People went in and out all night. I don't remember. If you ask me, all this palaver about Vivian is rubbish. I reckon Carol Connor was a little harpy. I reckon they wanted to kill *her*.'

'We will be investigating every possible line of defence, Miss Dodd,' David Breslin said, but he sounded politely skeptical of her theory. 'Perhaps the word harpy ...' He looked pained. He would be coaching her for court. As Max's character witness, he wanted her to come across nicely.

The cook laughed. 'Marrying a man for his fortune and

then expecting him to be in love with her as well.'

'You heard Kendell and Carol argue about his other women?'

'Every week,' the cook leaned forward, eyes gleaming. 'I heard her threaten him. Kendell's always got his eye out for other women. Some men are like that and there's no point in thinking you can change it. They had a big barny. Maybe a week before the party. People think I'm deaf or stupid. Carol told him he wasn't going to humiliate her.'

The cook smiled triumphantly as if she had just solved the murder, Poirot style, before a room of incredulous suspects.

'Did *he* threaten *her*?' Lenny asked.

'He wasn't in love with her,' the cook said. 'I know that much just from looking at them. I'm telling you she was a schemer. Trying to turn herself into another Vivian. Kimberly saw right through her.'

'Yes?' Lenny prompted. David Breslin was discreetly glancing at his Rolex. Must be lunchtime.

'Vivian told Kimberly to mind her own business. She liked Carol. They were as thick as thieves. Kendell would never have been engaged to that girl if his mother hadn't pushed it.'

'I want to know about the letters,' Lenny said. Six neatly typed letters promising a violent death. *I'll cut you up.* And that was exactly what happened. It appeared to be a crime of passion and yet the letters suggested premeditation.

'I told you! I didn't write them! Look, I'm just an old lady ... ' She pulled out a lace handkerchief and dabbed at dry eyes.

Lenny left Liz Dodd being served tea from a silver service. Bet those were cucumber and watercress sandwiches on the little plates too. Where was she living while the police still had the house sealed off? Was Henry Talbott picking up a hotel bill?

Downstairs in the lobby, Mr Silky gave her a pensive mew.

He sensed her antipathy. She took the box from the guard who had the overly familiar smile of someone who thought he was dealing with a fellow animal lover.

'He's been no trouble, have you, kitty?' The guard winked at Lenny.

'Great. Thanks.'

Chapter 20

MAX IN THE BIG HOUSE

Veronica Aaron was waiting outside her office door. Her cardigan was buttoned incorrectly. Something was wrong.

'I *had* to come,' her mother began.

'I see.' Lenny unlocked her door and strode in. She would not endure another scene in the corridor. She put Mr Silky's box on her desk. He mewed to be released but she ignored him. She faced her mother. 'What is it?'

It was her father, she thought suddenly. He was dead and she hadn't known it. She felt dizzy with fright. Her mouth opened to say something but her mother cut in: 'It's your granny. She's had another stroke.' Veronica stuffed a crushed tissue to moist eyes.

'Is she dead?' Lenny asked. She leaned against her desk and pulled out a cigarette. She was so relieved she almost cried herself.

'Not yet but they think ... oh, Lenny!'

'Tea?' Lenny reached for the *Sencha* tin.

'If ... if you're popping the jug on. We haven't had a cuppa together for ages.' While the jug boiled she looked around the office, took in the Japanese posters and the shrine.

'It's not right, all this Japanese stuff,' she said. 'It's going against your own kind.' She took the cup Lenny held out to her and sniffed at the Japanese tea dubiously.

'Chuck it away if you don't want it.' Lenny sipped hers. 'What do you want from me anyway? I visited her the other day. She was fine.'

'You didn't upset her, did you?'

'Once in my life I would really like to upset her,' Lenny said. 'But apparently I'm going to be denied that chance.'

'Lenny! Please come to the hospital to see her.'

'Nope,' Lenny said. 'I can't believe you think I'd consider it.'

'Please ...'

'No.'

'She loves you. She *does!* She's sick. She can't help the way she is. She's *sick*.' She hesitated. 'She loves us. She just can't control herself. She gets angry and frustrated more than other people. More easily. But she loves us, I'm sure. She's family.'

'I said no.' Lenny mashed her cigarette. 'Is that all then? I'm extremely busy.' She stood at her window, looking out, arms around her body. She was always afraid in these moments. Afraid that her mother would push past the clichés and ask her a tough question. She heard her office door click and turned, found herself alone.

There was a note on her desk, *Saint Vincent's. Ward 4B Geriatrics* and underneath: *Dad says hello*.

Mr Silky mewed and she peered in at him. Cats had no memories of their mothers. Most kittens were taken from their mothers from four to six weeks of age. If they ever met again, neither would recognize the other. It seemed to her a very satisfactory way of dealing with the family unit.

She dialled her parents' phone number.

'Hello?' Her father picked up on the tenth ring.

'Dad,' she smiled. 'It's Lenny.'

'Len.' He sounded ridiculously pleased and she rubbed watery eyes with her fingertips.

'You sound very weak.'

'No ... no. OK. You—?'

'I'm fine.'

'Careful ...'

'I am. I will be. Veronica was just here.' There was a long pause. He didn't like it when she called her mother Veronica.

'Len ...'

'I may visit my grandmother if I get time,' she lied. 'Shall I come and see you?'

'No. No.'

'Dad—'

'No. No.' He put the phone down, struggled for breath for a few moments. 'I don't want you ... to see me like this anymore.'

'Oh Dad ...' She spent the next half hour talking, keeping her voice buoyant. When she hung up she put her head down on her desk and cried for five minutes. Then she got up and washed her face. She had an appointment to keep.

At the Remand Centre, the guard didn't like the cat. He reached for a hankie the moment he saw it and gave Lenny muffled instructions through clammy sneezes. Lenny left the cat box under a tree. Mr Silky, hirsute allergen, settled down for a nap.

Lenny had visited the Remand Centre before, transporting prisoners to and from court. Max Curtis would not get an opportunity to grow champion roses here, she thought, taking in the grey walls and tiny, barred windows. There were exercise yards inside the complex but this was the only access to the outside for the inmates. Remand inmates were the most likely to try to escape or to harm themselves. Consequently, the Remand Centre was a high security institution.

David Breslin was waiting for her in a reception hall which boasted nothing in the way of hospitality. The hard-faced, muscular woman in the dark grey uniform asked to see some ID and made them sign a register.

During the short wait she and David Breslin made no small talk and the guard picked at her stained teeth with her little fingernail while her drip filter burbled.

Eventually another guard came to take them to Max. The guard was male, about thirty-five with a heavily pockmarked face and dark red hair. He said 'sir' to David Breslin and gave Lenny a nod. They followed him down the long corridors. All doors were numbered, grey walls lit by harsh fluorescent lights. Their footsteps echoed ahead of them, as if they were already where they wanted to be.

They were shown into interview room three. It was really two rooms: a tiny front office where someone could stand and watch through a soundproofed window, and a larger room where Max Curtis waited at a table.

The pock-faced guard left them with a new guard, a short squat woman with beady eyes, tightly curled hair and enormous breasts. She nodded at them as though answering a question.

'He's in there.'

'Thanks for pointing that out,' Lenny said.

Lenny sat across from Max, David Breslin at his side. Max had been crying, Lenny thought, noting the puffy skin around the eyes. He was pale, looked ill. He wouldn't last a year in prison.

'Hello, Max. Your father has asked me to investigate your case. I want to ask you some questions.'

'I can't allow you to call Mr Talbott my father.' Max shook his head. He met Lenny's eyes. 'I never wanted all this to come out. I was quite happy as I was.'

'Mr Talbott *is* your father,' Lenny said. 'You admitted it to the police. And there's your birth certificate and the letter your mother left for you when she died. It says Henry Talbott is your father.' She looked at him closely. The resemblance to Henry was there if you looked for it. But it was disguised by his pale colouring.

'I'm sorry about all the publicity you've had out of this,' Max said gently. 'It's a pity the newspapers had to drag up all that business with Michael Dorling. I hope you're doing all right.'

'I'm fine, thank you.'

Max smiled suddenly. 'I read all about your cat business in *The Age*. The RSPCA gave you a good review.'

'I didn't read it,' Lenny said. 'Max, what happened the night of the party?'

'Nothing happened to me, Ms Aaron. I was in my room having a cup of tea and a sandwich. Lizzie fixed me up with it earlier. They don't like me coming to the house if there's something on.' He said it without anger. Could anyone really be so accommodating, Lenny wondered. 'I was watching an episode of *The X-Files*. I tape them. Liz has got me into science fiction now. I watch everything I can. I think that young Ms Scully is a very fine woman.'

'So do I.' Lenny said. 'But I'm afraid the writers might force a romance between her and her partner.'

'Oh that would be a big mistake.'

'Yes.'

David Breslin growled and they both looked at him.

'Well,' Lenny said, 'you'd better give me some background. What happened to your mother?'

'She died when I was a teenager. She'd always been delicate.'

'She never told you Henry Talbott was your father?'

'No,' he agreed. 'She wanted to bring me up herself. I expect when she got sick she worried I'd have no one. No family. So she left me that letter with my birth certificate. It didn't mean anything to me at the time. I was just a boy. Later on I was angry. I was fostered and they were good people but I had a lot of anger then. Teenage stuff.'

'Why didn't you or your mother ever tell Mr Talbott?'

'My mother was proud. She didn't want his money and he'd been the one to end it. She didn't want him marrying her for the wrong reasons. She knew he didn't love her.'

'And why didn't *you* tell him, after your mother died? Didn't you want his money either?' Lenny was skeptical.

Max looked at his hands. 'I broke my own fingers, you know.' He placed his palms flat on the table. Lenny looked at the straight little fingers. 'They were bent. I hated him then. He never even knew about me and I still hated him for abandoning me. It was very unfair of me. One day I didn't want to look at them anymore. I used a hammer in my foster father's tool shed. It was easy to do the first one but damned near impossible to do the second. In answer to your question, Ms Aaron, I didn't tell him then because I enjoyed the drama of being the outcast. Teenagers are like that. We all look for something to define us, don't we? My particular role at that time was teenage misfit.'

'And later?'

'I went to gardening school and discovered there was something I could do well and that I loved. I always had a job and enough to live on. I never intended to contact Mr Talbott.'

'Max, no one will believe you gave up a chance at millions of dollars to work in a garden.'

'People will believe the truth,' Max said firmly.

'All right. How did you get the job at Brighton?'

'I'd finished up a six-month stint overhauling a big garden in Hawthorn. The employment agency had always had good reports about me so they set me up with a plum job, permanent gardener, live-in position. My own boss. I'd just hit my forties and I was looking around for a long-term job to see me through to my retirement. It seemed just the ticket. It turned out to be with Mr Talbott.'

'And you still didn't say anything?'

'I won't say I wasn't tempted. But shortly after I took up the position, Mr Talbott's new wife and children came on the scene and I knew it would only cause upset all around so I kept quiet.'

'You're really a saint, aren't you?'

'Really, Ms Aaron,' David Breslin interjected.

'Don't worry, Mr Breslin.' Max smiled. 'It's simply Ms Aaron's style. If you knew her better you'd like her. She's got a warm heart.'

Everyone paused for a moment to let this extraordinary statement sink in.

'What about Henry?' Lenny asked. 'Didn't he ever suspect?'

'No. Why would he?' Max rubbed his eyes. He was tired but dignified. It was hard to imagine a jury sending him down. But there were the police photographs of Carol Connor's head.

'Max, did you kill Carol?'

'No. I really didn't know the young woman. The police keep saying I was jealous of young Kendell. That I resented his beautiful girlfriend. Of course I didn't. I had no reason to harm her.'

'That's not true, Max. Carol doesn't like so many old people on staff. She told you to start looking for a new job.'

'Ms Aaron—' David Breslin again.

'Well, Max?' Lenny ignored the lawyer. 'You were so happy at Cedars Court. You had serenity, remember? And she wanted to take all that away from you. That's a reason to harm her, wouldn't you say?'

'Ms Aaron,' Max paused, sighed. 'My life has been a happy one. I have no complaints, no resentments. If I had lost my position and had to move on ... well, that's life. I did not wish to harm Ms Carol. I did not wish to harm Mrs Talbott.'

'You never resented Vivian?'

'No. I believe she's a little hard on her acquaintances. At least Liz seems to think so. But she was always gracious to me.'

'Who wrote the letters, Max?'

'I don't know.'

'Was it Liz Dodd?'

'No!' Max was emphatic. 'Ms Aaron, if they ever accuse Miss Dodd, I will confess to the murder myself.'

'Touching, Max. You're a romantic, aren't you? You've had the cook in love with you for years and you've kept your tragic secret. All this "we're just friends" stuff is nonsense. When did you tell her about your parents?'

'I shouldn't have told her,' Max said, 'but we were friends. I enjoyed her company. I've never been much for women as far as romance goes. Not that I'm ...' he blushed.

'I'm sure you're straight, Max. Go on.'

'I told her about ten years ago. I asked her to keep it to herself and, as far as I know, she did.'

'But she thinks you should have told Mr Talbott?'

'She has a strong sense of justice. Not my idea of justice, you understand? I don't want anything more than I have now. But Liz thinks differently. However,' he looked her straight in the eyes, 'having said that, I'm certain she had nothing to do with this terrible crime.'

'Max, how do you explain the blood at your door and on your clothes found in the tool shed?'

'Someone must have taken my things and put the blood on them. They didn't find any blood in my place or on my body. I was set up.'

'Max, if only you and Liz Dodd knew that Mr Talbott is your father, then who would bother to set you up?'

'I'm sure you'll find that out.'

It seemed their time was up as the squat guard came in and slapped Max's back.

'Up ya get, matey! Back to ya room now! Bit of TV'll fix you up!'

Max stood up. He nodded at David Breslin, smiled at Lenny and went with his jailer.

'I don't see that any of that was necessary,' David Breslin told Lenny. 'Frankly, considering your record, I'm appalled that Henry Talbott is allowing you anywhere near this case. A failed police officer turned cat catcher. Not a very reassuring curriculum vitae, is it?'

'Excuse me.' Lenny pushed past him and marched down the corridor.

Back in the car, Mr Silky began his mewing protests again. Lenny ignored him and gave the guard at the gate a wave. He nodded, kept his hankie pressed up to his nose.

In her wing mirror she spotted a tail, an old brown Holden with a dented fender. It stayed too close to her in traffic. It *had* to be a cop. She slowed down and, to her surprise, the Holden pulled alongside her. Ron MacAvoy was driving. He waved and gestured for her to follow.

She nodded and he cut ahead of her in the traffic taking the road to St Kilda.

MacAvoy found a park outside Greasy Joe's hamburger bar, but Lenny wasn't so lucky and it took five minutes to find a spot on the esplanade. Mr Silky sniffed the new location curiously.

MacAvoy had a booth near the back of Greasy Joe's. He was drinking a Carlton Draught. He never had any problems about on-duty drinking. Lenny guessed he was on duty now, all right. It was long past the social visit stage.

As she slid into the booth, his chili burger arrived and he wolfed into it. He grinned at the cat.

'The same,' Lenny said to the waiter and placed the cat box on the floor under the table. Mr Silky wowled and she kicked the box warningly. She glanced at MacAvoy. Past his prime but he was still a cop. And he wasn't stupid.

'Like the old days,' MacAvoy said.

'I don't think so. Why are you tailing me? Is it official?' She took her beer from the waiter and had three big gulps.

'Semi,' MacAvoy said, forcing a large piece of burger into his mouth. 'Mmm. I love this place. I gotta bring Jan here.' He peered under the table. 'This one yer own?' His tone suggested a pet would indicate a happy change in her life.

'A client,' she said flatly.

'Oh right. The business.'

Lenny's burger came and they ate in silence for a few minutes. She took a small piece of meat and pushed it into the cat box. Mr Silky sniffed it disdainfully but when Lenny sat back up again, there was the sound of greedy chomping.

MacAvoy wanted something from her. Let him ask for it. The burger was great—although Dr Sakuno would be disturbed by the amount of mammalian toxins she had put into her body in the last ten days.

'Lenny, you got something on the Talbott case we should know about?'

'No.'

'Lenny, if you're withholding evidence—'

'I'm not withholding anything,' she said. 'If I find evidence, it's yours. I haven't done that. Anyway, I thought you'd decided on Max Curtis.'

MacAvoy shrugged, finished his potato wedges and ogled Lenny's.

'Yeah well ... it's him.' But he sounded uncertain. He was not, despite his manner, a completely stupid man.

'But it's a little easy?' Lenny suggested. 'The blood outside his flat, the clothes in the tool shed. Ridiculously easy, don't you think?'

'He panicked. He was in shock. Or maybe he just wanted to be caught.'

'Or maybe someone else did it, MacAvoy.'

'Yeah, well ... D'you ever consider that the Connor girl was the intended victim?' he asked.

'Sure,' Lenny said. 'She didn't like the older staff members. She made it clear to them that their time was up. One of them could have been angry enough to attack her.'

'One of them could have been Max Curtis,' MacAvoy replied.

'I don't think so. And you know when Max goes on the stand, he's going to convince a lot of people that he's an innocent man.'

'Yeah, well I've got photos of a girl with half her head off and Max Curtis's axe in her back. But let's say for argument's sake, he's innocent. Who did it?'

'The security sensors on the garden walls were activated. It had to be someone at the party that night.' Lenny said.

'The boyfriend. Crime of passion.' MacAvoy believed strongly in crimes of passion.

'Motive?'

'She was cheating on him?'

'Other way around.'

'Argghh—' he reached out and took one of her wedges, then reddened at her look. 'Sorry.' He put it back. Lenny picked it up and tossed it onto his plate.

'I don't want it now you've had your fingers all over it.'

'Yeah, I forgot. Look, Lenny, a lot of people downtown think the old man's guilty. But you've been sniffing around and the boss wanted me to check it out.' He was a gumshoe in a cheesy thriller. He knew it and grinned at her.

'I have nothing to report,' Lenny said. She was ready to leave it at that but he ordered another beer. He looked at it, looked at her, looked at the beer again.

'You miss being a cop?' He sighed. 'You were one of the best young ones we had. You and Dan.' She resisted the bait but he answered the unspoken question for her. 'He's OK. Senior Sergeant now. Got a nice girl ... ' He wound down, embarrassed.

Of course he imagined she and Danny had been lovers. She said nothing.

'Len, if Max Curtis isn't guilty then the killer's still out there.'

'Your point?'

'Be careful, Len.'

'I can handle myself,' she said and saw his eyes on her arm. She felt a rush of anger, and embarrassment. This was the crux of it. He thought she was going to get hurt again and the arm was proof that she couldn't handle it.

She rose, picked up the cat box and walked to the counter. She never liked MacAvoy to see her angry, always played the ice-woman cop for him. Even in the hospital she didn't cry or in any way break down in front of him.

She paid for her meal and went out into the sunshine.

She put Mr Silky on the back seat of the Colt and sat quietly for a few minutes. She jumped as a hand rapped on her window and a head loomed through the glass. It was MacAvoy, beet-faced from running to catch her. She wound down.

'Lenny...' he said. 'Aw c'mon. You know I didn't mean to upset you. I say things the wrong way for you. I always have. What I'm trying to say is—'

'It's all right, MacAvoy.' She didn't look at him because she felt a little water sting her eyes. She started the engine and drove off quickly.

Mr Silky mewed. She took a cat snack from the glove box and handed it back to him. She went to her apartment.

Her answering machine flashed two messages and she replayed them as she fed Mr Silky. The first was her mother.

'Lenny? Lenny? It's Mum. I'm at the hospital but I'm going home now to pop Dad's tea on. She's ...' a pause for dramatic effect, '... she's all right. Still on the critical list but Dr Hinley says she's a fighter. Lenny, I really enjoyed our cup of tea.'

The next message was Kimberly Talbott: 'Ms Aaron, it's Kimberly. I'm at my father's condominium. Please call me today.' She could wait, Lenny thought.

She half filled a basin with warm water and baby shampoo. Mr Silky screeched when she immersed him but she had her leather gloves on and he clawed in vain. She wiped his eyes and sniffed his ears. There was an unpleasant smell.

Afterwards, she towelled the cat firmly and then used a hand dryer on the lowest warm setting to finish him off. His fur shone like glass and he settled on the armchair in front of the TV. Lenny flicked on the VCR and lifted the cat onto her lap. They sat together watching day fifteen of the Sumo. Takanohana in a shock defeat to Mainoumi. Akebono watched on the sidelines, no doubt guffawing inside. How did they keep it inside, she wondered. Weren't they sometimes just dying to let out a tiny smirk? Their faces were as blank as Lenny's account balance.

A year ago in a two-hour session with Dr Sakuno, she

had watched her first Sumo. At first she found it gross and ridiculous: fat men in diapers rushing each other, slapping, kicking and pushing. The fight lasted only a few seconds but the glaring and salt-throwing that preceded it could last up to five minutes. Intriguing.

Mr Silky had fallen asleep, his head against her thighs. He snored gently and his brown paws twitched. Dreaming of running free down a filthy alley with a half-eaten mouse or bird. It was the fantasy of all felines. Technically she should shove him off her lap and make him spend the night in his box. But she was still feeling—well, admit it, *funny*—about Cleo Harrelson. It had been an emotional day and the Birman was reaping the benefit.

She rewound the video and dialled the Talbott condominium number. Eric answered.

'Yes?'

'It's Lenny Aaron.'

He hung up. Lenny waited. From his perspective she supposed he had every right to be pissed off. When the phone rang she picked it up after the sixth ring. 'Hello?' Very coolly.

'Ms Aaron, it's Kimberly. My father asked me to call you and give you a message. Um ...' she hesitated.

'The message?' Lenny prompted.

'Ms Aaron ... Lenny, about last time we met. I hope you didn't think ...' she was whispering.

'I didn't,' Lenny lied. 'The message?'

'Oh, oh. My father contacted Mike and Sonny Buchanan. They'll see you tomorrow at two.' She gave Lenny a Brisbane phone number and address.

'I still need to interview your mother.'

'She's leaving the investigation up to the police now. She said it's best in the hands of professionals.'

'Ask her if she'll see me.'

'I did. She said no.'

Lenny's face warmed. She gripped the receiver. 'Then tell your father to *make* her see me.'

'I could do that ...'

'Do it.' Lenny hung up. Vivian still hadn't forgiven her, still blamed her for the murder.

She rang Qantas and made a reservation for Brisbane the next day. She also booked a rental car. Mr Silky stirred on her lap and she pushed him onto the floor. She wrote out an invoice for the Woodruffs. Seventy-five dollars plus a dollar-fifty for the Friskies. Mr Silky protested loudly at being woken and fleeced simultaneously. Lenny stuffed him into his box and headed for the car.

She parked down the street from the house in North Fitzroy. Mr Silky, sensing home territory, perked up.

'Calm down, stinky,' she said and rang the bell.

The door was opened by Mrs Woodruff's ginger-haired husband. His face lit up when he saw Mr Silky. He was carrying the toddler in his arms and the reunited threesome began a licking and stroking love-in.

'Where've you been, you bad cat?' Mr Woodruff gazed at Lenny, realizing who she was. 'Nella said you were good, but this is incredible! Listen, she's in the bath but she wants to thank you herself. Come in for a drink, won't you?'

'Thank you, but no,' Lenny said and handed him her envelope.

'Oh right. Shall I pay you now?'

'A cheque in the mail will be fine,' Lenny said. 'His ears smell. You should clean them out with rubbing alcohol on a cotton bud. If it persists then it may be an infection or earmites and you should take it to the vet.'

'Well, you're a wonder!' Mr Woodruff was impressed anew.

She got away from there fast leaving Mr Silky, who had forgotten she was alive, frolicking at his owner's feet.

The senior accountant was dead a few days later. Out on bail, he was gunned down on the way home from Safeway, groceries all over the street. His wife survived minus a piece of her jaw. An unusual Saturday in an otherwise geriatrically subdued Camberwell Junction, it made the papers all over the country.

Michael Dorling denied involvement. On TV he looked genuinely distressed, the unthinkable death of a dear friend.

Chapter 21

A COMA AND A TRIP TO BRIZZIE

Seven a.m. and the hospital was already too noisy. Breakfast trolleys were clanging and nurses were waking patients who wanted to sleep longer. Hospital, as Lenny recalled, was not a good place for sick people.

No one bothered to wake Mrs Sanderman for meals because she was in a coma. The withered body was hooked up to machines that beeped and flashed and there were tubes up the nose and down the throat. The mouth was not hanging open quite as grotesquely as it did in consciousness and, all things considered, Lenny felt her grandmother looked better than she had expected.

She had come deliberately early to avoid her mother. The nurses were not impressed.

'There are visiting hours, you know. People can't just waltz in when they please!'

'Should I leave then?'

'Well, you're here now. But stay out of the way.'

She stood at the bottom of the bed. Once more, she had brought nothing. The room already had a bunch of pansies. Courtesy of Veronica, she thought, who always brought pansies. There was also a big pink get-well card, signed 'from Veronica, Ted and Lenny xxx'.

She had come, she told herself, to witness the death scene. Standing at the bed, however, she did not feel any surge of victory. But neither was there a swing to compassion. This was it then, she thought. This was who she was now: a creature incapable of feeling.

'She's not long for this world, poor lovie ...' The old

woman in the next bed spoke. She was frail, translucent skin hanging off her bones.

'What?' Lenny jumped. The other woman had been asleep when Lenny arrived but was eager for a chat now. She had narrow green eyes and wore a woollen baby bonnet around her balding head. Her stainless steel side table was covered with cards and fruit.

'I'm not either.' The woman moved her head sagely. 'Cancer. I'm having chemo. The doctor says I'm doing nicely but I know my time's up. Is that your granny? Poor soul.'

'Mmm.'

'Could you switch the telly on for me?' She moved a hand slightly towards the remote control which was on her bed but still out of reach. Lenny flicked the TV on. Machines were easy. On and off.

'Going, dear?' the old woman asked. Lenny nodded. 'Well, you have a nice day and try not to worry. I'll keep an eye on her for you.'

Outside in the corridor, she found a nurse. Very young, very pretty and impatient.

'What is it? You're supposed to stay out of our way.' She was much younger than Lenny but had developed a nursing attitude that made her seem about fifty-five.

'What's the prognosis?' Lenny asked. The nurse rolled her eyes.

'Do I look like a doctor?' She raised the metal pan in her hands closer to nose level. 'I've got six of these to empty. Dr Hinley does rounds at nine.' She strode away.

Lenny had no intention of waiting around. She had an eleven o'clock flight. Before that she had a meeting with the two extra staff from the Talbotts' dinner party.

It proved futile. She met Sid and Nancy in a private study room at the university library. It was difficult to get past their excitement about the case. They made a show of concern but underneath there was the thrill of being a part of the murder of the year. No doubt they were campus celebrities.

They didn't remember anything significant. When not serving food or drinks, they had spent most of the night in the kitchen, watching the TV and nibbling leftovers. Liz Dodd kept them supplied with tea and coffee. They thought the old lady was sweet. They refused to believe she could have had anything to do with the murder. Neither of them had seen Max. Did they have their suspicions? Nancy hoped that Larry Burton was guilty. Apparently he had grabbed her bottom.

Munching her fruit plate and danish on the plane, Lenny put a line through their page in her notebook. The man next to her leaned across her body to open the window shutter and peer out at the land thousands of feet below. He grinned at Lenny.

'Do you mind?' She snapped the shutter closed. The man raised his eyebrows but he was handsome and she was not, so he didn't let it bother him too much. He smiled charmingly at the stewardess. 'Do you think I could trouble you for another whisky, my pet?'

It was humid at Brisbane airport. Lenny went to pick up her rental car and the breeze was a sticky mist. Brisbane was Queensland's capital city and, by its proximity to the Gold Coast, a tourist trap. It was famous for its houses, 'Queenslanders': white wooden squares with dark green tin roofs. They were built on stilts as a protection against floods. Wattle trees and a Hills Hoist completed the picture. The ones in better suburbs were renovated by yuppies; those in poorer suburbs demolished and replaced by flats.

The Buchanans' house was in Ascot, not far from the airport.

Lenny pressed the intercom button at the rococo bronze gates.

'Yes?' A woman's voice.

'Lenny Aaron.'

'I'll buzz you in, Ms Aaron.'

She parked next to a gross cherub fountain. Water spurted

from the baby mouth in a two-metre jet straight up into the air. There was birdshit on its cheeks.

A middle-aged woman in an ivory jacket and skirt met Lenny at the door. She looked cool and competent. Lenny was a sweaty mess. She followed gratefully into the air-conditioned foyer. It had an enormous curving staircase, the Tara of Aussie architecture.

'Mr Buchanan is waiting for you in the drawing room.' The woman led Lenny down a hall to the left.

Mike Buchanan was on the phone when Lenny entered the drawing room. It had spindly chairs in dark wood and heavy drapes. A King Charles Spaniel completed the picture of the peer at home. Mike waved Lenny in with a big smile, gestured for her to take a seat on the William Morris couch. The Spaniel, fat from over-indulgence, looked at her but didn't move from its chair.

'Lenny,' Mike hung up and thrust out a hand, pumped hers like an old friend or a game show host. 'Good to see you again. Quite a party we had!' He paused. After all, a girl was dead. Should he tone it down? 'So, what can I do to help? Henry's kid, eh? What a shocker!'

He reminded Lenny of his dog. Both had small mouths, too much hair and bloodshot eyes.

Mike leaned forward. 'So, what's the deal? You trying to get Max off?'

'That's right.'

'Tough job. But you look like you're up to it. How can I help? Anything for Henry.'

'Great.' She opened her notebook. 'A few questions then. You went to the party to get money from Henry, right?'

'Eh?'

'You wanted your wife to ask Vivian because of their special friendship,' she prompted. He remembered the conversation now and knew she hadn't been asleep.

'Now look, Lenny—'

'Did you get the money?'

'What the hell do you—'

'I don't think you did. Your wife had a spat with Vivian upstairs in the bedroom. Did she tell you that? I don't think you were ever going to get the money—and you knew it.' She kept her voice conversational. Only the words were provoking. 'Eric Hunter told me Henry might have helped you. But Vivian is going to have all the power through Kendell when Henry dies. And Vivian made it clear she was going to let you go under.'

'Eric? The fucking secretary cum wet nurse? What the hell does he know about anything? He's just a servant. When Henry dies he'll be down at the employment office checking the board. He doesn't know anything. You're not going to fucking pin this on me.' The big smile was gone. 'Why don't I just tell the police I saw Max coming down the stairs covered with blood, hmm?'

'The police didn't find blood on Max.'

'Well they found it on his clothes and on his fucking axe, didn't they?'

'Yes.'

'I'm still financially solid. Lenneee ... c'mon ...' When she didn't respond he cut the charm. 'You're reaching, Lenny. You're out of your league now, sweetie. Cats are your thing, right?' He lit a cigarette and offered her one. She refused and lit one of her own. 'No one at the party had the balls to go at Vivian with an axe. I mean ... I did. But I didn't.'

'Someone did.'

'Max.'

'I don't think so.'

'Yeah? Well, forgive me, but who gives a fuck what you think? Why don't you go and hassle Larry Burton? He's got nothing to do at the moment. I don't have time for amateurs.'

'Vivian is in danger,' Lenny said.

'Little orphan Vivvie?' Buchanan shrugged. 'She puts on the airs though, doesn't she? She was grooming that kid to take over from her. Do you think Ken would have married the kid without Mamma doing all the pushing?' Apparently not, Lenny thought. It seemed to be popular opinion that Vivian had pressed hard for the marriage.

Lenny rose, put out her stub in a crystal ashtray.

'I'll see your wife now,' she said.

The garden was filled with the lush scent of frangipani. She wandered down pink-tinged marble steps and across the lawn to an enormous yacht but didn't go aboard. She had never enjoyed sailing. She didn't like to imagine deep water underneath her. It wasn't particularly a fear of drowning. She just didn't like the idea of anything deep and dark.

She sat on a marble bench near the river and waited. It was quiet, only the odd boat puttering past. Lenny felt the sun burning her head and wished she had a hat. She wiped a hand across her damp face.

Sonny Buchanan teetered across the lawn in red heels and a red and white, skimpy sundress. From a distance she looked like an old style movie star with scarlet lips, yellow hair in fat waves and a push-up bra. Up close the image was less appealing. She was too brown. The breasts pushed over the bodice were freckled, her arms and legs scraggy.

She carried a glass of whisky in her hand and reeked of it. She sat next to Lenny, struck a pose, legs neatly and sexily crossed to the side, head thrown back to catch a little more sun under her huge hat. She waved a hand majestically at a passing boat and sniffled several times.

'I was the most beautiful deb this town ever saw,' she said. Her voice, as Lenny recalled from the party, had a rough, crackly sound from too much liquor. The nostrils were red again. But she was trying to hold it together. She was ten years older than Vivian but it looked more like twenty.

'I was supposed to find an establishment husband. I'm supposed to be Lady Buchanan,' Sonny smiled and patted Lenny's thigh with a brown claw. 'Oh, I have the right background: private schools, piano lessons, French, ballet, a year in Switzerland to Europeanize me, dilute the Aussie a bit. So why do you find me married to this pathetic *nouveau-riche* loser? And having made myself into a perfect wife for him to boot?' Her laugh was melancholy. Lenny was unexpectedly touched by it.

'Your father gambled,' she said. 'I read about it. He lost your family's money. So you married to regain it.'

Sonny inclined her head and studied Lenny, almost fondly. She finished her drink and tossed her glass into the river. It bobbed on the surface.

'You're a smart girl,' she said finally and stretched out her legs. Her knobbly knees were freckled but her ankles were delicate as were her wrists, a princess gone to seed.

'I tried to pretend nothing had changed,' Sonny said. 'I was seventeen when I married Eddie Bowman. He was very successful and only a little vulgar. Much too old for me, of course. That was something Vivian and I had in common. We used to laugh about it. But *I* didn't produce a baby. Vivian did that. Extra points.'

So Ed Bowman—'The King of Used Cars!'—had divorced her and married a fertile woman. Lenny had found it all in the gossip columns of the State Library newspaper archives.

'I suppose you think I'm pathetic?' Sonny asked. Lenny's sunglasses hid her eyes. 'Well, I suppose I am. I married Michael because he was up and coming and I needed the money. I went through Ed's settlement in six months. I used it to get Michael. He was really very unsophisticated. To him, I seemed like,' she smiled, 'a real lady. I didn't press him for children and thank goodness for that, hmm?' She looked arch. It was common knowledge that Mike Buchanan was gay.

'I didn't want to talk to you,' Sonny said. 'Do you mind if I have one?' She bummed one of Lenny's Marlboros. 'You're rather sweet.'

'Tell me about Vivian,' Lenny said. She wasn't going to be flattered or cajoled into missing anything. Sonny, though drunk and probably drugged, was no fool.

'We met in the early eighties. We were occasional lovers for about six years. Vivian initiated it. So, why not? I knew it wasn't really about me. She loved the success, the money. That excited her. But she was ... is the most beautiful woman in this country. I fell in love with her.' She shrugged.

'And Vivian?'

'Vivian didn't love me, if that's what you mean.'

'Did she end it?'

'Of course.'

'And?'

'Lenny—Leonie?'

'Helena.'

'Lenny, I didn't kill Carol. You wonder if I was drunk—I was—and couldn't tell the difference? I could never mistake anyone else for Vivian. I slept with her for six years. I adored her. She was the big romance of my life. Do you remember the 1984 Melbourne Cup? Vivvie and I in those ridiculous crinnies? With those enormous black hats? That was the most glorious day of my life.'

'You had an argument with Vivian last Tuesday at the party,' Lenny said. As it happened she didn't need to remember that Melbourne Cup scene. Her library search on Vivian had included photographs from the social pages. One in particular had caught her attention: Vivian and Sonny at the '84 Cup charming the TV cameras, naughty best friends with endless charge accounts. The highlight of the social calendar was 'The Cup', the second Tuesday of November each year. The horse race that stopped a nation. The rich and famous appeared at the track with baskets of gourmet goodies to eat from the back of the Merc before they mingled with the rest of the hoi polloi and the royal personage rented for the day. Not to make an appearance at the track was a sure sign of slipping.

'Yes, I had an argument with her,' Sonny looked out over the river. She squinted, lines deepening all over her face. 'Michael's panic is contagious. So I begged Vivian for help.

She's the one with all the real power. Henry's dying. Kendell's bound to get the lot. Vivian has him wrapped around her little finger.'

'And she laughed in your face.'

'I see you already know. Well, I was not very discreet. I was furious. She was crueler than before. I'd never experienced that level from her—and, really, Vivian is the cruelest person I know.' She kept her eyes on the water. 'I was deluding myself. She's not going to help me. On the contrary. Less power for me is more for her. That, finally, means everything to Vivian.'

'Did you know Carol Connor well?' Lenny asked. She kept returning to the fact that Carol was the body on the floor.

'We met once or twice at social engagements. I didn't like her. She was charmless, just sat there and let everyone run around for her.' It was said without malice. 'But Vivian had taken to her, so it was a fait accompli for Kendell.' She shrugged. 'She reminded me, of course, of Vivian. Part of it was calculated. The hair and clothes. But she had Vivian's ruthlessness too. A tough cookie.' She smiled and faced Lenny again. She looked tired and uninterested in pretence.

'I think,' she continued, 'that she'd have done anything to become Mrs Kendell Talbott. Vivian probably admired that. Kindred spirits.'

'Do you think Vivian and Carol had a relationship?' It was the first time Lenny had said it out loud. It had been on her mind from the start of the investigation. Vivian and Carol. They were so often together. A team. Vivian guiding and Carol imitating.

'Do you mean sexually?' Sonny was surprised but she gave it some thought. 'I doubt it. What would Vivian have to gain? She already had all the power in that relationship. As far as I know, sex was always motivated for Vivian. Even with me.' She stubbed out her cigarette. 'Michael and Henry were both so successful in the eighties. It was like a dream. Vivian was just attracted to the idea of the two most powerful women in the country being together. I know it now. I knew it then. It didn't make any difference. I was obsessed with her.'

Lenny felt her face beginning to burn. She took out her sunscreen and rubbed it on her nose and cheeks. Too late, of course.

'What time was your fight with Vivian?' she asked.

'Nine-thirty. Ten o'clock maybe. Are you trying to establish the time of death *Detective* Aaron?' It was said with unexpected sharpness. 'Did Vivian know your history when she hired you?'

'No,' Lenny said. Know what? That she was a loser, incompetent, afraid?

'Really? That's a surprise,' Sonny got up. 'You'd better come out of the sun. You're burning.'

Lenny followed her up the gangplank onto the yacht. Sonny fixed two whiskies. She tossed her hat onto a chair. Her stiffly waved hair was sweaty around the hairline and her lipstick had bled. Old lady like, she had forgotten the lipliner.

'My advice, for what it's worth,' Sonny said as Lenny savoured the coolness of her environment and fought off the sensation of wanting to take a nap, 'is to stop investigating. Just accept that Max did it.' She smiled thinly. Lenny saw that Sonny had learned the hard way about life's little expediencies. 'Henry's love child. Let Max go to jail. He'll be a model prisoner and get an early parole. I'm sure Henry has contacts.'

'Max is innocent.'

'Oh, Lenny, does anyone care?' Sonny kicked off her red heels and placed manicured brown feet on the couch. 'Henry, maybe and the old cook. But they'll both be dead soon. I can *smell* Henry's cancer, for god's sake. He won't last the year out. My husband will go to prison. And I'll get myself another divorce. If I'm really lucky, another husband.' She closed her eyes. Her mouth trembled a little and she finished her whisky in a gulp.

'I think Vivian's still in danger,' Lenny said. 'Whoever tried to kill her may try again.'

'Well it wasn't me,' Sonny said, 'in case you're asking. I can't answer for my husband. He's a very unpleasant man sometimes. Or did his charm fool you?'

'No.' Far from it, Lenny thought, but she wondered if Mike Buchanan would go so far as to kill to save his business.

Sonny looked around the yacht's bar room fondly. 'This is a nightmare, isn't it? We have to sell it, of course. We'll put the cash in my name so the bankruptcy courts can't touch it. Michael thinks I'll look after the money for him.' She laughed at the idea.

'Lenny, I'm going to go on believing that Max killed Carol. And I think you should do that too.'

It wasn't spoken like a threat. More like good advice. It was something Lenny already knew. If Vivian was in danger, then she was putting herself in equal danger with her investigation.

'Did you see anything on Tuesday?' Lenny asked.

'I heard Kendell and Carol arguing.' Sonny shrugged. 'Out on the terrace. I listened at the window. I couldn't see them but Carol's voice carries. She was very upset. I couldn't get the details but I doubt Ken was a faithful fiancé. Still, if you're marrying a man for his money you can't complain.' She spoke dryly. How many boyfriends had Mike Buchanan brought home over the years, Lenny wondered.

'Vivvie's been unlucky with her children,' Sonny continued. 'Ken's a nice boy actually. Sweet, very polite. But at the mercy of any woman who comes along. And zero head for business. And Kimmie is a psychologist's dream. Not that I blame her. Neither Henry nor Vivian gave her a scrap of attention from the day she was born. I know all about them, used to be a regular in that little circle. The twins, Vivian and the hench ladies.' She meant Annie and Margaret Gross.

'Tell me about them,' Lenny said.

'Annie and Maggie Gross?!' Sonny laughed loudly. 'You don't suspect *them*? You're on the wrong damn track if you do. They're her real family. They were both at the home with her, you know. They worship her. Vivian once told me that they'd both die for her and she meant it.'

'Does Annie have lovers?'

'Annie?' Sonny laughed. 'I always think of her as the last of the fat virgins. Annie is grateful for the chance to be an honorary Talbott.'

'Did Annie and Maggie know about your relationship with Vivian?'

'Of course. Sometimes Annie phoned me to arrange things. Maggie treated me like a protective mother treats her daughter's biker boyfriend. Yes, they both knew. But I wasn't Vivian's only lover so it wasn't a shock to either of them. I should think Vivian is indulged.'

'Have you ever known Annie to be violent?'

'No, though I'm sure she could be if she thought Vivian or the children were in danger. She's odd-looking, don't you think? That big body with those spindly arms and legs? Creepy. Vivian says its left over from the Cushing's Syndrome but personally,' she held out her own chicken wing arm for appraisal, 'I've always thought fat people are disgusting.'

'Have you talked to Vivian since the murder?' It was her wind-up question.

'I *saw* her. Yesterday. Our taxis crossed in traffic. She was headed for the airport. I had a moment's fantasy that she'd come to see me. I imagine, Lenny, you've discovered that a lot of people wouldn't care if Vivian died. But I'm not one of them. I'd still care very much. However idiotic that may sound.' Her eyes watered helplessly. 'But I have made a decision to put this behind me. For better or worse, Vivian is a part of my past now.'

Yeah, yeah, Lenny thought, brushing aside the melodrama.

Vivian had been in Brisbane yesterday, not hiding out in her Toorak mansion. What did that mean?

'Was anyone with her in the taxi?'

'No.'

'How did she look?'

'Lovely, poised, our dream girl.' A harsh laugh and penetrating glance told Lenny that Sonny knew exactly how she felt about Vivian.

The flight back to Melbourne was delayed an hour. Lenny was impatient for action. She rang Henry's St Kilda Road condominium. No answer. She left a message. She wanted him to force access. Vivian had to see her.

Chapter 22

ANNIE AND MAGGIE

She taped pieces of white card onto her living room wall and onto these she printed the names of the key players. Lines radiated connections between suspects, blue for family, red for others. She flicked through her notes again. She couldn't see the connection yet, although logic and experience suggested that, in a case involving this much wealth, she would find the answer if she followed the money.

She got an apple from the fridge and put it on the plinth in front of her home shrine, lit incense and put her hands together. At home she prayed to the eleven-faced, thousand-armed bodhisattva, a copy of the 900-year-old gilded statue in Kyoto. There were two requests today: the death of her grandmother, the life of Cleo Harrelson. Oberon Wellington had left a message on her machine. Cleo was doing fine. He would add the price of the call to her account.

She was going to have to deal with the cat issue once and for all. She knew she said that about so many things: her parents, Mike Bullock. She put things off until they reached crisis point. It was not sensible to shell out hundreds of dollars in vet fees for a cat nobody wanted.

The Cosmic Exchange, as so often happens when you really need it, was engaged. Lenny ate the apple grumpily then took a small handful of Aspirin before falling into bed.

She dreamt about Sonny and Vivian. It was Melbourne Cup day with herself as jockey. She wore jaunty red and green silks and rode the winning horse. Sonny looked young and happy and Vivian gave Lenny a cool kiss on the cheek, whispering something she couldn't quite hear. Then a Sumo wrestler muscled past Sonny and threw salt at Lenny's horse. She stared in amazement and woke up. It was morning.

The shower water hurt her sunburned scalp. The phone rang while she was drying herself and she let the answering machine get it. Who rang at six-thirty in the morning anyway? Maybe it was her mother with news about Granny Sanderman. Not on an empty stomach, she thought.

'Ms Aaron, this is Margaret Gross,' said the machine tersely. 'Please come to Mrs Talbott's Toorak home at ten a.m. I believe you have the address.'

Lenny dressed with more care than usual in baggy black jeans and black, slim-fitting, soft leather waistcoat over a black and white striped t-shirt. She tried a lipstick and then wiped it off impatiently.

She knew the Toorak address. She had driven past it several times in the past nine days, watching the press and the security guards. It was Vivian's fortress until Max was officially incarcerated.

Lenny parked around the corner to avoid creating a scene. A security guard and two young reporters lounged outside the house. The reporters knocked each other over sprinting to get to her. They had had little luck. A few snaps of Vivian at the window. There had been no interviews and no quotes.

'Why are you here today, Lenny? Weren't you fired? How's Vivian? Are you seeing her today? Listen, we can pay good money ...'

The security guard checked her licence and let her past. Margaret Gross was waiting inside.

Lenny saw at once that the housekeeper was not going to be an easy interview. There was a high spot of colour on each cheek and her breath was minty. She wore a black dress, high necked and long skirted but too tight in the sleeves. Her upper arms were pinched, pink salamis.

'You'd better come in then,' Margaret said, and Lenny followed her into a room at the front of the house. The blinds were drawn. Margaret clicked on the lights. The room was decorated in soft yellows and ivories.

Lenny took a seat near the window. The housekeeper sat

opposite her on a couch. She sat forward, placed her feet close together and dropped her hands into her lap. The movement looked rehearsed.

'Ask your questions and let's be done with it,' she said, eyes somewhere above Lenny's head. 'Vivian said I was to answer anything you asked to the best of my knowledge. Then Ms Baron will see you. Then Vivian herself.'

'What did you see at the party last week?' Lenny asked.

'I was in the dining room, as you were. I saw what you saw.'

'You'll have to do better than that. Do you believe Vivian is still in danger?'

There was a long pause. 'Yes ... yes, I do,' the housekeeper said finally. She pressed her lips together and smoothed the dress on her knees, glancing at the liquor cabinet briefly. 'Vivian told me all about those letters. After that fuss in the kitchen with Liz Dodd's pink paper I knew something was going on. I made her tell me. Why would she keep it from me for so long?! She can trust me with her life. She knows that!'

'Annie knew from the start,' Lenny provoked.

'Why would she tell her? Just because—' Margaret reddened and stopped.

'Is the danger from inside the family?' Lenny asked.

Margaret shrugged. 'I'm worried about her,' she said.

'Then you'll want to help me.'

'You're the one who's hurting her,' Margaret said. 'If you'd just leave it alone! She fired you, didn't she? The police have arrested Max, so that's that!'

'He's not the killer.'

'Max Curtis pretending to be a gardener!'

'He *is* a gardener,' Lenny pointed out.

'He's dangerous.'

'I don't think so,' Lenny said. 'Does Vivian really believe she's safe now?'

'Yes, she does,' Margaret nodded firmly. 'She told me

everything will be all right. And I believe that. If you'll just leave it.'

'So what's the danger?'

'Nothing! No one!'

'You said she's still in danger—'

'I didn't! I—' Margaret reached into her pocket, pulled out a packet of peppermint Lifesavers, put two into her mouth and crunched on them as though they were sedatives. 'I just said it. I didn't mean anything.'

'What happened the night of the party?'

'I don't want to say anything. There's been so much publicity. The press won't leave it alone, you know.'

'Just answer me!' Lenny had made a fist with one hand and Margaret stared at it.

'Mr Burton,' she said, disgusted. 'He threatened Vivian's life.'

'You heard him?'

'She told me. He's got some mad idea that she's to blame for his dreadful show being taken off the air. It was about time, I say. It was lewd.'

'Anything else?' Lenny asked. 'I mean anything *you* actually saw?'

'No.'

'Margaret—'

'The answer is no.' The housekeeper turned her eyes to the ceiling.

'Maggie,' the tranquil voice from the doorway made them both pause.

Had Vivian been listening the whole time? Her hair was tied back in a loose ponytail, a few strands around her face. She was thinner. Stress? Fear? Her violet eyes were overly bright like a child who had had too much excitement.

'Maggie,' Vivian soothed her housekeeper, 'Lenny's trying to find out who killed Carol. We have to help her. I want you to do that for me.'

She smiled at Lenny. 'I'll be in my room when you've

seen Annie.' She hesitated. 'She's been upset by all this.' The message was 'so be kind to her', but Vivian didn't press it. She waved a hand and left them. The housekeeper took a shoulder-lifting breath, fortified by Vivian's visit.

Lenny paused. Certain subjects seemed bound to produce hysteria. Perhaps she could lead up to it gently. First she went to the liquor cabinet and poured two gin and tonics. Should have thought of it before. Margaret looked at the glass, knowing she was 'on duty', and then took it anyway. 'I shouldn't really,' she grinned.

'Oh, spoil yourself.' Lenny drank half her G & T. It was heavy on the G.

'Tell me about Vivian,' she said.

'She was head and shoulders the best-looking girl in Gympie,' Margaret said. From what Lenny knew, Gympie was not a mecca for starlets or pageant winners.

'And Annie?'

'She was all right, I suppose. Pretty but not special like Vivian.'

'When did she get sick?' Lenny asked.

'After Vivian had the babies they moved into Cedars Court. Annie was already getting heavy then. I told her she looked terrible. But she said she'd be fine. Then she got bigger and bigger and her face and neck were all red. Vivian took her to a specialist and he said it was Cushing's Syndrome. It's a pity for her because she'd always been slender before. At the children's home she was as skinny as Vivian.'

'Do you have any pictures of the children's home?'

'No.' Margaret sighed. 'And it's gone now. Burned down a few years after we left. Mr Denny and the kiddies got out. He retired. He was sixty then. I suppose he'd be eighty now. Goodness! Maybe he's not even ...'

'What about your own photographs?' Lenny dragged her off memory lane.

'Vivian took them. She said she didn't want to remember a time before she was Mrs Henry Talbott.' She tutted, but fondly. 'She was such a sweet little thing.'

'You're very close to Vivian, aren't you?' Lenny smiled. Margaret beamed, easily set up for the sucker punch. 'Only Annie's closer to her than you.'

'Oh, I'm much closer! Much, much, much closer! Did Vivian tell you that Annie is closer?'

'No.'

'Vivian's like my own little girl!'

'Who do you think killed Carol?' Lenny changed tack abruptly.

'Max,' Margaret said firmly.

'What happened when I left Vivian with you, after the murder? Did anyone come into the room?'

'A doctor popped in and examined her. And the police, of course. It didn't do them any good. I'd given Vivian a sleeping pill. She slept like a baby the rest of the night.' Margaret's hands clenched around her empty glass. 'She was in shock.'

'Did she speak about it, did she say she knew who did it?' Lenny pressed.

'She said it was Max.'

Lenny wrapped up the interview, wondering if her interrogation skills had slipped. She couldn't get a grip on this case.

Ten minutes later, Annie Baron entered the room carrying a tray with a Japanese teapot and two cups. There was also a plate of mouse-sized *mochi* and flower-shaped sugar sweets.

Annie hadn't bothered to put on make-up. Her hair was up in the familiar bun. The blue eyes darted around the room, and the hands, nails nibbled, moved restlessly. After she poured the tea she sat on her hands.

'I'm upset,' she said quickly and lowered her head for a moment. 'This is awful. You have to leave us alone now. Vivian says if we go to Europe and have a holiday, everything will be all right again.'

'Annie, tell me what you know,' Lenny sipped her tea and

ate a *mochi*. It was superb. What did they put in these things?

'Carol's dead.' Annie said.

'Yes,' Lenny said. 'Did you like her?'

Annie nodded then shook her head, hesitated.

'You're trying to trick me! You're trying to hurt Vivian.'

'No I'm not.'

'She said not to trust you.'

Lenny should have been prepared for this. Who trusts a cat catcher with their life?

'I know you had a hormone problem,' she changed the subject. 'You're fat now because you had Cushing's Syndrome, right?'

'Yes ... '

'I read about it. You put on weight and there's hair growth and skin rashes.' And mental deterioration too.

'You're trying to upset me.'

'Annie, Max will go to jail for the rest of his life and I think he's innocent. Are you protecting one of the children?'

'I love them,' Annie said.

'Kimberly doesn't like you.' She was being cruel because it got results.

'I love Kimmie.'

'Does their mother love them too?'

'Yes.'

'Would she do anything to protect them?'

'Yes.' Annie nodded, on solid ground again. She pulled out a large hankie. 'Of course she would. How can you ask that?' She blew her nose long and loud.

'Tell me about when the twins were born. You were with Vivian, weren't you?' Lenny said.

'At St Anthony's,' Annie agreed. 'It was terrible!' She covered her mouth for a moment with a trembling hand, remembering. 'They couldn't stop the bleeding. Dr Brown was wonderful.' She smiled faintly. 'And then the babies were so pretty!'

'Was Vivian happy with them?'

'Of course.' Annie smiled and the tension fell away from her. 'We were so happy. Then Vivian married Henry ... Mr Talbott. We had a big wedding.' She smiled, lost in her memories. 'Henry was handsome at the wedding.'

'I saw the photos,' Lenny said. Henry, at sixty-nine, had been a bull-necked old man.

'Tell me about the children's home.'

'I liked it,' Annie said, 'but I like it here much better.'

'Maggie was the nurse, right?'

'Yes. She took care of us when we were sick and needed to go to the doctor. Mr Denny took the boys but Maggie always went with the girls. She waited outside for us.'

Annie squeezed the damp hankie in her lap. 'I'm so fat. I'm ugly now. I used to be pretty. I don't understand it. But I'm healthy. Everything's all right.'

'Tell me about the Gympie doctor.'

'He was nice ...' Annie said. She shook her head and stood up. 'Vivian said you'd try to trick me. Are you tricking me now?'

'What about the dog?' Lenny asked. Her coldest voice. Annie stopped in her tracks. Her mouth opened. She shook her head.

'The dog in Gympie. The one you killed,' Lenny pressed.

'I never,' Annie whispered, frightened. Her hands made fists that rubbed against her thighs. 'That dog frightened Vivian!'

'Did you like killing it?'

'No!'

'Did you ever burn anything?'

Annie squeaked in fright and stuffed a hand into her mouth. 'I won't tell you!' She ran out of the room.

Chapter 23

REFUSING THE UNREFUSABLE OFFER

The house was silent. Lenny walked up the staircase. It was lit by a skylight allowing her to admire black and white photographs of Vivian all the way up the wall. They were glamour shots by famous photographers. One was deliberately blown out so that what remained was a hint of dark hair and huge eyes. It was compelling, reminding her of someone she couldn't quite place. Of Kimberly perhaps. There were no photos of Henry or the children. The staircase was covered in thick carpet on which Lenny walked soundlessly.

At the top she heard a TV, followed it to an open door and went in. Vivian sat at a desk near the window. She was waiting and didn't pretend to be doing anything else. Her eyes dwelt on Lenny's perky outfit and she smiled slightly. The mini TV on the desk was peddling a news program. The sound was low.

Vivian had loosened her hair and it hung around her shoulders. The slight frailty added to her beauty. Her slim hands lay perfectly still in her lap and she appeared calm.

'I'm stuffed to the brim with pills,' she said. She sighed. 'The doctor thinks it's best. I mean, I don't take as many as he thinks I should. But I have had a *very nasty shock*.' She used pompous doctor tones.

'People have been saying things about you,' Lenny said. It was her planned opener. Vivian accepted it with a laugh.

'All true, I'm sure,' she drawled self-mockingly. 'I did warn you at the start of all this that I'm a bitch. So I don't suppose you're surprised to find the proof of it.' She lit two

Dunhills and handed one to Lenny. 'Were Maggie and Annie any help?'

'Sort of,' Lenny said. It was an evasion and Vivian knew it.

'Maggie has a drinking problem and Annie is, as you know, no rocket scientist. I doubt either of them could be relied on. In court, I mean.' It was said in a whimsical tone but Lenny didn't mistake the penetrating eyes. She was being warned off. Vivian *knew* who the killer was.

'I guess so,' she said. 'You know that victims of Cushing's Syndrome can become mentally unbalanced?'

'You've mentioned this before.' Vivian shrugged. She tapped some ash into her ashtray.

'She's very close to your children. She's interested in your husband and she's unattractive. She has plenty of reason to be jealous of you.'

'I agree,' Vivian said.

'So?'

'Annie doesn't hate me.'

'You don't believe she could hurt you?'

Vivian chewed the inside of her mouth. She shook her head.

'I won't believe that,' she said after the longest pause so far. She sat up straight. 'I'm not going to talk about Annie.'

'Are you afraid of her?'

Vivian averted her eyes. 'Of course not.'

'Did she always have psychological problems? Even before the Cushing's Syndrome? Perhaps the disease only exaggerated problems she already had?'

'I won't discuss Annie any further with you, Lenny.' Vivian was cool.

'You're withholding information ...' Lenny tried a tough police interrogation voice but it was a pathetic failure. Vivian began to laugh.

'Yes,' she agreed.

'Have you had any more letters?' Lenny changed tack.

'Why would I? Max is in jail.'

'We both know Max didn't write the letters,' Lenny said. Her palms were moist.

'Liz Dodd wrote them,' Vivian said finally.

'Are you sure?'

'Of course. I've thought about it. I think they're in it together.' Vivian crossed a leg man style—ankle over knee. She managed to make it incredibly sexy. She was a subtle but exquisitely successful flirt.

'Tell me about the night of the party,' Lenny said. She felt colour in her face. Was this how Sonny Buchanan felt? Intoxicated?

'It'll be the most famous of all my dinner parties—and it was going to be so dull too!' Vivian smiled wickedly then looked angry with herself and a little ashamed. 'Lenny, I try to cope with things by ... I'm not very good at dealing with loss. Carol was very special. I'm not the kind of person who goes all sentimental, you know ...' She paused, collecting her thoughts. She finished her cigarette and lit another one.

'First of all,' she continued, 'I feel so guilty about Carol.'

'Did you have a relationship with her?' Lenny asked. Vivian raised her eyebrows.

'What a dirty little question. Is this your police gutter training? You know, I've always despised the police.'

'That's not an answer,' Lenny pointed out.

'A sexual relationship? Certainly not. She wasn't my type at all,' Vivian shot back. She was angered by the question. 'You really think I'd sleep with my son's girlfriend?'

'I think if you fancied her, you wouldn't let Kendell stand in your way.'

'Well, perhaps that's true. I don't pretend to be a great mother.' Vivian smiled grimly. 'But the last thing on my mind was sleeping with Carol.'

'So why the guilt?'

'It's my fault. You know that better than anyone. I made a joke of those stupid letters. I should have hired a professional security team. It was too much. For you, I mean. I read about you in the papers. All that stuff with that man, Michael Dorling? God, what a monster! I know that it must have been sickening for you ...' She paused again, choosing her words carefully as Lenny hid her reaction: 'I shouldn't have been angry with you. It was too much to expect that you—'

'No it wasn't,' Lenny cut her off.

'Lenny, you know how I feel about you. But I was in shock. I don't blame you anymore. Not really. After I read about you in the paper, I knew you must be suffering too.'

'Fine.' Lenny gritted her teeth for a moment. 'You fired me. I'm working for your husband now.' *You know how I feel about you*?

'I didn't *need* a detective anymore. That's why I fired you. Max was in custody. The investigation is finished.'

'No.'

'Henry knows Max is guilty,' Vivian continued. 'The police have arrested Max and I'd like it left at that.' The violet eyes narrowed a fraction. 'Do you think it's easy for me? This scandal with Max? Kendell and Kimberly have a man who's old enough to be their grandfather telling anyone who'll listen that he's their brother. You realize he could have killed any of us at any time? We trusted him.'

'Henry believes Max is innocent,' Lenny insisted.

'No. He's had a shock and he's old. He feels remorse for the past. Dying men try to make amends.' Vivian paused. 'If I thought this was about money, I'd match his offer to you, ask you to stop. But it's not about money, is it? You're on a mission, the comeback trail.' Their eyes locked, then Vivian smiled and touched a hand to her brow briefly, regretfully.

'I'm sorry,' she said. 'Why shouldn't you do as you please? I always do. Why anyone would want to be a detective, though ... Ask your questions. Let's be done with it.' It was said gently and fondly, as though they were old friends resolving a minor crisis.

'You fought with Sonny Buchanan,' Lenny said. 'Do you believe she or her husband are capable of killing you?'

'You were a policewoman, Lenny. You know anyone is capable of killing given the right motivation and convenient circumstances.' Vivian shrugged, looked bored. 'But I doubt Mike has the brains to set up my gardener. And that's what you're suggesting, isn't it? Would he kill me because I'm standing in the way of a big business reconciliation with Henry? I am. Henry's money will go to Kendell. All of it. There's no space left for Mike Buchanan. And, believe me, if the boot was on the other foot, he wouldn't be offering me any charity either. But it's just business.'

'And Sonny?'

'She's become everything she once hated. Too much hair dye, too much suntan, too much everything.' Not a scrap of leftover affection there.

'She loves you,' Lenny said, pretending to peruse her notes.

'That doesn't obligate me, does it?' Vivian said flatly. 'Lenny, Sonny is an old lover. She makes a fool of herself sometimes but, as you say, she still loves me. She wouldn't hurt me.'

'Did she threaten you?'

'She said "I'd like to kill you", but she's said that before. I told you, she gets drunk. She makes an idiot of herself.'

'Maybe this time she decided to do it.'

'No.' Vivian was certain. Lenny didn't believe it either.

'Larry Burton?' she asked.

'Larry?' Vivian was surprised and amused. She definitely didn't consider the TV host a threat.

'Kendell heard him talking to you in the hallway. He seems to believe that you're responsible for his show being cancelled. That if you were out of the way, Henry would allow the show to extend a couple of years.'

'Oh *that*!' Vivian laughed and lit another cigarette. 'His

show was shit and that's why it's been cancelled.' She shrugged. 'He's a toad. He seduced Kimberly. Can you believe it? The little idiot. She's nothing to look at, so she's an easy target.'

'Did he threaten you?'

'Maybe. Sometimes he does. He was drunk. He's looking for someone to blame. Look, Lenny, Henry asked my opinion about the show and I told him to go ahead and cancel it. But whatever Larry may imagine, Henry just wanted his own opinion verbalized. It was never my decision.'

'Did he *threaten* you?'

She thought about it again. 'Yes, he did. But only in an "I'll get you, you bitch" kind of way. That never means anything.'

'Someone got Carol that night.'

'The little idiot wanted to be me. My style, borrowing my clothes—' Vivian was subdued suddenly. 'I encouraged it. I thought it was cute.'

'I heard Carol in the garden,' Lenny said. 'Did she often fight with Kendell?'

No hiding a genuine reaction. Vivian's eyes widened and she took a tiny breath. She was afraid, Lenny thought. Why? Because she knew *Kendell* was the killer?

'We're all in black here for Carol,' Vivian said finally, face set. 'Except Kimberly, who refuses to.'

'Kendell isn't either,' Lenny persisted. 'In fact, he already has a new girl on display.'

'Kendell, like his father, has a sexual ... compulsion,' Vivian said coldly. 'I tried to explain this to Carol. But she thought Kendell was humiliating her. They fought occasionally. It was nothing. She would have learned to live with it.'

'Would Kendell hurt her?'

'Don't be ridiculous!' Vivian was furious. 'Lenny, Kendell is not a perfect boyfriend but he is not violent. Whoever murdered Carol—and I believe it was Max—did so because they thought it was me. No one had any reason to hurt Carol. I told her parents that.'

It was a tangent but Lenny followed it.

'You went to Queensland?' she said. Vivian nodded, unconcerned. 'Were you visiting the Connors?'

'There's been a delay over the release of Carol's body,' Vivian said. 'The Connors want to bury her but they can't. I wanted to see them. In a way, I was closest to Carol. I thought I could comfort them. Especially Mrs Connor.'

'As one mother to another?' Lenny said, not hiding her disbelief. She didn't see Vivian holding hands with Mrs Connor and fighting back the tears.

'It's the truth, Lenny,' Vivian said. 'I did visit the Connors and I did try to comfort them. I miss Carol.' She seemed surprised, as if she was realizing it for the first time. 'She was a lot of fun.'

'Vivian, I believe you're still in danger. And I think you know who the killer is.'

'And if I tell you, you can save me? Forgive me, Lenny, but you had your chance and Carol is dead.' Vivian finished her cigarette and straightened her posture, uncrossed her legs.

'You told Annie not to trust me,' Lenny said.

'Oh, Lenny, stop it!' It was a return to the warm smile of earlier, accompanied by a graceful shrug of the shoulders. 'Come to Europe with us.' The invitation came as the ultimate seduction. 'After the trial we're all going to the house in Vienna, then Florence, Paris and London. London in summer—you'd enjoy it.'

'As what?'

'Anything you want.' Vivian smiled and fluttered her lashes again.

'Why?'

'Because you're a very sweet girl.'

This was ridiculous enough to make them both smile. Lenny knew what was on offer—paid companionship or paid lover. Her choice. Her life in comparison was pathetic:

sniffing out cats for a living, her grandmother and father both dying, neither quietly, and her mother ever an unresolved problem.

'Who are you protecting?' she asked.

'I'm the only one who can save my life, Lenny,' Vivian said. 'That's the truth. It's you who is putting me in danger.'

'Larry Burton saw you arguing with Eric Hunter,' Lenny cut in. 'I suppose *he* threatened you too?' She was sarcastic, wanted a return to toughness, rejected the seduction.

'I threatened him,' Vivian corrected. She didn't register disappointment. She just went blank again. Like she had an internal switch, waiting to click to the next required emotion.

'How?'

'His self-confidence—based on nothing—is beginning to bore me. When Henry dies, he's fired. I told him that.'

'Because he's homosexual?'

'Because he's a two-faced, disloyal, back-stabbing creep.'

'He could be favoured in Henry's will.'

'Not a chance.' Vivian was certain. 'He's doing a nice little routine: the caring companion. Maybe he even *does* care. But when it comes to money, nothing is more important than family. Eric will be lucky if he scores a gold watch and a stuffed platypus.'

'When did you last see Carol alive?'

'Around eleven o'clock.' Vivian had anticipated this question. It was one of the first the police would have asked. 'So I imagine I was one of the last to see her alive. She was upset after a tiff with Kendell. She wanted to go upstairs for a while.'

'Did you go up with her?'

'No.'

'Why was she in your room?'

'She liked my room. She was always in there. I don't know. Do you suppose Max was waiting in there the whole time?' She shivered.

'I don't know,' Lenny said. She had thought about that

question a lot. The killer hiding in a wardrobe or behind a door. Then Carol entering, the killer seeing only the slim figure, long dark hair and black dress. Already confused by anticipation, blind to the little clues that showed the woman was Carol and not Vivian. Then the first blow. The thwack against bone and the spurt of blood.

'Is one of the twins the killer?' Lenny asked. She felt now that this must be the answer. There was no other reason for Vivian to protect anyone.

'No.'

'Would you do anything to protect them?'

'They've given me everything in my life,' Vivian said simply and stood up to indicate the interview was over. They walked down the stairs together.

'This one is good.' Lenny stopped before the big eyes portrait. Again she had a feeling of recognition.

'Is Maggie your mother?' she asked at the door, as her hand was on the door knob in fact. The old eleventh hour trick. The Colombo question: *Arrgh ... just one more thing, Ma'am*, the crumpled look on the killer's face. But Vivian only smiled.

'How unflattering! You can't think we look alike? Of course she isn't. She's my old nurse, that's all. How very peculiar you can be.'

They held hands at the door for a moment. Officially a handshake but neither moved their hand away. Lenny glanced at the long cool fingers.

'I may need to ask you more questions,' she said. Vivian shook her head.

'Max will be convicted. This will all end naturally and you'll be left with nothing to investigate.'

Lenny slammed into her car, switched the radio on loud then pulled out too quickly and was honked by a passing Volvo.

She drove to Oberon Wellington's office. He was busy amputating a dog's hind leg and couldn't see her. Two guilty parents and a dirty six-year-old were sobbing together in the waiting room. They held a bloodied dog blanket in their hands.

'Mother backed over it,' old Mrs Wellington giggled as she led Lenny through to the side office where the patients were kept. There were two cat cages with low baskets in them. One contained a Somali with all its paws bandaged.

'Stepped in spilled cooking oil,' Mrs Wellington explained as she unlocked Cleo Harrelson's cage. A bandaged head raised at the clang and a blue eye peeked out at them. An eye, Lenny thought, not eyes. She was relieved to see that there were still four legs though.

'I'll leave you two alone for a little moment,' Mrs Wellington said. 'I'm having a cuppa. Can I get you one?' Lenny thought about the grease-stained kitchen. She shook her head.

Alone with the cat she didn't know what to do. Cleo was still splinted and couldn't stand. Did the blue eye look mournful? Accusing? Lenny reached out a hand and stroked the warm body gently. Cleo pressed against her hand. *Oh god!*

'Look,' she said, 'I didn't mean you to get your eye out. I thought you'd just go off somewhere.' Not true. Cleo should have been hit by a car and killed. That was what happened to strays. Cleo mewed very softly and a scratchy tongue licked Lenny's fingers. She pulled her hand away.

'I'm not keeping you, get it? I'm not. When you're better you'll be going to the ...' She couldn't say it and turned away angrily. Mrs Wellington came back into the room with a chipped Bunnikins mug of tea.

'I thought you needed it, dear,' she said. 'You know it'll be seven hundred for the operation plus care? Oberon wanted me to tell you. Drink up now.' She offered the cup but Lenny didn't take it.

'It's chipped,' she said. 'I can't drink anything from a chipped cup. Don't you know that germs breed in chips?'

'Eh?' Mrs Wellington blinked.

'This place is filthy. You've got a nerve calling it a veterinary clinic. I could have your licence.'

'Oh goodness,' Mrs Wellington slapped her side. 'If Oberon could hear you, dear, he'd add an extra fifty to your bill out of perversity. He's a one.' She looked into the cup. 'I'll give this to Mrs Herbert then. She's hysterical. I don't suppose a few chip germs will worry her.'

Lenny drove home miserably. She sensed dirt everywhere and spent two hours cleaning the venetian blinds. To get at the parts between the strings she had to use wadded-up tissue paper and toothbrushes. She was pouring with sweat when she finished but the blinds sparkled.

The phone rang while she was drinking tea. She expected Vivian but it was Eric Hunter, his voice hollow, shaking.

'Henry's dead,' he said.

The dead accountant and the shredded ledgers made conviction a problem. The two junior accountants were unwilling to testify against a beloved employer and had no knowledge of the second set of books. Lenny was beginning to feel the case would never go to court. She could testify to the senior accountant's fear and that she had seen the second set of books before they were partially destroyed. She was eager to try. Until Michael Dorling snatched her from the car park, knocked her unconscious and threw her into a car.

Chapter 24

A FUNERAL

It was not raining on the day of the funeral, three days later. This would have been the weather's chance: tears and raindrops falling as Henry Talbott was buried among the trees and flowers of the private Talbott burial plot. But it was not to be. In fact it seemed the sun shone brighter and hotter than it had all summer. The faint breeze was warm and dry and only added to the loveliness as it rustled silky green leaves and floated flower petals and butterflies. Telephoto-lensed press cameras whirred non-stop.

Henry's social and business acquaintances had been requested to make charitable donations in his name. In light of the Talbott family's recent troubles, however, it had been announced that attendance at the funeral was by invitation only. Consequently the mourners were few: Liz Dodd crying into a large linen handkerchief, the twins, Vivian, Maggie, Annie and Eric. A white knob of bandage covered Eric's entire nose and it was impossible to see if it had been restored successfully. Perhaps the surgeon wouldn't even try until the swelling reduced. It was massive. He looked exhausted.

Max had been let out for the service and burial but was in the custody of two uniformed police officers, chunky men with spare tires and aviator sunglasses. They nodded at Lenny although she did not know them. They obviously knew about her.

All heads were discreetly lowered during the church service. Lenny peeked at the others. Kendell wiped tears from his cheeks, Kimberly looked tense and Vivian kept her expression a secret behind large dark glasses and a black lace handkerchief raised to her mouth. Only Eric cried long and loud. The others intermittently glanced at him as though he was behaving in the worst possible taste.

The service was brief and distant despite the lavish coffin and an abundance of lilies. The coffin lid was open and everyone in turn went up for a look. Eric said something to the skilfully made-up corpse but so softly no one could hear. Max placed his hand over his father's for a moment. The police guided him back to his pew. Liz Dodd peeked into the coffin and shook her head. Vivian, on the other hand, barely glanced in then returned to her seat next to Annie in the front pew. They didn't look at each other once or exchange a word.

Lenny took her own glance at the body. The guys at the funeral parlour had done a fine job. The old man was rosy cheeked and cherubic. The family was lucky the police had permitted the burial. In a case with so much ongoing drama, they could have insisted on an autopsy.

Lenny followed the hearse, the limousines and the police car to Hawthorn cemetery. The posse of journalists followed her and she thought she saw MacAvoy.

The gravestones were ornate and clean. Someone was paid to keep fresh flowers on each grave. No wilted petals or weeds here. Dead Talbotts took up a quarter of the cemetery, with plenty of space left over for the next couple of generations. The family stood around the hole expectantly, waiting for the body to go into the dirt, trying not to enjoy the sunshine too obviously.

Lenny stood on one side of the hole with Kendell and Eric. Opposite them were Kimberly, Margaret, Annie and Vivian. Max and his two police friends, Liz Dodd at their side, were at the far end of the hole opposite the priest.

Wearing an old-fashioned grey suit, Max was not cuffed but he stood as though he were, hunched forward and tired. He was frail, she thought, an old man. His eyes dwelt lovingly on the flowers and occasionally he lifted his head to catch the sunshine. Max and Liz Dodd were the only ones in the group, including the policemen and the priest, not wearing sunglasses.

Kendell, standing next to Lenny, kept leaning forward to look into the hole. Eric continued to cry gently.

Vivian, once out of the church, had placed her handkerchief in her bag and taken a long breath. She looked disinterested, turning her profile to let the photographers catch a better shot, raising a languid hand to fan a tiny yellow butterfly from her face.

Next to her Annie Baron was sombre, hands clutching and worrying at her purse. She stared into the grave. She shook her head once and her lips moved silently. Vivian said something to her and she nodded.

Maggie Gross had obviously been at the bottle early and was pink. She tugged at the too-tight black lace collar of her clingy cocktail frock. Even Annie's bulk covered in simple black linen wasn't so offensive.

Kimberly played the part of bereaved princess, dressed in black Lacroix with a short lacy jacket. Her skirt was micro mini, her heels grew five inch spikes. She wore no hat but had a large diamond choker. An unfortunate choice for a bulldog face, Lenny thought. She used a scrap of black linen to dab under her sunglasses.

The priest spoke again of Henry Talbott's devotion as husband and father. Then the usual blather about dust and ashes and he was lowered into the ground. Max looked at the sky, Liz Dodd, Kendell and Eric gulped, the rest were blank. Max locked eyes with Vivian briefly.

David Breslin appeared about halfway through the burial speech. He hovered uncomfortably away from the group and when the coffin was in the dirt he made his move to join Max briefly and pat his arm before moving on to Kendell. They spoke together for a moment. A tasteless cemetery grab for cash, Lenny thought. She gave him a mock cheery wave which he ignored.

Then Vivian was at her elbow, serene-faced for the probing

cameras but up close a little pale. She rubbed a finger gently against Lenny's jacket sleeve. It was publicly intimate and noticed by just about everyone.

'Walk with me a little, Lenny,' Vivian sighed, and the two of them moved away from the others. Lenny heard the camera action hot up. She also felt the hostility coming off the little group they had left behind.

'This is ridiculous, isn't it?' Vivian gestured back towards the grave. 'Eric's putting on quite a display, don't you think? Or is that too nasty even for me?' She sighed. 'I suppose it's wrong to imagine no one loved Henry just because I didn't. Henry told Kendell he wanted Max at his funeral too.' She smiled. 'I don't really mind. An old man's last request. Kimmie is outraged. Don't let the sniffling fool you. We had to fill her with Valium this morning.' She sounded as though it was not an unusual occurrence and, at worst, an inconvenience.

'Is she ever violent?' Lenny asked, arms folded across her chest. She didn't want this to become another intimate moment and she certainly didn't want any more touching.

Vivian laughed at her question, her head tilted back giving Lenny a long look at her pale throat.

'You never stop with the detecting, do you?' she said. They were under the trees and in cool shade so she slid off her sunglasses. 'Why?' she asked. 'Do you think Kimberly killed Carol now?' She shrugged. 'Kimmie has a temper. But we control it with drugs and she sees her psych every couple of weeks. It doesn't mean anything.'

It meant plenty, Lenny thought.

'Has she ever seriously hurt anyone?'

'Not for a long time. At primary school she bit another child. Not seriously. A couple of stitches.'

Nice, Lenny thought.

'Lenny, she and I are not close. My fault probably. We don't confide in each other. But she tries hard to be a good girl. Let's not spoil it for her, hmm?' Vivian took a seat on a marble bench. Lenny sat next to her. They were at the far side of the cemetery.

'What about Kendell?'

Vivian opened her black Prada purse and pulled out a small white envelope which she handed to Lenny. 'I don't want to talk about Ken or Kimmie,' she said. 'I want to talk about this. It came this morning.'

It was addressed to 'V. Talbott' at the Toorak address. Inside was one piece of stiff white card with red print. It read: *Bad timing. Next time no mistakes.*

Lenny turned the envelope over. It was postmarked Toorak. She didn't express the frustration she felt.

'It's stamped yesterday,' Vivian said. 'Max had no opportunity but it could have been Liz Dodd.'

'Who do you really think it is?' Lenny demanded crossly. 'Why haven't you given it to the police?' But there was an obvious answer to that: Vivian didn't want the police to release Max. Despite even this absolute proof that she was still in danger, she preferred to let Max go to jail.

'Lenny, come and stay in the Toorak house and then come on to Europe with me.'

'Why do you keep pretending that you're interested in me?' Lenny said flatly. It was the last line of defence because her heart was pounding. 'I don't have money or power. What do you want from me?'

Vivian reached out and touched her hand for a moment. Lenny yanked it away.

'Stop touching me.' She could imagine how this was going to look in the late afternoon newspapers. Vivian sighed.

'You're very clever and determined. I admire you,' she said. 'Lenny, it would never last a lifetime. You already know how I run through people. But for a while it would be lovely. Don't you think?'

A while ... six weeks, six months, even six years. She tried to imagine the two of them together. Vivian would 'go Japanese' and be very amused and amusing about it. They would stand on the balcony of a hotel in Kyoto, overlooking the Kamo River. Lenny would learn a few basic phrases to ask the Japanese maid to bring more green tea. Except it wouldn't be a Japanese maid, it would be Maggie and Annie.

'And I want you to stop your investigation.'

'You know who did it. Tell me.'

'Lenny, come with me.'

'I'm going to Queensland,' she said. 'When I get back I'll consider it.' But she already knew the answer was no.

'The letter ... I need you.'

'I need to finish this,' Lenny said. Vivian nodded but was agitated.

After a long pause while they both looked at the trees, Vivian began again, resigned: 'When do you go?'

'Tomorrow.'

'All right.' She sat forward, eyes hidden. 'Lenny, I'm scared.' Vivian's shoulders moved a little. Lenny realized she was supposed to make a comforting gesture, something physical. She didn't move. Her tongue was drying on the roof of her mouth.

'Tell me why,' she said.

'I want to,' Vivian replied, 'but I can't.'

They walked back to the others who were waiting in various stages of impatience.

Vivian went straight to her car, followed by Annie. The journalists screamed questions but she only smiled in return. It was the picture for the evening editions. Glamorous young widow shows no grief at husband's graveside. This would do nothing to help her reputation.

Kimberly approached Lenny, hands mangling her handbag.

'This is disgusting,' she said. 'Kendell's got a real nerve having Max here. It's just like him to be soft about it. The next thing you know Max will be expecting his own plot here.' She hesitated. 'Are you busy after this? We could go for coffee. Or tea. That Japanese stuff you like. I bought some.'

'I'm always busy,' Lenny said.

'But not for my mother, right?' Kimberly's raised voice turned heads to her.

'*Are* you?' Kimberly asked. 'Are you with my mother?' The handle of her bag was going to snap under the strain, Lenny thought.

'No,' she said. Kimberly glanced back at Vivian.

'I don't believe you.' She looked very young, betrayed. 'She's glad my father's dead, you know.' She ran away and slid into the second car next to Maggie. She had arrived with her mother but for the return trip was rejected. Vivian had asked Kendell to ride with her.

Lenny cursed herself for not nipping it in the bud earlier. It was the legs. She was always intrigued by stunning legs but she should have made it clear to Kimberly that she was never going to be interested.

She waited until the limousines had driven off. Max and his two policemen stood at their car. They were discreetly recuffing him for the trip back to the prison. He glanced across at Lenny.

'Ms Aaron,' he said. 'It's good of you to come to pay your respects.'

'I'm sure you know that's not my reason for being here, Max.'

'You underestimate yourself.'

During the service the family had ignored Max with the exception of Kendell, who gave his brother a smile. The two of them, separated by forty years, were not at all alike physically and yet there was a connection. Max could be a good influence on his brother, Lenny thought. She wondered if they and their uptight, lonely sister could ever be a family.

Eric Hunter waited for her at the edge of the grave. Tears still drizzled down his face but he didn't wipe them away.

'I'm free of them now,' he said. 'I'll get my money now. Henry changed his will, you know.' He laughed at her surprise. 'That's going to shock a few people. He had the lawyers in before he died. I don't know what he told them but he would've looked out for me. I'm sure of that.' He reached for her arm then remembered and laughed again. 'It's not him anymore, is it? Down in the coffin? It's just a body. Where do you go when you die, do you think, Ms Aaron? Do you go anywhere?' He covered his mouth to stop his laughter. Lenny left him standing there.

As she drove through the remaining security men and flashing cameras, she saw MacAvoy clearly although he was trying to hide himself in the crowd. He had always been useless at surveillance. She decided it was flattering that he continued to tail her. It meant the police still thought she was competent and might discover something worthwhile. She resisted the urge to wave at MacAvoy. Let him think she hadn't seen him. That way it would be easier to lose him when she wanted to.

She drove back to her office, watching his car following all the way. She drove past the hospital but decided against another visit to Granny Sanderman. Best to wait a few days. Either death or recovery must come soon.

Chapter 25

HER KNIGHT IN SHINING ARMOUR

There was a cheque at her office. It was from the Woodruffs. Also enclosed was a polaroid of the smiling family with Mr Silky front and centre and a nice letter of thanks on lilac floral paper. Lenny opened her filing cabinet, found Mr Silky's file and tossed the letter and photo inside.

She cleaned the office. It looked very bare without the bonsai. She sat at her desk going through the junk mail and bills and listening to three messages: all cat related. The warm sunshine heated her neck and shoulders. She opened the window a little to get some fresh air although it meant the conversation of the shoppers in the car park was audible. Her answering machine messages competed with chatter about ice-cream flavours and what-to-have-for-dinner.

She flipped her desk calendar a week forward and wrote down the cat owners' telephone numbers. Doing it, she realized she was anticipating some free time, as though the Talbott case was ending. Events were moving beyond her control. Vivian was right.

She rang 0175 to get the Connors' Queensland telephone number. There were six and she took them all.

The first was an old man who, enraged, demanded to know how she got his number. He said he was going to go to the TV stations to protest the invasion of his privacy. His daughter came on the line and apologized for 'the old bugger'. He was senile and no, they were not related to Carol Connor and she had already told that to about ten journalists. The second Connor was an old lady who was profoundly deaf and managed only: 'Hello? Hello? Could you speak up, dear?

Is anyone there?' before hanging up. The third Connor was Carol's father.

'Yes, I want to fly up tomorrow,' Lenny explained. 'No, I'm not the police. I'm a private investigator. Mr Connor, may I visit you tomorrow?'

He said yes and gave her the address. It was off the beaten track a little, he explained. There were no brothers or sisters, he said. Just him and Cindy and the cat. Come any time. Always someone home. Great, she thought, a cat.

She phoned Qantas and booked a flight for seven a.m. She also booked a car. She'd have to drive to Gympie. She couldn't get an economy seat on the early flight so had to take business. That would just about finish her financially, she thought. Vivian was right though—it was not about money.

When she left the office it was deserted in the corridor. Anastasia had one client in the chair with a hot towel on his face and two quarrelling old Italian men waiting. She waved her scissors for Lenny to wait and hurried over to the barber shop door.

'So how is the Siamese?' she demanded. She had pinned her curls back with multicoloured bobby pins and her cheeks were rosy with good health.

'It lost an eye but it's going to pull through,' Lenny said. She took a breath. 'Listen ... thanks for looking after it for me.'

'You paid me, remember?' Anastasia grinned. 'Take down that sign for the free cat. You will keep this one, I'm thinking. Anyway, who's gonna take a one-eye cat?'

Lenny nodded. It was time to stop kidding herself she was going to take the Siamese to the pound.

'We'll see what happens,' she said.

'You take care.' Anastasia had half an eye on her shop where the men were becoming restless. 'I'm hating cutting hair, you know? These old men, all they want is the basic cut. I'm looking for a challenge, you know. If you need an assistant for the cats—' she waved a vague hand.

A middle-aged man clutching a bag of videos to his chest rushed out of the porn shop, giving Lenny a nervous glance. She walked out into the sunshine.

It was a perfect day. Lenny, still in her funeral black, felt she should be relaxing but she couldn't shake the feeling that she was being followed. Of course she knew it was MacAvoy,
but somehow she had lost sight of him on the drive to her office. She stopped walking and pretended to look at her watch. She scanned the street. Footscray residents were out in force. MacAvoy remained incognito.

It was late in the day so the bank was crowded. After she had deposited the Woodruff's cheque she ate falafel and drank a cappuccino back in her office. She was loath to go home. There was something pleasant and reassuring about her office and she wanted to *catch* MacAvoy. She kept peeking out into the car park to see if she could spot him. Nothing! All the way back from the bank she had felt his eyes boring into her. She wanted to scream at him to come into the open.

After sculling a large glass of Alka Seltzer with a double Tylenol chaser, she tilted back in her chair to read through the rest of her mail: advertisements for lotteries where she was 'already a winner!' and department store catalogues with the 'new autumn line'. She didn't plan to take a nap. She didn't even recall closing her eyes.

Sometime around eleven p.m. a noise woke her. She yanked her head up off her desk and stared around. She hadn't fallen asleep on the job for a long time. Once, during a particularly dull stakeout, she and Danny had dozed off in the unmarked police car. The small time robbers turned over the jewellers right before their closed eyes.

She switched off the lights and hurried out of the office. Her shoulders ached from napping in an awkward position. She wanted to have a quick shower and hit the futon. She had to get up early for the Queensland trip. The corridor was quiet, the only light coming from the still-open porn shop. Everyone else had gone home hours ago. Lenny had worked late before and wasn't afraid.

However, when she reached the car park, she sensed something. It was very dark outside. The street light was flickering. She made out about five cars in the car park but she didn't see any people out there.

'MacAvoy, give it up,' she said under her breath and stepped forward grimly. He was a fucking bastard trying to scare her and she wasn't going to give him the satisfaction. She wished she had a cat with her. Cats had a vision range of two hundred and eighty-seven degrees and, with their pupils dilated at night, light was magnified forty to fifty times for them. While Lenny could see almost nothing in the car park, a cat would have been able to see everything. And might then have hissed some kind of warning.

She was almost at her car when she sensed the person come at her. It was a nightmare flashback to two years previously and she screamed. Later she would wonder where all that noise came from. She also swung her body left so that the 'thing' hit her on the right shoulder rather than the head. Still it knocked her face-forward into her car door and she would certainly have been easy to finish off if her rescuer hadn't made his move.

'Hey! Hey! Hey you—'

She was in a state of semi-consciousness that lasted only a few seconds but each second amplified her pain, fear and confusion. She was aware of the soft slap of sneakers running away and a loud thud of shoes coming towards her. Then gentle hands turned her over because her face was still plastered against the car door. She yelped in pain and, when she saw the face of her rescuer, burst into tears.

Mike Bullock burst into tears too. His face crinkled. He touched Lenny's cheek. 'I'm all right,' she sniffled.

'Mate ... mate ...' he was crouched next to her on the bitumen, shivering.

'Did you see him?' she asked. Mike shook his head.

'Great. Let me get up,' Lenny said but found she couldn't and had to accept his help. He was concerned, wanted to call an ambulance. Lenny shook her head and regretted it as pain sliced her right cheek. Was she cut? The cheek felt burning hot. Must be bleeding. She fished with her left hand for her car keys, lumbered to her door and opened it. The pain in her right shoulder was making her sweat and her head was pounding.

She slid into her car but couldn't drive. She couldn't raise her right arm to the wheel. Mike Bullock hovered by her open door, sniffling. His perm was awry and his beige and chocolate ensemble was rumpled. Her hero! Just her luck.

'You'll have to drive me to the hospital,' she said reluctantly. She had never in her life imagined Mike Bullock inside her car. She had to clench her teeth to get out of the car and go round to the passenger side. She waited in a semi-swoon as Mike hurried back into the mall to lock up the porn shop.

The drive to the hospital brought back memories of that other drive. She tried to avoid it. She turned on the radio to drown out Mike's nervous attempts at soothing chatter. Nothing would soothe her now except high dosage tranquillizers. She stared vacantly out of the side window. She wound it down to let the cool air hit her hot face. She cursed herself for blubbing. She never seemed able to overcome the shameful ability to cry when it was the last thing she wanted to do.

In the hospital car park she had to suffer the final indignity of Mike rushing around to help her out of the car.

'Look,' she said, left hand nursing the right arm because to leave it dangling was too painful. 'You don't have to hang around. I'll be fine now. Thanks.' He had saved her life but he was just about the last person she would have chosen for the task. Where the hell was MacAvoy when you needed him?

'Right ... right ... I'll get a cab. No worries.' Mike agreed.

'Great.' She was being severely ungrateful. Why did this have to happen after their last conversation when she told him she would never be interested in him! She tried to think of something pleasant to say.

'See ya tomorrow then?' he said.

'Sure. Listen. Thanks ... a lot.' She limped away from him to the emergency doors and was set upon by nurses.

Nurses never shrieked when they saw your wounds. Somehow they didn't show any of the shock or repugnance they must feel. So Lenny, lulled by their blankness, was startled to catch sight of herself in a mirror in the X-ray room.

Her right cheekbone was cut, though not badly, she thought, but the cheek was purple and puffed to about twice its usual size. If the blow hadn't been deflected she'd have had a smashed skull. Whoever hit her had intended to kill. It had been no warning. There was another bump on her brow. This was from where she crashed head-first into the car. The lump was egg-sized and very red. Head wounds always looked worse than they really were, she told herself tearfully.

The X-rays showed that she had not sustained any skull fractures but that her right clavicle was cracked. This was not the kind of thing that could be plastered. Instead they used tight bandages to wrap her shoulder to try to steady the bone. She could move but very stiffly. Her right arm was then placed in a sling. Her cheek, to her surprise, took four stitches and the gauze and sticking plaster they used to cover it made it ridiculously large.

They kept asking her if they should call someone and looked worried when she said no. They wanted to admit her for shock and probable concussion. Lenny, wearing only her black bra and jeans but wrapped in a soft, baby blue hospital blanket, shook her head.

'No.'

'Ms Aaron, you've been seriously injured.'

'Bullshit. I've got a cracked collarbone and a bruise and I want a taxi.'

They had to know how it happened—for the records. She looked, she supposed, like a domestic violence victim. She told them she had fallen at home and hit her face against the sink. They didn't believe her of course.

She didn't want to make a police report. It was bad enough to have gotten herself beaten up without drawing attention to it.

She staggered to her feet. It was difficult because of the bandages. She was becoming nicely muzzy from the drugs they had pumped into her. She hadn't told them to hold back on the pills, that she had a history, a tendency to become quickly dependent. No, she just said give me something quick. They noticed her arm of course.

My goodness, that's quite a scar. What happened?
None of your business.

The doctor argued with her, insisting that she stay overnight, but she was willing to walk out and get her own taxi so he had to give in. They compromised. She'd go home in an ambulance. So she did, sitting up stiffly, smoking a cigarette and scowling at the ambulance man who sat in the back with her. He quickly caught her mood and they said a poisonous nothing during the ten-minute drive to St Kilda.

She was home by two a.m. She was glad of the late hour. Her neighbours didn't need more reasons to single her out for attention. She hadn't tried to dress herself (couldn't get her arm back into her shirt and jacket). Her jacket hung around her shoulders, her shirt tucked under her good arm.

She was standing on the kerb, shuffling for her door key and watching the ambulance pull away, when she saw MacAvoy's car parked across from her block of flats. His face was lit by a street lamp—as was hers—and she saw his look of shock at her appearance. He bolted over to her.

'What the fuck happened to you?'

'Where were you? Aren't you supposed to be tailing me?' She leaned against the bricked-in mailboxes wearily.

'I saw you at the funeral,' MacAvoy said. 'I was gonna talk to you but I got a call this afternoon. I had to go out to Frankston. Drug bust. Jesus! You look terrible! Who did it?' MacAvoy was not going to believe any 'fell into the sink' story and she didn't try it on him.

'I don't know. I didn't see them.'

'Lenny, you're not cut out for this kind of work,' MacAvoy said. He was angry but not with her, she knew. Angry with whoever had hurt her. It reminded her of his reaction to Michael Dorling's attack. His sympathy, the unexpected gentleness. She had resisted it then and she did again now.

'Bullshit,' she said.

'Dorling broke your nerve—'

'Fuck you!'

'You're going to get yourself killed.'

'Look, MacAvoy,' she shoved him in the chest with her left hand so he fell off the kerb onto the road. 'We used to work together but you were half-arsed then and you're half-arsed now. I didn't ask you to tail me or help me or give me your stupid advice. You just concentrate on your retirement package, OK?'

'I'm going to forget you said all that.'

'Don't forget it.' They glared at each other. MacAvoy, under his bluster, was the worst kind of overly sensitive male. She had cut him and he would suffer for a long time. But he had hurt her too. She always believed her police colleagues thought less of her after she'd quit the force. Of course they did. But hearing it confirmed so brutally was a bitter pill.

MacAvoy rubbed his chest where she had prodded him and gave her a contemptuous look.

'I'm sorry for you, Lenny.'

'You piece of shit.'

He slammed back into his car and drove away, engine

roaring. A light came on in the flats behind her. Great! She hurried upstairs, shoulder protesting on every step, and unlocked her door.

In a few hours she had to be in Queensland. She couldn't afford to go into a drugged sleep so she sat upright on the futon in front of the portable TV, propped up on pillows. She allowed herself to doze but not to sleep. She watched a late-night news program. Henry's funeral was the lead story and the camera teams were back outside Vivian's Toorak house. Lenny watched sleepily as the camera zoomed in on the upstairs window, searching the closed blinds. Was Vivian standing there, looking out and then glancing back at her TV to see if she could be seen? Did she know about the new will? What did she think about her husband's death? Was it the freedom she had longed for? *Come to Europe with us.*

Lenny was dimly aware of watching an American sports round-up, a documentary on whales and an episode of *Dr Kildare*, but they merged together. Dr Kildare, holding a bat between enormous flippers, struck out twice. She was almost unconscious when Bugs Bunny took on Yosemite Sam. When the alarm clock went off at five a.m, it took her a full minute to register that the buzzing meant something.

Her painkillers were wearing off. She cried as she sat in a half-filled bath to sponge herself clean, self-pitying and exhausted sobs that left her even weaker. She had to avoid wetting the bandages, so the bath took some time. Trying to brush her hair and teeth and then dress was a nightmare. Somehow she got a white shirt and olive pants on. She pulled on a loose jacket and by then her arm felt like it was radioactive. She slipped the sling back on and, since her car was still at the hospital, called a taxi.

Chapter 26

GYMPIE

The flight to Brisbane was blissful. She popped a double dose of painkillers and allowed herself to sleep. She was aware of snoring rather loudly but was too exhausted to wake herself. Eventually a steward shook her good arm gently.

'Miss ... Miss!' Lenny opened her eyes. 'We'll be landing in fifteen minutes. Please place your seat in the upright position and fasten your seatbelt.'

'Sure.' Lenny struggled upright, wincing. She had been a focus of attention when she boarded the plane. Time had only increased her bruises. Her cheek was hidden by the wad of gauze, but her forehead was now solidly purple.

After the landing she went straight to the ladies' room and washed her hands and face with cold water. Her stomach churned; too little sleep, no food and a gut-full of medication. She bought two cups of coffee and two doughnuts and wolfed them in the airport lounge, following that up with two sticks of Wake-Up gum. Then she went to pick up her rental car.

The girl at the counter looked at her sling questioningly.

'Are you OK to drive?'

'Sure,' Lenny said, although she had no idea. She wriggled out of her sling, hiding the stab of pain and flexed her hand and fingers. 'It's just a precaution.'

'I see ...'

At the wheel of a brand new Mazda, she lifted her right arm. It was extremely painful but not impossible. She could balance her right hand on the wheel and do most of the work with her left. It was an automatic, which helped.

It was a couple of hours to Gympie but once she'd negotiated the Brisbane inner-city traffic and found the highway, she made good time. It was very different to driving in Melbourne. The highway narrowed abruptly to a long tunnel between thousands of rows of fir trees. Road signs warned of kangaroos. Lenny's Mazda had no bull bar and she imagined a kangaroo impact, like being hit by a sofa.

When she reached Gympie, she stopped at a petrol station to buy a Coke and check her directions to the Connors' house. The girl at the counter was simultaneously watching *The Midday Show* on a portable TV, eating Doritos and filing pointed nails. She wore a stretch halter top in lemon poplin and had greasy hair, pimply skin and clear lip gloss. Time tunnel.

'What happened to ya face?' the girl asked, taking the Coke money.

'What happened to yours?' Lenny quipped, walking out as 'Bitch!' and 'Ugly mole!' flew after her like haunted-house bats.

The girl's charming brother was working the petrol pumps. His shirt was tied around his waist as he worked on a suntan and gave Lenny a good view of his muscles. He swaggered towards Lenny. His eyes, like his sister's, were anaemic blue and crossed.

'Getcha petrol?' He made it sound like a threat. His breath smelled of hamburger.

'Nope.' Lenny slid into the car carefully. She showed him her map. 'I want to get to the Connors' house. George and Cindy Connor. Do you know it?'

The boy's eyes rolled back out of sight as he thought.

'Go down the main street then take the first right. Just keep going.' It confirmed her map. He slapped a hand on her boot as she drove away.

The main street of Gympie wasn't breathtaking. A small supermarket, a post office, a few coffee shops and boutiques like 'Celeste's—Est. 1958'. The window mannequins were prehistoric: the breasts were too large, the hips miles across and the faces smiled warmly instead of pouting and sneering.

She popped another painkiller into her mouth and swigged

the Coke. The long drive had worn her out. She recognized that her personality was on extra high burn. Had there been any need to insult the petrol station girl? Get a grip! Control. Control. She fantasized about finding a motel and sleeping for three days, but she needed to finish this. Someone had tried to kill her last night.

She drove east until the road became a dirt track. On one side was open farmland and on the other, trees and overgrown bushes. Cows were resting under a tree. Did that mean rain? Veronica Aaron always said so.

The Connors' abode was a whitewashed, one-storey house with an aluminium roof and three cars in the front garden— two of them obviously bombs that someone was fixing up. There was a budgie in a cage on the verandah wall perched over a pile of its droppings.

Cindy Connor met Lenny at the front door. The fly screen slammed noisily behind her. Mrs Connor resembled her daughter though her hair was short and badly permed. She wore a light blue summer dress which looked dated but was possibly a 'this season's latest model', from 'Celeste's'. She smiled warmly.

'Goodness! Your poor face! You must be Miss Aaron.'

'Yes, I am.'

'Come in then.' In contrast to the white light outdoors, the interior of the house was at first pitch black. They had not invested in skylights and the windows were small. As her eyes became accustomed to the darkness Lenny noted that the furniture was old but not antique and Cindy Connor liked to crochet. On top of the piano was a photo of Carol in a bikini.

'Isn't she lovely?' Cindy said.

'Yes. You don't have a TV.' Lenny scanned the room. Perhaps it was in the kitchen or their bedroom.

'We have the radio.' Cindy pointed at an old cabinet that might have passed for a radio in a World War II film. 'George likes the ABC news every night.' She sat opposite Lenny. 'George!'

Lenny jumped. George Connor put his head around the kitchen door.

'Miss Aaron's here,' Cindy said with a smile.

George Connor entered the living room, a fat tabby at his heels. He didn't look like her idea of a doctor. He looked like a tramp. He wore old trousers cut off at the knees, a blue work singlet covered with paint stains and oil, and filthy Blundstone boots. His hair was thin, his jawline jowly. Like his wife he looked friendly.

'You're not Jewish then?' he said. 'I treated a few of 'em. So did Dad after the war. He said they had all sorts of problems. Not the ones I treated of course. I was much later. Just the usual coughs and colds.'

'Right,' Lenny said and took out her notebook.

'I've taken early retirement,' George said as though in answer to a question. 'Carol's death made me think about things. I didn't need to keep working and life's short, isn't it, Miss Aaron?'

'Do you have any idea why Carol was killed?' Lenny asked.

'Carol was our pride and joy,' Cindy Connor said. 'Pretty as a picture. We only had the one so we spoiled her.'

'She came to expect it.' George took up the tale and the couple nodded at each other. 'I'm a country doctor. There's no real money in it. Not for the kind of life she wanted. All her friends were rich. From the school we sent her to.'

'She told us she was going to get a rich husband,' Cindy said, nodding, hands clutching knees, eyes overly wide, smile too big. 'There's nothing wrong with that, is there? We met Kendell the once. He seemed nice. We didn't have a chance to meet the rest of his family. Except when Vivian came up here after Carol passed away.' She blinked back tears.

'What did you think of Kendell?'

'No brain surgeon,' George Connor said immediately. His cat mewed and he rubbed its ears affectionately. 'Shaddup, Chester.' He chewed his cheek. 'I read in the paper that you're a bit of a cat expert. You might like to examine Chester if you've got the time. He's had a bit of a blockage. I've examined the back passage and it looks clear but—'

'I'm not a vet,' Lenny said. No way was she shoving her digit up that monster's butt. She had Vaseline, eyedroppers, hydrogen peroxide and a rectal thermometer in a kit she carried around for show. She never used it and didn't plan to start now. 'Are you alternating canned food and kibble?'

'Well,' Mr Connor looked coy, 'we let him have the table scraps most nights. I suppose that's not good?' They all glanced at the obesity before them.

'Miss Aaron, the police told us Carol was killed by mistake—because she looked like Kendell's mother?' Cindy said.

'Do you believe it?' Lenny asked.

'Do you?' George replied. He was suddenly and disconcertingly sharp-eyed, like a Womble that reveals it has a PhD in astrophysics.

'Vivian feels terrible about it,' Cindy said. 'She spent hours talking with us. She's a lovely woman.'

Chester's stomach made a noise and a foul smell filled the room. George patted the monster sadly.

'What did you talk about?' Lenny asked.

'Vivian said how much her son had loved Carol,' Cindy said. That had been a lie, thought Lenny, although under the circumstances a white one. 'We looked through Carol's old school photos and things.'

'Did she take anything?' Lenny asked.

'Goodness no,' Cindy sniffled. 'I thought it was odd, Kendell not coming with her.'

'Vivian was interested in everything about Carol. It's not right, is it? The young man should have come,' George said.

'Can I see Carol's things?' Lenny asked. She wondered why Vivian would make the effort.

They took her to Carol's bedroom. The furniture was small and white with appliquéd pink flowers and rabbits on the quilt and a pink crocheted pillowcase. There were posters of movie and pop stars on the walls.

While they watched, George holding the fat feline like a hefty baby, Lenny rummaged through the desk drawers. It held letters from school friends. She scanned a few. They wanted to know all about Carol's huge country estate. Carol had not been completely honest about her roots. Her father and mother watched in silence. Had they read the letters? At any rate, there was nothing in them that had any connection to the murder, as far as she could see.

'I'm sorry,' Cindy Connor said, because Lenny didn't disguise her frustration.

Lenny, George and Chester sat out on iron chairs in the garden while Cindy got drinks. It was hot. Lenny's cheek stung under her plaster. George nodded at the cars on the lawn.

'I'm fixing 'em up,' he said. 'Small commission. I could never decide between mechanical engineering and medicine but Dad was a doctor ...' He chuckled. Lenny had missed it the first time he mentioned his father but now the penny dropped.

'Was your father a doctor here in Gympie?'

'I took over his practice after he passed on. He was the doctor in this town for thirty years. Everyone knew him. I think the patients took to me eventually but I could never replace Dad.'

Cindy Connor brought out three glasses of pithy, homemade lemonade and a dishful of milk for Chester.

The four of them slurped. Lenny wondered if Vivian had sat out here with Cindy's lemonade.

'Did you get beaten up?' George asked eventually.

'Yes,' Lenny said.

'You're unlucky, aren't you? Cindy and I read all the papers. Cindy's keeping a scrapbook. You might think that's morbid but she was our daughter. It's all we have of her now.'

'Your poor arm.' Cindy patted Lenny on the left shoulder. It was obvious she was referring to the old scar.

'Why'd you let Dorling get away with it? You should've taken him to court.' George Connor gave her a sharp look. 'Are you a loose cannon like the papers say?'

Was that what the papers were saying? Was she still identifiable as the ex-detective gone mental?

'George, that's not polite,' Cindy intervened. 'Another drink, Miss Aaron?'

'No, thank you,' Lenny said. George was waiting for his answer. Lenny looked straight at him. 'I lost my nerve.' It wasn't the first time she had said it. Dr Sakuno made her say it regularly in therapy. Confront your hurdles and in doing so climb over them. But it was the first time she had said it naturally in conversation—and to strangers. She felt relaxed. A little pressure valve had opened. Their ratty garden suddenly looked homey. Even their horrid, obese cat was attractive.

She was persuaded to stay for tea. It became one of those situations when, for a brief moment, you find something in strangers that is familiar and a comfort. So it was with Lenny and the Connors.

She spent the rest of the afternoon outside in the sunshine. Mrs Connor set up an old white sun lounge and a faded umbrella. Lenny took more pills and dozed while Mr Connor energetically whacked at a tennis ball pegged into the ground on an elastic band. He was very good. He could hit that thing fifty or sixty times without missing. Once he hit it so hard the peg came right out and the whole contraption flew into the bushes.

Mrs Connor did a roast beef dinner in honour of the occasion, with Yorkshire pudding, roast potatoes, peas, baby carrots and gravy. Lenny, who had eaten only the doughnuts and various pharmaceuticals all day, gorged herself. They both looked pleased.

'Carol ate like a little bird,' Cindy said. 'Finish the gravy with bread. That's the way.' Lenny mopped obediently.

'You think Kendell killed her, don't you?' George said. His wife looked ready to intervene for good manners again. 'That's why he hasn't come.' He had washed his hands before dinner but not tamed his tennis-wild hair.

'Perhaps,' Lenny said. Although she was beginning to think something quite different.

George shook his head. 'I'm sorry for the mother then. Do you reckon she knows?'

'Oh no! Vivian was very kind!' Cindy said and put a big home-baked apple pie and jug of cream on the table. 'She was a Little Pines girl,' she added. So local people still remembered. Cindy saw Lenny's surprised look and smiled.

'Most people in Gympie our age know it,' she said. 'Mrs Talbott's our most famous old girl. She never comes back to visit though.'

They were about the same age, Lenny thought. Cindy was perhaps a few years older.

'Were you at school with Vivian and Annie Baron?'

'I was,' Cindy smiled, 'but I was much older. I was nearly seventeen when they came up to the High. Vivian and I had a nice talk about the school but she didn't remember me personally, of course. To tell you the truth, I never had much to do with them. They were too young. Anyway, we didn't talk to home kids. In case they stole something.' She blushed. 'That sounds awful.'

'Do you remember them?' Lenny asked George. He shook his head. He had been educated out of town at Brisbane Grammar.

'They were both pretty, I remember that. Two little matching dolls,' Cindy said. 'Annie wasn't nearly as pretty as Vivian though. Some people said she was a bit slow. I saw in the paper that Annie was at the Talbotts' house when Carol was killed. It's nice that she and Vivian are still friends after all this time, isn't it?'

Lenny didn't answer because her mouth was dry. *Matching*

dolls. Her spoon hovered on the edge of her lip but she didn't take that bite. She was thinking about the photograph of the eyes in the Toorak house. The black and white blow-up of Vivian's eyes that had reminded her of someone else's.

'Were Annie and Vivian best friends?' she asked. She ate voraciously now.

'Oh look, I don't know. I only remember them being pretty.'

'Does the Little Pines director still live in Gympie?'

'He'd be over eighty by now,' George said, lethargic after his meal. He put his cream-filled bowl on the floor and the tabby began to lick.

'That's Mr Denny,' Cindy said. 'He's over at Pine's Cottage.'

'And your father?' Lenny asked George. 'When did he die?'

He smiled, surprised. 'Dad's been dead for twenty-odd years now,' he said, yawning.

Lenny fought off a yawn too. She had slept all afternoon but she could easily nod off again. She rummaged in her purse for medication. She had the hospital painkillers but they acted as tranquillizers. She wanted to stay awake. She found three Sudafed and took them.

'Carol never knew her grandfather?' she asked.

'He died before she was born. In a fire at his surgery. He fell and hit his head, knocked himself unconscious. That's my opinion, anyway.' George looked at her intently. 'There was nothing left. Cabinets, instruments—all destroyed. The police said it was arson. Dad would never have destroyed that business. I told them again and again. But he had a nice insurance policy on the place, that was the thing they were interested in, you see. They thought he was after the money. Or maybe Cindy and I were. Everything Dad had passed on to us.'

Cindy was tearful as she remembered. 'Policemen—people we've known all our lives—asking us terrible questions. Of course it never came to anything. Eventually we got the insurance because they couldn't prove it was us.' She realized what she had said. 'I mean, it *wasn't* us!'

'Nothing survived the fire? No records?' Lenny asked. She had to see the medical files for the children from Little Pines.

'There aren't any records. I told you, everything was destroyed,' George Connor said.

'Is there any other record of those times?' Lenny pressed. 'Perhaps you've forgotten something.'

'Dad's notebooks,' George said suddenly, slapping his thigh. 'He worked on them here in the house. He liked to record some of his more interesting cases in detail. I think he fancied himself as a bit of a writer. I haven't looked at the stuff for years. Do you think there could be something in there that might help you?'

'Did Vivian read them?'

'No.'

The notebooks were in the bottom of the linen chest in the corner of the Connors' bedroom. There was a bag of old photos of George Connor senior in his heyday. He looked much the same as his son. Lenny's attention went to the notebooks. There were three of them: ordinary blue lined with 'G. Connor' printed on the cover. Over a thirty-year period he had covered a surprising number of unusual cases in this small town. His notes were detailed and, presumably because they were for his own pleasure rather than for use as official records, he had added sketches and comments. He had not, however, included the names of his patients.

'There are no names here,' Lenny said.

'Dad was very careful about protecting his patients' privacy. This was something for his own interest. He didn't think it was right to include names. I mean here you are looking through the stuff twenty years later.'

'Did Carol read this?' Lenny asked. Neither of them knew for sure.

They left her alone. She sat on the satiny bedcover, the

notebooks by her side. Through the window she could see a grove of pines across the road. There had been a hot breeze all day, but now there was no movement in the spiked branches.

It took some time to read through and dismiss the first two notebooks. Lenny finally found what she was looking for in the middle of the third notebook. It was the case of two orphan girls. One of the girls suffered from severe but not unusual menstrual cramps. The other also had menstrual pain but Dr Connor diagnosed something more serious.

... I could feel the endometrial lesions in the pelvic exam. It suggested the growth of tissue outside the uterus. This combined with the severe lower back pain during menstruation, the irregular bleeding and the premenstrual spotting made me immediately suspect endometriosis. I advised the young woman to consult a specialist to confirm the diagnosis before we began treatment. I reassured her that while 30–40 percent of women with this condition became infertile, there was a still a chance she would be able to have children. She was not unduly troubled by the news but she asked me to keep it to myself which of course I did. An odd young woman though. Something almost disturbing about her. I've always felt it. About both of them. Unusual girls.

The accompanying sketch of the two girls showed a similarity in the shape of the face and the eyes. Both had dark hair. But one was a classic beauty, the other merely attractive. This was more than Lenny had expected. This was Buddha giving, big-time.

She took the notebook into the living room. The Connors were setting up dominoes. They looked up, hopeful. It was time to leave.

'Can I take this?' she asked.

'Can I trust you with it?' George gazed into Lenny's eyes for a moment. He nodded, reassured. 'If it will help.'

Lenny slipped the notebook into her bag. 'Did Carol ever visit Mr Denny?'

'Yes, she did!' Cindy was enthusiastic. 'She joined the volunteer group that visits old people.'

'Didn't you think that was odd?' Lenny asked.

'I thought it was a lovely gesture,' Cindy said and dared both her husband and Lenny to say otherwise. 'Then she went off to Toowoomba to be a nurse.'

'Not really a nurse,' George corrected. 'A pink lady.'

'Pink lady?' Lenny said.

'They're volunteers at the hospitals,' Cindy explained. 'They sit with patients who don't have any visitors and help the nurses a bit. They wear pink uniforms so they call them pink ladies.'

They must have hoped it would lead Carol to a career in nursing, Lenny thought. But after only two months at St Anthony's, Carol took a summer vacation with her high school friends, met up with Kendell Talbott again, and that was that. She never returned to Gympie.

'Did Carol have many boyfriends before Kendell Talbott?' Lenny asked.

'High school romances, I suppose,' Cindy replied. 'She never talked about it. She never went out with any of the boys around here. There was a doctor from St Anthony's who rang for her once but she was already engaged to Kendell by then and I told the doctor that. He never rang again.'

'What was his name?'

'Tom Brown,' Cindy smiled. 'Like the book.'

Mrs Connor waved to Lenny from the porch. She was tired but she kept up a brisk wave whenever Lenny looked back. George walked her to the car. Chester had long since fallen asleep on his crocheted pouf in front of the old radio.

'I'll want that notebook back in one piece, you know,' George said.

'I understand.' Lenny slid into her car. Her shoulder ached badly.

'I could use something for my shoulder,' she said. 'Do you have anything that won't make me sleepy?'

George glanced back at his wife. He leaned through the window right into the car and scanned her face.

'Ms Aaron, I'm a doctor and therefore it's my job to recognize types. Stay off the drugs.'

'I'll try,' Lenny said with a grim smile.

'Are you religious?' he changed tack.

'I'm a Buddhist.'

'Oh well ... I don't know about that.' He held the window frame. His nails were oily like a mechanic's and a couple of knuckles were skinned.

'I think I know who killed your daughter,' Lenny said.

'Who?'

'Let me prove it first. I'll be in touch, don't worry.'

He walked back to the house as Lenny drove off. She wondered if he really knew what she was thinking. He had read the notebooks but it was Carol, some twenty years later, who put it all together. A pink lady! Carol Connor had never planned to be a nurse.

She stopped the car on the side of the road and took four Sudafeds with the flask of lemonade Cindy Connor had given her. She felt immediately better. She burned on into town but it was deserted. Only the video rental store was open. She found the Connors' clinic. It had been remodelled after the fire twenty years ago. Lenny wished she was still on the force and able to 'pull records'. It had been arson all right, but the police should have pursued it further.

Little Pines was a burnt-out shell on the outskirts of town. The signpost was still hung at the entrance gates but someone had lavished graffiti on it. The buildings were silhouetted between stands of yellow box.

Lenny turned her headlights off. It must have been quite a night, she thought, with children screaming, Mr Denny desperately counting and recounting. But they all got out alive. Had the killer been nearby in the darkness?

There were several hurdles to face if she was going to prove her theory. For one thing, the killer was ahead of her and had been all along.

It was all about family, of course, and it had been beautifully orchestrated. By someone who was—and had been for years—pretending to be something they weren't.

The cicadas creaked loudly. Lenny smoked a cigarette. She was thinking about secrets and loyalty and terrible, evil betrayal. She was thinking about Annie Baron.

Chapter 27

TEA FOR TWO

Mr Denny lived in a small prefabricated house in a south Gympie estate. There was a garden gnome near the front door, and a sign that said 'Pine's Cottage' mounted on the wall.

She knocked gently. It was still reasonably early in the evening and she couldn't wait until tomorrow. She had to know now. Her hands felt the familiar shakiness at the fingertips and her lips were numbing. Pharmaceutical intoxication.

'Who's there?' It was spoken through the closed door.

'Mr Denny, my name's Lenny Aaron. I'm a friend of George and Cindy Connor.'

'I don't know them.'

'Yes, yes, you do. Their daughter, Carol, was murdered in Melbourne.'

'The girl in the paper?'

'That's right.'

'What about it?'

'Mr Denny, open the door, please. It's the police.' After a pause the door opened very slowly and revealed a pair of striped blue pyjamas under a faded brown dressing gown.

Mr Denny was extremely small and bald as a cue ball, but he had a sweet, wrinkly face. He had an inch of glass over each eye which made them cartoony. He looked her up and down.

'Young lady, you are not with the police.'

Lenny slipped in and closed the door behind her. 'I want to ask you some questions. I'm a private investigator,' she risked what had become the truth.

They wound up in the little kitchen at the back of the house. It was filled with lime green cabinets. Mr Denny put the kettle on. A brown, Cymric tabby with alopecia swept around his ankles.

'Mr Denny—yes, I will have tea—I want to ask you about Little Pines,' she began. He had lemon wafers and she ate one. 'You were the director of the orphanage, right?'

'I didn't do anything wrong.'

'Mr Denny—' She wasn't feeling patient. She took a breath. She was not going to bully him. There were other ways. She thought of Max's words suddenly: *You underestimate yourself.*

'I want to know if you remember two little girls at the children's home,' she said. 'They would have been there in the nineteen fifties and sixties: Vivian Leonard and Annie Baron.'

Mr Denny smiled. The kettle squealed and he grabbed for it with a teddy bear oven mitt. He made orange pekoe tea in a little china pot and let it brew.

'I chose those names,' he said.

'Vivian was abandoned,' Lenny prompted.

'They both were,' the old man agreed. He warmed two cups with hot water and prepared a strainer and a Peter Rabbit milk jug. 'It was like a fairy story. We found them in a basinette, squashed in together. I'm surprised one of them didn't suffocate.'

'And the mother?' Lenny watched him turn the teapot three times to the right.

'The police never found her. A city teenager, probably. She left a note but it just said "take care of my babies".' *Matching dolls.* Sisters. The eyes on Vivian's Toorak wall might just as easily have been Annie's.

'You gave them different surnames though.'

He poured the tea and it was worth all his fussing because it smelled delicious. She needed something. Her stomach was beginning to writhe. 'At first we just called them Vivvie and Annie, Nurse Margaret and I. This was a small town then. Forty years ago ... There wasn't so much fuss with red tape in those days. But when they grew it was obvious—'

'That one of the children was less intelligent ...' Lenny continued for him. 'This is the best tea I've had in my life and I usually prefer Japanese tea.'

'Fresh milk,' Mr Denny said. 'Benjamin won't go near it though ...' He looked fondly at the cat at his feet. 'Isn't that odd, a cat not liking milk?'

'The children?' Lenny prompted.

'Annie was always a bit slow mentally. Nothing terrible. Just slow. Vivvie was so quick and bright we couldn't keep up with her, but Annie just sat in the cot watching. Nurse Margaret spoiled Vivvie.'

'The names?'

'We ...' he hesitated. 'We didn't think anyone would adopt them both, not with Annie being so ... quiet and everything. They weren't identical. I mean we never did any tests. How could we know for sure they were related? Anyway, we registered them as unrelated children.' He sipped some tea and dunked a lemon wafer. He sighed. 'I always knew in my heart they were sisters. I always felt wrong about the names. That's why I told them later on.'

'When exactly?' Lenny asked

'I told them on their tenth birthday. I chose their birthday. We had to approximate their age. I thought they might as well have each other since neither of them had been adopted. No one wanted to take Annie and Vivvie was a strong-willed child, crying and such. Nurse Margaret could probably remember better than I ...'

'Were either of the sisters ill?'

'They both had troubles when they became young ladies,' Mr Denny blushed. 'Nurse Margaret dealt with that sort of thing. Really, I don't recall. The usual troubles ...'

'You mean they had problems with their menstrual cycle?' Lenny asked flatly.

'I believe so. In my day a gentleman didn't talk about things like that. Especially not in front of a lady.'

'Don't think of me as a lady,' Lenny said.

'They were in and out of George Connor's office. I never asked. Look, I'm tired and I'm an old man.'

'I'm tired too but this is important.'

'It's all a long time ago.'

'Do you remember Dr Connor's death?' The question frightened him. His fingers closed around his cup.

'George was a friend,' he said. 'That was the worst night of my life. We got the children out. Nobody hurt. Then they told me about George ... '

'Two fires on the same night,' Lenny said. It fitted. 'Didn't anyone think it was strange?'

'It was summertime. Dry as a tinder box,' Mr Denny said. 'They took all the kiddies away. I was pensioned off.'

At least you were alive, Lenny thought. He was lucky.

'Did you tell anyone about the sisters?' she asked.

'No, I did not. That was private information. Nurse Margaret was also very much against telling anyone. She agreed with me that we should keep it between the two of us.'

'Have you been here all week?'

'No.' He smiled. 'I visited my sister, Marilyn in Brisbane. One week every other month I go. She's elderly. Enjoys the company. I came home yesterday.' It all made sense to Lenny. What amazed her was that nothing had happened before now.

'I heard Vivvie married a rich man,' Mr Denny said. 'Is it true?' Lenny nodded. 'I'm glad. She was a lovely little thing. I miss all my children.'

'Including Annie?'

'Oh indeed. Indeed, indeed. I would have kept her myself. But Vivvie took her of course. It was only right. For the best. There would have been terrible times if she hadn't. Annie would *never* be away from her sister. She wouldn't have survived without her Vivvie. She worshipped her.'

'Was there any jealousy?'

'You mean was Annie jealous? No. Oh no. Goodness no.

I wondered. Because Vivvie was far the prettier and, of course, smarter. But no, she followed Vivvie like a lamb. Do anything for her.'

'Was Annie ever violent?'

'Goodness me!' He was about to deny it then thought again. 'She was very protective of Vivian. When they were little she would sometimes smack the older boys if they were too rough. Is that what you mean?'

'And Vivian?'

'Vivian allowed it. Commanded it.' He smiled. 'She had a presence even as a toddler.'

Lenny's stomach flipped again. She rubbed it gently.

'What did you tell Carol Connor?' She tried to shake off the lethargy.

'Eh?'

'Carol Connor. George's granddaughter. She visited you.'

'No—'

'On the old people's volunteer program?'

'I am *not* an old person.'

'Look, I don't care about that. Just tell me about Carol.'

'No need to be unpleasant.' Mr Denny said. 'Young ladies who don't mind their manners know what happens to them.'

'Carol—' She experienced a rush of nausea and swallowed hard. Her face and shoulder hurt. Perhaps the Sudafed had been a mistake. Suddenly the memory of the Connors' tabby licking at the cream leftovers was forefront in her mind.

'There've been a few young people visit here. I don't request it.'

'Carol was the pretty one with dark hair. She was about eighteen. Bitchy.'

'That is inappropriate language.'

'Mr Denny, I'm not an easy-going person.' Lenny tasted hot bile. Her brow was starting to sweat. 'I apologize for offending you, but you tell me about Carol, hmm?'

'I'm going to get you some Mylanta. You look bad.' Mr Denny stood up and left the room. When he returned Lenny was barfing tea, lemon wafer and the half-digested remains of a roast dinner into his kitchen sink. Mr Denny, now in his element, held a towel and sponged her face with cold water. He led her into the front room and made her sit on a low couch.

'There, there ... ' he said as she whimpered, her oesophagus still aching. He patted her hand gently. 'Too much excitement, that's all. You sleep now. That'll fix you up.' He placed a little bucket on the floor next to the couch.

'Carol ...' Lenny said as he tucked a pillow under her head.

'I remember ...' Mr Denny sat by the couch on a little stool. 'She was pretty. She asked a lot of questions about the home. She wanted to be a nurse at St Anthony's.'

I bet she did, Lenny thought. It had been a long shot but Carol followed it through ruthlessly and it paid off.

'What did you tell her?' Lenny's eyes closed to keep the room from spinning. She was too tired to move. Perhaps she would Hendrix and drown in her own vomit. Mr Denny would save her though. It seemed she had a penchant for being rescued by unlikely heroes.

'I ... nothing.' But she heard the lie in his voice and smiled against the cushion.

'You told her they were sisters,' she said.

Lenny imagined Carol sitting at the kitchen table, trying to look like the sort of girl who wanted to be a nurse. Mr Denny would have made tea for her too. And eventually, through flattery, sentiment and cunning, the girl would have tricked everything out of him.

She woke up in the dark, still on the couch, sling strangling her. She sat up painfully and pulled open a curtain. Streetlight lit the room enough for her to see her watch face. It was four a.m. She turned on the old radio, lit a cigarette and sat quietly in the front room until dawn, listening to some farmers talking about a crop subsidy.

When Mr Denny peered into the room at first light he

looked uncertain. He had thought he dreamt her, Lenny realized.

'Still here,' she said.

'I'll make toast,' Mr Denny nodded. He sniffed the tobacco air unhappily.

They sat in the kitchen again. He made himself a soft-boiled egg. Lenny's stomach refused anything but a piece of dry toast and a cup of Earl Grey tea. He had a big plastic container with all the Twinings varieties in it.

'Should be tea leaf ...' he said but Lenny shook her head.

'This is good.'

She needed a shower but didn't want to use an old person's
bathroom. She straightened her hair with her left hand. Mr Denny watched, slurping egg from a teaspoon. She supposed she looked a sight.

'Margaret Gross—Nurse Margaret—works for Vivian now,' she said, wiping her crummy fingers on a blue table napkin.

'That woman always got too involved. Unprofessional,' Mr Denny said disapprovingly. 'You know she couldn't have any babies of her own? Turns a woman crazy.'

'We're not all breeding machines, Mr Denny.'

'Eh?'

So in the end their final parting had none of the visit-to-grandpa warmth it could have had. Lenny used her left hand to shake his.

'Will you be coming back?' he asked.

'No. I'm sorry for vomiting in your sink.'

'Oh, think nothing of it.'

'Listen, maybe you should visit your sister again for a few days.'

'Goodness no! Once every other month. Our little ritual.'

'I meant for your safety.'

'Isn't that kind?' He began a doorstep wave that lasted until her car was at the end of the cul-de-sac.

It occurred to her that she was now following in Carol Connor's footsteps and that for Carol this path had led to death.

Toowoomba, reached several hours later, was situated on top of a small mountain plateau. Lenny was looking for St Anthony's Hospital. Carol had come here for confirmation. It was a neat, grey building with a wide, glass entrance. There was a solitary ambulance parked outside.

'Ooh Miss!' A chubby nurse jumped up as she took in Lenny's injuries. She offered a wheelchair and Lenny (Why the hell not? She *was* exhausted!) sat in it and allowed herself to be wheeled into examination room five.

'You wait here and I'll be back with a doctor,' Nurse Judy said.

She returned ten minutes later with a handsome young man in a crisp white jacket. He was ash blond and deeply tanned.

'I'm Dr Patrick,' he said. 'Worry about that later, Judy ...'

'Yes, Doctor.' Nurse Judy put down the pencil and file obediently.

'Actually, I'm here to see Dr Thomas Brown. He's a friend of a friend,' Lenny explained.

'Oh.' Dr Patrick and Nurse Judy were disappointed so she allowed them to change the dressing on her sutured cheek. Dr Patrick, fringe flopping across vivid blue eyes, made a great show of examining the stitches. He was so fresh and clean he crackled. Nurse Judy swooned with admiration.

'So you know old Tom?' Dr Patrick said, applying neat surgical strips over a gauze pad that was thankfully smaller than the previous one.

'Yes. Is he on duty? Ouch,' as Nurse Judy, hovering with a little metal tray for leftover gauze, bumped her injured shoulder.

'Really, Judy!'

'Sorry,' she whispered. To him, not Lenny.

'He'll be on in another hour,' Dr Patrick said. A noise in the waiting room sent the nurse scurrying out to check. She ran back, eyes bright.

'There's a broken leg, I think! There's so much blood!'

'Well, don't panic.' Dr Patrick stood up from his stool, loving it.

Lenny looked at herself in the examination room mirror. She was pale and her hair was greasy. Her forehead bruise was eggplant coloured. She took off the sling because she wanted to look strong.

From examination room one she heard the stentorian tones of St Anthony's finest: 'I'm sorry, this may hurt ...'

It took thirty seconds to find Dr Brown's location on the hospital directory board. She found the stairs and walked up two flights. It was quiet and shadowy in the corridors. Once or twice a nurse passed ahead of her, crossing from one ward to another. But, like an invisible woman, she went unnoticed until she reached room eleven: Dr T. Brown, Obstetrics. The door was not locked so she went in.

The room, though decorated in the stereotype of a successful doctor's office—degrees on the wall, antique wooden desk, executive chair—looked faded and threadbare. The skeleton was dusty. It was an old man's room.

Lenny picked up the framed family photo. Dr Brown, for surely this was he, was about fifty with wavy grey hair and a big face. His wife was the same age and pretty. The children, a boy and a girl, were in their late teens or early twenties and resembled their parents. The girl was holding a Persian cat.

When Dr Brown arrived, Lenny had made herself comfortable in a chair opposite his and was smoking her second cigarette. There was no ashtray in the office so she had wadded up several sheets of his notepaper and was using that.

Dr Brown, at least five years older than his photograph, looked hard at the cigarette and then at Lenny. Surprise and pomposity fought across his face. He took in her injuries in a swift assessment.

'Please put that out.' He was brusque, going immediately and dramatically to open the big windows. Sunlight shafted across the room in a wide stripe. 'I don't know how you got in here, young lady, without any sort of appointment. If you need medical treatment I suggest you take yourself down to casualty. It's on the ground floor.'

'Dr Brown, I'm Lenny Aaron.' Lenny put down the cigarette. It sizzled through a couple of layers of paper. Dr Brown's eyes stayed on it, lips pursed. 'I knew Carol Connor. She asked me to speak to you.'

He sat down and picked up a pen to twiddle with.

'Carol Connor?'

'An ex-pink lady.'

'I don't recall the name. I have little to do with the pink ladies. Admirable hobby.' He pretended to examine his calendar.

'Carol told me you slept with her—' She hadn't really known for sure—it had been a hunch until his face went purple.

'Who are you?! How dare you!!'

'I'm Lenny Aaron,' Lenny smiled.

'Ms Aaron, I will call the police.' Hand reaching for the phone.

'How do you know I'm not the police?'

'Are you?' He was worried for a moment, then slapped his chair arm angrily. 'I've already told my wife—you can't blackmail me!'

'Oh shut up,' Lenny said. He was lying. They never told their wives. They got caught and *then*, sobbing, confessed all. She lit another cigarette. He opened his mouth to complain but didn't.

'Look, Doctor,' she said, 'I don't care about your wife. Really. I want to know about Carol. How long she was here. What she did. What you talked about. If she was sleeping with anyone else. You tell me all that and you'll never see or hear from me again.'

He was speechless for a moment and she realized he was genuinely taken aback.

'Sleeping with someone else?' he said weakly.

'Tell me everything you remember about her.'

'Carol's dead,' Dr Brown said. 'She promised she'd never talk about us.'

'Can't trust young girls,' Lenny told him.

'Look, I really won't answer to this! This is preposterous!' He jumped to his feet, used to being the authority figure for young women with their panties off and legs apart.

'OK, OK,' Lenny said. 'So I'll call your wife and I'll tell her you were fucking a girl younger than your daughter.'

'You can't!'

'Stop screaming.' She lowered her voice a little. 'You'll have a nurse in here. Sit down and talk. It can't matter to you to tell me. I give you my word that if you cooperate, I'll protect you. Keep you out of it.' Dr Brown sat down.

'Really?' he said. Lenny nodded. 'All right ... all right ... but it was two years ago. I haven't seen her since then. She got engaged to another man ...' Yeah, a single, young, rich man, Lenny thought.

'I don't know what this is about. But *she* came after *me*,' Dr Brown said firmly. 'She was ... voracious.'

'And sometimes she waited for you in this office? Alone?'

'Well ... yes ... I suppose ...'

'Do you keep all your records in these files?' Lenny gestured at the cabinets. 'I mean old ones? Twenty years old?'

He nodded.

'Pull out Vivian Leonard's file,' Lenny instructed. 'You delivered her twins twenty years ago.'

'Now look here. We can't have that sort of thing. It's not on. Confidentiality.'

Lenny blew a line of smoke at him. 'The file or I call your wife from the pay phone downstairs,' she said.

'This is an outrage!'

'Think of it as the most exciting moment in an otherwise dull day,' Lenny quipped and held out her hand. 'The file.'

He stood up and foraged in one of the cabinets. 'A lot of the details are on disc now, in Archives,' he said. 'I only keep the basics here.'

Lenny grabbed the file from him. It was a beige manila folder with V. Leonard printed in red ink in the top right-hand corner. It *was* basic: twin babies, their birth weight, the genetic deformity of their crooked little fingers, their mother's high blood pressure due to weight gain. It had been a twenty-two hour labour. The babies were blood typed A+, the same as their mother. Vivian was admitted for a week but all three of them left the hospital twenty-four hours after the birth. There was no follow-up, no address and no contact number.

'You'll have to provide the details,' Lenny said.

'I don't understand what all this is about. Who are you?' Dr Brown said. 'I know Vivian Leonard married Henry Talbott but it's old news if you're some kind of journalist. Quite a scandal at the time. Old enough to be her—' He realized his hypocrisy and stopped. 'The babies' fingers. That's why he married her . . .'

'Were the fingers crooked at birth?'

'Of course!' he thundered. 'Do you think I'd sanction something like that?! How dare you!'

'Keep your wig on,' Lenny soothed him. 'I'm sure they were. Tell me about the birth. From the start.'

'She was here less than forty-eight hours,' he said, gesturing at the file for confirmation. 'She didn't come here for prenatal.'

That supported Vivian's story, Lenny thought: hiding out in the country to avoid publicity, Henry repulsed by her fatness, not wanting to visit her, taken care of by the long-suffering Annie. No check-ups. A rush to the hospital when the contractions became severe. In and out before the press could wake up to who she really was.

'The second baby, the girl, came out quite quickly in

comparison.' Dr Brown wound up his explanation of the birth of Kendell and Kimberly. 'They were both big and healthy. Ms Leonard was very weak, though. She'd lost a lot of blood. Normally we wouldn't have discharged her so early.'

'Was anyone with her?'

'A woman. Dark, I think.'

'Did she speak to you?'

'Yes. I do remember that. It was a disappointment. A bit slow, I thought. Wouldn't meet anyone's eyes.'

'And Vivian? Was she beautiful?'

'Well ... not then, of course. I never believe pregnant women are beautiful. That's just something we tell them because—' he shrugged, smiled again. 'They have such an unpleasant time, don't they? Vivian had a lot of water retention. Some of them balloon.' He shrugged. 'But I saw her a couple of months later in the wedding photos. She looked spectacular.'

She had woken up in a shed. Pitch black outside and silent. The 'middle of nowhere' scenario. Tied to a wooden chair, both arms and legs strapped tightly. But not gagged. Her face felt swollen. He sat opposite her. He wore corduroy pants and an ivory Shetland jumper. Blond tously hair. Like a model from GQ or Esquire.

He smiled. She realized she was going to die and started to shake, teeth rattling.

'Lenny, you're not going to testify.'

He opened a string bag and took out a Stanley knife and a large metal mallet.

'We're in the middle of nowhere, so scream away.'

Then he cut her arm. It was tied to the chair at both wrist and elbow so she couldn't move it. He used the Stanley knife to slice neatly through the tissue and muscle then parted the skin with his fingers so the white bone was exposed. He was as impassive as a surgeon at his two hundredth incision. Through all this she screamed. She never realized it was possible that your own voice could make your ears hum.

'Have a look,' *he said in the same casual voice. There was blood over her arm and legs and the floor. But the whiteness of the bone sparkled up at her. A gorgeous, virgin white against the background of scarlet.*

'I want you to have the scar so you can look at it and finger it and remember,' *he said.* 'But that pain will go away. I want you to have a more permanent pain.'

He raised the mallet and, while she watched, he brought it down on the exposed bone. It shattered on the first impact. Blood sprayed up into her face and hair. Somehow she didn't pass out. Unimaginable that the mind could allow you to remain conscious through pain and horror—but it did.

He took out a bandage, used his fingers to squeeze the skin together and wrapped her arm tightly. St John's Ambulance, he said. The circulation was gone from her fingers.

'You'll have to make it over to casualty yourself, Lenny,' *he said when they reached St Vincent's Hospital. He drove off with a smile and a wave.*

She remembered the walk to casualty; coming through those swinging doors like Carrie on Prom Night. Then X-rays, gurneys, bright lights and the merciful amnesia of drugs.

Chapter 28

CAT CATCHER

Her office answering machine had three messages. MacAvoy was first. He sounded gruff and apologetic. She fast-forwarded. Her mother was next.

'Lenny? Are you there? Lenny?' Pleading, a pause. 'Lenny Aaron, you pick up that phone!'

'Lenny, hi.' The last voice was Vivian's. A long pause. 'Are you listening and just not picking up? Are you screening me?' The voice was a little sad. 'Listen, I want to see you. We're going to Vienna this week. I want to see you before I go. Please, Lenny.' Another pause. 'I'll wait for you this afternoon, in Leonardo's. It's a coffee shop on Toorak Road, near South Yarra station. I'll be there at three o'clock. I can wait until four. Please come.'

There was another pause. 'The police have *finally* opened up the Brighton house. You still have your security access for the gate and your house keys, don't you? If you have anything there you want to collect, you can drop by. Today would be best. The house is empty so you won't be disturbing anyone. Meet me, Lenny. Please.' She hung up.

Lenny pulled Dr Connor's notebook out of her bag and flicked through it. It wasn't really any kind of evidence. Without names and an official case file, it was just an old man's story.

A familiar voice from the parking lot outside her window made her leap out of her seat. She stuck the notebook back into her bag, grabbed her keys and, ignoring the pain in her shoulder, ran out of the office. She made it to the car park before they got away. It was Dr Sakuno and a young Japanese girl of about fifteen loading boxes into the back of the Crown Majesta. They looked up as she approached and their identical movements and faces gave them away: it had to be Dr Sakuno's daughter.

Unlike her father, the girl dressed casually. She wore sneakers, baggy shorts and an over-sized Prodigy t-shirt with the sleeves ripped off and a lime green bikini top as a bra. She had five silver rings in the ridge of her right ear.

'Dr Sakuno! What a surprise!' Lenny said. 'I thought you were on vacation.'

'Ms Aaron.' He was clearly horrified to see her.

'There's a cyclone in Guam,' the girl said, staring at Lenny's sling and bruises. 'You're one of his strange ones, aren't you?'

'Kumiko!' her father thundered.

' "Mickey",' she corrected.

'Could be,' said Lenny. 'Lenny Aaron.' She held out a hand. The girl took it, trying to mask her curiosity.

'Mickey Sakuno.'

'Ms Aaron, this is hardly the time.' Dr Sakuno manoeuvred his daughter towards the passenger door but she twisted away.

'Isn't Footscray a little out of your way?' Lenny asked.

'We bust a *shoji* door. There's a Jap carpenter out here,' the girl chipped in. 'Cheap supplies.'

'I need to talk to you,' Lenny told Dr Sakuno. 'I've got to pick up my car from Western General Hospital, then I could come in to your office.'

'Wanna lift? We're going past the hospital,' Kumiko offered.

'Kumiko, that is not desirable.'

'Why? Is she really a psycho?' The girl looked Lenny over. 'Did ya get beat up?' Lenny nodded and the girl looked pleased.

They drove across the bland city sprawl. Lenny asked Dr Sakuno to drop her at the hospital. He made no attempt to speak to her. He was outraged that a patient had wriggled her way into his privacy. Kumiko chatted over the noise of her Oasis tape.

'Has he started you on the Buddha shit yet?' Lenny nodded. 'You're so predictable, Dad.'

'*Otosan*,' Dr Sakuno corrected her stiffly. 'Call me *Otosan* and with respect. Ms Aaron, please do not speak with my daughter. She is impressionable.'

'Dad won't be happy till I'm in a kimono and married to a salary man,' Kumiko laughed. 'He reckons I'm off to Tokyo to uni. Like I would, right? I'm not,' she paused, 'Japanese.'

'Kumiko!'

'I don't even speak Japanese.'

'Yes, you do!' Dr Sakuno fired off a volley of angry Japanese. Kumiko made 'over my head' gestures, egging him on.

'It's all Greek to me. Tell me, Lenny, is he a good psychologist?'

Dr Sakuno gave her a nasty look and turned the music up loud. Kumiko began to chew on a thumbnail that was already down to the quick.

At the hospital, Dr Sakuno got out and walked with Lenny to her car, which was still parked in the emergency area. Kumiko, having won a minor familial victory and feeling quite independent now, ignored both of them.

'Do not approach my family again,' Dr Sakuno said. 'The last thing Kumiko needs is to be influenced by you.'

'Look,' Lenny sighed and pulled off the parking ticket attached to her windscreen wipers, 'I'm in danger. Can we focus on me for a minute?'

Dr Sakuno muttered in Japanese but drew a breath to calm himself. He looked at her battered face seriously for the first time.

'I saw the papers. I would never have advised all this.'

'You said be your own lamp!'

'I was going out the door on vacation. That's the sort of advice people give to get rid of people.'

'Thank you, Doctor.'

'Look,' he shrugged, a western gesture, 'it's a long way from cats to murder. Too far.'

'I've solved the case,' Lenny insisted. She felt annoyed and disappointed. She wanted him to be proud of her.

'So tell the police, not me.'

'I want to follow it through myself. I think that would be a good idea for me, don't you?'

'I think you'll get yourself killed.' Dr Sakuno stepped away from her and glanced back at his car. He was still angry with his daughter and not interested in anything else. 'I have no time on my schedule today. Make an appointment. And whatever happens, don't blame me. I do my best, but you're incurable.' He jogged away. Lenny watched him begin an argument with Mickey.

She looked at the ticket in her hand: thirty dollars for parking in a restricted area.

She drove along St Kilda Road towards Elsternwick and Brighton. It was time to rescue her bonsai. Dead bonsai, she amended. Cedars Court was just as she remembered it: peaceful and elegant. No cricketers today though.

The garden needed mowing. Grass was ragged and a few weeds had already staked claims. The police scene-of-crime tape was gone.

She unlocked the front door and went in. In the hallway there were signs of packing, crates and boxes filled with valuables. She punched a code into the security key pad by the door to deactivate the motion sensors and then moved through the house.

She found the bonsai. Someone had over-watered them. They'd drowned. She was loading the pots into a cardboard box when she heard a noise and spun around. Annie moved into the doorway, filling the exit with her bulk. Vivian had said the house was empty.

Annie looked tired and confused. She was dressed as always in a loose dark dress, with her hair scraped back. Lenny looked at her with new eyes. This was Vivian's twin. Despite the weight, it seemed clear now.

'Vivian says you know everything,' Annie said slowly. 'Are you going to tell?'

'Yes, I am,' Lenny said.

'You'll spoil everything!' Annie started to weep. 'Henry would be so angry.'

'Annie, Carol is dead. Someone has to pay for that.'

'Max!'

'No. You know who's responsible.'

'I don't! I don't!' She looked ready to spring. Lenny prepared to jump sideways.

In the end she did nothing because Vivian appeared at her sister's shoulder. She was smiling.

'Annie, wait for me downstairs.'

Annie hesitated then walked away. Vivian was calm. She must have known this day would come.

'Come to my room,' she said and Lenny followed her.

Vivian wore a white jacket and pants with no blouse. Her feet were bare and her hair was blown around her shoulders. She stood at the window, watching the sea, near the same balcony where Carol had been killed. The edge of the white carpet was still tinged musk. Lenny stood across from her at the antique dresser.

'I'm sad to leave this house,' Vivian said, turning around. 'But we must. Your poor bonsai. I'll replace them of course.'

'You said the house was empty. You said you'd meet me at Toorak,' Lenny said, cursing herself. She had to get out of there as quickly as possible.

'Your poor face,' Vivian continued softly. She looked concerned now and regretful. 'Will there be a scar?'

'A small one,' Lenny said.

'It will suit you. Lenny, did you find anything at the Connors' house?'

'Yes.'

'Are you going to give it to me?'

'No.'

'What are you going to do with it?'

'Give it to the police.'

'Do you have it with you?' Vivian laughed and sat on her bed, white against white. 'I suppose you haven't told anyone either? Did you plan a big finale where I begged you not to reveal everything? Is that what you want, Lenny? Do you want me to beg you? No one will accept Annie as an axe murderer. No one will believe you!' She laughed again.

Lenny laughed too because this was the final betrayal. 'Annie's been with you all your life,' she said more bitterly than she'd intended. 'She's done everything you could possibly ask of another woman.'

'Of a sister,' Vivian said softly and covered moist eyes with a slim hand. 'I didn't want you to find out. Lenny, help me to protect her. Please! She was confused! I have to look after her. She isn't clever like me.'

'You made her your servant for twenty years.'

'I wanted a rich husband,' Vivian said. 'I never realised how much she resented me until it was too late. She had been moody at first with the Cushing's Syndrome, but you were right about her. She was always moody, even when we were kids. She had a temper. I knew she sent the letters but I never thought it would go beyond that. I didn't *know*!' Her hands tensed. 'How could I know? That's why I let you stay with us. I mean, I didn't care about Kimberly's bloody cat, but I thought if Annie felt I had an investigator, it might scare her into stopping.

'I didn't realize she was dangerous. You have to believe that. She had started to become jealous of me. She began to act as though Henry and the children were *her* family. Sometimes she was quite normal. But sometimes she frightened me.

'Obviously not enough to take action. I never thought she'd

really try to hurt me! When she mistook poor Carol for me, I had to help cover it up. Lenny, I know you think it's wrong ... but Annie is dearer to me than anyone alive. I won't let you send her to jail.'

'Bullshit.'

'No. Lenny—'

'Shut up,' Lenny said coldly. Vivian was silent, the tears suddenly gone. 'Annie was right. I do know everything.'

'Lenny, don't say anymore. She's dangerous. I know that now. She'll hurt you.'

'Shall I tell you everything?' Lenny kept her peripheral vision on the open door. Where was Annie? Was she close by, listening, waiting? She leaned back against the dresser.

'It's a strange story from the start, isn't it? Twin baby girls abandoned. One was always so much prettier than the other. And smarter too. Annie loved you but she was a millstone. You would have offloaded her if she hadn't been useful. If you didn't have to keep her around.

'Nurse Gross worshipped you too. She'd do anything for you. She took you to see Dr Connor all those times but she waited outside. She didn't know Dr Connor told you he thought you had endometriosis. He advised you to see a specialist to confirm his diagnosis. And he suspected you were infertile.'

'You mean Annie,' Vivian said. 'That was Annie.'

'No,' Lenny said. 'You were sisters. You both had trouble with your menstrual cycle. You both visited Dr Connor. But Annie's was no more than regular cramps. You were the one who had endometriosis. I'm betting you saw a specialist and you found out his diagnosis was correct. You were never going to have children.'

Vivian said nothing. She watched Lenny.

'Tough break,' Lenny continued. 'But no one knew except you and Dr Connor. You didn't tell Margaret. You went off to get a rich husband and you found Henry Talbott. You wouldn't sleep with him. You were holding out for marriage but he wanted children and you couldn't give him that. Then you got lucky. He was drunk. When he came to your room, you were out but Annie was there. It was dark. She resembled you. He raped her.

'When Annie was pregnant, you told Henry *you* were. You convinced Annie to keep quiet. You told her she'd never be allowed to keep the babies if people knew the truth. At the delivery you disguised yourself as Annie. You kept your head down, you mumbled. No one was really looking at you anyway. They were all looking at Annie.'

'Annie and I *are* twins. The rest is ridiculous,' Vivian said softly, her eyes wide on Lenny's face like violet lenses, like some animal's eyes at night, like ...

'You can't have children. Kimberly and Kendell are Annie's. When you took the babies to Cedars Court you were disguising yourself to look heavy, but Annie was the one recovering from the pregnancy. If she'd become thin again, if Henry had recognized her ... I wonder if you'd have killed her before that happened. But you didn't have to, did you? Your luck always held. Annie developed Cushing's Syndrome. A million to one shot. She never recaptured her looks. Henry was never going to recognize her. So you let her live.'

Vivian reached for a pile of letters on her bedside table and began slitting them open with a stainless-steel letter knife.

'All right,' she said. She shrugged. 'I went to Brisbane and had the tests. I used a fake name. The doctors there said the endometriosis had already caused severe damage to my fallopian tubes and ovaries. They said there was very little chance I would ever conceive.' She shrugged again. 'It meant nothing to me emotionally. I didn't want children. And I took a course of drugs to help the pain. But I needed to produce a child for Henry. He made it clear nothing else would get me what I wanted.

'So,' the cold smile. 'I'm asking you not to tell anyone. You think I *stole* Annie's babies? Henry would never, *never* have married Annie. My way we all got to have everything we wanted. Believe me, I allowed Annie to be happier than she had any right to expect. I'm the one who's been betrayed! I'm the one you should be outraged for! She tried to kill me—'

'Why?'

'Henry's illness has something to do with it. When she knew he was dying she had some kind of mental breakdown. One minute she's the old Annie, loves me, the next she's ... She thinks I have everything that should be hers.'

'Don't you?' Lenny demanded.

'She killed that poor child—'

'Because she thought it was you?'

'Yes.'

'Couldn't she tell the difference between her own forty-year-old twin and a twenty-year-old girl? Oh, I know Carol was dressing like you and doing her hair like you. I wonder who encouraged that?'

'Carol wanted to step up. She imitated me.'

'You encouraged her?'

'Yes.'

'And then you killed her.'

There was a long silence. Lenny watched the letter knife slide along another envelope. The gold embossed invitation was tossed onto the bed with the others.

'Annie killed her. She'll confess it. Shall we ask her?' The violet eyes that met Lenny's were no longer guarded.

'I know you could get her to confess,' Lenny said. 'She loves you. That's her weakness. I suspect her only weakness. All that stuff about her temper, her moods. I think that's your character. You wanted me to think it was Annie's. But it's not true and I won't let her go to jail for you, any more than I'd let Max.'

'I had no reason at all to hurt Carol Connor,' Vivian protested mildly. 'I was the one who encouraged Kendell to marry her. I was her friend.'

'No,' Lenny said. 'Once I stopped believing you were the intended victim, it was much easier. You tricked me with your stories though. About Kimberly and Kendell and Annie. You wanted me to think they were all dangerous. Everyone except you. That story about the dog that Annie killed. I think you killed the dog.'

'You'll never prove any of this,' Vivian said.

'Carol Connor was a nobody,' Lenny said slowly. Was it too late to dash for the door, too late to realize that Dr Sakuno was right? *She was going to get herself killed.* 'But she was smart and ambitious. And her grandfather was Dr George Connor, the one man who suspected you couldn't have any children.'

'He's dead,' Vivian said.

'Of course. You killed him twenty years ago. You destroyed your medical records and burned the orphanage—'

'Lenny,' the slim hand gripped the hilt of the letter knife again. Lenny kept her eyes on it. She prepared to move at the first sign of attack.

'But Dr Connor kept personal records at home,' Lenny continued. 'Carol found his case history of two Gympie orphans. Her mother often spoke about Gympie's most famous old girl: you. She figured it out. It was easy for her to seduce Kendell, then all she had to do was tell you that if she didn't get to marry him, the story would be out.'

'I was the only one who ever liked Carol,' Vivian protested mildly. 'Everyone will tell you that. I supported her.'

'You planned to kill her from the start. You sent threatening letters to yourself. You had Kimberly find the letters in your bag. You even went through the charade of hiring me. You stacked the party with people who hated you but that was a back-up plan, right? You always intended Max to be arrested. You always knew about Max.'

Vivian laughed softly.

'I went into Max's room one day while he was out shopping,' she said. 'I was curious to see how he lived. The birth certificate wasn't even hidden. He kept it in his top drawer.'

'You took Max's axe from the shed,' Lenny said, eyes never leaving the knife. 'You hid it in your room and arranged to meet Carol upstairs. She was upset. I heard the two of you arguing in the garden but I thought she was speaking to Kendell.' *It's time you realized you do what I say. Things are going to change around here.*

Vivian pulled white gloves from her pocket and slipped them on, wiped the knife handle. Lenny was torn between the urge to run and the urge to finish this. She had taken the next step. She wanted to go all the way. If she didn't, Dorling had won.

'You met her in your room, waited until she had her back to you then you hit her with the axe. You took blood down to the shed. You stole Liz Dodd's pink paper to write one of your letters. I don't know why, except I think that you liked the game. You wanted to see how many elements you could draw into it.'

Vivian put down the knife. She smiled, raised her hands in a little gesture of submission then reached into her pocket and slid out a tiny pistol. The first bullet hit Lenny under her right knee cap. She fell sideways. The second bullet hit her right shoulder, sending pain waves through the cracked collarbone.

Lenny scrambled for the door. She was bleeding but not profusely. The bullet holes were small and Vivian hadn't hit any arteries. But she would. Lenny kicked against the carpet with her left leg and pushed herself backwards. She took a breath to scream for help but felt a smashing blow to the left side of her head and collapsed onto the carpet, shards of vase around her. Her mouth and nose dripped blood and she turned her head to spit. Was there anyone other than Annie in the house?

Vivian, smiling, came round to her left. She lifted Lenny's left arm gently. Almost as though she intended to help her up. Instead she struck down hard with the paper knife, through skin and tissue into the old wound. Lenny lashed out with her right arm, the pain of the bullets engulfed in this new horror. It was unendurable—pain and memories of pain together.

She used all her weight and the last scrap of strength to swing forward into a head butt. Her forehead cracked into Vivian's. Vivian fell backwards, yelping in surprise and put a hand to her head. She dropped the knife and pressed her fingers to her brow, bewildered. She crouched next to Lenny who was struggling to stop the blood pouring out of her arm. She pinched the ripped skin together. It didn't help. She was going to bleed to death.

Vivian smiled, blood on her hands and all over her cool, white Armani suit.

'I lost control the night of the party,' she said, amused by Lenny's ridiculous attempts to stop her bleeding.

'The second time I hit Carol was obviously unnecessary. But after the first time I wanted to do it again.'

'Vivian, help me ...' Lenny was dizzy, she was lonely and she was going to die. It seemed as though her blood filled the room.

'I'm not going to go through all this and then save you, my darling.' Vivian smiled. 'No, no, no ... When you're dead Annie will come up and she'll leave her fingerprints on the knife and the gun and then she'll confess. I'll say she hit me. I tried to stop her ... ' She touched her forehead. 'So thanks for this.'

'They'll investigate.'

'Oh, Lenny, they're stupid, aren't they?' Vivian laughed. Then she leaned forward and took Lenny's jaw in her hand, hard like a vice so that the split lip spilled opened again. 'I tried to kill you in that parking lot but you just wouldn't let go, would you?' She pushed lightly. This time Lenny had no strength to sit up. She didn't release the grip on her cut arm, she clung to it, but she felt herself drifting somewhere else, where arms and scars and cat catchers didn't matter.

Vivian sat by her, knees up to her chin, arms wrapped around them, talking softly, soothing.

'You're right about everything. I want you to know that. I'm completely surprised and very proud. I chose you deliberately, you know. I knew about your arm and your breakdown.' She smiled. 'I killed Kimberly's cat. I needed a way to bring you in.

'I knew Michael Dorling. We met socially. I recognized him at once for what he was as he recognized me. Nothing ever came of it. When you almost got him, I followed your career, the attack, the nervous breakdown, even the cats. I was fascinated that you'd been hunting him but that in the end *he'd* caught *you*. Still, I might have never given you any further attention. But then Carol came to me with her threats and blackmail and I had to think things through.

'I needed people to believe I was in danger. I thought an investigator would be a nice touch. I spent some time considering how to find someone suitable and how to bring them into my plan. And then, quite out of the blue, two weeks ago, Michael Dorling gets himself shot in the head. Well, I thought of you at once: the fallen, ex-policewoman, the cat cop. I remembered how much your story had interested me. And I thought how perfect you would be for the chump.' She showed her teeth again. 'All I needed was a missing cat. But that was easy. Kimberly had bought Marie Antoinette a couple of months ago. It seemed, Lenny, almost fate, that you and I were being drawn together. I took the cat into my room, rolled it inside a towel, and smashed it against the bathroom wall. Of course Kimberly wanted someone to find the cat and *of course* she chose you. I'd already rung the RSPCA and the pound and a handful of vets myself to see what would happen if someone had a missing cat. *Everyone* recommended you. You're the best. I hid the cat for a couple of days until it got too ripe and then had you find it on the beach. You surprised me with the autopsy though. So thorough, Lenny!

'I think it's a neat ending to kill you this way, don't you? The same wound? You should've died the first time. I used to wonder how Dorling felt when he had you trapped and he could do anything he wanted to you. You couldn't stop him.' She moved suddenly, Lenny had no strength to react.

She felt the long lean body press on to hers. Vivian lay on top of her, their bodies fitted together, faces close, mouths almost touching. She pressed her smooth cheek against Lenny's bandaged one for a moment, sighed. Breath mingled. Lenny felt Vivian's lips nibble gently on her own swollen, torn top lip and then a caress from a hot tongue. Lenny's eyes ran tears from the corners.

Vivian sat up again with Lenny's blood on her mouth. 'You've done yourself proud, Lenny. You should be happy.'

Lenny's eyes hurt from the light. She blinked, but the only escape now was to close her eyes and let death take her.

'I did kill Dr Connor. I had to. He was surprised to see me, asked me if I ever followed up on the endometriosis. I pretended I was driving through town and suddenly had terrible stomach pains. It was easy. I was the last patient. When he turned away for a moment I slammed him into his desk. He was old. He wasn't dead though. He looked up at me. His forehead was bleeding. He tried to get up but he passed out, poor thing.' She smiled. 'I torched the place.'

'Mr Denny?' Lenny said. She thought, why do I keep wanting to sort it all out, even now? Am I mad? She was cold and her grip on her arm was slipping, sticky with her blood. But she knew she didn't want the old man to die because of her.

'Mr Denny was lucky he escaped the Little Pine's fire and lucky he kept his mouth shut afterwards. Margaret kept in touch with him. She warned him to say nothing. She's been invaluable. She gave me a sedative that night after Carol was dead. But not straight away. I had to go and check Carol's things. I didn't find anything, of course. Maggie never even asked me why. Loyalty like that is hard to find.

'Do you think Mr Denny's a danger to me? Shall I go back and kill him? I thought about it last week but he wasn't in. Lucky old sod. You found him though, didn't you?' Her eyes hardened, violet-grey. She turned to the door and called Annie.

Lenny heard the thuds on the staircase as Annie huffed and puffed her way up. She appeared in the doorway and began to shriek, husky whines that sucked in great gulps of air.

'V ... V ... Vivian!'

Vivian stood up, eyes wide as if from fear.

'Lenny tried to hurt me, Annie! She wants to hurt your babies too. You watch her now while I call the police. You pick up the gun and that knife and watch her.'

Annie grabbed the weapons. The gun shook in her hand. The knife hung at her side.

Lenny's head lolled and she knew that she had released the grip on her arm. Voices got louder in the distance. Chattering. Women. Someone else in the house?

'Shoot her! She'll kill Kimmie!' Vivian's voice, filled with rage and panic. There was another gunshot but Lenny's eyes were closed now. She didn't feel the bullet but surely somewhere it entered her body. It didn't matter.

Then screaming and voices again. Annie was saying Vivian's name over and over. And someone was squeezing Lenny's arm hard. Another hand was slapping her face and when she blinked to catch the last glimpse of world-light, she saw Kimberly's bulldog face, grey like graphite and mouthing in digital slow-mo.

Her head turned. Vivian was lying on the carpet, violet eyes wide open and a tiny spot of blood over the heart of her white suit. Annie was screaming over her and pounding the carpet, hitting the floor like an ape, her knuckles bleeding into the white wool. Behind her Maggie Gross cried into a telephone.

Lenny closed her eyes. There was another sharp slap.

'Don't you die, bitch!' It was Kimberly. The reliable fascist. Lenny smiled but her mouth moved oddly. Her lips must be swollen. Did she get hit there? She hurt everywhere.

It was the pounding that kept her alive. She could feel its bass rhythm through the floor; the dual action of Annie's thumps to the carpet and Kimberly's slaps on her face.

The ambulance men arrived. Lenny knew they must be moving fast and yet everything was too slow, too drawn out. There were some police, she saw blue legs and cheap, shiny shoes. Hands reached down to lift Annie away from Vivian's body. Vivian's body.

Lenny tried to reach out when they lifted her, but they took her arm firmly and tied it down against her. They strapped her onto the gurney and took her away while Annie screamed and smashed the floor.

Chapter 29

A MEZZED UB CAZE

Lenny remembered little from immediately after the attack. There were days of sleeping then waking, her intravenous bag being changed, her bottom gently wiped: indignities quite soothing under heavy medication.

The first thing she noticed was her mother sitting near the bed. Veronica Aaron looked ten years older.

It was her mother who filled her in on the details of the missing week of her life. She was called in as the next of kin on that first day a week ago when it seemed like Lenny might die from shock.

Apparently it had been the full drama. She had bullets removed from her shoulder and leg. Her nose was badly broken and her lips needed ten stitches inside but that, the doctor assured her mother, was purely cosmetic and would not leave a scar. Her left arm, however, was a different story. The ripped muscles and flesh, old scar tissue re-torn, was going to take a long time to recover. In fact it was unlikely she would ever regain full mobility of her hand. She had seen the unbandaged flesh when the nurse changed the dressing and it was nothing like the neat, surgical cut Michael Dorling had given her. Her forearm was a web of purple, puckered skin crisscrossed with sutures.

The arm was semi-plastered to prevent movement. Her palm had a tingle of awareness but there was nothing at the fingertips. She was, they told her distraught mother, going to be an outpatient for a long time.

Veronica Aaron had kept all the newspapers. She read them aloud while Lenny listened and dozed. When she was awake she was in pain and grumpy. Her mother popped in and out from the hospital cafeteria. Knitted. Kept up a light chat.

'You gave us a real scare but you're going to be just fine. Dr Ogden—he's lovely, married—told me just this morning that he has high hopes for you. You just don't worry about anything. Just concentrate on getting better.'

The police who came to interview her had a different line: 'Just concentrate on the facts.' Lenny had the feeling they envied her celebrity. The newspapers had dubbed her the detective who solved the crime of the decade; that is until the next crime of the decade came along.

She was in the same hospital as her grandmother who was—a miracle!—out of her coma and off the critical list. The old lady was in fine spirits apparently, had asked for Lenny quite distinctly on regaining consciousness. The ward sister relayed this to Lenny as she sponge-bathed her and wanted to know if Lenny would like to be wheeled round for a visit. Lenny's mother buried her head deeper in *New Idea*.

Ted Aaron had joined the family in hospital. His left lung had collapsed. Lenny felt no connection to this news. Her mouth tasted of chemicals. She was drugged. As she had been the night of the party. Drugged by Vivian. The champagne cocktail supposedly whipped up by Annie. All bullshit. Vivian had drugged her—not enough to make her suspicious, but enough to make her careless.

It didn't matter. She didn't care about anything. Just sleep. Sleep.

'My cad,' she whispered. My cat.

There was an enormous, floral card from Ron MacAvoy and his wife pinned on the wall. And one from Danny, who hadn't visited but whom she had hallucinated at the foot of the bed, reading her chart and laughing.

Mike Bullock was genuinely distraught. He brought a bunch of red roses and a poster of Mount Fuji with pink Japanese writing. She could see where he had cut out two figures fucking in the foreground—there was still an ankle left. The nurses taped the poster to the wall.

'Lenny, mate ...' He cried like a baby. Veronica Aaron was horrified—was this gingery slob her daughter's beau? Lenny struggled to move, to speak, to deny.

Mike moved in. 'Yeah, mate? What is it? Anything. I'll do anything for you.'

'My office. Keeb an eye on my office.' She let him sit with her for half an hour, knowing that later she would have to deal with the consequences of encouraging him.

Anastasia brought fruit, chocolates and a handful of second-hand romantic novels. She kissed Lenny on both cheeks.

'Twins! Always they are trouble, no? My god, we had a pair in my family in Moscow. Never trust them! You are looking like shit. Come to me later, OK?'

She was also taking care of Cleo Harrelson again.

'Don't worry about payment this time, OK? Now we are truly friends.' She visited every afternoon and Lenny began to look forward to seeing her.

She saw Max too. He visited her at the hospital, brought soft yellow mountain buttercups.

'You have been my saviour, Ms Aaron. Perhaps, if you don't mind, this once I might call you Lenny?'

'All ride.'

He had been released from prison and was living in an apartment with Liz Dodd. 'Merely friends,' he insisted. They were just fine. It seemed important for him to convince her of that. Margaret Gross, however, was not fine. She had taken Vivian's death very badly. Max explained that she was currently living in the Toorak house alone, a situation that could not continue for long. He worried about her, was going to try to help her.

'I've seen young Kendell,' he said. 'He's taken to visiting me. There's a good heart there. We're going to visit Annie together, the two of us. He wants to stand by her. I can never thank you enough, Lenny. You're a very dear girl.'

'Thang you, Max.'

Lenny's news of the Talbotts came mostly from the TV. Annie was in custody. She had confessed everything. She said she killed Dr Connor, Carol and Vivian and she wanted to die.

Lenny figured it had been bad timing. Vivian's plan went wrong. Kimberly, expected at the house later to find the body, turned up too early. Vivian heard her and Margaret on the stairs. She lunged for the gun because Annie, terrified and confused, was taking too long to fire, and then it discharged. Into Vivian's heart.

The newspapers also reported the contents of Henry Talbott's will. The *new* will had not, as Eric anticipated, provided him with a fortune. Rather, as Vivian had suggested, when it came to money, nothing was more important than family. The new will therefore had simply provided a large annual allowance for Maxwell Curtis until the time of his death. Kendell had inherited control of the company but announced his intention to share joint CEO duties with his sister, Kimberly. A letter for Lenny had arrived at the hospital. A forty thousand dollar cheque signed by Kimberly Talbott.

Eric Hunter had inherited twenty thousand dollars, a set of leather books and—again Vivian had been right on target— a selection of Henry's favourite stuffed Australian wildlife. In response to the less than lavish bequest, Eric negotiated a tell-all book deal with HarperCollins.

Mike Buchanan had escaped his debts, becoming something of a celebrity fugitive in South America. Sonny remained in Brisbane auctioning the trinkets and showing a brave face in the social pages.

Dr Sakuno came to visit, eventually. Lenny hadn't asked for him but as he stood before her, looking at his Rolex watch, with his bad hair and severe face, she realized that she had wanted him to come very much.

'Mrs Aaron,' he bowed to her mother who blinked at him.

'Are you another doctor?' she asked.

'A psychologist, Mrs Aaron. You must know Helena san is a disturbed young woman.'

'Oh ...'

'Some time alone with the patient, perhaps?' He gestured to the door and her mother allowed herself to be bundled out with her knitting.

Dr Sakuno moved closer, narrow eyes narrowing. He was holding a bonsai and slipped it onto her bedside cabinet. 'This is for you.' He paused. 'Get well soon.' It was a Kingsville Boxwood, Lenny realized, the best of the indoor bonsai. He had already completed the basic pruning and limb-wiring. He had also brought a spare set of bonsai tools, saying he would help her now as she could only do so much one-handed. It would be their hospital project.

Then he just waited.

Lenny sobbed on cue and for the next half an hour Dr Sakuno simply sat at her bedside, holding her good hand and saying there, there and now, now, occasionally in a very stiff voice.

'I mezzed ub the caze,' Lenny said, her face stupid with tears.

'You solved the case,' Dr Sakuno returned. 'You're very famous now. You should become a real detective before people forget about you. Make some money.'

'My arm'z cud ub ... ' Lenny said fishing for a way out.

'Better cut up than cut off,' Dr Sakuno quipped sagely.

They ended their meeting formally—he bowed from the end of the bed, she tried to bow up from the pillows. He wanted to see her once a week for a while and she was, on his orders, off all pain-relief medication.

'I've told the nurses that you're a drug abuser. You'll get no more sympathy from them.'

When Lenny's mother returned, she found her daughter attempting to step out of bed, attached to an intravenous stand which dragged after her arm.

'Lenny!' Veronica cried. 'I'll get a nurse.'

'Mazzaaa!' Lenny said. She saw Veronica's face droop at her tone. She paused for a moment and continued softly. 'Don'd fuzz. I'm fine. I wand to ged oud of bed.'

Her mother nodded. She began to gather her magazines and knitting. 'I should pop over to Dad's ward for a little while if you're feeling better. Will you be all right by yourself?'

Lenny nodded.

'Right then.' Veronica hesitated. 'I'm off.'

'Ride.' Lenny said. 'Mazzaa . . .'

'Yes?'

'Thang gyou for sidding with me.'

'Shall I pop in later?'

'Yes.'

She was discharged a month later. Anastasia was standing outside the hospital holding Cleo Aaron. The cat was wearing a little jumpsuit that Veronica Aaron had knitted. It looked ridiculous. One eye socket was squeezed shut but the remaining blue eye blinked at her. Cleo mewed a noisy greeting.

'I told you, she's fine. You see?' Anastasia handed over the cat and Lenny balanced it against her sling. 'Do you need a lift? My new boyfriend.' She gestured towards a Ford. The driver was a muscleman with a deep tan who preened when he saw them looking.

'I like them big,' Anastasia laughed. 'You should try it yourself, I'm telling you. We can double date.'

Not in this lifetime, Lenny thought. She held out the bonsai.

'Keep this in your shop until I get in this afternoon,' she said. 'Do you have the stuff?'

Anastasia handed over a large bag from the chemist. Inside it was Lenny's requested shopping list: Aspirin, Tylenol, Codral, Sudafed and a carton of Marlboro. Her body had recently begun to feel rather healthy, the result, Dr Sakuno said, of a clean digestive system. But she was out of hospital now and she was going to need a little help.

'No problems,' Anastasia said. 'Didn't they give you painkillers in there?'

'Oh, hmm, yes. Just extra ... you know ...'

Lenny took a taxi to the MCG. Dr Sakuno was meeting her for an Australian Rules match, an exhibition between Footscray and Hawthorn. It was a good day for it. Later she would go home and clean her flat. The thought of the dust build-up there and in the office was daunting, but it had to be faced. For now she was going to relax. She would eat a meat pie and watch the big men fly. Cleo Aaron purred softly in her arms.